Wake Me Up

The first literary crime novel
by critically acclaimed author
Justin Bog

"If you enjoyed The Lovely Bones by Alice Sebold, you'll LOVE Wake Me Up by Justin Bog."—Melissa Flickinger, *Goodreads*

"Although Justin Bog is a member of International Thriller Writers group and his new book *Wake Me Up* is a crime story in general, it's not an easy-going page-turner about catching and bringing criminals to justice . . . The story unfolds from a very unusual point-of-view: from the depth of Chris' coma, the narrator is Chris himself. This is an original approach to tell such a complex and intricate story!"---*Portland Book Review*

"Wake Me Up is an amazing book, leaving this reviewer in awe of the writer's skill. The point of view is stunningly complex, both omniscient and limited. At times, while Chris slips into various characters' consciousness and reconstructs the attack, he acknowledges that his understanding of other's actions and what happened may not be correct, due to limited perspective and damage to his brain. In a subplot, his father's lover, fiction writer Deepika, constructs her stories based on local people, and Chris's unreliable narrative becomes tangled with hers. This theme of perspective, of how much we can ever understand others and events, is connected to notions of fate. The assault on Chris was fated as he was propelled into it, by forces he didn't understand himself, when, contrary to his nature, he confronted the assailants. That "choice" set off a series of effects that also seem fated, changing everything in a way that may have been intended."—Stacia Levy, *San Francisco Book Review*

"Four students from Chris Bullet's Middleton, Montana, high school viciously beat him up because they earmark Chris to be gay. It is 2004, an election year. As "the Presidential cycle warps into full-blooded hatred of anyone gay, anyone different, and fills political campaign war chests," Chris lies comatose at a children's hospital. In an out-of-body experience, Chris views various people and their situations, such as the goings on in his school and also the fictional story loosely based on Chris' demise written by Deepika, his father's lover."—Anita Lock, *Manhattan Book Review*

"Some reviewers have compared this story to The Lovely Bones and I'm not exactly sure if I agree with that assessment. I believe this story goes even deeper than The Lovely Bones for it demonstrates the destruction that one tends to lend to himself . . . Great read and one that I most certainly would recommend adding to your reading shelf. Bog is the conscious voice of literary reason and socially adept to handle whatever story comes his way! Well done! I'm impressed! I'd love to see this made into a movie. It would be so fitting for today's movement."--*Mello and June, It's a Book Thang!*

"Wake Me Up is a powerful story. Justin Bog is a special writer. He has a unique writer's voice. I find the way he structures his stories to be a breath of fresh air . . . Buckle up and get ready for the emotional roller coaster ride through a torn family's drama. A mother who has experienced a cheating husband and now a dying son, a father whose depression and choices have brought him to the verge of death, and a boy who is just trying to survive."—*Sage's Blog Tours*

"(Wake Me Up) is Justin Bog's most extraordinary book

to date, and an absolute masterpiece! Intensely written, this is the tragic story of a teenage Montana boy who lies, at the heart of this tale, comatose after a brutal beating fueled by hate, and the chaos that ensues after the attack. All told through the eyes of our victim and hero, Chris Bullet. The author weaves the story together as a group of individual stories as witnessed by Chris almost supernaturally in his altered and ethereal state. Brilliantly crafted, complex, and beautifully written! I cannot say enough great things about this fine book, and happily encourage everyone to read it. It is a story of the injustice of our times, and I believe it will be a story that will stay on the shelves long after our times have all passed. If you read nothing else this year, please read this. five + stars."—Bradley Knox, *Hogwash*

"A Kafkaesque literary trip through the brain of a brutally assaulted teenage boy whose supercharged perceptions expose the secret sins of those he wants to love and hopes to believe in . . . The genius of author Justin's Bog's first full-length novel is that though everything Chris "knows" and recounts in his inner monologue is mysterious, maybe mystical, there is no hint of hocus-pocus, nor of the vague disjointed dream sequences one might expect from an unconscious protagonist . . . In the brief lead-up and denouement we see reality clearly: the attack and the aftermath. In between, everything that "happens" to Chris in his shut-off state is just as real and just as believable—but impossible. It would be hard to identify a literary precedent for this method of construction—Franz Kafka, perhaps, meets Lewis Carroll."—*Chanticleer Book Reviews*

"Wake Me Up is ultimately a novel about how lives connect and disconnect. Its theme centers on a pivotal moment in time, one that can reconnect fractured relationships or pull them farther apart. The intelligent, original, and heart-wrenching storyline is one we will all relate to, as it asks the difficult questions: Do we choose love and forgiveness, or do we judge and hold on to the pains of the past? How we proceed will define the meaning we give to our lives today . . . It's and important and enduring theme throughout the book, one that is told masterfully. Wake Me Up by Justin Bog is an extraordinary debut novel."—from Eden Baylee, Author of Stanger at Sunset

Books by Justin Bog

COLLECTIONS

Hark: A Christmas Collection
Sandcastle and Other Stories
Speak the Word

WAKE ME UP

Justin Bog

Copyright 2016 Justin Bogdanovitch

ATTRIBUTION: You must attribute the work in the manner specified by the author or license (but not in any way that suggests that they endorse you or your use of the work).

NONCOMMERCIAL: You may not use this work for commercial purposes.

NO DERIVATIVE WORKS: You may not alter, transform, or build upon this work.

Cover Design by MadHat Covers

Art detail taken from the painting "Ocean Boy" by the artist George Bogdanovitch with permission.

Published September 2016 by The Author's Advocate.

Previously published January 2016 by Gravity.
Reviews taken from the first edition.

This is a work of fiction. Names, characters, places, brands, media, and incidents are either the product of the author's imagination or are used fictitiously. Any resemblance to similarly named places or to persons living or deceased is unintentional.

PRINT ISBN: 978-0-9854751-4-7
EPUB ISBN: 978-0-984751-5-4

Library of Congress Control Number: 2015921021

CONTENTS

- DEDICATION 13
- PART ONE 15
- THE GREEK CHORUS I 17
- PART TWO 45
- APATHY 47
- DISTANCE 93
- DEAD 137
- DARKNESS 167
- PART THREE 213
- FRAILTY 215
- COMPLICATIONS 251
- MORBIDITY 289
- HUBRIS 333
- PART FOUR 379
- THE GREEK CHORUS II 381
- TRIAL 395
- ACKNOWLEDGEMENTS 405
- ABOUT THE AUTHOR 407

AUTHOR'S NOTE 409
A READER'S GUIDE FOR BOOK CLUBS 411

DEDICATION

Always for Deepika Bahri—a light shining bright.

*For Cheryl and Chapter One Bookstore—
you will always be the boss of me.*

PART ONE

One thought fills immensity.
~William Blake

THE GREEK CHORUS I

NEAR THE END I no longer see the baseball bat, keep track of who holds it as they toss the bat to another ready, grasping hand. I trip into the bat at the exact instant when one of my classmates swings like a steroidal homerun hitter. I'm not saying I'm to blame either. I got in their way. In the wrong place at the wrong time. Of course, when the final blow splinters my skull I'm a gibbering mess and I blank out like a light, convulsing on the asphalt, bleeding from my ear, nose and arm. My elbow lays twisted like a pipe cleaner, my eyes flutter in spasm then close.

I have three days—the doctor says this, three days, nights, to watch my swelling brain struggle. They take a piece of my skull, a cutout—a surgical procedure I'd struggle with watching on one of those medical surgery shows if I had to watch. My mom would have no problem storing the clinical bloodbath away in her absorbed brain and also no problem teasing me about being so squeamish—a way to help relieve the swelling and cross their fingers. Keep me unconscious, they say, to help get me over the proverbial hump of pain and brutality. The surgeon tells my family (what's left of it) that, at this point, it's touch and go, up to God, up to fate. I hear this doctor's voice, spouting worry-laced probabilities all around me in the pitch darkness, somehow, saying to leave my life to fate in his emotionless tone. He lacks a warm, bedside manner. His clipped formal medical jargon grates and he's barely able to say: "I'm sorry for your troubles" before exiting the waiting room.

* * *

Here's how it happened: my father, my mother, my father's lover, weren't there—so how can I blame them—they were off pursuing their own dreams and demons and isn't life about running towards something? In the mid-'90s, my parents moved us all the way out to Middleton, Montana, following my mother's poetical yearnings, and Big Sky College of Montana is the central, #1 with a bullet, economic force in Middleton. This college town is close enough to Missoula to be a rival, but hardly as distinguished. A river runs through this city, too. If you close your eyes, imagine herds of sheep, ranchers spitting chaw, Australian shepherds barking and keeping the braying woolies in line as they race through the downtown square. Wish that still happened. Now it's fake Oktoberfest celebrations and mooning fratboys on midnight streaking runs.

It's 2004, and the Presidential cycle warps into full-blooded hatred for anyone gay, anyone different, and fills political campaign war chests. I stay where I am. I don't think of myself as a sexual being, but those who tease maliciously, bully, punch, spill innuendo, name-call with vitriolic bravado, can spot the weakest member of any herd, and will always, eventually, move in for the kill. Being gay in Middleton wasn't an option open to me or to anyone, and I deflected bent insinuations with the best retorts, or ran away, dug a deeper hole, climbed into a darker closet.

What happened, I can only imagine, may have happened anywhere, in anytown, USA. Bullies are born every single ding-dong-damn day. They seek popularity, belonging, a higher class social ranking, inevitably fall short and must take out their frustrations on somebody they perceive to be weaker—I've known several people with the bully placard hanging around their necks. I pity them.

Middleton, the Lumber City, certainly has its fair share of frustrated teenagers. It's a college town, really a small Western city of close to 40,000 people, near the Idaho border, the thin upper peninsula part, where mountains begin to rise up on all sides and clash, forming Glacier National Park to the north. This side of Montana is unlike the flat farmland and plains blanketing the rest of the state. In junior high I had to do a report on a county in Montana, and the teacher assigned one of the farming blocks on the eastern side of the state, Custer County, all dull 3,793 square miles of it—over 11,000 people, at the time, called Custer County home, the racial makeup 97% white (and proud of it). The bulk of the people come from strong German and Norwegian descent. At least I have neighbors in Middleton who don't ride tractors or milk cows, not that there's anything wrong with that. I just know I'd make a terrible farmhand—I'd be teased as mercilessly by all the ranchers and their stolid rancher kids for being soft, clutching at my mother's hemline as she skins squirrels for stew. Middleton has a downtown center with mid-rise buildings that try to look modern, most under seven, eight floors with the open-plain height restrictions, a movie theater, a view of the mountains in the distance, a river that runs through it (as I said), decent chain restaurants and steakhouses, places to hide in, be alone with yourself, to engage with, or disengage. It became the perfect town for my family.

The four boys, the bullies from my high school, shout and laugh as they crack and shatter windows out of the parked cars on the back road of a middle-class neighborhood. People come out onto their poorly lit porches, warily, after the damage is done, too late, but they venture no further because of the sheeting rain and the threat of violence inherent in the sound of shattering windshield glass. Most of these adults shake their heads and think the world's going to hell in a handbasket, assume the kids vandalizing their street are all on drugs. Three of the vandals run faster than the fourth boy who doesn't want to run and acts disinterested in catching up with his friends. When I cross their path I'm already so angry. Angry, not because the boys are in my way and vandalizing cars; I could care less about the damage they're doing; deep inside I want them to ask me to join in, take up a rock and throw it through one of the Jeep windows. I'm angry with my father and the woman he sexed up all last Spring; Deepika's pregnant with my father's love child, and she never thought to tell my father until today. She keeps secrets like a fortune teller: only when convenient for her—the lies he told all of last April to cover this up. Weeks later (June?) I can see him begging my mother to let him back in the house: let's become a family again. And she let him back. The weakness in her makes me even angrier. I don't want to believe what's happening to my family. I've never had a death wish before. I haven't inherited that particular trait.

Steaming, fists clenching, I enter the street shouting at the boys to stop—maybe because Ellis is one of them. I foolishly believe he'd somehow step up before any of them threw a punch.

I know I won't remember any of this if I even survive to wake up—and if and when I wake up I'm concentrating on this memory, trying so hard to get all the details right—in case I'm questioned later by the police officer who tells my mother to get to the hospital quick. I'm fed up with my parents, and Deepika most of all and the child she will give birth to early next year, my future half-sibling. I'm pissed at how the cold rain saturates every piece of clothing I have on. I drip like a sponge, and then Ellis Pallino arrives, lagging behind his three buddies and causes my distraction and destruction.

Are they all on drugs? There's a rumor floating around school that one of the three boys who circles me, baiting me, yelling, is going to bring a gun to homeroom. Look at the bullies now. They want revenge because someone started another rumor about the drugs they sell. Who could possibly predict they'd go off on me like a delayed bomb in the middle of a dank October evening? I never even speak to them at school, only pass them in the hallway and try to act invisible and small and unthreatening, a part of the background scenery, everyday wallpaper. All of them, except Ellis, are upperclassmen.

I don't understand why my anger pushes me to confront them, and this is my boldest mistake. The largest one shouts at me: "Fag."

I'm stopped short by one awful word. To me it's worse than the other freaking F word, has more hidden potency. It's not the first time someone called me this. Again, in the school hallways, catcalls, you hear people using this word all the time, sometimes as real ribbing, sometimes just a catch-all insult not meant to offend too much, describing an inanimate object, or a thought, as gay, weak, lame, just joking, and still unforgivable. In the rain I hear it and my stomach tightens before they even punch me there.

His buddy chimes in: "Hey . . . Faggot."

I couldn't think of anything to say, the word lashes into me and I go mute, a rabbit stilled by a headlight. I definitely can't move by this time either. They circle me, a sacrificial target. I try to keep all of them in my sight.

I'm not a faggot. I mean, how can they know I am when I'm not even fully aware of it myself? A denial. I'm filled with so much self-hatred? Is that a lie?

Ellis steps into the picture too sudden and intense. He's the strongest and smartest, hanging back, wiry. How could he be with them? Is he on drugs? I stare at him. Too long for the rest of them, which of course makes them feel uncomfortable, creeped out. I try to answer my own questions—see if his stare is blurry and diffuse—a pout, a parting of his lips I keep thinking about whenever we cross paths in school. A school baseball hat shadows his face too much for me to tell. Long sideburns push through the haze, dark against the white of his chin. Yes, without speaking, it's freaking obvious I'm attracted to Ellis. Crush city.

"What's the fag looking at?" The one hefting the baseball bat sneers as I stare at Ellis. The leader's in Ellis's face—"You want this punk to be your girlfriend? You want to be his boyfriend? You his boyfriend, Ellis?" The others whistle and hoot at me, calculated, annoying, aggressive comments splashing onto Ellis. I imagine Ellis's pale face turning red in the darkness.

I want to ask Ellis what he's doing with these punks—stop time. Don't you know they're crazy, violent dicks? That one of them used to string stray kittens up to a tree for batting practice? Is that the same bat? We just helped each other with algebra during lunch, and now there's rage and humiliation controlling his face, egging on group mindlessness.

"You like what you see?" The third boy joins the verbal battle. He's the one who grips the baseball bat, catching it as his friend tosses it to him in an arc through the air, choking up on the bat, leaving five or six inches showing beneath his hand. He smacks it against his palm. I know they're not putting me on. I've seen destruction and tripping and pushing in the school hallways. Usually, I shirk away or turn and take detours to the classroom I need to be in. I swerve around them like roadkill.

If I knew how this situation would end for me, I would've had enough guts to go back and laugh in their faces instead of acting scared. Why would they hit me? If I knew how to be strong, why would they even pick on me? I didn't give them a reason until they saw me staring at Ellis. People in the school hallways call each other fag, queer, sissy, and worse—no, there's nothing worse—all the time. I hear it all the time—directed at everyone—a universal putdown. No one—teacher, parent or principal—ever does anything to stop it. I hide in the closet because I know I'll never have the guts to come out, not in my school—that's my confession. I keep asking myself this time and time again; it becomes circular and devouring: why would they hit me so hard? Don't they know they could kill someone swinging the bat the way they do?

The namecalling breaks my stare and I get one more look into Ellis's shadowed face before one of them punches me in the stomach and I huddle over clutching from the blow. All oxygen disappears and I stumble to my knees sucking wind, spittle, and rain as the second bully hits me with the bat. I see it coming and try to deflect it with my right arm and the bat crushes my elbow and I see brilliant flecks and sparks of light and an overpowering blackness for a split second. The pain is enormous and I struggle to remain aware as the bat passes to someone else. I don't know who has the weapon now but when I open my eyes I'm on my knees searching for Ellis.

That very morning I watched Ellis as he dressed in gym class. His aloofness brought people to him, his looks being judged on a higher scale—and not just by me. His newness wasn't offputting; he made friends at an enviable rate. He seemed harmless, popular, and untouchable.

It's Ellis who swings the bat last as I start to rise from the street, a shadow delivering the last blow. Someone else trips me. The blow alone shouldn't cause me to check out so completely. The four of them react by running away—now they're scared shitless. They run because they know this faggot bleeding on the ground means big trouble if they get caught. Why didn't they realize this possible outcome when they started taunting me? They run fast, the slap of their shoes echoes on the slick pavement.

In my last cogent moment, the bat swinging to crush, there's no doubt they want to kill me. I see this. I can call it an accident. I can rationalize the whole sorry mess away into something it's not because Ellis is there and doesn't really mean to betray me. We barely know each other anyway. I always try to keep to myself. I reign in any tendency to appear to the left of manliness, and the label of sissy has never really fit me. I'm a good actor whose ruse has cracked; I've been exposed, raw, found out. I'm slipping away.

* * *

I speak to you from total blackness. I rest now in a private room, on a hospital bed in the children's wing of a Middleton hospital. A security guard paces outside my room, up and down the hospital hallway. The press, local, soon to be national, is huge, candlelight vigils, a strident call for less violence, a peaceful mankind—a bleating new age twist of pablum too, save the world, save yourself, find your inner broken child and relate to this poor, poor, poor child in darkness—we're all to blame. If I could throw up, I would.

The guard speaks to the nurses who flit back and forth delivering medicine and checking bedpans. Even though my eyes are closed I can see. Even though my skull and ears are bandaged like a mummy I can hear. I know everything that's happening around me but I don't know why I know all of this. The word coma blinks there in neon, a truck-stop diner sign. Severe brain trauma. I'm in a coma.

"He's comatose from the trauma to the brain." A doctor tells my mother this and encourages her to keep speaking to me to help make a connection: "It's so important that you try to continue any form of connection between you and Chris. Ask your family and church members to pray for

Chris's awakening recovery." The doctor just assumes my family goes to church.

A presidential election rumbles beyond the froth stage. We, my government class, the easygoing, seemingly nonpolitical teacher, talk about it all the time. October. Fighting is in the air. Distorted into a tawdry back-and-forth. Polarizing, the most heated and harsh respond to anyone who is feared to be gay and I sink in my seat at the back of the classroom. Why should we let them marry? The teacher asks this since it's a huge component of the social issue war cycle between the two groups of disingenuous candidates, fomenting the fear—Bush vs Kerry. Here's why we shouldn't let Mo and Ho marry, says someone to my left, a mumble from another jock with issues . . . and these thoughts are there too.

* * *

I can see everything occurring at once. Somehow, the past is the present to me and will merge with my unknown, blurry future. It's a strange, elevating experience because I can't prove this is happening. I hover within myself and outside myself, all at once, and time splits into a multifaceted gemstone. I lie on a thin mattress plumped up by thin pillows, prone and to the outside world totally unaware. I want to wake up. I want to hold my mother's hand like a toddler. I want to speak to my father, but, of course, he's not here. I need someone to wake me up. Please. Odd—I'm not scared. I can't sense any panic within and this alone would terrify me if I could feel.

I have a story to tell.

Somehow, the day after the attack, a moment forthcoming, I sense, I see, I'm there watching as Deepika sits in her green Saab down in the hospital parking structure contemplating getting out of her car. She then walks into the hospital with her composure a bit off. There's no explanation why I'm able to do this—I imagine a ghost feels like this and I know ghosts exist, now . . . I'm a wraith. It just is.

Deepika's a few years younger than my mother, late thirties perhaps, but I've never been very good at guessing anyone's age. It's too late to sign me up for carny work. She's thinking about what she can possibly say to my mother in her defense if they happen to cross paths but she hasn't come up with anything of substance yet. Ghosts can read minds. Just kidding.

When I say she's thinking, I'm only guessing, but making a better than average guess since I sense what compels people in my current state. Gift or curse? I'm the one in a coma. When people say: "We know what you're thinking." Or: "You think you're so great, smart, funny," they're only making guesses based on past behavior. Does this color how I tell my story? You be the judge. I know what you're thinking, too.

Also, Deepika thinks of her fictional characters, the ones she's writing about—placing them in a series of interconnected short stories—back in her cozy office, centered on Sai and someone named Mrs. Plesher. She wants them to rise above conflict. She concentrates so hard on these characters during this time I picture her with multiple personality disorder.

She's set a few of her stories in Sun Valley, Idaho, the ski resort, The Queen of the West. Once, not too long ago, Deepika met Andy and Terry in Sun Valley over Presidents Week for a ski vacation. Terry was a bit too standoffish, officious, to warm up to Deepika (why be jealous of her—she wasn't a gay man—but, nevertheless, Andy and Deepika had once been married to each other, as short-lived as that union was, and Terry knew that a warm connection remains. Deepika kept Andy's last name of Webber after the divorce) and, after that trip, Deepika moved to Sun Valley, loved the blue sky, the 300 sunny days a year. She learned to snowboard, lived in the mountains for two years before taking the two-year Visiting Writer teaching position in Middleton at the College over a year ago, and a day's drive north along Idaho mountain roads to Montana. She learned all about Ketchum, the small mountain town that fed the Sun Valley resort economy, got an honest feel for the character of the people there, the lay of the land, how white it is, the mountains in winter and the people too—how she stood out. The most common thing people said to Deepika was: wish there was an Indian restaurant here—using a tone of voice she questioned because it always sounded like they wanted her to whip up some Bombay potato curry and pick her brain about gods and Kali and the Dalai Lama—that's Tibet—easily confused. Buddha then? I'm Hindu. The whole town needed a boost in ethnic hospitality.

Sai, the main character in *A Great Distance*, her short stories, is gay, Hindu, but not from Calcutta. Sai was born in America and raised by immigrant parents who wanted a better life but got a child instead. Deepika's driven to talk to the admittance desk and find out how badly I was hurt even though it's none of her business. It's not her fault either. Deepika remembers her ex-husband Andy and how he always complained to her about his family accepting all the blame because he turned out gay, as if they were martyrs, how sorry they felt for him having to live such a hard-knock life where everyone hates you because society thinks you're abnormal. I hope I can find out, wake up like Deepika, that straight parents and friends and acquaintances often blame themselves when a family member comes out of the closet, as if being gay somehow rubs off of them and their actions or inattentions, the father isn't around enough, the mother is too smothering, distant, overbearing, emotionally distant or browbeating—don't forget to bring your umbrella, and, Chris, stop listening to that Nine Inch Nails crap and clean up your damn room—and, he's always been an overly sensitive boy—remember when he would run with his legs pumping but toes pointing way too high? Like a band majorette or something. His father saw that once and put a stop to it and the boy never ran again like that for fear he'd be labeled a sissy.

In Deepika's current writing I will have an influence so large I wonder if she'll dedicate her book to me. Her characters will be a channel for her own unacknowledged guilt and anger. When reality becomes fiction. Never become friends with storytellers because they will pick over your life like mockingbirds, take all the shiny bits. There will be too many similarities in Sai's memory wall, his fictional world of life and death: the four attackers who put me in the hospital will become three men and one woman in one of her stories—Ellis will be the woman—and all four of them will murder the put-upon mother, Sai's grandmother, in a grocery store in North, Georgia. It's Deepika's story—murderous violence, a defeating circle of parental hatred, a yearning to figure out why people act the way they do.

* * *

While I blink out, the bat rushing into temple and bone crunch, my father rests in the upstairs bath, a rectangular, white, deep, soaking bathtub. He hasn't filled the bath with water; he still has on the wrinkled suit he wore all the livelong day, the suit he slept in. I ran away hours ago and he's worried about me for once, and not himself. That worry doesn't stop him from drinking huge sips from the long large Grey Goose bottle and swallowing acetaminophen tablets one at a time with each vodka sting.

* * *

Somewhere else, not too far away, my mother laughs as she picks up Chinese food she promised for our dinner. A dinner we'll never eat as a family or otherwise. Red-stencilled packages will sit on the kitchen counter and rot. The Chinese woman behind the counter has no way of foretelling this and she smiles overly friendly, twice asking if my mother wants chopsticks. Bowing thanks. My mother gives a small nod. Her body's still stiff, uncomfortable, and she barely manages the large bag of white cartons. The Chinese woman stops herself from asking if my mother needs help. My mother is happy; there's an ironic cheer stiffly contained.

* * *

Hours after the attack, Ellis Pallino, his t-shirt stained and wet green, sits behind a gray metal table at the police station spilling his guts. At this very moment he tries to shift all the blame to the three redneck druggies he befriended at school because he's seen as a responsible type, good enough grades, popular, a future star of the football team, always helps his grandmother out of her wheelchair, anything he can say in his defense; his parents are also seen as the responsible types who do good things for the community; his father is on the city council and was the one who took Ellis out of the private school he was attending and enrolled him in the public high school for his freshman year to make a good impression with his constituents. I never met Ellis before our freshman year, but I'd see him around Middleton, near the swimming pool or tubing down the river. He'd turn my head even then—I wanted to know him. We were all new to the high school . . . going from junior high to the much larger high school—trying to remain invisible. That's me. Get by. Ellis's father doesn't listen to him and doesn't want to hear the truth if it's really bad. His father tells him to come clean but blame the other three who are deadbeats with sealed juvenile records a mile long: firecrackers in mailboxes, animal cruelty—never proven—driving without a license, caught with marijuana, a joint or two, not enough to prosecute but enough to keep an eye on them, spray painting the new high school theater seats, two entire rows of them with archaic graffiti. Ellis's father knows the list goes on and on, privy to the information because of his political ties to the city, and, thinks: How the hell could my son be messed up with these three shits? Ellis folds under the persistent questioning, and knows the police don't believe a word he says even when he points to the other three who are then picked up systematically. When the others are questioned all three point the finger squarely back on Ellis and then on me, saying I came onto them, all at once, out on the street, propositioning glass-shattering thugs for sex. All four of them are cunning liars and do it so effortlessly it makes the lead detective's head spin into one of the worst mind-splitting headaches of his life.

* * *

Andy Webber watches Terry Elias, the man Andy calls his longtime companion, as Terry speaks on the wireless telephone in their small, yet cozy, inviting, San Francisco Potrero Hill apartment. Terry speaks to his mother, who lives in Las Vegas. She's forming a plan, trying to get her only son to fly down for the weekend to see a circus show. Terry and Andy both loathe Vegas. Andy wonders if she includes him in her plans. He's in love with her son. They even went so far as exchanging rings in a commitment ceremony two years ago on the lawn in front of The Palace Of Fine Art while California went through its own battle over their largest social issue: a union backed by the government—in 2004, utter failure, if not futility, became the norm. He's now part of Terry's family. Terry moves out onto the balcony and Andy stares at his back and the Union Square city skyline in the far distance. He and Terry want to marry each other for real, legally, and who knows, rumors in the city are flying this fall, San Francisco may yet get its act together and allow them to do so, but people still have to be convinced no harm will come when wedding bells ring for everyone.

Imagine that day. Realistically, Terry and Andy cannot, not in their lifetimes.

Terry will get off the phone and act like his mother really cares and is accepting of the life she still says he's chosen to live.

Andy will say it's not a choice.

Terry will say his mother didn't mean it that way.

Andy will counter that his mother only tolerates them and is far from accepting and Andy will go so far as to say he's ready to not tolerate anyone who doesn't accept him for who he really is; he's sick of hiding. He did that once. He even got married once, divorced two years later.

"That doesn't count," Terry replies. "It was a marriage of convenience to a woman who wanted a green card and you were available."

"We exchange Christmas cards. We're still close. I

thought you liked her when you met Deepika on that ski trip?"

"How close can you really be when you don't even speak to her more than once a year?"

"Some friends you don't have to. I could pick up that phone right now, call Deepika, and she'd answer and we'd talk for hours, but you and I don't have time to argue about this anymore—you can go to Las Vegas without me if that's what your mother wants; I won't be insulted."

"You will be."

"Okay, but what if I try my hardest not to be?"

* * *

Ms. Phyllis Deafers, well into her sixties, snoozes in the teacher's lounge the morning after I'm beaten to a pulp. She doesn't remember me from study hall where she monitors the room like a weary battleship. No one remembers me; I'm only a freshman, but after the principal requires a moment of silence in my reflective honor, the whole class body tries to remember who I am, and fails. That won't stop the most savvy and college-bound from coming up with plans for candlelit vigils and bake sales to help defray hospital costs and pleas and testimonials will rise daily as my coma deepens: I'll have many best friends recalling how they passed me in the halls, helped me with my homework, cut class with me, pumping my loner image into school rebel territory. Ms. Phyllis Deafers will fall asleep that night watching Jeopardy without being able to answer anything in the form of a question.

* * *

Amos Morataki, a classmate, studies at home the evening of the attack. He was even gloating, just the littlest bit in his tone, about my father earlier at school until he saw how his words struck me: "It's too bad your father lost his job"—telling me something that I didn't even know (one of my father's secrets—not well hidden), that set me off on a path of my own destruction. I wanted to flee the school, get home, to witness my father lie to my face again. Was Amos the catalyst? Amos can tell I didn't have a clue my father had been lying to me about work, to Mom, still dressing every morning in his false and battered suits. Amos won't even know about my hospitalization until the next day at school when the principal makes an announcement over the P.A. system during homeroom. The principal's tone will be practiced sadness with a hint of resignation and the creeping worry of lawsuits. He's checking with the school superintendent about the school position on the protection of gay students and where liability lines are crossed. Is the school to blame for not protecting me? Is it a hate crime like the newspapers suggest in bold print, emblazoned across the front page? Another desert State wants to do away with all bullying protocols in public schools because their right marching guard says protecting gay kids means the schools condone the gay lifestyle of these same gay kids. Take the protection away. Other kids are bullied, why single out them?

* * *

Anger—it's my driving force, and it's an insatiable emotion. I give into it freely. I seek justice, vengeance, revenge against those who continually do me wrong, choose bad paths to follow down darkening woods—ghosts in horror films are always driven by vengeance against the living. And this simmering anger spurs me to want to wake up, heal, get better. And to remember.

* * *

Mary Follick sits in another cubicle at police headquarters spilling her guts, crying and hysterical until her parents arrive. She's a witness to the fight and the end of the attack as the four boys took off and she knows the name of two of the attackers and clearly heard what they were calling me and would tell all of this to the reporters outside in the rain three hours later.

Did you know the injured boy?

Yes.

Did you know he was gay?

No. Smug with a self-important air of satisfaction Mary will reveal she has always suspected I am gay—closeted. I wouldn't go to the seventh-grade dance with her, she says to the reporter, and this is her proof. She kept chasing me and chasing me until I left the dance, frustrated.

Mary hands the detective her cell, one of the off brands, that takes bad quality digital pictures. She explains how to forward the photos she hurriedly took while behind the car, hiding from the fight. The detective smiles and thinks the case will wrap itself up. In one of the snapshots, through the rain glimmering like a sheet reflecting the streetlamps, the baseball bat swing blurs, highlighted in mid-swing, in the hands of a kid with long sideburns, a trucker hat shadowing his face—still too dark to rely on in court, but not blurry enough to show to Ellis and start a teary confession that will last for years.

From Mary they get the names of two of the attackers. She doesn't tell the police these two boys call her slut, ho, whore, make moist kissing sounds as she drifts close. Whenever she passes them in the hallways of the school they make her feel like shit. Ellis has never called her anything. She can't believe Ellis was an active participant and imagines him frying in an electric chair wearing an orange jumpsuit, heavily tattooed and bald as an eagle. He'd deserve it if Chris (if I die) dies, she thinks, and for once I'm in her corner rooting her ire on.

* * *

Edy Augustyn, Ellis Pallino's biology lab partner, finds

herself alone in class the day after the attack. No one will be her biology partner now as if she tainted Ellis somehow. The minds of teenagers, all the stupid decisions made everyday, seldom amuse me to action. She sits behind the black counter and asks the teacher if she can join Mary Follick—who is also alone, branded a different kind of traitor—if he'll place both of them together, since I'm now in a coma and won't be coming back anytime soon, and Ellis is in jail. There isn't any delicacy in her voice; she just wants help with all the lab work and will beg and mewl until she gets her way. I'm not coming back. No freaking way.

* * *

At the same time I fight for consciousness, beaten to within an inch, Dr. Fusil waits for the results of my mother's blood tests, as we all wait, as we all waited in separate areas of the hospital: a terrible coincidence? Fate? My mother and I, my father too, if you count his crazy bullshit maneuver that got him locked up; he's the only one who has an ugly death wish. Lock him up and throw away the key. All too much to be coincidental? It happens. When more than one person is sick in a family, or hurt, or undergoing psychiatric evaluations, which just about covers us. If I was able to speak, move, I'd high-five my mother on the way to get a CT, join the party. My sense of humor isn't that cruel, I know this isn't funny. The doctor, my mother's ER doc, even though she's still only three years out of medical school, knows the tests won't reveal anything. Dr. Fusil still has to run the tests, cover every little step, but what she's most interested in is the MRI and what she intuitively knows will show up on the films: the little black spots, a marker for MS—100 to 1 that's what's been causing my mother's separation from her physical being, her rigidness, her mystery frailty. Dr. Fusil remains upbeat and positive when she's around my mother while waiting for the shoe to fall after she tells Maddy what she doesn't want to hear. With everything around her collapsing the last thing my mother wants to hear is: take care of yourself—she's been distracted and involved with herself for too long now.

* * *

Travis searches his apartment for a blank greeting card he bought at Target the other day. He's composing a sympathy card for my mother, for the hardship she's now going through, for the way he can be there for her if she'll only open her eyes. He senses her sadness and wants to help her if not for all the right reasons. He sits at his kitchen table with the card and can't think of an opening line.

The Greek Chorus pauses a breath and then resumes, gathering strength, shielding the weaker members.

* * *

In Boston, Deepika's eldest brother (there are two younger brothers and a sister back home in India tending to their own growing families and their parents, grandparents), Ananda, sits in his Medical Clinic office going over charts. One of his patients, a woman who started bleeding in her stomach lining, almost fainted, and needed four pints of blood, is in full recovery. Ulcer.

The woman's husband says: She's a lucky woman.

She says in reply: I get a second life now.

Ananda says to them both: I firmly believe in fate. I don't fear anything. Things come and things go.

Deepika would roll her eyes and tell her brother he's laying it on a bit thick.

The man and the woman don't have anything to add.

Ananda thinks about his sister, Deepika, and the child she carries and tries to apply his easy-going philosophy to her situation. He's trying hard not to judge her. This is her fate.

* * *

Liv opens her Big Sky College Logo Shoppe, a place to buy kitsch of all shape and form, Team Spirit candles set into little horned bulls with Big Sky College written on the sides, ceramic matadors in school colors, copper, silver, and gold, stemming from Montana's history of mining, although blood red, because it's easier to duplicate and print, became the official substitute for copper in the early nineties and no one ever remembers this fact—We Are The Matadors—shot glasses with clever sayings, silver jewelry from Bali, multicolored scarves, t-shirts and hoodies with school emblems blazing. Liv calls Deepika the morning after the attack to set up a meeting for tea in the late afternoon. Just the daily ritual Liv goes through, walking through the campus center to her little store, saying hello to the other shop owners on her street, griping about the morning's headline, some boy from the local high school in critical condition at the hospital, what a shame something like this happening in her city. Deepika tells Liv she can meet later after subbing for another teacher. She doesn't tell Liv what teacher and Liv can sense Deepika's departure—one of these days, soon now, saying a teary goodbye to her and Montana and never looking back and never returning—Liv won't cry. She never does. A campus population is too transient to shed tears over. Deepika and Liv make a point of meeting once, twice, sometimes more, a week to talk and enjoy each other's company ever since Deepika met Liv when Deepika signed the first rent check on one of the five small rental homes Liv owns in and around Middleton. They made fast friends immediately and laugh loudly together. Deepika has been gone most of the summer and only returned, pregnant, to finish her book, and, because of her pregnancy, asks to be let out early from her winter term teaching obligation. Liv hasn't even asked Deepika about the baby. She'll get around to it.

* * *

Doctor Gapestill, my neurosurgeon, stops his rounds to check on my progress almost every hour. He worries and frets and consults other specialists about and has upgraded my condition to beyond critical. The swelling will not go down and this is the main concern. The night after my attack, post brain swelling surgery, skull removal, after spending one whole 24-hour period in a coma, after Doctor Gapestill hurriedly rechecks the settings on the respirator because my breathing is even more labored, something blocking my airway, the doctor will inform the media of this sudden downward change and they'll go off and write it up for tomorrow's story:

CONDITION STILL CRITICAL FOR BOY IN COMA

Doctors fear the worst. The spin will be negative and depressing and I'm lying in blackness living with the knowledge I could die. The day after that the headline will read:

HATE CRIME HITS MIDDLETON

The police involved in my case will cringe and follow procedure. Everyone will think they're not doing enough and make them feel hollow. That night hundreds of college students, teachers, high school parents and their children will hold a candlelight vigil outside the hospital—let us shine a light on hatred so ingrained it makes all of us culpable. Pray for me. Hold your light higher. Bring me out of the darkness of hatred. The light of innocence will shine when I open my eyes. My ass. The Burn In Hell crowd, smaller, vocal, are there too.

* * *

Harry, the psychiatric nurse, is sleeping so he can get up early for his day shift. I won't be able to sleep until I wake up. When Harry does awake he'll wonder which patient he'll have to shut up today. Who he'll have to yell at, who will scream at him, who will give him trouble about taking the medication and who will try to play him. The Psych Ward is full of manipulation and deceit, Harry thinks, including the doctors on staff.

* * *

Lance and Sheila sit at the Detroit airport waiting for their flight to be called. They don't know the specifics of what my father spoke about but they're worn and very willing to see what kind of trouble my father has gotten into. My father practically begs Lance to fly out and save him. They want to help even though my mother tried to put them off the day before when Lance called full of concern for my father and his lost job. They weren't really my mother's friends to begin with. They arrive the night after my attack bursting to take charge of the situation; there's nothing they can do; they're stuck in the waiting room with all the rest. I think my mother will let them try to take over if only to see how they fight for control with Nell.

* * *

The night of the attack my mother's only sibling, Rhea, watches the news with her husband. She's following the election like a bee after honey. It's three weeks to the Presidential election and she lives in red San Diego County. Her two kids play in the backyard with the neighbor kids. Her first dirty martini hasn't loosened her up a stitch and she's bitterly complaining about both candidates whenever one or the other appears on the television screen. She asks her husband, Carl, to make her another drink. He goes to the bar to do so and hears Rhea's running commentary on the state of the nation from the kitchen. Carl shakes the martinis. Rhea, Carl, and their kids will speak to Nadine the next day. Rhea is mom's younger sister. Rhea will get off the telephone after hearing about me and start ripping into my mother and her character and how holier-than-thou she's always been. Carl will ask if she wants to take a flight to Middleton and Rhea will contemplate this all night before deciding to wait until she hears from her parents, my grandparents, Millie and Frank.

* * *

Mrs. Gallows sits and reads her high school students' English compositions the night of my attack and rolls her eyes and points out the misspellings to her husband time and time again; there are so many.

* * *

Mr. Roffiger, my algebra teacher, sits at his kitchen table with all of his children. He named them all so he isn't at a loss at remembering how each of them came into his life, eight and counting. His wife serves grilled cheese sandwiches and iceberg salad with under-ripe tomatoes and they say a prayer. He thinks of the tests he has to grade after dinner and with a twinkle in his eye listens to his youngest as she tells a knock-knock joke. He won't remember my absence from class until he finds out he has no test from me in his stack of papers. He'll then wonder where I was and why I wasn't in school; I'm one of his stalwarts, one of the kids who doesn't need to practice more and more just to get things right. I can read something once and know the information. I'm no genius, but math has always been easy. I understand the complexity. He'll mutter and cluck when and if I reappear in class, and, in front of everyone, give me a demerit for missing the math team quiz, as if I don't have enough on my plate. Maybe I won't even go back to school; I have the biggest excuse in the world not to.

* * *

Millie and Frank, my mother's parents, drive through Alabama in their used Winnebago Ultimate Advantage with rose accents and cherry wood interior trim. They vacationed in Gulf Shores, Alabama at the Gulf Shores State Park where Millie took a picture of Frank in front of the sign that says: Please Don't Feed Or Aggravate The Alligators. They've been on the road for two months and are ready to get back home to Ohio. They're not prepared for the news of the attack the next day when Nadine, mom's best friend, calls them from the hospital. They're just one of many family members Nadine shakily calls from the hallway in the hospital's children's wing. They'll make plans to beeline-it home to New Albany; take a flight out of Columbus with two connecting flights in Minnesota and Salt Lake. At least they'll arrive on the second day of my forced sleep.

* * *

Glynnis, my dad's former personal assistant, doesn't have a clue about what's happened to my dad or me, but when the newspaper arrives on her doorstep the next morning she'll head straight for the office with tears at the ready. He was such a good man, she'll justifiably pronounce, and all this tragedy is such a shame, shame, a crying shame. What a poor, poor boy. She'll ask my father's former partners if the law firm should send flowers or not . . . to be tacky and righteous or not to be? In an interdepartmental memo they'll okay the flowers with short, to-the-point embarrassment.

* * *

Within this growing Greek chorus—these lives I am forced to witness like a moving picture, a film of intersecting and mostly unknown and unknowable characters popping in and out of the blackness, stories visualize and disappear, and I hold onto them. Often, it's people I didn't know at all—Valeria Brandow takes off all of her clothes five hours after my attack and streaks into the drizzling, Middleton, Montana, October nighttime chill. She "borrowed" her ranch-neighbor's horse, Pennywhistle, the horse she fed carrots to almost daily, but still a huge legal blunder if the neighbor wanted to pursue charges, and Nancy, her sister, prostrated herself at their feet—please, it won't happen again—how many times had she already said this? The police pick Valeria up, wrap a blanket around her cold, wet, naked body, and take her to the same hospital where I lay sleeping. They wrangle Pennywhistle back to the corral without a scratch, bristling with excitement. The doctor in the E.R. will try to send her up to the Psych Ward for an evaluation. The Emergency Room nurse calls Valeria's sister, Nancy Followatta, listed in the computer system as an emergency contact person (Valeria's been there many times), to come get her when they find out Valeria's insurance won't cover the locked, overnight stay. Nancy will end up taking Valeria home with a sour promise to the police she won't allow Valeria to do this again. She'll also bring her neighbors a fancy bottle of their favorite whiskey to apologize.

The police will shake their heads and tell Nancy her sister could end up in jail if it does happen again. The Middleton police have a long file on Valeria listing similar episodes but their hands are tied; they want to do the right thing but don't have the heart.

Nancy glares at Valeria on the short car ride home, berating her, and finally touches her hair, as if petting the fur of a favorite pet, and says: Val, this has to stop. I can't take it anymore. You have to take your medicine.

Valeria has long since stopped caring about taking anything anymore.

* * *

Along with his partner, Officer Pardue, Officer Ken St. Amour will end his night filling out the paperwork on my case and my father's. It'll take him three extra hours to get everything down to his satisfaction. He's exhausted after he checks out and heads to a bar frequented by off-duty police officers. They ask him if the fag will live, but they don't mean it as a slur; it's just the way some of the older cops talk. Officer Ken St. Amour could get angry; he doesn't show it as he drinks another draft. He knows he won't sleep well and he'll be jumpy all day at work tomorrow. He orders a shot of tequila for Officer Pardue when he arrives and waits for the bartender to tell him a new joke.

* * *

Mr. Abrassini, a colleague of my mother's at the college, hears the news, like everybody else, the next day over coffee. He reads the paper with a sense of righteousness and entitlement. He thinks my mother is getting knocked down a peg, and justly. He doesn't like her writing at all, doesn't get her poetic stance (he hasn't produced anything of merit in eons) and she gets more respect, acclaim, than he ever will.

* * *

Marjolaine, the Big Sky College English Teaching Coordinator, sits in her office the night of the attack and tries to get her desk in order. She thinks if she can just work three more years she'll get her pension and be able to leave Middleton for a better place. She hates the winters and her joints ache and she believes everyone in the department makes fun of her behind her back. She'll be left out of the loop on my attack and what's happened to my mother for a long time but she'll put a happy face on and try to coordinate all of the class schedules so that my mother, if she misses a lot of them, won't suffer in any way.

* * *

Nell, my father's only sibling, will not be called until the next day after my attack. She'll want to know everything, in amazing detail, and Nadine will try to tell her but Nell won't have any of it. She'll hang up on Nadine and book a flight from Palm Springs the next instant. Then she'll call her neighbor and say, Reggie, you're going to have to look after the dogs and don't over-water my orchids.

She's on her way, Nadine will tell my mother as she sits at my bedside. My mother and Nadine, her best friend, will both roll their eyes and try to talk me awake. My mother will kiss my face like sleeping beauty, but I won't wake up.

* * *

The Chess King, my father's father, my absent, banished grandfather, will be traveling back home from London. He's in his eighties, but fit as a fiddle. I don't remember ever meeting him. I must've way back when. I was just a toddler, perhaps. While in the UK my grandfather visits old friends from the fifties, friends who stood up for him at his wedding long ago. He plays chess for a month with a lot of the genius-level chess players and then books a flight to New York City after spending another week of solitude roaming the coffee shops and Indian restaurants on London's West End. He hasn't spoken to my father in well over ten years, since his wife died—my dad never mentions his mother or her death from high cholesterol and blocked arteries. I remember her light; she had enough kindness, humor, to bless any room with her infectious luminosity. The Chess King knows his son lives in Montana because Nell keeps him informed but he's too stubborn to interrupt his son's life any more—the rift widened, a natural geographical occurance. He's already done enough meddling for one lifetime. On the flight back to the states The Chess King amuses the flight attendants by making up dirty limericks using their first names: There was a young lady named Cheryl _____.

* * *

I see all of these people. They're living and breathing and acting on their basest impulses. I lay in a coma. They live. I hover over all of them, all at once. I can see my body, motionless, wired up, adrift. And I can find out why this happened. This is my story and I won't remember any of it when—if—I wake up. But I'll try to remember—I'll try damn hard.

PART TWO

*I was angry with my friend: I told my wrath,
my wrath did end. I was angry with my foe:
I told it not, my wrath did grow.*

~William Blake

APATHY

"YOU'RE STILL MY SON," my father says to me last July after he comes crawling back home, disgrace lingering around him as an almost physical attachment. Now, I can't respond—I didn't think it okay to respond at that time either—trapped above it all, in darkness; all I can do is remember and observe, the past and present colliding in my cage. I remember my father's imperious tone, as if he owns me. I'm either his jester or his serf, meant to either entertain or serve. It isn't the right time for him to lay claim to me anyway; he's in deep shit in our house. Mom has told me she's welcoming Dad back into the house, "welcoming" is my satirical word. I don't really know what to think. Mom has her own secrets, the reason she won't give me any specifics: I don't want you exposed to your father's weaknesses. She can't protect me forever. My father has an affair with a visiting writer from India. He moves out of the house for two months and into a hotel suite downtown. That must've been expensive. He says he never moved in with Deepika. My mother tells me he and she will work it out, get Dad some help, get us all some help. I tell her I don't want family therapy; television shows dealing with family therapists always make me want to heave.

Back to my father's weakness: my father is handsome, and some would say this is his strength, but I know better; it greases agreements, people pay attention quicker, some openly fawn at the prettiest who walk amongst us. He has charisma, but there's darkness there as if he tries too hard to show everyone he's happy.

I remember him all summer trying too hard. Anything Mom wants done, he does it, without question. He's in the doghouse. I suppose I get my way, too, but I never ask my parents for much. They're too busy. Not now, my mother says to me a lot, I have to get all these writing samples back and get ready for the conference. How about renting a movie? You pick. And I'd be off to Blockbuster on my bike, spend the summer reading, surfing the internet, playing Nintendo, Xbox, watching movies at night. My mom and dad worry I don't have any classmates to hang out with; I never cultivate lasting friendships. The distant and affected nerds like me are loners. I can see how I acted during this tenuous détente between my parents all summer, and I ache. They don't confide in me. My mother's too busy, a shell, too brittle to allow anything to come close for fear of breaking it. My father tries to demand my respect, which didn't help the situation, since I cannot respect him or see a way back.

Fast forward to right before the attack. There I am in my bedroom. It's a couple weeks before Halloween, and it's later than I thought it was. My father's locked away behind his office door. He acts even more distant and aloof. He smiles too widely, which makes his handsome features distort enough for me to see the cracks, and I hate looking him in the face. We can't make eye contact. I'm above the scene. This is my near past, the night before I meet up with Ellis and his brutish, bat-wielding buddies.

* * *

My father, Geoffrey Bullet, sits in his desk chair and stares out the upstairs office window at his backyard where the aspen trees bunch into an impenetrable wall and close off any glimpse of the river. His wife, my mother, Madison, Maddy to those really close to her, has planted a perennial garden running along a low stone fence ending at the tree line. The magpies, large, black, white, bluish, annoyingly aggressive birds, strut across the garden and fly back through the aspens as if they own the airspace. The birds act bothered and shriek to fill the sky with their buzzing cry whenever Geoffrey, Maddy, or their only child, me (Chris), steps into their territory. Geoffrey thinks about imaginary borders, lines the birds fly past in patrol, crossing back and forth, puffed up.

Long ago, Geoffrey cleared a path to the river by downing the ailing aspen trees and hauling the deadfall away. He let the path meander and take a natural curve away from the house along a dry streambed and back to a grassy knoll bordering the river's shore. On the far side of the river are gnarly trees, ornamental fruit trees gone to seed in the wild, and their reflections on a still day lay dark on the water. Geoffrey and Maddy keep dreaming of building a small gazebo there with screens to keep the mosquitoes out, but they never seem to get around to it. She fancies writing out there one day if they ever become ambitious and extend electricity to the nonexistent gazebo and Geoffrey once dreamt of taking naps in a secondhand chaise lounge, falling asleep to the trickling river sound. Bronzed planter boxes stand in welcome at the entrance to the forest path. She picked them out of a catalog and he hauled them over to the path and into place. Not this last spring. He wasn't home to help her. Somehow the job got done just the same. Alone, Maddy filled them in spring with salmon geraniums and silver dusty miller. In the middle of October, the skeletal remains poke up from the containers. Maddy hasn't made time yet to pull the withering flowers out and cover the boxes for the long winter. Geoffrey thinks about going out and doing this job right now but only for a moment. It wouldn't help. The flower boxes are Maddy's job. Geoffrey can't see the river, just the path, but he hears the water humming at the edges. And this inability to view the rushing water, so beautiful, something so close, has always bothered him. He doesn't remember the last time he took a walk down the path and sat at the river's edge alone or with Maddy or, me, his son.

* * *

Wednesday afternoon Maddy kills time in her office at

the college writing and responding to her agent's plea for new material and pushes thoughts of her family away. She never works well under a deadline. She takes a break for dinner at the Union Café and walks to her night class to teach her graduate school students the current Norton Anthology of Modern Poetry. The book is the size of a cinderblock and has pages as thin as cellophane. It's a book the students hate lugging around and Maddy does also but the book is practical and covers all the major poets. She won't be back home until late, sometimes eleven at night, well after the three-hour class; she must answer all the busywork questions by the territorial few who need handholding by the professor. Most of the time the graduate students are nontraditional and some are even older than Maddy, who is in her early forties, her last birthday celebrated without her husband, just me and her, in a downtown restaurant, mud pie with a candle, a broken family. I remember her wish: to be a family again.

* * *

Ever since Maddy left two hours ago Geoffrey fidgets a lot but never budges from his seat. He needs to go to the bathroom to relieve himself with some urgency but he stays seated and vows to keep sitting until the pain becomes too unbearable. He imagines his wife as a ship he passes in the night, every night. Her ship, really a yacht or a boat, has clean lines and a sleek bow knifing through the water carrying the glitterati to literary festivals. His ship, a tanker carrying boxcars of garbage and toxic waste, plunges through the water without anyone in view on deck. He imagines dumping his trash out at sea, but he knows he'll get caught. The main body of the ship is the color of mud, rust, dull green, and murk. No one notices either ship. I'm not even thought of as a dinghy.

A cloud passes over the sun and he thinks about his name, Geoffrey Bullet, and how his elite, elitist, upbringing figured into the middle of the mess he believes he's caught in. His wife didn't take his name when they married, twelve years past. She keeps her own: Dakota. At times, Geoffrey thinks Madison always wanted him to take her name; she believes it has a harder edge, like The Old West; it can give her some credibility or a roughhewn image suitable to market her name as an author.

Geoffrey and Madison buy a house on the river, a river the house cannot be built on but near, and the taxes don't follow that way of thinking. It's almost three acres, a river lot regardless of whether he can see the river from his house or not; his taxes rise and they will keep rising like a body of water after snowfall until the state of Montana takes all it thinks it deserves. For a state with no sales tax, one of its selling points—Come live here—the government tries to get you by stealth. Geoffrey complains to anyone who will listen. Only the rich complain anyway about such things, say Maddy's parents, Millie and Frank, who remain comfortable on their perch with Ohio's middle class. Geoffrey remembers talking to Maddy's father about how Geoffrey could try to circumvent the tax law for Frank who was about to purchase a motor coach. If we put the coach in our name you'll save a lot of money, Geoffrey said. Frank thought about it and declined. I can afford the taxes, was Frank's reply.

Geoffrey wants to figure out how to kill himself. He tells himself he's not allowed to get up from his desk until he figures it out completely. He nixes all the easy scenarios because he's exposed to far too much pain. There doesn't seem to be an easy way.

He's read an article about a group of young adults in Japan who create websites to inform others on how to be successful at suicide. Someone begins by posting a note on the web. Where to meet? When to meet? Usually, someone else has a van. A group of six gathers in the van and kill themselves with a linked hose. Suicide pacts worry the establishment, but not enough for them to act upon their worries.

Geoffrey thinks about all the people he will leave behind, all the people who will worry about his family and what would make him turn to suicide. Maddy, the passing cruise ship, will eventually find another passenger to take on. She surely will. The cloud floats on and the sun pokes out quickly before an entire sky of cloud takes over. It'll have to be a gray night, a gray week, he ruminates, and there will have to be an appropriate environment in order to do what he feels he must do.

After three hours of thinking, and at the same exact time his wife's office hours finish, Geoffrey stands and stretches the stiffness out of his legs. Then, he races for the bathroom down the hall at the top of the stairs. The physical relief he feels doesn't transpose itself into his psyche and he fastens his khakis as if detached from the act. As he walks back to his upstairs office, the last room down the darkening hallway, he passes my room. He realizes he must not disturb me; he can't face me in his state of mind. The door's open a crack and if Geoffrey turns to look he'll see me lying on my bed with my headphones on. At that moment I'm listening to French language tapes for the beginner year. I'm a freshman in high school and French is the language my mother continues to tell me she wants to learn if she ever clears enough time—and despite what half of America thinks about the French at this time, 'Let Freedom Fries reign,' Maddy still likes to romanticize the language, the people, the rich history.

Why don't you take that? Anyone can learn Spanish, Maddy tells me, after all, it's so easy—and yet only people who don't speak Spanish say it's easy to learn how to do it.

Geoffrey doesn't chime in with his opinion so I add Latin to my course load and then drop it a week into the school year without consulting anyone except one of the three harried guidance counselors, which is a requirement, and takes up less than two minutes of her time: Who are you? Are you sure you want to drop Latin? Fake and frustratingly resigned, the counselor stamps the drop form as if she knows me enough to care. She sees only a student composite, a puzzling illusion distorting and vibrating away from her desk after she hands me the piece of paper I now have to file with the assistant to the vice principal. My father doesn't have a comment as he passes in the hall either but he isn't racing back to his office with the same urgency he used to flee to the bathroom. I know taking Latin, following in my lawyer father's footsteps—you get a good basis if you want to study law like your old man—isn't in my deck of cards.

From the coma I can see all this. Somehow I know what my father is thinking when he comes close to interacting with me before he departs. He doesn't know my secret, any of them, and I'm not fully aware of them either, some of them. In death, do we relive the moments leading up to our deaths—is this what's happening to me? Is there a way to change the past? Live? I'm lying here in my hospital room, clueless. Everything is before the fall. I know so many things I shouldn't but there's no way for me to tell anyone as long as my body stays broken. I can't even warn myself. I try in this state, concentrate on changing fate, but fail.

In this past I listen to music after the French cassette ends. I wonder if my father's on vacation again. It's hard to tell. He works all the time. When mom comes home I hope I can find enough enthusiasm to ask about dad. Wishful thinking. I know I won't ever ask.

Geoffrey places his hands on top of his legs as he sits behind his desk again. His bitten and ragged fingernails scratch across the denim. He really has convinced himself he doesn't know what to do. His mind stuffs itself full of branching pathways and he's tried to follow each one. His logic always carries him to a doom so great it will overwhelm him even more if given the chance. Currently he thinks about Maddy and the mileage she's received over her last published book of poetry, now two years in the past. She's since found a larger publishing house and has taken on an agent who wants her work seen by a wider audience. The agent sought her out using the website in the back of Maddy's book of poems—Have you ever thought about writing prose? A novel? Maddy's written only sixty single-spaced pages, a novella, in the two years. Maddy says it's damned hard for her to write fiction. Geoffrey knows better; it's damned hard to write poetry, too, but somehow Maddy has seven highly respected—In small, regional circles anyway—books of poetry on the shelves.

The Purple Sparrow Press published her novice book of verse while she was still finishing up her B.F.A. years ago from Bowling Green State University. *Mirroring Medusa* sold the requisite 1 copy out of 10 printed of a very low print run. Enough attention paid, however, to place Madison Dakota's picture in the paper and a regional poetry tour of the bookstores in the Ohio, Indiana, and Michigan area. The poems speak of a hardship no one can guess the poet has ever experienced. A cutting of all life support, growing up in a family of philosophers, being a lesbian—or, really, in Madison's case, imagining being a lesbian, which was the rage at the time in college—being poked and prodded by doctors with too much glee, and the latest diet to take hold of her body, the female body corrupted into thinking it had to be thin at all costs, the usual poetic themes written furiously in the dead of Ohio ice storm winter nights at the homes of colleagues and the pacifists of the day.

Madison Dakota, the poet, would, after a two-year break, get into the two M.F.A. programs she applied to: Emerson, in Boston, and Iowa. Stay close to your roots. She decided on Iowa's program in Iowa City; it was most like Ann Arbor, the University of Michigan town she always loved to visit since it was only ninety minutes north of Bowling Green. Her parents, who weren't really philosophers, were very proud of her. They always seemed too normal to Geoffrey. When Madison introduced Geoffrey to her parents, Millie and Frank, for the first time, they shook hands like old buddies and confidants, a wink from Frank with a pat on the back, too.

Maddy's two-year break between undergrad and grad school was spent working in Ann Arbor, Michigan part time at a bead and jewelry shop and for a small used bookstore in the evenings. One of her undergraduate professors had suggested that Maddy not go right back into the school mill after she graduated; she inferred Maddy will only get used up, ground down to bits by the workshop system of trash and slash if she doesn't clear her head and see the world a bit first. The mentor actually described the world by saying: in all its complexity—which almost made Maddy realize she might need to follow the advice of someone else. Take some time to figure out what you want to do with your life and then pursue it with the right amount of enthusiasm. Give yourself a break.

Maddy remembered the long drive to Iowa. After saying

goodbye to all of her friends, she celebrated by drinking cheap sparkling wine with her neighbor well into the night, moved to flat Iowa and never looked back. Full steam ahead the writing continued at every spare moment not working, and sometimes during work, cooking for her friends and screwing the occasional sad castoff boyfriends of her classmates. After she received her M.F.A. in poetry from Iowa she moved back to Ann Arbor, Michigan. She had dreams of finally being The Writer and Ann Arbor had always felt like the best place to accomplish this dream. Most of her friends from the past were gone, moved on and into their own futures. Maddy had always liked the atmosphere in the town and liked her freedom. She could teach writing there. She'd make new friends. This was where she met Geoffrey.

Maddy floated around Ann Arbor and spent most of her free afternoons writing in her notebooks by the river in the arboretum, sitting on a bench overlooking the ponds and the Japanese bridges curving into the distance. When she wasn't making poetry of her life, she kept to herself—that is, when she wasn't casting her lot with Geoffrey Bullet, a green lawyer with little time for her because he was working for a firm that had him by the balls. Keep the new guy busy was a rite of passage. He called Maddy late and they would meet at his apartment for sex. There was little foreplay. When the door shut behind Maddy he was all over her, taking her clothes off for her, not quite ripping them in the quickness but enjoying the rush and an hour later they were both asleep.

* * *

Now, several years later I witness my mother as she finishes up her Modern Poetry class and tries to quell a developing migraine. One of her students, a man of indeterminate racial background—my mom thinks Native American—sits in the middle of the long conference table as he always does and sounds off on the subtext in the poetry. He also likes to proclaim as fact what he believes to be the poet's intent in a voice so sure of itself that everyone, including my mother at times, tends to just let him speak his mind and draw his pictures without argument. With his large stack of blank paper and his heavy black pen he's always ready to draw something in order to explain his ideas to the group. The pen never leaves his tight grip. Pictionary Poetry one of the other students called it once.

"See," he says, as he draws squiggly lines from left to right across the widest part of the page. "There's a forest of aged conifers the poet speaks to."

Maddy tries not to roll her eyes. She can't allow her emotions to cause her to lose control of the discussion.

"What about the rawness of the couple?" Another grad student, a woman across from the artist, speaks up with the question. "I don't get the forest. I mean, I don't think the forest is all that important. It's in the background. Just scenery. The couple and what they're doing remain central to the poem."

"I'm drawing the forest now," the artist says with determination.

The woman continues, "But the sex is the basis of the poem. The symbol."

"Does anyone else have a comment?" Maddy tries not to direct the discussion too much but she wants the scribbling on the notepaper to stop. She feels the beginning ache above her right eyebrow and knows if she doesn't drink a lot of espresso soon and swallow two Tylenols she'll have a monster headache to contend with. It's getting late and the class is restless. The two first-year students fidget, pass notes, and glance at each other, try to do so without anyone noticing, but Maddy is a teacher after all and the note-passing thing didn't work well in high school. Why do they think it's okay to do it in her class?

The woman who poses the question about sex comes back: "The longing in the poem is so fertile and if he, The Artist, thinks they fuck near a river—"

Maddy lets out a laugh, almost a snort; she can't believe the woman actually called the man The Artist. Just like that.

The swearing is normal for this student and no one is shocked by it; they know she uses it for effect. All the other students and Maddy believe she doesn't need to swear, ever. The Artist says, oblivious, "I can draw that too."

A quiet student, a boy who everyone listens to last because they believe he's too shy, finally breaks in and says, "Please don't draw the fucking couple!"

Maddy finally loses it and starts to really laugh and then everyone else joins in while The Artist places his pen on top of the squiggles. The rounded shape of the joined lovers remains unfinished next to the row of conifers and will stay that way.

"I think that's all for today," Maddy announces. Dismissing the class, she smiles at everyone, even the sullen artist, as they put away their books and notes. The large poetry volume doesn't fit in some of the backpacks so they carry it against their chests like bulletproof vests.

"Goodbye," Maddy calls out, "See you next week along with your class project and paper ideas." She gives the students free rein. She's never liked grading academic papers. The number one topic in the teachers' offices? How much they hated all the time they had to devote to grading their student compositions. Some just graded without comments and never below a "C" so the teacher wouldn't have to ever see the poor student again. Maddy would rather be writing her own poetry, inventing her own sexual longing, and that, among other things, is part of what settles in her mind along with her headache when she realizes she cannot move.

* * *

Geoffrey still sits behind his desk and I can't muster enough will to go see if my father wants any of the canned Santa Fe Corn Chowder I heat up on the stovetop. I do this weekly when one or both of my parents are out working late. Open a can or a bag or heat up leftovers from the weekend casserole, or take-out dinners. Someone needs to go to the supermarket soon. My father's upstairs and quiet. The answering machine keeps blinking but I haven't heard the telephone ring. Two messages show a blinky red light and I press the play button.

"Mr. Bullet. This is Susan Aplington from the Bluff Trust Bank in Traverse City calling. I need to speak to you about your payment for the Good Hart property. This matter is urgent! You can reach me at . . ."

I press the skip button to go to the next message.

"Geoff, I hope you'll return my call. I've left a couple messages. Hey, buddy, call me."

It's Lance Copler, an unrelated "Uncle" of mine, an old college friend of Geoffrey's trying for the third or fourth time in two weeks to get ahold of him. It has something to do with the beach lots they bought with two other friends back in the late eighties. They were young and just starting out and thinking about real estate as a good investment in the Harbor Springs, Michigan area. When he hears them, I know my dad will quickly delete the messages before my mother has a chance to hear them, probably. I don't know why my father won't call these people back, but I worry about it as much as I worry about asteroids hitting the earth. This Chris, me before, has no way of knowing the reason my father doesn't return the calls is linked to why he's upstairs contemplating suicide. I know that in my family things will eventually all come out. I've learned not to ask too many deep questions. The last year has been a testament to that. Mom? Hey, Mom? Why did you kick dad out of the house? The Chris in the kitchen then thinks: Hey, Mom? Why did you let him back into the house?

Geoffrey hears the muffled voice of his best friend, good-ole-boy Lance, his buddy, from his upstairs office and realizes it's almost ten p.m. and he needs to erase the messages from the machine before his wife returns home. Lance keeps trying to reach him. They get their families together still, once, sometimes twice a year—spring breaks, New Year's Celebration.

In college it used to be an everyday thing. Geoffrey and Lance would hang out, read law books, study for tests, drink cases of beer and watch the lacrosse team lose. If the lacrosse team wasn't on the field they'd go watch the soccer team. Geoffrey appreciated the players' stamina and skill with the ball. Both sports had the guts to be just what they were without the padding and self-adulation of the other louder sports.

Geoffrey didn't want to speak to Lance and thinks about never speaking to his old buddy ever again and shivers. Maddy will arrive and take stock of what he's accomplished and say nothing at all. She'll finish the bottle of wine she opened the night before while reading her student papers until midnight. She'll believe her son is in bed and asleep for the last hour and loosely regret not being home sooner to wish him a goodnight. I'll make sure my door is firmly closed. Geoffrey will hole up in his office. Maddy will take a bath and be in bed reading her own work, make editorial decisions, slice her own verse to shreds by one in the morning. Maybe Geoffrey will be dressed for sleep by this time, too, or, maybe not.

* * *

Usually, this scenario is the norm during the workweek. But my mother can't move her legs. She's stuck late Tuesday after class with no one to help her. On Wednesday, Maddy recuperates by sleeping in. She doesn't have to be back at the college until noon where she meets with the other people on the board of directors of the English Department. Then at 1:30pm she teaches the undergraduate 400-level Creative Writing course. Maddy thinks about her upcoming morning (will she still be there), keeps her mind drumming through her organized life, and wonders why she can't budge her lower extremities. She wonders if Geoffrey and I even worry why she's so late.

All the Modern Poetry students have long-since filed out of the classroom. There isn't anything left on the tabletop, not even a drawing from the mad artist.

When she stops the class she answers all the usual questions and chitchats with the brownnosers about nothing interesting, she moves her hands, arms, neck, facial features, and her upper body but her legs are useless, except for a tingling sensation, almost a burning, but not painful, warm. The funniest thing. A bit strange, Maddy thinks, as she says goodbye to the last student.

"So long. Have a great week. No, I think I'll stay a bit before heading home."

"You can join us down at The Basement if you like," says the quietest student with real yearning in his voice. "A few of us are heading there to talk about writing and play darts. I never did thank you for letting me take your senior-level writing class."

"Well, it's nice to have a graduate student there to show the other undergraduates that writing can be pursued in different ways. But, even though a drink at The Basement sounds fun, I'll take a rain check. I've got to get up early." A contradiction, Maddy thinks, of what she'd just said previously, but he'll go away. Won't he? But he hangs around, leans in the doorway against the frame like a scarecrow, the skinniest boy she's ever seen. His name is Travis and Maddy can easily tell he likes her. This is his problem, his crush. He quietly flirts with her after every class. Joking really, and she humors him and laughs about his intent. Was this her crush? He's been polite but his eyes burn into her the glance of a militant.

Travis bows his head and somehow keeps his eyes on hers. He has a beard, full and scraggly, a beard most people would characterize as Southern as if he ran a still in the backwoods, but this is small-city Montana. Somehow the beard fits and Maddy likes his attention. It makes her feel as if she's back in grad school again. He doesn't say anything else just stays silent and stares at her for another half minute.

"Can I help you with anything else?" Maddy asks.

"I'm just thinking," Travis speaks quickly, a bundle of nerves.

Please go, Maddy begs inwardly, I can't get up and I don't want you to see me like this. Her mind takes her to a vision of where she would like him to see her. What if she could get up? Would she go to The Basement with Travis? Who were the other people he said were going? She doesn't care. She has a vision of him leaning against her and not the doorframe and she lowers her palms to the tabletop and sighs. She tries to sound resigned to a long night of reading.

"I've got a lot of work still."

"May I ask you a question?" There's a sense of humor attached to his voice, bubbling below the surface.

"Not now. Please."

Travis's body language changes instantly and the slouch is gone as he straightens up. He looks almost physically wounded.

"Okay," he says. He turns to leave. Has Maddy detected the slightest tone of concern in the boy's voice?

"Stop by my office hours this Thursday. Travis. Please. I'm at a loss right now. Maybe it's the late hour." She's on the verge of plain begging the idiot boy to go away.

Travis salutes her, brings his right forefinger up to his eyebrow, and finishes with a wave.

"Sure thing. I'll try to make it. See you next week if I can't."

Then he is truly, and finally, gone.

Maddy groans. She sweats under her clothes and she isn't sure what exactly causes her to do so. She wonders if she's lying to herself. She knows better.

* * *

Geoffrey waits until he hears me climb upstairs to my room before venturing out of his office again. Once more he uses the bathroom and washes his hands, spending too much time staring at the water coming out of the faucet. He splashes cool water onto his face and lets the drops fall without toweling them off. He's older, most would say distinguished, well into his forties. The skin of his face has started to wrinkle and loosen just the littlest bit, but no one really notices this except Geoffrey. His dark hair turns gray at the temple, dusting his short sideburns. Maddy, two years past, says she finds this distinctive, and very handsome. You could've walked off a movie set. Take my breath away stuff. Back in one of the happy stages.

Down the stairs he walks, stiffly, as if his legs have just been pushed into the sockets. The constant sitting he's been doing hasn't made him the most flexible. What is he thinking now? Death by sitting.

First, he must erase the telephone messages from the Bluff Trust Bank and his good buddy Lance. With the press of a button he's done and thinking about eating to quell the hunger in his stomach. There's some leftover soup in a bowl and he notices the goldfish crackers I left out on the counter. This perturbs him to no end and he files the snapshot away for later when he'll remind me to pick up after myself. At least he's planning on sticking around long enough to share his pet peeve.

I have no clue my father is so lost, and that's the hardest part of being so self-absorbed (both of us), not knowing what you're missing, clues. My father, my mother, and me, each into what's so important. I've only been thinking of my life, feeling sorry for myself, for thinking about possibly being gay in a country that's supposed to be giving to all and touts the unbelievable right to allow everyone to be free. People can take gay people if the issue is played for laughs in sitcoms and movies, but not if it crosses the line into real feeling or has emotional depth. I keep hearing how abnormal gay people are and I want to crawl into the walls so no one will point fingers at me. No wonder so many top actors feel they have to hide their gay secrets. Some of the biggest actors in the world are rumored to be gay and don't want to come out of the Hollywood Closet; it's in all the supermarket tabloid headlines. If the actor's that good at his craft and can command millions, doesn't he, or she for that matter, know his career will continue? The roles will change, but at least the energy used to conceal the secret will be put to better use, show the confused gay teenager it's okay—See? Being gay, like being straight, is okay and life gets better— just get through the high school gauntlet. Everyone has the same dreams and wishes. Everyone rolls with the punches. I just can't duck fast enough.

My father scoops up the cracker bag, opens the pantry door, and throws the fish onto a shelf. They spill out of the open top, and the door shuts before the last cracker lands on the shelf, food for a stray field mouse seeking indoor warmth.

It is now past eleven and the house barely makes any noise. The whirring of the forced-air furnace is it. That's why I can hear my father return from his kitchen foraging. I know he's made a double espresso from the jarring sound of grinding beans and the clanking of the automatic machine. My father carries the espresso cup and saucer in his left hand as he approaches my room. He stops in front of the door but doesn't move to open it. I don't want him to open it. I hold my breath until he walks away. My father thinks of me, his son, in the abstract, and this only makes him more depressed for some reason.

Geoffrey returns to his office and opens one of the windows. There's no moon in the sky and he imagines the darkness seeps in like a cool wind to extinguish his computer light. It isn't until he sits behind his desk that he takes the first sip of his strong espresso. Still hot, but very bitter. Someone will have to check the machine, clean it out. He buys the organic espresso beans from a dingy coffee shop in downtown Middleton close to the building where his law firm set up shop on the top three floors. The light of his desktop computer remains alien blue in the darkness.

With the flick of a switch the screen changes to announce Geoffrey's email. He has a couple from Lance—Boy, he's really trying—but Geoffrey doesn't give him any credit. Spam email of the latest books, Shrek 2 and Spider-Man 2 DVDs to ponder from the 2014 summer blockbuster now in the past, CDs, naughty women and men, ads for losing weight without worrying or how Matilda can change his life with the shifting astrological chaos-reading she has in store for him if he'll only log on. Give it a whirl. The email's piled up in only two days' time and without reading any of the letters Geoffrey systematically deletes them until his recent mail cache is empty.

He finishes his coffee quickly and sets the cup aside at the edge of the desk. He turns his computer off and swivels to face the open window. He thinks of Maddy again and where she is. He wonders if she's been having an affair, and good for her, a get even thing. Her latest book is taking shape, what she keeps saying to him, prose this time, her first novel, how many times will she tell him this as if she believes he hasn't heard her the first time. Not another book of slim angry poetry—thank God, Geoffrey thinks—and she'll be too busy to take notice of what he's been up to. She's too smart to keep the blinders on for much longer. He's been caught out of his own affair long past at the beginning of spring. She'll want to hurt him back, but no, she still loves him. Be charitable. He won't accept her pity when the time comes to break even.

* * *

The migraine escalates, throbs, and makes my mother keep pressing, with growing dread, against her forehead, rubbing with pressure in a small circular motion. At the same time Geoffrey runs through the many scenarios of doubt and blame, Maddy still sits in the English building classroom, and he's the furthest from her mind.

All she can think about now is her immobility, and the pain in her head. Her legs can't function and Maddy tires. The door to the room remains open and she smiles at other people as they walk by on their way home or to the bars or the undergraduate library that never closes. The people who glance in see a woman in her early forties who's seriously occupied and straining. She rubs her head while these people pass by and this just makes them think she's studying too hard, burning the midnight oil. The custodian pokes his head in the doorway at 11:30pm. Her class ends at ten. He usually cleans Maddy's classroom by 10:30. He hates when his schedule is broken, but he isn't about to interrupt a professor.

He says, "Putting in a long night . . . looks like."

Maddy forces a smile, shuffles through the papers in front of her, and replies, "Yes. I only wish someone would deliver coffee. I have a bomb of a headache, too."

She and the custodian chuckle (grumbles that he can't help with her headache), and, alas, he moves his workstation-on-wheels down the hall after wishing her a goodnight.

With her hands balled into fists my mother smashes her thighs. Hard, and then harder still. Nothing. She doesn't feel the pounding but she knows she'll have bruises in the morning. The morning. The next day. Will they find her the next morning? She doesn't know what class has control of this room the next day, first thing at 8am, some early, freshman comp class where everyone will be too drowsy or just plain missing—Skipped another class today, Ma!—to enjoy the teacher's rhetoric. She doesn't have the water bottle she usually carries so Maddy takes a few Tylenol capsules out of her purse and dry swallows them with a gulp.

She concentrates her thoughts on something she always picks away at: her husband. Maddy wonders if he'll step out of his funk long enough to worry why she hasn't come home. Will he call someone from her department? Will he dare to call Deepika? No, she left, and my mother doesn't even know Deepika is back in town for the month of October (I'm not even aware of this, but it's true in my new state of knowing). She thought Deepika has left until the next term, but wishes she left for good.

No, after everything, he won't do that. If Maddy had brought her cell phone with her she'd call him herself but she left it on the car charger; she doesn't ever want to be caught disrupting her own class with a cell phone, break one of her strictest rules: there are no cell phones ringing during her discussions. If one rings, Maddy asks the offender to leave and not to come back until the next class. She doesn't want to risk asking herself to leave.

A young girl with long blonde hair pulled into a tight braid passes the room and then backtracks. "Are you okay?" the girl asks, "I heard crying."

"I'm perfectly fine," Maddy says so sternly the girl leaves with a surprised sneer and an abrupt turn.

No you're not, Maddy thinks. I did cry out. She calls herself weak. Do I need to draw you a picture? The pain of her headache starts to make sparkles, little white digits—that's what Maddy calls them—in front of her eyes. The digits dance and undulate without rhythm in a constant swirl of pain and then fade with the pressure, the pain changing form. Maddy hopes her impaired visibility doesn't take the next step and begin to upset her stomach. What else can go wrong?

Maddy realizes she does need help. She pushes herself away from the table by gripping the table's edge. The legs of her old, graffiti-scraped wooden chair make a squeal as she inches further. She can bend at the waist and does so until she finds herself looking down at her brown loafers. She wraps both hands below her right knee and lifts her lower leg. She can't touch her toes but Maddy is able to lift her calf up until her heel rests on the table's edge.

Propping her left leg on the table gives her some hope but she realizes she won't be able to lift up her other leg. She's never been an exercise queen but vows right then to start taking yoga in the mornings—here I am making vows. What's next? An appeal to God? That'll never happen. Her friends always tell her yoga and stretching will really save you if you take the time and give yourself freely to the meditation part. It'll help with the stiffness caused by the accident. She's too impatient to allow silence to take over. The counting will get to her, too. Hold, breathe, pause, release, and again. Now: Think Serenity.

Maddy grasps her left calf again and drops her leg down. It snaps back into sitting position with a bang. She still doesn't feel a thing, no underlying core strength.

The building is completely quiet when my mother feels a tingling in her feet, moving upwards. The tingle fires small and tight and then Maddy feels fiery pins, as if her legs have only fallen asleep, ripping into her muscles. The pain is excruciating and she starts massaging her thighs, then her calves and, when the pain becomes a dull ache, she finishes by rubbing her feet. She can feel though and that's all that matters. Her migraine softly pulses in the background, and Maddy's relief almost brings tight tears. The Tylenol usually staves off the worst effect of migraine nausea. She collects all of the papers in front of her and puts them in her briefcase.

Should she drive to the emergency room? Can she drive? What if her mobility vanishes again? Another car wreck is not what she needs. She decides to walk out the kinks in her legs before chancing the drive home. Nothing to worry about. Only the stress at home, and her new book, which remains stalled in the long middle section, causes her body to disobey her mind.

The air stays crisp and the sky jumbles to overflowing cloud cover. Without any moon to guide her steps Maddy tries to be careful as she walks tentatively down the English department steps. She glances across the main quad of buildings and finds she's not alone out there late at night.

Of course she isn't alone. This is a college campus, after all, and students, like zombies, haunt the darkness. A third of the undergraduate library windows remain lit and the silhouettes of bowed heads reading and researching visible in the darkness. Maddy takes another step. The staff permit parking lot is another two blocks away. Her green Audi A6 is close and Maddy uses the image of her year-old car to keep her legs moving. She still feels a deep tingling in the muscles of her thighs and hamstrings. She tells herself not to panic. There's nothing wrong with her—nothing really wrong with her. Of course, being where I am, compared to my situation, I can say this.

* * *

Even though I should be asleep and dreaming of high school terrors and insecurities, I knock on my father's office door. Geoffrey doesn't make a sound so I open the door. My father faces out the window into the darkness and his office chill focuses his inner pain.

"Dad?"

My father's chair turns slightly towards me and his eyes look shadowy and dark.

"Are you okay?" My voice a whisper.

Geoffrey nods. He thinks of Deepika. That long night. For the last hour, Geoffrey's been dwelling on the woman he approached last April. Her image taunts him and depresses him even more, inviting a forgotten feeling of recklessness, blossoming in his mind, too numb to forget.

"Mom isn't home yet," I say, a little louder, short. A tone meant to convey: Don't you care?

"How are you, Chris?" My father sits, crestfallen, in his chair, as if momentarily stopped from shrinking away to bits.

His words are tentative and yearning as if he doesn't know what to say, as if he's gone through all the selections in his computer banks and come up with the best possible question. There isn't any concern in his voice for his wife, for my mother, and I almost turn around without answering, slam the office door off its hinges, my unseen anger spikes so quickly within. Don't make a scene. It's late and there's nothing he can do anyway. Not in the state he's in.

"I'm fine"—I finally answer with a shrug—"but mom should've been home by now. I'm starting to worry."

"You've grown a lot."

I can tell this conversation isn't going to go anywhere. There's too much sadness in my dad's voice. He has his own private problems to deal with.

"I'm going to call her office again. She hasn't been answering her cell either." I turn to leave as Geoffrey swivels his chair back to face the open window. The office door clicks shut and the house embraces quiet again.

It's so late and there's an algebra test I've barely studied for. The teacher, Mr. Roffiger, is gung ho about the current story problem equations that will help everyone out some day. I think: only if you love mathematics and go that way with your career. So far I haven't met any real genius mathematicians with all the mental problems like those characters in the movies and I don't see how algebra enhances anyone's sanity. Why are brainy people usually portrayed as having a screw loose on film? I use the telephone in the kitchen to call my mother's office and let it ring and ring and ring. The cell service says there's no room for more messages. Have I left that many?

I'm not hungry but I eat a handful of Pringles, then another, almost finish the can, and taste the starch as it coats my mouth and throat until I feel a thickness within. I pull out my algebra book and skim over chapter four and the few errors I made in class. Mr. Roffiger's a nice man. I keep telling myself he's too nice to teach such a ball-busting course. He's always smiling and happy and I start to feel—how can you blame him?—there's no way he wouldn't be happy. He has eight children at home, the oldest two years younger than me, but I've seen the whole brood coming and going, at the movies, out to dinner at some fast food place where you can't push tables together to accommodate a family of ten, including two toddlers who still need high chairs, and two more who insist on using the booster seats to be as tall as their siblings in one of the two booths they finally, always, have to take. "Older kids here, and be good, let's keep the young ones with us. Do you have Little Annie?" Mrs. Roffiger holds the youngest under the arm tightly. Little Annie squiggles and her extremities pinwheel but Mr. Roffiger's wife doesn't care and stands unruffled until her family is seated. She shoves into the booth and waits for the many trays of hamburgers and special order chicken fingers and fish sandwiches to arrive. Mr. Roffiger flits back and forth to the counter, as a few of his children miss something, ketchup packets, a toy in the kid meal, and he sweats to make everything right and perfect.

    I sit at the kitchen table in what my mom calls the breakfast nook with my schoolbooks spread over the surface and I think about all the children Mr. Roffiger deals with daily. Since I'm an only child it's hard for me to fathom the need for such a large family. Maybe the youngest are insurance children—just in case of emergency. My grandparents, my mother's parents, live on a farm in Ohio and they have at least eight cats running around the barns and the main house. Always that many cats, give or take, in case some of them get run over on the highway or killed off by the foxes and coyotes. They call them insurance cats. Grandfather wakes before the day begins, and feeds all of the cats first. They flock to him like chickens. They cry and meow and rub up against his legs and he takes care of them in the barn by filling up a huge trough with dry cat food. There's always a momma cat who is pregnant or one that's just given birth. Once, when my family was visiting over the 4th of July there was a litter of seven kittens, striped in patchy browns and orange tiger, and grandmother gave me a large basket with a brightly colored hand towel for lining. She put all the kittens at the bottom and we went downtown for the holiday parade.

"Walk up and down the block and give them away," Grandmother said to me. My mother got me all dressed up really country in cutoff dungarees and a local grocery store hat and I yelled 'Free Kittens' at everyone. They were gone in an hour. And I thought of these large litters and how easily they were given away.

Am I really missing anything? The cat barn still stands, but it has turned into an R.V. storage shed and I'm pretty sure there aren't as many cats to take care of. My grandparents, old and retired now, drive their motor coach from one end of the country to the other to visit their kids and grandkids. They get a neighbor's son to feed the cats when they're gone.

Mr. Roffiger must love all his children; why else would he want to be a teacher? I find something suspect about his ever-present smile, too, and have a hard time looking him in the eye. Maybe he's a fool because algebra seems like fool's work to me.

Sometimes it's just too easy. The homework takes me little time and my classmates seem to grasp all the answers so slowly, out of reach at the tip of their fingers, unlike magicians. I seldom miss a step and rarely need extra help filling the spaces in logic. School feels simple to me, every subject a slow heaping of knowledge I pick up as if I'd already known the answer all my life. I retain everything. Not photographically, but my retention of information after I read or listen to something, is phenomenal. The teachers who judge me as a slacker because I sit in the back and wear dismal-colored hoodies, know my secret after the first few tests come back. Could I be valedictorian? Possibly. Maybe I picked up the genius gene from my grandfather. Of course, this is another secret I never advertise. I'm bored in every subject but gym, and there's talk there won't be a gym class after the new budget cuts roll down the line. It's only the second month of school, mid-October. I look ahead and there's a long road winding away in front of me. Some of my classmates, the ones who looked stupefied, are already mumbling about summer school, just to catch up, and they have to do well so they can get into a good college.

I remain dumbfounded. Most adults tell me I act too old for my age. In private. When given this type of compliment, I hide within myself even more, act against this description, make incorrect guesses on tests on purpose. I want to fit in too badly.

As I sit at the breakfast table going over the chapter review questions the clock ticks making me aware of the time and I start to really worry about my mother. What's the use. I close my algebra book and slump up the stairs to my room. I'll stay awake until I hear my mother come home.

* * *

When Maddy finally makes it to the car, her legs feel normal and her migraine is gone. She lets out a chirp of a laugh. She will laugh again tomorrow when she wakes up as if this episode was but a dream. If she was a superstitious woman she'd conjure up a hex to protect her and her family from harm, but she's not and she begins to laugh, silently, again. Her car windows show a film of moisture coating them; she turns the defroster on high and waits for them to clear.

It's been hard, she knows, to think of anyone else lately. It's late and she wonders if Geoffrey missed her and this makes her bark out another laugh. She picks up her cell from the car charger hidden in the middle compartment and finds all the messages from me. Where are you? When are you coming home? Plaintive whining. There isn't a message from Geoffrey. She'll be home soon enough so she doesn't call. In the stillness of her car she grips the steering wheel tightly until she can't feel her fingers. Her legs are fine. She presses the gas pedal and revs the engine. It's the only sound in the empty parking lot and this alone gives Maddy a chill and goose pimples form along her spine. None of the other teachers are up this late. Why should they be? We've got it easy: the nice and cozy life on the Big Sky dole.

Maddy places the car in drive and inches her way towards the parking lot exit. The tenderness of her right foot on the gas pedal almost makes Maddy start crying because she feels it. To think she almost lost it back in the classroom. She's so happy she didn't ask anyone for help. That would've been richly embarrassing. She can picture the polite, mumbling custodian lifting her up and trying to massage her muscles, and then she pictures Travis rubbing the same areas, drawing heat.

Skinny Travis pleads, a puppy willing to do anything for her—right—right? She wonders if this really is the case. How far would he go to help her? If she'd told him she couldn't move, what would he have done? He'd stutter and walk back into the classroom, and finally, when confronted with too much reality, paralysis, migraine, how unsexy, he'd leave to find someone else to help her. "I have to get to The Basement. I'm meeting Reggie. Darts, you know," he'd say. Then he'd write about it in his worn journal of longing. Later he'll turn her infirmity into a poem; all life he uses as his palette. His tallness such an eye-catching feature he doesn't need the beard to make people aware of him. Maddy has to force herself in class not to look at him longer than any of the other students. Must be proper and rigid. Not that being rigid is hard for her to do.

Audi A6, green, sleek, the roofline slightly rounded, and very safe. The car purrs as it shifts to a higher gear turning out of the parking lot. Maddy worries about safety the most. She must drive a car highly regarded for safety. Torn between the Audi and the Volvo. If the Germans do anything top-of-the-line it's car manufacturing. She chose the Audi over the Volvo based on safety first and then power and finally on cuteness. How the car looks isn't really that important to Maddy, but the faculty parking lot has more Volvos and she felt pulled the other way. Every car speaks stories embedded in the subconscious. She knows people who will not set foot in a German car to this day; too much history.

Maddy used to drive a small, maroon Subaru station wagon, low to the ground with good fuel economy. It was given high marks for safety also, and Maddy believed this at the time—and she still does; it's what saved her life—when a Ford truck ran a stop sign ten miles north of Middleton. The truck T-boned into my mother's side, right into Maddy and me, when I was just a six-year-old kid strapped in the back, on the way to Flathead Lake for a family weekend getaway. The car left the ground. All four wheels jumped off the pavement, spiraling up and around into the drainage ditch, parts of the car pinging away, flying into the air. The man in the truck was high on bad temper, not booze, and of course he walked away from the wreckage without a physical scratch, the front end of his truck smashed like an accordion too old to play.

Ever afterward, Maddy remained rigid. The accident happened when I was still a squawking child pestering my mother with innocuous question after question from the back seat. I can remember the whirly-gig feeling of accident freefall and that's all. Now I look back on the accident and crave that same physical tumult—only because I survived. Like an amusement ride you can keep riding knowing the safety bar will be raised so you can get in line again and again if you want. Maddy was in the hospital unconscious for hours, and spent most of the day in surgery, with a concussion, a broken back, a nerve in her neck pinched, and a multi-fractured left leg, where the door parts ripped into her. Haven't you noticed how she walks with a slight limp? No? Well it's there and she's better now, but she's still very rigid. The pinched-nerve in her neck is what gives her the most trouble and if she smiles you can barely tell anything happened at all. She becomes her old self. When the ambulance brought us to the hospital Maddy was in the emergency room for three hours before she could be stabilized and taken first to the O.R., followed by a dreary term in the Intensive Care Unit. Someone said I couldn't stop crying. Later, as years passed and the story came up, I was embarrassed, but not now—I was just a kid. Even when Geoffrey came from his office to be by our side I wouldn't stop crying.

My father had planned on meeting Maddy and me at the Flathead Lake weekend rental later on in the day. He told

Maddy earlier in the week he had to do something for one of his important clients and he couldn't be with us to drive up as a family. "We'll take two cars." Maddy wondered about this case, this client, so important, and how Geoffrey's day became interrupted regardless of planning. After Maddy was revived enough to speak and long afterwards she never asked about this client of my father's. He didn't say much at the hospital as I clung to his middle and pressed and wouldn't let go, his gaze blank and unforgiving. A look you could get used to and do nothing about.

* * *

Geoffrey doesn't get up from his office chair when he hears the garage door rising and Maddy's car enter. Geoffrey feels too adrift and unaware and totally alone. He can hear the car engine sputter off and the garage door lumber closed. It catches with a loud hitch halfway down and Maddy has to press the button twice to get it going down again. The door to the mudroom closet opens and he imagines Maddy taking off her fall jacket, a black windbreaker too old to be stylish but not nebbish and out-of-date. It's what her students, the ones who live as if they invented fringe, call retro and compliment her on it just to be speaking, to curry favor. The sound of her large briefcase and another bag of books being dropped on the kitchen table reverberates through the ductwork of the house. *Smack smack smack* Maddy takes the notebooks and papers out and sorts them into upstairs/important and table/tomorrow. She'll drag the important work with her and the glass of wine to act as a sedative. Even after the migraine she thinks she deserves the wine. She told her doctors she wouldn't give up red wine, even though it's on the list of migraine triggers. Now that her headache had been expunged, somehow, she needed to de-stress.

He wants to walk downstairs to break her pattern. What took her so long coming home, anyway? Let's see how she likes the confusion, Geoffrey thinks, but he stays seated and straightens the office equipment on top of his desk.

Then Maddy starts up the stairs, slowly, feeling each step, tentatively at first, and Geoffrey hears a little laugh as Maddy runs up the last ten steps to the landing. She's tickled her legs are normal. That's what they are, she thinks, and laughs again: normal. It's the sound of the old life, a couple of months after she finally agreed to marry him. Just giving him an adjustment period. The child's almost three and Maddy's finished her writing program years before and he wants to finally tie the knot. She keeps putting it off and doesn't think anything of living together out of wedlock. Even her parents—to her face anyway—really didn't mind the arrangement. They must've hidden what they thought very well. They'd never show their loving concerns or true feelings to the potential in-law anyway.

Maddy stops outside my room and stands quietly debating whether to open the door or not. I turned the small bedside lamp off when the garage door opened. I heard her race up the stairs and her genuine laughter and I lay in the dark trying to see the door across the room. I will her to open it and tell me where she's been all this time and ask what's so funny and after a minute I hear her move away down the hallway. I close my eyes to sleep. My alarm is set.

* * *

Deepika sits at her writing desk and listens to the weather outside her window. She opens her laptop and finds the short story she's been working on, the part of her new collection she's been trying to get just right. She's never written autobiographical, thinly-veiled, stories before, consciously anyhow. There's her main character, Sai, who feels abandoned and dropped into the United States, as if it's the deep end of a swimming pool, by parents too twisted up to have a child. Will her parents even care? They've never read her work before. She can imagine the scandal press and the local gossips reading the tabloids back in her hometown asking her parents for input on their behavior. Deepika hopes to shed light on her upbringing, twist the facts because it's fiction, but sometimes the reality is much harsher, too unbelievable. She's been writing stories about real people back home and these subjects rarely complained, but Deepika worries about her stories now. She presses her hand against her forehead for an instant and then her fingers caress the keyboard.

She writes: (Part one follows here. Read it now like I do or read it later. See if I care. I do. I think what Deepika writes is important. She's definitely hurting. This mistress of awareness. She has a lot of anger, too, and needs to take it out on someone. I can pinpoint the exact moment I became her main character. I am Sai).

* * *

A Great Distance (excerpts from)
By
Deepika Webber

There's the rotting smell stuck in the walls of the rental apartment Sai stayed in for the winter season. His clothes reek of it and when he opens the refrigerator the rot stench ratchets up ten degrees. The fridge shakes when Sai slams the door shut. It must be leaking Freon.

He'll be moving into another rental apartment when he returns; he's not leaving Sun Valley, Idaho, for good (he loves the thin air and the sun shining on below-zero days, the free mornings spent snowboarding, hanging outside Seattle Ridge Lodge on top of Baldy, eavesdropping on vacationers and locals whose job seems to be skiing every single day with their Season Pass showing like an elite badge). The rental apartment he lives in is a horror and there won't be anyone to take his place for at least three months because the landlord's a bastard and a Peeping Tom with a nosy complaint complex. So, when Sai's estranged father died and indulgent memories slivered into his mind, drawn up from martini-fueled depths, rage isn't too far behind.

He'll use this family crisis as a break, a chance to move into something nicer, bring his mother out and take care of her. She needs someone to do this and he's her only son.

I can't stand this place, Sai thinks. I wake up this way every morning. I wake up asking: Why? When I'm older the question will change to: How?

He'll find a better rental in Warm Springs; he has several options, friends from the paper who will help him out until he lands a caretaking job, a house or pet-sitter position, save rent, live out of a suitcase if his mother doesn't want to leave Gladys.

Sai's next assignment is to write a news bitch-n-moan article about a woman who takes in stray animals, cats and broken-winged birds mostly, more than the housing code allows. If she can't save the wild birds, she makes her brother take them to the vet, who extinguishes them mercifully. She lives in Elkhorn and is a widow.

Widowhood probably suits her and her obsession with the animal world. Sai imagines the woman telling him she's a healer as she serves him green tea steeped too long and bad molasses cookies. Death turns a lot of people into true believers, turns some into drunks or thieving liars; for some, the very few, it's an awakening after a long life of servitude and endless roadblocks, self-imposed or not. The woman with the thirteen cats seeks a new age.

A small town believes it is different in all ways from the largest city and superior because of the difference, but Sai knows better. Everyone has the potential to become fucked up, big or small. Sai hasn't even started to pack his bags. A farce, really: how can he be about to leave? Just tying up all the loose strings.

Sai can't say this enough. In his mind, leaving is a light bulb blinking on and off repeatedly.

After the snow melts in April he'll be looking for something, someone new, maybe even a roommate beyond his mother; the rents are so high in the Sun Valley resort town it's hard to find affordable housing, which is an oxymoron.

I'll save some money for a rainy day, he tells himself

once more. Why can't I get this out of my head? It'll rain on my father's grave.

The woman with the cat complex is named Mrs. Alice Plesher, but she doesn't reveal her first name to him and Sai only finds out by accident, later. Mrs. Plesher calls the paper and is put through to Sai. He has no idea why although he could guess the green guy gets all of the drudgery assignments until proven worthy. Alice speaks very slowly as if hardened by age and she has a rasp. Sai pictures her in a long house dress from the fifties, pink-and-white stripes fading with age—a smock of beige over the dress, a multitude of cats clinging to the fabric like stick-ons.

"I want to speak to a real reporter."

"I am a real reporter, Miss—"

"Mrs . . . Mrs. Plesher. I was married thirty-two years when my husband died."

Sai wants to tell the dotty old bird he got his job the same way—death the great equalizer and the beginning and ending of all stories. Even though his partner, Joe, hasn't died at all, just grew apart, bored, left Sai for a younger version without a lifetime of accumulated baggage. Which spurred on Sai's escape to the high desert atmosphere of a ski resort town, a place he can't help but view as another temporary safe house.

"Mrs. Plesher, my name is Sai Amrashi."

"What kind of a name is Ashrami?"

"Amrashi."

"Whatever. You're not supposed to correct your elders. Just answer the question, Mr. Amrashi."

"I'm not sure." Who is this woman? Sai wonders. He's supposed to find out so he keeps this question to himself and lances his interior thoughts with sarcasm.

"Indian or real Native American Indian?"

"Indian," Sai replies, stifling the need to say, the fake kind.

"I need to tell someone about those people trying to kick me out of my home. I've lived here more than twenty years. They can't just do that without a fight and I'm fighting them with everything I've got and they still keep bothering me."

"That sounds horrible. Why don't you give me directions

and I'll come out and take your story."

"It's not a story."

"I mean interview you. I'll ask you all kinds of questions and see if there's something the paper can use. Stories like this take a lot of background work. I have to approach both parties to see what is happening, from both sides, objectively." Mrs. Plesher isn't digesting what Sai says and he knows she isn't but he can't help himself. He thinks about his father dead on the stairwell and Gladys finding him there and cursing the man, maybe even spitting on his corpse as it chilled and stiffened in front of her in final repose.

"You come see me now."

"I'm free in two hours. Would that be possible?"

"Just don't send anyone who's allergic to cats. Last time I had to stand out in the cold. A woman my age." She says the last as royal queen outraged by the unscrupulous creeping closer to her kingdom.

Last time? Sai wonders what the hell she's talking about and can only imagine ruin and damnation and personal letters to the editor spewing vitriolic injustice. Happens all the time in every local paper in the world. The letters to the editor are a mix of complaints and bitterness. Someone passes a law-abiding citizen on the right so a local writes in about the degeneration in driving of everyone who has come to visit or put down roots from another locale. If you're from California, forget it, you'll never be a local and everyone will detest the sight of your black bruiser SUV. One word of advice: change your license plates as soon as possible. The latest gripes are about the new hospital cutbacks, the lowering of the speed limit on the highway, the pettiness of the city council and the mayor and the battle to put up a grand hotel blocking the view of the ski mountain from Main Street, while other major developments lay stranded, parking lots filled with weeds, since the tech bust and 9/11 fears shook everything up, the amount of time it takes to get to town from Hailey (now up to 45 minutes on a snow day), and everyone knows skiing takes precedence in a mountain town, how people with dogs are so inconsiderate about picking up after them, and how to say it in a letter so they come across as the saintliest of gadflies. Judge not the people who may help you when you slip on the ice outside the post office one bright sunny winter's day. Sai thinks, it's an election year to boot and the bulk of the letters to the editor denouncing the process, the unfairness, the hatred, makes me want to scream. He doesn't know if he'll vote, sometimes he tells the most spiteful campaigner for either presidential candidate he refuses to vote because it's his right, just to watch the wheels come off the bus. He likes to sit and listen to the debate. It's an American right to vote. Yeah, yeah, yeah. Sai's an American, even if some people don't believe him after they ask where he comes from: New Jersey.

Sai hangs up on Mrs. Plesher after she winds up and then down. He finally decides to delay telling his editor-in-chief he needs to fly home to wrap up his father's estate until later in the day. Imagines saying: I just got the news last night, and I can't believe I still feel like coming into the office. True avoidance issues bloom. I'm the only son, the only child, and the one to whom this task falls. When you hate someone so much there isn't anything you can do about it but try not to expend any energy on that person, become indifferent. Time doesn't heal wounds—new age bullshit.

* * *

Sai arrived in Ketchum nine months ago. He wanted to live in a mountain town, learn how to snowboard, maybe find a semblance of peace, escape from the fiasco he made in northern California; write the great American novel. Sai's thoughts: If Hemingway could do it here (drunk off his ass) why can't I? Lofty pipedreams. Was Hemingway always into whiskey like me? No, but Sai imagines Hemingway as a bit light in the loafers, those macho denials, playing for Sai's team, which always makes Sai laugh; after all, The Old Man and the Sea did have a home in Key West and loved Fire Island's dunes way too much.

* * *

Sai, middle-life. There's still so much rage. He doesn't want to think about it anymore and he's been hiding it so well everyone at the paper thinks of him as the sweetest guy in the world. Most of his coworkers want to set Sai up with someone. Sai lets it be known he's definitely not interested, but most keep trying anyway. Then he, with great humility, tells these people he's gay and that still doesn't stop the most persistent of them. "I know a great guy for you. Gay. Nice. Lives alone, poor thing, in an old hunting cabin. Blah. Blah. Blah." Sai wonders about these potential boyfriends who escape to the wilderness of Idaho. Sai escapes a past life, a past partnership; why would he want to get involved anew? This mountain town isn't kind to single straight people so you know the pickings are slim if you happen to be gay and single; hook up on the spotty internet, turn yourself into a sexy Indian cowboy with your own sensual website, get lots of hits, or take the long drive to Boise if you need to get your rocks off. If you click your ruby slippers three times, you won't be taken home.

The editor isn't in her office. Sai puts off telling her about his dead father for another day, but he knows he can't wait too much longer. Sai doesn't want to discuss his past or his weary, messed-up family with anyone right off the street, especially to someone he barely knows or respects.

* * *

With withering judgement in his tone, Joe would always tell Sai that Sai doesn't let anyone ever get close enough to really get to know—for the thousandth time. Does that make sense? Joe always pouts after ripping Sai a new one. You can be so insensitive, Sai, he'll say, and then stalk off. Two hours later he's back insisting, insulting, and cajoling Sai to go see his analyst; he'll pay of course, for someone to listen to Sai's problems, because all the problems in their relationship are Sai's fault, and then they'll go out to dinner with friends and pretend none of what they fume about ever took place. Maybe dancing at the current, flavorless bar will follow, smiles all around and lots of Cosmopolitans, too many for anyone but the newly sober to keep track of. When Joe and Sai return home to Joe's apartment (Sai moved in when Joe wanted Sai to be his permanent boyfriend), Joe will give Sai the silent treatment the second the front door bangs shut. Off to the bedroom without a word, now miffed by something else Sai has done or said or witnessed but doesn't do anything about vocally.

* * *

Inside his black Jeep Wrangler, Sai feels safe even though it's the size of a shoebox and the door wings back and forth because the doorstop mechanism has been broken since Sai bought it used from a shifty woman who wouldn't make eye contact. He needed the Jeep and it was cheap. The woman said it had good karma (instantly thinking she wasn't being racist by saying "karma" in front of a real-to-goodness Indian who thought of himself as a lapsed Hindu); the Jeep never left her stranded. There're only 76,000 miles logged and it's been a good car to go to Tahoe in, back and forth from Larkspur. Never a problem, she says, with not a little strident pride. Look me in the eye when you lie to me so effortlessly, Sai imagined saying, but he bought the car and believed its pedigree and named it Sanjit after one of his father's ancient brothers who still exists somewhere in a nursing home in Massachusetts. Sai and Sanjit on the road again and in trouble.

Sanjit starts right up but quickly sputters out with a sigh. Sai rubs his hands together and curses himself for giving Sanjit too much gas. Sai is famous for having a lead foot, one of the many arguments Joe picks (picked) with him; Joe always insisted he drive. The car won't start and Sai bangs his hands on the steering wheel. When he's really mad Sanjit becomes a car again, just a rusty piece of junk. Sai pictures Joe laughing at him, his mouth curving into a laughing frown, and Sai's father's there in a flash spitting tobacco juice at Uncle Sanjit's feet the last time they spoke. Harsh words flew like thrown darts and made them impossible to return to sender, yelled them with a relish so ulcer-intensive Sai hid in his room for hours.

Uncle Sanjit wasn't doing anything to me, Sai said, later. Sai cried. He treated me like an equal, and the foul, inhuman assumption, now that Sai was an adult, really pissed him off royally; he never saw Uncle Sanjit again because his father thought his own brother was doing something despicable to Sai—the two of you alone—Dad, all the lights were on bright, after a revisionist: in a dark room together—sitting on the bed together—and Sai wasn't even old enough to understand what his father was raving about. Later—No, he never touched me. Father. No. What're you talking about? Mother so far gone at this point, forever silenced by her fall, Sai believed she cast no shadow.

Life's a bit of a magic act and Sai feels the lingering effects of his escape. His goddamn car won't start, and he made a promise to old bat Plesher he'd be at her house in less than an hour. He stumbles out of Sanjit and grabs his shoulder pack. There's a free bus system in the valley but he has to ask directions to the closest station and when the next bus will be by to take him to Elkhorn. He ends up getting on the wrong bus to Sun Valley and is forced to get out near the Sun Valley Lodge where he waits for a different bus to take him on the circuitous route from Sun Valley back into town where the driver tells Sai he has to get out and stand at the bus stop on the other side of the street where the bus to Elkhorn will be by in twenty minutes. By this time Sai is already fifteen minutes late and he can picture Mrs. Plesher's lips screwed up tight as she counts cats to pass the time, a snarl issuing from between her too-plump-they-can't-possibly-be-real lips. The first thing she'll say is: No one makes me wait. Sai has his fair share of doors slammed in his face.

The right bus drops Sai off in Elkhorn, as close to Mrs. Plesher's road as possible, which means half a mile away. Everything out in the real West means longer, bigger, brighter, better, cleaner, a wider horizon. Sai curses The West and the way the developers have continued to hack up this pristine valley and put homes designed by romper room's space-age division all over the hills with no care, the hubris of man. Sai isn't against the homes being built, exactly, but, aesthetically, enough (bad apples) of the homes are butt-ugly and caught in the '70s and '80s and make him wince as he walks by on his way to Timber Frame Road.

Because of the street name Sai makes the correct turn and expects to see lovely homes of timber frame construction but again he feels jarred by stucco homes the color of pencil lead with gables going one way and not matching the roofline of the guesthouse stuck on top of the garage which is also 2,000 square feet. There's always way too much room in these houses for one family and all their extended family to descend upon them during high ski season. A pack of legal and illegal immigrants and migrant workers clean the homes weekly and mow the Midas-size lawns and feel lucky to be living in the valley where, for housecleaning, they can easily charge $25 or more an hour, laugh about their employers all the way back to Hailey and Bellevue in the part of the valley where all the workers live. Let them take enough of everything to go around for everyone.

The people at the coffee shops discuss their housekeepers and landscapers as if they're indentured servants without families and problems of their own, in voices filled with dismay, indignation, overly worried about breakage and theft and how hard it is to find good help these days—boy does it cost them an arm and a leg. One woman with hair platinum, perfect, and blinding says she hates paying for the privilege of living here in Sun Valley and then stands up from the table intent on taking her purebred dogs to the groomer who charges $85 per dog if the dog is really, really dirty. She turns back to her friend, sits, and says, in a shrill voice: Can you believe that C.E.O. moving here and getting permission to put up that 30,000 square foot concrete and glass monstrosity on top of that hill? Wonder how much money changed hands? Did you hear about that?

Her friend says, Or that one celebrity who thinks he can peep into private windows whenever he wants, who totally disregards the No Trespassing signs—as if they don't apply to him? Or the comedian with Saddam's forehead who thinks he's too much the Star to even say hello or thank you or anything polite to the people he passes every day in this small town—he won't last long; it's hard to be a Republican in this Democratic town anyway; I hear he wears the most ridiculous safety helmet when he goes ice skating.

And the rich, ah, their full time job is managing the help and most are so bitter about the cost of everything they take it out on them in many small ways, mostly by appropriating a tone of voice never suitable in polite company and only slightly understandable when reprimanding a dog caught piddling on the carpet.

Mrs. Plesher's sprawling ranch-style house comes into view up on Sai's left. Again, it's also gray but not stucco, just faded cedar siding to give it a real faux-Western feel. Her landscaping, just the sage fields and a few pine trees, remains nonexistent for her having lived in the house over a decade and Sai realizes she doesn't want tall pines planted to block her view of the ski mountain or the perpetual White Cloud Mountains to the north. Sage dots the hills behind the house in waves, patterns broken by the strip-mining veins racing to the peaks thousands of feet higher than the homes.

Besides her inflated lips, the next physical detail Sai notices about Mrs. Plesher is her stern figure. She carries herself in a formally rigid manner, with her arms crossing a flat landscape of chest the majority of the time. Her shirt is such a plain cornflower blue it could've come off of a pharmacist's back. She's happy, Sai deduces. Her seriousness is her way of showing this. At one moment in her history with but a glare she stops the boys from laughing and making fun as she walks by.

* * *

Her parents grew up in Wyoming on a farm that raised hay, sugar beets, and barley, and there were so many horses it could've doubled as a horse ranch. When Mrs. Plesher was a young girl following in her mother's footsteps, a dart of a shadow behind the quickness of adult strides, she could measure up because she learned to take control of every situation. Her mother, a firm disciplinarian, wouldn't cotton to frivolous acts or phrases.

"You can be a silly nitwit, Alice. Don't let me catch you playing with the hem of your dresses anymore. You wear them to church and you sit beside your brothers and act like a lady."

"I'm not."

"A lady doesn't backtalk her mother either."

"I'm not playing with my dress."

The slap would spring into Alice's field of vision quick as a pinball bumper. Alice learned to be her mother's plaything. She was the oldest and only daughter of five children and her mother always told her she had to set an example. If her four brothers acted up and destroyed the carpet in the back hallway with their muddy pig shoes it was her job to make sure her mother never found out. She'd yell at her brothers, Lionel, Shorty, Curtis, and Forrest in that order until they got used to it, and would do whatever she wanted. Alice wouldn't fight or slap her brothers; her words would cut into them.

It was a hard life in Wyoming in the '40s and '50s with few neighbors to speak of near Laramie but far enough away to make every childhood trip to the town seem like a special event. Alice would help her mother with the baking and the feeding of the chickens and the egg collecting and the other chores too easy for anyone else to do, but her mother always wanted her to have a mind sharp and brilliant and sent her to the school with a warning for her to learn her lessons. Always unspoken was the OR ELSE. Alice's studies would prepare her for a life beyond the farm. When her mother said this to her the first time she was only ten-years-old. You're old enough to know there are few ways for a woman to find something of her own to hold onto, out here especially.

Alice studied and memorized and learned how to manipulate the teachers, and her mother helped her.

"You're going to be respectable one day, a teacher perhaps, someone a sterling gentleman will fall for like a stone down a well," said her mother with her flat tone. The heaviness in her mother's voice Alice learned never to forge barriers against. At first Alice thought her mother just wanted to get rid of her. She was competition after all. Her father doted on her in many small ways, never overtly, never so that the other children would make a cry of bitterness, but he did. Alice read to him at night after she read stories to the boys and helped put them to bed. She'd get books from the school's teachers on loan: Steinbeck, The Bronte sisters, and Fitzgerald and Hemingway, one after another, the stories coming out of Alice's tight, serious lips. Her mother would sit listening while she knitted or mended the socks, sewed back buttons, and patched holes in the family's laundry. Soon, Steinbeck would grow too racy and Alice read them in secret; his stories about wanton women in the West of the past didn't smooth anything at the farm, biblical parable or not. Her father loved the true stories about the land and Hemingway filled the bill and Alice's brothers even liked them too, but not as much as they liked Zane Grey Westerns or the space operas from the pulps at the drugstore.

The life of Alice Plesher was planned out from the beginning days on the farm as if God had inhabited her mother's flesh on one of His bad days and a tiny part clung to her when He had to go put a crack in a dam somewhere across the world to teach the people caught in the flood a lesson about sticking together, helping your neighbor, in hard times. You did what you were told. The family didn't go to church often. Alice always wondered why and imagined her parents balking at religion the same way they dug into the sand when anyone tried to tell them what to do or how to live.

A girl had few escapes on the hay and horse farm. Alice would follow her brothers around when they were goofing off, finished with their chores and school and trying to get away. They all ran to the woods bordering the river to escape. Her brothers weren't stupid either so much. Too many times the five of them would get to the bank of the river where they piled up broken branches and logs into a shelter and after an afternoon building and supporting the fort they'd collapse under the makeshift roof sweaty and smelling of rot and dirt and molding leaves. They all felt the weight of their parents and they'd talk about it till even the youngest, Forrest, the sunniest of the children, could be trusted to never repeat what was said to their mother and father.

"I'm going to California when I get old enough," Shorty said.

"You don't even know the right direction to start such a journey," Alice replied.

"You'd help me then. Just like in that Eden book. I'd wander the world."

Alice swatted Shorty because they both knew he was the only one she read that book to. This was the early '50s when all the children except Forrest were about to be teenagers and so much of the world outside their farm seemed like a fantasy world, someplace like Oz or the wicked forest where Ichabod Crane met his fate. The boys only saw the good though and could never believe people had to face true evil. "I'd get myself whipped from here to Laramie if I helped you run away. Besides, you're the one Dad counts on to run the farm."

"I'll run the place if he doesn't want it," Lionel said without any hesitation. They all knew Lionel had his eye on the place. He wanted to follow his father everywhere. Make him proud. Always did what he was told. Alice called Lionel a simpleton whenever his back was turned.

"You know Dad wants all of you to run it."

"Why not you?" Curtis asked. Lionel pushed Curtis and he fell backwards and raised himself off the bed of leaves with a sneer.

"I'm still only a girl and Mom has other plans for me."

"You're lucky."

* * *

Sai greets Mrs. Plesher with a wry smile and an outstretched hand, which she refuses and fades back into her home with her arms crossed. Her hair is cut short and cradles her forehead closely as if formed by a bathing cap, and then he realizes she's wearing a wig and has a hard time not staring at her hair from that point on. When Sai follows her into the front entryway the dimness of the lighting strains his eyesight.

"You're not here to do anything but take down my story. I have a lot to tell you about my neighbors, my lovely backbiting, son-of-a-bitching neighbors, and I don't have time to do anything else. I've made coffee if you want some."

Sai shakes his head no while saying, "No, thank you. Let's get started."

He can't help but notice the cat smell as Mrs. Plesher leads him into the kitchen, a small galley-sized room facing the sunrise with the end of the galley made into a breakfast nook with windows—a bright room in the morning. The cats laze on the ledge, but seem ready for action at the slightest provocation; they watch the sparrows and the magpies bounce around the feeders Mrs. Plesher has installed like temptresses on the other side of the glass. Most of the cats are black or solid white, but there's one large tabby and a calico who sit like bookends on the floor eating food out of two of the six red plastic bowls spread out in front of a row of Formica kitchen cabinets.

"So," Sai starts, "are all of your cats indoor cats or do you let them go outside?"

"How long have you been a reporter?" Mrs. Plesher asks with the faintest hint of condescension.

"About three years off and on. My background is in English with a minor in Journalism. A town this small could afford to hire the best."

She catches Sai's sarcasm but asks another question with the same tone of voice. To get through the next hour Sai knows this interview will take all of the skills he acquired while growing up with the parents he somehow got stuck with. Maybe he can cut it short and write nothing. Go back to the editor and reveal Alice's wacky scheme to create an army of cats so one day she can lay siege to the hills, burying her neighbors in cat-box smells and scratched antiques.

"Where're you living?"

"Warm Springs. In a rental condo."

"So they pay you well."

"It's just a hobby. I've been fortunate enough to be raised

as someone who has learned how to save every penny."

"Which means you learned how to be cheap, too." Mrs. Plesher snorts, and maybe with a slight approval; snorts are hard to define sometimes, could've been derision.

She is interviewing Sai.

"Cheap is a state of mind. I prefer the word frugal."

"Don't get smart with me."

Sai has a vision of Mrs. Plesher taking a whack at him with one of the many kitchen knives hanging magnetically against the wall.

"I've got far too many smug neighbors as it is to deal with someone else who's trying to get the truth to tell the whole world."

Sai has dealt with a regular kaleidoscope variety of manic people in his life. He can spot them in a hurry with enough time to sidestep the clinging compulsions fueling the paranoia. It isn't fun. And he knows his sense of humor is too much for Mrs. Plesher; not many people appreciate good sarcasm anyway. He won't underestimate her either; he knows she's sharper than most of the people who sat next to him during composition class at the only community college in New Jersey he could afford.

"Okay. Why don't you start at the beginning and take me through the events you spoke about on the telephone from the past to the present."

"Chronological is the way you want me to tell my story."

"I think the simpler the better. News writing is usually right to the point."

"Don't patronize me, you little shit."

Sai feels goosed. He stands abruptly, clutching his notebook. He doesn't let anyone speak to him in such a manner not even if Mrs. Plesher is mildly entertaining in a falling from a tall bridge fashion.

"Oh, sit down."

"You cannot," Sai says, and repeats, "You cannot speak to me like you just did, nor in that tone of voice; I think it would be best if I got somebody else to take down your grievance."

"I said sit down." Mrs. Plesher blocks the small exit and the way her fists grind into her hipbones Sai just wants her to back up. He also wants to take a photograph of her just like that, arms akimbo. She reminds him of his own mother's mother: old and too mangy to put out to pasture quietly.

* * *

"I'm not lucky," Alice said to Curtis with a grave smile.

"Yes, you are. You're the only one of us who'll get off the farm and see the world."

"I'll let you visit all the time." Around the fort they'd hung blankets too ratty to be missed by mother or father, but just perfect for the privacy of their meeting place.

Lionel looked sullen and Alice could tell he was withdrawing. "Lionel will take care of you. I'll give that job to him when I leave. I'm sick of wearing that crown anyway."

"Lionel will get a crown?" asked Forrest, who from the tone of his voice was kind of miffed he wouldn't be getting one either.

"There's no crown, you goofball." And Curtis smacked Forrest on the back of his head. She'd seen her mother do that a thousand times to all of the boys and they'd seen mother smack the back of her head too. Once so hard and by surprise she'd lost her baby tooth when it slammed against the rim of her cereal bowl. There wasn't a scratch of money for the tooth fairy anyway; she scolded Alice not to expect it either; I'll never understand the things you do to wind up everyone in this family.

* * *

"I was the eldest of five. Did I tell you that?" Mrs. Plesher asks as she folds a cloth cocktail napkin and lays it in front of her. Sai keeps his seat and doesn't mind listening as she runs through her past. Stories fill his head and Sai makes most of them up anyway. It's good to get new ones and the tone of voice Mrs. Plesher uses, honestly, puts him on edge;

he's heard it all his life; hackles up.

"Blood splattered all over the table. When Shorty brings it up he always says I filled that cereal bowl to the rim. My mother really had a great swing. But who knew about tennis then out in Wyoming? The rich maybe . . . a different time a different planet perhaps . . . smile and tell me everything will be okay. The happiest day of my life? Do you want to know what that day was like? I remember it because I got away. There was the train out of Laramie and I had one new dress and a lot of hand-me-downs from my mother even though I had to take them in a lot, without complaint."

One of the cats, a Maine coon with a head the size of a grapefruit starts scratching Sai's pant leg. He kicks it away without actually kicking it.

"Best to not anger The Main Puss. She'll rip you a new one without regret, and don't expect a condolence letter from me."

* * *

Deepika always feels weak after a long writing session. Her forearms and wrists ache and she dreads the possibility of getting carpel tunnel syndrome, something one of her former colleagues at Big Sky deals with daily. He wears wrist guards on both arms and always asks Deepika or anyone available to open doors for him. Even the lightest of swinging doors give him problems and he's become a burden to her and most of the staff. When Deepika spies him up ahead she'll do anything else to avoid opening the door for him. Sorry, my hands are full. She's off to wash her face in the restroom sink. It's such a small matter, an irritation, Deepika thinks about. She'd put him in a story if she didn't think he'd sue.

Her characters, Sai, and Mrs. Plesher and Sai's parent all have appearances to keep up and battles to wage. So does Deepika.

DISTANCE

THE NEXT MORNING my alarm buzzes and I smack the snooze button with my palm, another ten minutes of pre-awareness. The house rests quiet, still. Maddy and Geoffrey are mice in their own separate cubbyholes behind the walls of the house. I haven't laid eyes on my mother in so long; I can't remember the last time I saw both of my parents in the same place; the three of us keep missing each other.

"Life is tough, Honey," my mother says the week before, "and we're both in school and your father has a job that makes him work such long hours." Maddy likes to act as if she's forever in school even though she's on the teaching side now. She hopes to make me feel better, as if we're both still in this educational hamster wheel together. I always say: You do my algebra then . . . write my stinking term paper.

The shower wakes me up better than caffeine. Listening once more, nothing moves in the house except me. I don't waste time washing my hair; just stand under the shower spray to wake me up. My hair will hang limply all day but the grunge look lasts forever in my school. I try not to make too much noise as I dress in jeans and a snowboarding t-shirt. At my high school baseball hats, any kind of hat, are banned.

I glance down the hall to my father's office and instead of going to the kitchen I walk to his door and muster the will to open it. My father curls asleep on his small sofa. His suit jacket covers his upper body. His blue-and-white, striped tie rests on the floor near his right hand. He looks like a crumpled puppet. I know if I nudge him he'll awaken quickly, with a shock, and part of me wants to do it, just run right up to my father and give him a smart kick with my padded, midnight blue Skechers. He'll wake up all right. This small college city awakens slowly. I turn and shut my father's door.

I don't need to open my mother's bedroom door to know how she sleeps; she's always on her left side, curled into a ball with her arms wrapped around a buffer pillow and her legs pressed into another longer king pillow. To take the pressure off her back, she says, the doctor told her to start sleeping with pillows, bolsters, all around her. After the car accident this little bit of advice helps her. There she'll be on the bed in the middle of her own cocoon, as if all the safety bags have been deployed once again.

I don't eat much for breakfast, just an apple cut into slivers with the apple cutter. Most mornings my main goal is to get out of the house as fast as possible without any confrontations. An inherited trait: I like my alone time. The high school complex is less than two miles down the road and a turn to the left on Dorma Street. I'm one of almost three hundred students in my freshman class alone so it's hard to stick out. I'm not one of the popular kids. I got the opposite gene from both my parents.

* * *

While I change in the locker room for first period gym class my mother awakens but doesn't move. She feels the same stillness I felt an hour earlier although she doesn't feel the same panic of the night before. She tests and presses down on every muscle in her legs even before she moves them slightly to check. She has to reassure herself nothing is wrong with her body. An empty wine glass sits on her bedside table and Maddy realizes she drank too much. She can't remember drinking all the red wine. She knows she shouldn't be drinking at all. She's read a book on headaches and the author lists all the foods and drinks she should try to avoid. It's a long, long list. Life's too short and she laughs at the thought of eating only carrots and celery and drinking water the rest of her life. If everything good is taken away, she thinks, what's left?

In a second she moves. Tick tick tick tick . . . tick. Moves like she always moves in the morning: slowly and deliberately. Her eyelids are crusty with sleep and barely open. What would it be like to wake up blind? Maddy thinks this and doesn't crack a smile, her dark sense of humor again just not funny. She does laugh inwardly at all the physical problems she's dealt with since the crash. Once again: she knows no one wants to hear it. Most of the time she keeps her aches and pains to herself. Maybe she really has pushed Geoffrey away; she really is to blame for his weak choices. They've had their problems, like any couple, she thinks, and the car crash happened almost a decade ago. She's long over it.

After unfolding the covers and pushing the leg pillow away and then sliding to the side of the large sleigh bed, Maddy hangs her head. Her brown hair is long and straight, usually; now it has kinks and sleep swirls and juts out and away from her head. She runs her fingers through and then pulls her hair back into a ponytail she fastens with a large tortoise hairclip from the nightstand drawer. Light passes through her windows and Maddy knows the sky remains cloud-covered, threatening rain—another day in the Montana fall season.

Maddy didn't hear me moving around earlier, getting ready, and she doesn't hear Geoffrey moving at all and she wonders if he's already left for work. He's up and gone on Wednesdays well before she awakes. She thinks she has the house to herself.

Maddy studies her feet and then cringes at the shape her toenails are in: ragged and uneven. She wonders about the last time she cut them. Are they turning yellow? What does she do to damage her feet so much? It's just the way it is, and then she lifts each foot and wiggles each toe. At least they're moving this morning. The scare of last night's situation comes back full force and Maddy stands and leans against the far wall. She presses her palms hip-width apart, and stretches her legs out behind her until she's leaning diagonally. She hasn't done these stretches in so long she hears the popping in her knees as she tightens. What if they lock up now? She thinks: Excuse me, officer, I realize it's awkward you finding me here like this, can you be a dove and just prop me in the hall closet.

With a laugh, Maddy turns and lets out a shriek when she faces the open door to her bedroom. Geoffrey stands there like a scarecrow, staring at her.

"I didn't hear you come in. You scared me," Maddy says, with a hint of anger. Geoffrey doesn't reply but moves over to the bed and sits. "How long were you watching me?"

"Are you okay?" Geoffrey asks instead of answering his wife's question.

"This isn't about me!" Maddy realizes her tone of voice has an edge to it. She thinks: I hope he's awake enough to understand it's just because I'm grumpy when I wake up. No espresso yet. Keep the bitterness away. He's only asking how I am. He looks horrible even though he's probably been up for an hour making me breakfast with an industry I don't believe he has in him. Is he going to wear the same rumpled suit a second day? He looks like he slept in it.

"I'm working on a new case today."

"I thought you already left for work. That's why you scared me. Funny. I forgot you were home with the flu."

"I don't have to be in for another hour. I'm feeling much better."

Maddy realizes Geoffrey is lying to her, again, and it's so simple for her to see through him.

His words stay tentative when they should be the same old direct Geoff and his uneasiness rests heavy in her chest. Maddy inches away from the wall and sits cross-legged on the floor. She has a hard time looking at her husband. When will it get easy again? What was he thinking? Another writer, she thinks. He had to pick another writer from her department. Why did Geoff have to pick Deepika? And these thoughts of Maddy's bubble forth six months later, long after the affair has been put to bed, so to speak, but less than half a year from the time she let Geoff back into the house—a reconciliation—in early July. If this happens again—If this happens one more time, our marriage is over and Chris and

I will leave. One more time. It's like double-daring Geoff and in the past he was always up to the challenge.

Geoffrey tries to convey eagerness with his tone but fails and scolds himself internally. Maddy's stretching irritates him to no end but he won't reveal this fact. He just stays on the bed with his palms flat beside him on the blankets for support. Now he wants to ask where she was last night, why she came home so late.

"You seem distracted"—he says; and he cringes . . . what a stupid thing to say—"I mean, we haven't been spending that much time together lately."

"You have so much work and I'm in the middle of my book."

"It's a good thing Millie and Frank didn't call from your sister's to set up a surprise visit after their trip to La Jolla to vacation with their other grandchildren," Geoffrey says. He attempts irony to lighten the mood.

"They will soon enough." This brings back the old Madison. They can both bitch about each other's parents and extended families until the end of days. The ups and downs and the putting up with in-laws, the slights and irritations of childhood memories brought up to teach lessons oozing condescension, and it's where Maddy and Geoff can always start.

"I ran into Glynnis on campus," Maddy says. Geoffrey doesn't respond, keeps his silence, but the wheels go around and around. His personal assistant, Glynnis O'Toomey, probably has a lot more free time. It's inevitable. What does Maddy want him to say?

"She hopes you feel better soon. She waved from a distance, and when I caught up to her she barely said anything. We both know Glynnis is a talker. Did you get the flu that was going around last week? Because, Geoff, I'm sorry I've been so self-involved. I used to notice when you got sick. I thought there was time for us to get this year's flu shot."

"Don't worry yourself. I'm okay." The biggest lie of them all.

"Well, in that case, I have a lot of work to do and you probably need to get back to the office."

"Glynnis didn't say why she was on campus?"

"No. We bumped into each other for all of ten seconds, if that." Geoff's fishing for information so tentatively is curious. Glynnis wouldn't even look her in the eye. Maddy aches to go to Geoffrey on the bed and hold him . . . make him hold her. She'll say: Crazy thing, I lost the use of my legs last night, Geoff, temporarily. Tell him everything about the strange episode and see if he can comfort her for once, but his secretive nature, easier to spot now, pushes these thoughts away. Maddy's coldness returns; she would know it if he'd had the flu. So she doesn't know what he's been playing at, and maybe it's become easier to tell when he's lying to her. She wants to get through this morning without a fight. She itches to get out of the house.

"Oh."

"Do you know when you'll be back tonight?" She forces a smile. "I thought I'd bring home Chinese from that new restaurant on campus. Despite the cheaper than cheap prices and the closeness to the student hive, I hear it's great."

"Sounds good." And then Geoff plunges ahead, trying to create an explanation for his presence. "I'm going to start working from the home office in the afternoons. The case I'm working on for the Glacier Park contingent is taking a lot of time, but all my files are here."

"Maybe you'll see more of Chris," Maddy says. "But what about your personal assistant? Glynnis? You always said you wouldn't know what to do without her." Geoffrey knows Maddy is baiting him, trying to get him to say he needs another woman.

"She's going to work for a colleague of mine. I need more freedom." Maddy changes the subject. What her husband was saying didn't make sense to her. The last thing she wants to talk about is his need for freedom. He's had too much of that this past year.

Maddy tells Geoff that I won't be home until after the chess team meets and that there's an advanced math team practice the algebra teacher mentors on Wednesdays—I won't be home until dinnertime.

"I've got to get in the shower and back to campus for my

twelve o'clock class and I haven't finished grading the papers yet. Same old story and I keep putting the kids off."

Geoff replies, "I'll let you get to it. Can I make you some eggs? Scrambled on toast?"

"That'd be great."

"I think we still have some raisin and a couple bagels."

"Raisin." Maddy remembers to say: "Please." It's still very awkward between them but they push through. Both of them try to be pleasing and not step on each other's toes.

Geoffrey moves away from the bed and stretches his back into an arch, his long arms curving up and behind his head, fingers interlaced. Maddy walks to the master bath. She passes Geoffrey without making eye contact or touching him or even acknowledging they just had a conversation. That's all she can muster. She considers the rest of her day while she closes the bathroom door behind her and leans against it. She tallies her evening: an inexpensive—could it really be all that good—carry-out Chinese meal later in the evening. A long writing session after that; her main characters, a married couple who live on the Oregon coast dealing with the death, by bee sting, of one of their three children and how spare her prose has become. Slow going. In over a year she's only accrued sixty-one pages, each word and sentence constructed by sloth. The agent she keeps in touch with still wants to see her work but time hasn't put a bee, so to speak, in her bonnet. She doesn't feel like she has a deadline.

Geoffrey leaves the bedroom without a thought and moves on autopilot to the kitchen where he whisks eggs in a small metal bowl. He places the last of the raisin bread in the toaster and microwaves four bacon strips on paper towels. He hears Maddy making her bed—it used to feel like their bed—the floorboards on his side of the bed squeak like a broken rocking chair, and for the first time in a long time he can see how wrong he's been. All of the pain he's continued to cause over and over again. All the pain he feels is normal, but he won't allow it to show. He bites his fingernails and throws the refuse into the trash.

What did Geoffrey think my mother was doing last night when she came home way too late? She wouldn't do anything to get back at him just for revenge—an affair of her own, perhaps – would she? She looked too genuinely spooked when he startled her earlier but it isn't just that moment. There's something else in her voice. They've known each other too long to dance around like this.

* * *

I'm not the best athlete in the world. The gym teacher-slash-basketball coach still favors the boys over the girls in this equality world, and the ones who can play basketball over everyone else regardless of gender. Most rainy days are spent inside the auditorium divided into teams to play basketball and I hate it with every fiber of my being. I can dribble a ball; I'm not stupid; an idiot can do it, but I'm never going to be the first kid picked and more often than not I'm one of the last few squatters on the bench chosen with the rest of the misfits, Goths, nerds, geeks. The ball seldom finds me and everyone tells me to play defense as the teacher stalks the sidelines scouting the freshman class for his next b-ball star. I can run. It's the one thing I do well and I always use my swift feet to get me out of trouble. The playgrounds of yesterday would've been torture if I couldn't run away from the many bullies who plagued me every school day. No one can catch me and as I grow older the track team wants me. I say no to that right away after trying it in seventh grade. The track coach is an imbecile who never teaches anyone how to run, increase speed, what your hands, arms, feet should be doing, how to control breathing; he just throws the kid out to the starting line and yells a lot. I need more structure and I excel at solo sports where it's only one person against another opponent, or time. Tennis, running (if only there was a thoughtful coach), swimming, bicycling, and chess, if you count that, are the sports I can do something with.

I run up and down the gym for forty minutes and the teacher breaks it up and tells the class to hit the showers. I dread this time most of all, but know I only have five minutes to undress, shower, and change for my next class, Introduction to Biology. I race to my gym locker and swiftly take to the showers. The water's always on the verge of icy and it takes too long to warm the spray so I shiver under the nozzle while everyone else enters the musty tiled room.

 I'm not that close to anyone in gym and a natural pecking order has developed over the first seven weeks of school. The most athletic jock, Ellis Pallino, comes in swinging his arms out, high-fiving his buddies with a natural joking ease, already formulating manliness in his fifteen-year-old stance. He's jocular with most of the other team players. I never get caught staring at Ellis or anyone. I catch micro-glimpses of Ellis's physique (like everyone else does— I know better than to stare at anyone; I keep to myself; I'm hiding), and that's the only saving grace in gym class as far as I'm concerned, but he'll never know this. Ellis has everything I lack except the skinniness and I can't help the comparison. Most of the boys let their jeans hang off their bony hips with their boxers showing above the jeans. The kids who play football bulk up their bodies to hide being thin and small. I'd have to lift weights for a decade before my body began to reveal any shape other than the skeletal outline. I can eat and eat and not gain an ounce. My mother keeps pushing me to eat more but I don't let her pushing get to me.

 Ellis looks around the shower room, even stares for a split-second at me because there aren't any showers available and his niceness surprises me when he actually asks if I'm almost through. I'm finished but I can't say anything; I just walk out of the shower room hanging my head, eyes diverted down to the moldiest tile floor and wonder why Ellis thinks he can take his time. The bell's going to ring any second and there's only another four minutes to race to the far science building for Biology. We share the next class too.

* * *

Maddy walks into the kitchen wearing her worn flannel

bathrobe with her hair pulled into a loose ponytail. Her face doesn't appear taught and stretched. There's a hint of tan from the lost summer sun on her skin and Geoffrey thinks she's never looked better. He doesn't tell her this observation, and I wish, from my hovering state, I could force him to act, to speak his mind. Maybe this would change fate.

"Thanks for making coffee," Maddy says. They sit at the kitchen table. It's getting harder and harder for Maddy to think of anything to say beyond pleasantries.

"You're welcome. I know you like it strong."

"I'm going to need it today after the night I had." She wonders if she should tell Geoffrey what happened to her. He wouldn't understand her fears, her immobility.

"You were burning the midnight oil. I'm doing the same thing," Geoffrey says, rubbing his face.

"Are you getting any sleep?"

"I've been preoccupied."

"That's putting it lightly, Geoff." Maddy doesn't mean anything smart by her comment even though it comes out that way, a slight condescension.

Hurt, Geoff says, "If I could go back in time and not make the selfish choices I made, you know I would."

"That's just it. I don't know that. Not for sure."

Maddy clutches her coffee mug with both hands and stares into the darkness within. The coffee is strong and black and she hasn't lightened it. She shouldn't even be drinking anything with caffeine in it. Again, her headaches; she should make the right decisions. Maybe she'll start today and ask the questions she knows Geoff has the answers to. I'm not going to reassure him, she thinks; he looks so pitiable.

"Did I have any messages?"

"No. Not a one."

"I need to call my parents today, but my schedule at school is so busy I don't know when I'll get around to it."

"Are they still in La Jolla?"

"No. Gulf Shores, Alabama. I got an email. I think they've just started the long drive back to Ohio." She's not going to get irritated at Geoff again; he knows her parents were down in California. They just talked about this. Let it go. "They want to be home well before snow falls."

Millie and Frank visited Rhea and their other grandkids. Maddy's younger sister Rhea and her husband Carl have two kids both under the age of ten. Every even year, in the fall, Millie and Frank spend three weeks at Chula Vista RV Resort outside San Diego. They visit Maddy on the odd years. It's the system they like. They have a 36-foot Winnebago they bought used from another retired couple who became less mobile. It only has 15,000 miles on it and the interior décor's less garish than most. It has two slide-outs: one moves the entire kitchen area out almost two feet, and, the second moves the wardrobe the same amount in the bedroom area so they describe the area as spacious.

When Millie and Frank are done with their fall R.V. trip and say goodbye to Rhea and the kids, they start the long driving trip back to Ohio. This time they'll take the more scenic southwestern way back through Arizona, Texas, and all the way to Alabama and cross the Florida border for luck. Take their time and then head home up the middle of the country. Maddy always worries about her parents on the road. What if they meet up with the wrong people—the kind you read about in newspapers who beat and rob and disrupt and destroy without compunction or ounce of guilt? Millie and Frank travel with a cell and Maddy calls every chance she gets. Usually this time of year she can call her sister's house and speak to the whole family but she doesn't like to do it; she only wants to talk to her parents.

"Have they called?"

"Not in the past couple days," Geoffrey replies. Geoffrey can't remember if they called or not. He listens to the answering machine every day and presses the erase button so easily trying to remember who has called mystifies him. He remembers right then he has to call Lance back. Maybe he'll feel up to it today.

"Strange." They extended their California stay by a week to take the grandkids to Disney. Rhea's kids are on the whole-year school plan and get long breaks each season. In October they're off three weeks. Back in school the week before Halloween and another break for Thanksgiving and

Christmas before receiving another long break in February. Her younger sister, Rhea, always has it together. And Maddy believes she and Rhea have switched roles; Maddy should be the one in control, not her younger sister Rhea, who has to arrange everything to perfection.

"Maybe," Geoffrey says. He knows he can't really say what he thinks about Maddy's sister. She can't speak plainly about his sister, Nell, either.

"I've got to get going," Maddy says in response, keeping it light. "Thanks for making me breakfast; you didn't have to."

"I wanted to."

"Well."

"Do you think Chris is okay?" Geoffrey asks. He wants to keep Maddy there. He wants more time to build up his courage to tell her what a mess he's made.

"Why do you ask? What's wrong with Chris?" Maddy isn't going to take Geoffrey's question the right way. His way.

"I don't know. I saw him last night a couple times. He was doing a lot of homework. He just seems quiet."

Maddy wants to get out of the house now. Fast. Not sit there and answer Geoff's questions the way he wants her to. She knows he wants her to think about the possibility that I'm as messed up as he is. My mom's not going to let him deduce anything of the sort. I know I'm not depressed, clinically anyway, and my mother knows this, too. She doesn't need to see me every moment to know this. You're the one who gets quiet—she wants to yell this, make Geoffrey jump in his seat—you're the one who always gets quiet. If Geoff doesn't listen to her problems why should she listen to his? They aren't going to drag me into the middle of their tug of war.

Instead of rushing away from the kitchen, Maddy says, "I have so much prep to do. I think starting high school and all the homework the faculty loves to pile on . . . No matter how brilliant Chris is, he's still adjusting to it. That's all."

"You must be right."

What does Geoffrey mean by that? Maddy doesn't want to ask and finally she finds the strength to say, "I'll pick up dinner and we'll all sit down and catch up tonight. We've had problems with Chris being too bored with the school's offered curriculum. We can simply ask him."

"Sure. Tonight."

He's being so weak Maddy happily flees the kitchen.

* * *

Even though I showered, twice now this day, by the time I enter the science building and dart through the door to the Introduction to Biology classroom, I'm starting to sweat again. The bell rings in my ears and I wonder how far behind Ellis is. I take my seat at the third table from the front. I share the long table with three slackers—I pretend to fit in.

Mr. Van Allen stands at the front projector. He rocks back on his heels eager to begin. Mr. Van Allen is almost 6'6" tall. He's one of the few male teachers here with a full head of hair and he obviously doesn't care about haircuts and keeping it short. His brown hair is wispy and flies away from his head when he turns fast. To go along with his increased height Mr. Van Allen has very long arms, legs, hands and fingers.

Behind his back, the snarkiest wonder how long his dick is. The girls who take part in this speculation laugh and whisper about shoe size. Most of the students in my freshman class are virgins like me. The rest are braggers who talk the current lingo about hooking up with so-and-so—it doesn't mean anything when they say we're still friends, we just like to hook up, and no one seems to have boyfriends or girlfriends that stick anymore, they all just talk about and want sex so badly. The second bell rings and Mr. Van Allen starts class. By this time all but a few have pulled their laptops out of backpacks and Gap computer bags and opened them up. The kids, like me, who don't have the latest and fastest models with all-day battery capacity, are grouped around the few outlets at each lab table.

Ellis saunters in and hands Mr. Van Allen a small pass the school uses to excuse tardiness. He must've gotten it from the gym teacher. Buddies. In the same situation the gym teacher would only shake his head no at me and tell me to run. Mr. Van Allen places the slip of paper on his desk and Ellis takes his seat at the lab table to the left of mine. His hair's still wet, shiny, and I can't help glancing at him. He sits there surrounded by unknowns. Even seven weeks into the school year I can't get a handle on the many names of the other students; there are a lot of people at the high school, almost fifteen hundred kids. There are a couple junior highs and the high school took everyone from those and made one large school. There are two other high schools in the system and then the surrounding towns outside Middleton, but most went to my high school. There are too many kids in the classes and I can feel new just like everyone else because of the lack of recognition.

Since I'm not in the popular crowd I didn't bring a keen memory of hanging out with buddies from junior high. In my entire school history I was only ever invited to one birthday party and that was in third grade and it was the neighbor boy—I still remember his name now: Jeremy Egglestone—who lived four houses down from me. This had been on Crater Street, a small neighborhood on the East side of Middleton where my parents rented a house the first couple years after the move to Montana. The neighbor boy was also a single child with no siblings and I remember that Jeremy stuttered. Jeremy's mother invited everyone from the class at school and everyone came too, including the girls who made fun of him for his speech difficulty, and they only came because they were bored. I played games and kept quiet and watched the others. Jeremy seemed happy but I knew he wasn't. Now I remember how forced the party must've been and I could hear his mother's voice exclaiming how everyone loved a birthday party. Foolish.

Jeremy's father also taught at the College, Economics, and most of the other neighbors did too. The Faculty Ghetto on Crater Street became well known. Big Sky College owns the land the homes are built on and the idea is that new professors can come and buy a house even with their paltry beginning salaries. Whenever someone in the F-Ghetto is denied tenure, or dies, a vacancy soon appears. No one who doesn't work for the College is allowed to live in the homes on Crater Street. Widows of faculty members are the only exception. Jeremy moved away a couple years later when his father took a better offer at a private college back in the Midwest. I imagine another faculty ghetto in Indiana, the same cheaply constructed two-by-four homes painted brown with aluminum window casements and cinderblock basements, where Jeremy hangs out and smokes dope to stifle the clingy yammering of his mother.

"Everyone. Pair up with your lab partner"—what does he think we were going to do—"and we'll start the next project." Mr. Van Allen sings this out to the class. His voice ranges up and down from low to high. This teacher must love his job more than Mr. Roffiger. Maybe it's a conspiracy; the Freshman English teacher, Mrs. Gallows, also has the sunny disposition thing down pat. With a name like hers it's kind of funny to think she's always so happy. What's in the water in the teacher's lounge? They don't realize how easy their daily lessons are for me. I sit in most of the classes as if stuck in solid sludge, time passing slowly. Doing time in Montana. The tests breeze by. I don't respond to the high marks, but my classmates know, and treat me differently. Some are brave enough to ask for help. I keep to myself.

For my lab partner I'm stuck with a mousy girl named Mary Follick. I feel a kinship with her though because she remains the butt of many jokes from grade school on up through junior high, an outsider. Her clothes are never the right kind and she stays silent even when asked questions by the teacher. She's a petrified girl. Mary and I get along just fine; she's smarter than anyone else in the class, even gives me a run for my money. Mary smiles at me. Twice this year already, an historic accomplishment, we've had to work after school to complete assignments and her brick-wall guard began to crack around me, the wall she put up when I ran from her obvious crush back in 7th grade. She asked me to dance with her and I ran like my life depended on it, and now, it somehow seems to. I like her despite my own shallow ego. High school is just as tough as it ever was—not the classes, but the human interaction. Adults say we have it tougher now.

Ellis Pallino pairs up with Edy Augustyn and I know she isn't the brightest lab rat on the block. They'll both be lucky to keep their heads afloat. I'd give anything to trade places with Edy. Ellis transferred in from the private school in Middleton and he's been testing the waters in the school since his arrival. The rumor around school is that the private school kicked him out, but no one ever asks Ellis if this is true. Something rebellious became the story—drugs, perhaps the more realistic reason. He's instantly popular and there's been a drive behind his body language different from the usual slacker. He'll have to carry the lab for Edy; I hope he's capable.

"Are you feeling all right?" Mary says as I slump further down in my seat. I wonder why she even cares?

"I'm fine," I mumble back. I want to tell her to pay attention to her own self. The Dell computer in front of me is one of last year's models and I'm pissed because it's already so ancient I have trouble saving a lot of the homework with any sense of reliability, limited by its memory capacity on the hard drive. When I ask my father for an upgrade in laptops he just stares at me and finally says, "I'll buy you more memory but there's nothing wrong with the one we got for you." The computer jacks into the lab table, which is wired to the front projector Mr. Van Allen uses. He writes notes on the transparent surface and the class is supposed to pay attention when he writes. We don't need to take notes because all of the information he writes will instantly download into our laptops with a press of a button at the end of the class. Mr. Van Allen has heard Mary's whispering and gives us a stern look but doesn't say anything personally; he isn't that retribution-oriented.

The class studies invertebrates today and cellular structure and who can keep me awake? I stayed up too late. Look what happens to me after expending all my energy in Phys. Ed. At least I'm clean when I slouch in my seat.

Near the end of the class Mr. Van Allen downloads the study questions, homework assignment, and notes into our computers and I remain unimpressed by how instantly the file pops up on my screen. The school received a grant from the state, and with gifts from several dead alumni,

Middleton High School got the cutting edge. Only the science teachers fully grasp the new technology.

The bell rings and my eyelids grow heavy regardless of the clamor to escape the science building. Now I have to haul myself to study hall and force more algebraic equations into my brain for the test Mr. Roffiger has threatened to deliver in the afternoon. I feel so tired now but there's no use sleeping in study hall anyway.

The study hall monitor, Ms. Phyllis Deafers, runs the large cafeteria space as if she teaches astrophysics. Sharp-featured with arms and legs like broomsticks, Ms. Deafers snaps awake anyone she catches sleeping fast with a flat palm smack to the tabletop of the tired student. *Bam* and you're going again, better than caffeine. I just don't get it. So a student has a free hour to work on reading, writing, and arithmetic. Big deal. Let the student use the time how he or she wants to. Notice me writing this down in my computer journal where Ms. Phyllis Deafers has no chance of reading it and laying one of her famous smacks on me.

I stay awake by writing in my notebook computer. It's a journal of sorts and I censor what I write because I'm not a fool; I know someone can look over my shoulder, and my secret (one of my secrets) can easily be revealed to the whole student body and I picture a ridiculous misery commencing. I use multiple passwords in case my laptop is stolen—but who'd want to steal my old computer? I just hope it isn't my parents who ever discover my journals. Before I got the computer I filled up five paper notebooks. I try to hide them as best as I can in my room, in the closet, behind the trunk inside an old faded red Nike bag. Five books so far, since sixth grade, filled, line by line, with my very small and circular writing. My mother gave me the idea. She always wrote in her bound college notebooks, carried one everywhere she went, and jotted down idea after idea. The only difference being she wrote sketchy untruthful poetry and fiction of her life and I tell the truth, what I struggle with.

On the way to study hall I catch Mary staring back at me as she walks down the long hall a short distance in front of me. I write about Mary. Her backpack's full to bursting with all the heavy textbooks and she carries three more books and notebooks against her chest. She realizes I caught her watching and ducks her head, averting her gaze, and pushes on through the crowded quadrangle. The air remains cold, the sky gray, but at least it isn't raining yet so most of the students walk on the grass and escape from the covered breezeways that make them feel like hamsters in a tunneled cage. The midway bell hums out and I speed up, knowing I only have enough time to get to my locker and exchange my biology book for my algebra and history notes. I refuse to carry every class textbook like Mary or any of the other turtles scurrying with so much weight on their backs. My locker is centrally located and I make the time to switch out the old and only carry what I need for the next two classes: study hall and History. These books alone are the size of a glacier and can substitute for weights to build up the biceps.

As I write about this in study hall I think about Ellis and then write about him, imagine a life different from my own. When Ms. Deafers walks behind my desk I switch the computer to sleep mode and study my algebra equations.

* * *

Maddy races up the stairs again keeping her knees high and laughs with the same feeling of happiness and abandon. Her muscles act normally. Look at her move. She showers, takes her time, enjoys the smell of her lavender skin softener. She rubs the soap along her legs, behind her knees, and then massages her calves—even though I know this is happening, I look away—I'm not that creepy, even in this blackening state; I only see what I see. There's no pattern to it. Here I am one second, if it is a second, and then I'm somewhere else entirely with no control. Someone, some thing, wants me to be here now.

When my mom finishes she tempts fate by daring the tingling sensation to return. There's enough time to get where she's going and she hasn't yet woken up completely. When she exits the master bath she hears Geoffrey closing the pantry door. It rubs and sticks most of the time and she smiles when Geoffrey opens the door again and shoves it closed with another hitch. She hears the dishwasher start with a series of beeps and realizes he waited to start it until she'd finished with her shower. Thoughtful. When she first met Geoffrey he always seemed so kind and giving and would do anything for her and then me—but lately; it's only been in the last year—he's been preoccupied and tries to make up for his lapses in judgment. She reserves judgment.

Geoffrey finishes the breakfast dishes and listens to his wife as she races around the upstairs bedroom. She's doing everything at such a clip this morning. Then the telephone rings and before Geoff realizes it he himself races to answer it.

"Hello." Geoffrey keeps his voice low, speaking almost in a whisper.

"Geoff? It's Lance."

Geoffrey stays silent. He hasn't spoken to Lance in over a month.

"Are you there, Buddy?"

"Sure."

"Are you okay?"

Lance is always direct. One of the few lawyers out there who stays on point, it's very hard to fool him. Geoffrey says, "Everything's fine."

"You've been hard to get hold of."

"You know me, Lance, busy busy busy. Look. Now's not a good time to talk. How 'bout I call you from the office?"

"We both know that's not possible anymore. Geoffrey, I spoke to Glynnis last week. And I've been getting calls from the Traverse bank. You're two months behind on your share of the payments."

"Listen. Lance. I can't talk now." What will it take to get Lance off the phone? Geoffrey almost hangs up on his old friend. Lance figures things out in an instant and Geoffrey's situation changes from what it was a minute ago, after a civil breakfast with Maddy, pretending everything was normal and okay.

"When then?"

There's silence on the line and Geoffrey leans his head

against the kitchen cabinet above the telephone. He can hear Maddy coming down the stairs. At least she isn't running this time.

"Geoff? I want to come out there."

"You've got to be kidding. I don't need checking up on. Stay in Michigan, Lance. I'll call you in a couple days."

"I paid your share on the property."

"I'll pay you back."

"That's not what I meant. Don't worry about it. Sheila and I have a couple days. We both want to come out there to see you and Maddy. Chris, too."

He's only being a friend, Geoffrey thinks.

"Who's on the phone?" Maddy asks as she walks into the kitchen and places her briefcase on the counter. Geoffrey straightens his shoulders and nods, finally holding up a finger to make her think he's listening intently and won't be able to hear if she makes another sound.

"Uh huh. Okay. Fine then. Whenever you want."

Maddy doesn't pay any attention to Geoff's words and she waves goodbye as she hurries out to the garage. His secrets aren't her problem anymore and this irritates her to no end but she's not going to wait for him. He's lost that privilege.

"Listen. Geoff. It's Lance here. What are you into? You and I tell each other everything. I can help. Whatever it is."

With Maddy gone—Geoffrey hears her Audi engine start and the garage door finally nearing the top . . . open now—Geoffrey says, "What did Glynnis have to say?"

"She's a professional. Absolutely nothing. You got one of the few personal assistants who won't gossip. But she wanted to tell me something. I know you're no longer on the Calston and Meyers case."

"There you have it. I can't get into this now."

"You're not working anymore."

"Lance. Listen to me."

"I'm trying."

"Don't come out here. Maddy and I are going through a hard patch. We need to sort through something here and the job isn't important compared to that."

"Okay."

Why can't he leave me alone? He has to tell Lance something. Just enough. But why does he have to lie? Make it sound like it's all on Maddy, like it's partly her fault Humpty Dumpty fell off the wall.

"I'll call you next week. I promise," Geoffrey finally says.

"Geoff—"

"Next week, Lance. I appreciate it . . . for the land payments too. I'll pay you right back." At least he can say that much; he doesn't want to hear how he's been letting everything slide for so long. That's just one of the many things he doesn't have time for.

"I'll give you one week. Sheila sends her love."

"Back at her."

"You need anything I want you to call me. You have my cell number."

"Yeah. Goodbye."

"Bye."

After he hangs up Geoffrey thinks about collapsing to the floor, and is so out of himself he doesn't realize his behavior has become melodramatic. Tears sting his face and have throughout the short conversation. Geoffrey barely hid them from Maddy. She's gone and he thinks of how she bounced right out of the house with a renewed energy. Maybe she'll be okay. Should he leave? His planning of the night before creeps in and he once again contemplates all of the ways to kill himself, giving in once again to his dreary solitary thoughts. He shouldn't be in the kitchen with all the sharp objects and he knows then he can never do it. Just thinking about it makes him queasy.

He picks himself up and heads upstairs. He passes my room and doesn't even think about me. On the way to his office Geoffrey detours into the master bedroom and takes off all his clothes. On autopilot he steps into the shower. The tile walls are still wet from Maddy's shower and he breathes in her scent. I don't want to be here and in another instant, I'm not.

* * *

The cafeteria (easy to be here and this is where I learn the beginning of my end) is a huge space that can be divided into two smaller spaces with an accordion wall when there are special events. The school rotates lunch periods with freshman and sophomores eating at 11:40 and juniors and seniors eating at 12:30. Most seniors are allowed to leave campus for lunch anyway, one of the best privileges to look forward to; plus, they get a full hour to lounge and shoot the shit in the parking lot, drive to Domino's near the town's center for a quick slice before driving back to school. The locals who live close to the high school hate the lunchtime traffic and there's a push by this concerned segment of the neighborhood to stop everyone from leaving campus during school hours. Someone always has an axe to grind.

The study hall is in the smaller space of the cafeteria. The accordion-like divider has been pulled to close off the other areas and the sound of an industrial vacuum hums closer to the kitchen and cafeteria line. I study algebra again at the table and it's maddening. I know all about the chapter Mr. Roffiger's about to cover on his test, but in my mood I'm indifferent to the specifics, something that should be so easy for me right now—no light bulb goes off in my head yet—and the whole endeavor becomes pointless. Most of the other students spread out along the tables act twitchy and lack manners. Phyllis Deafers continually walks the aisles of the room with her roving eye. She makes people sit up in their chairs, turn down the volume on their music devices—what about that vacuuming roar? I want to shout at her. Can't you shut it down—She settles into a circular table near one of the exits. Her throne of convenience, this table is key to her getting out of the study hall before any of the students can run her over.

I close and then reopen my laptop to check the remaining battery power and there's not enough to take notes in History next period. The paper notebook and pen will have to do. Five minutes before the bell rings everyone starts closing down and putting books back into packs. Phyllis Deafers stands and stretches, her large breasts heaving upward, the reading glasses she needs periodically now dangle between them. Some of the boys watch this but

I cringe. She yells out across the room: Wait for the bell! I wince at the crow-like sound of her voice, too. High-pitched enough to give fingernails scratching against chalkboards a pleasant ring, her voice at full volume snaps everyone to attention.

The 4th-period bell rings. The din and clamor start again and I'm pulled and pushed along the hallway by the crowd. I have five minutes to get to world history with Mrs. Janeese.

Someone, a dark shadow of a boy in a paint-flecked blue t-shirt and scuffed jeans, trips the boy in front of me and he falls quickly, like a flyswatter smacking, onto the industrial beige carpet. He lets out a yipping noise. I'm almost pulled down with him but steady myself and back up quickly. Two other boys, older, with long sideburns and scattered acne—just like the rest of the class—hover over their victim and I try to skirt around them but an elbow digs into my side and I stumble over the backpack of the kid on the ground, another victim in the middle. One of the three has pushed me into the mix. Instinct can deliver trouble, too; I swing an arm to stop myself from joining the kid on the ground and grasp the forearm of one of the hovering bullies on the far side.

"Sorry," I say, mumbling.

"Get off me, Asshole!" I let go and skip a foot sideways and out of their reach but not before the three sorry-looking teens give me the once-over. They scowl and I can barely see their eyes under their trucker hats. I don't say it, wisely, but I think: Hey—you aren't allowed to wear hats. The boy on the ground is near tears, frightful, as he tries to keep track of his fallen books and papers. I hold my palms up as if to appease the group and say, "Sorry"—again, like an idiot. Ellis Pallino passes me, isn't even aware of me, and gives a high five to the rank who tripped the other kid. How does he know them? He steps backwards; they're bad kids, kids you cross the street to avoid, which I've done in the past out on the streets, in daylight even, to avoid their radar. Does Ellis do drugs? Meth and E are big on campus, pot always, and there's nothing the school system can do about it. I think about all of these things instantly.

The boy on the ground scrambles, hunches up, and

skitters between the legs, like a scuttling bug, and he's gone. I can hear an announcer in his head yelling: What a sacrifice play. Divert their attention away from him and onto you!

All of the older boys now focus on me. Why not Ellis? The boy I used as a crutch stares at me as if he's trying to burn my image into his memory and then he turns away, his head still facing me, as if to say: You'll get yours. All of them depart. I glance behind me and a teacher is coming down the hallway. Ellis follows the burnouts down the hallway. Did he even recognize me? Not really. I somehow want Ellis to stare into my eyes, too. I stand quickly and flee past the arriving teacher.

Now I'll be late. I dread the scowl on Mrs. Janeese's face when I enter her History classroom. She waits with the pad of demerits and a grin of satisfaction as she scratches my name across the top of the pink slip. It's one demerit every time you're late. Five demerits get you a detention and every five days without a demerit takes one of your demerits away until you have a clean slate again. The new principal has thought up this system with the help of the penal society. More paperwork for the teachers, but only the teachers with little compassion for teenagers and their problems and excuses hand them out with glee. I try not to show my disgust when Mrs. Janeese wiggles the demerit slip at me. I act bored by it and succeed—she'll keep marking my papers with 'A's and wonder why. I hope this act pisses her off. She doesn't know I've been targeted by a group of rough sharks in the hallway and she doesn't care. Ellis knows them.

Why is this information important? I imagine my life at full speed, stuffed to the gills without a break. My parents can't be with me in the day-to-day. The excuses. It's their jobs, always their important work schedules. The silence in the house is sadly enervating. I usually come home after school, vegetate in my room, search websites as soon as I hit the bed. All the classes I take make me too busy to honestly care what my parents do. I always find out much later—or not at all; the cover-up being too good—about every bad thing while the good things come more infrequently in the form of notes posted on my door with Scotch tape: Honey, My book is done! I'll be home late tonight but we'll celebrate this weekend. Try to keep one of your nights free. Love, Mom.

Gym class, Introduction to Biology, study hall, History, break and lunch period, English, Algebra, and finally French to end the day, a full schedule with a major change at the beginning of the year when I dropped Latin because it added too much work. I almost need a wheelbarrow to move from school to home. Why do I hide; is it in my nature? I don't even tell my parents I dropped Latin. I want them to think I can handle a complex world but the teachers don't let up—maybe next year.

Mrs. Janeese will never go for laughs in her class. She appears rigidly patrician—not like my mom who tries to keep her sense of humor through the rigidity left after the accident—and enjoys the role of teacher. Why do so many teachers embrace being strict? I wonder this all the time and then think about the type of students they have to deal with every day, the cutups, the cell phone abusers, the back talkers, narcissists, the swearing, the disregard and the serious lack of manners, compassion, empathy, and I don't blame them.

Mrs. Janeese is asking for bad behavior; she always dresses in earthy tones, some of her skirts designed with mini-flowers or zigzag patterns running down to her tightly laced boots with pointy toes; she's never worn pants as far as I know. I'd like to catch her in the garden, discover her Victorian tendencies are only a professional cover. I sit, numb, as she drones on about the battles against the British. In every History class the British, the French, or the Germans figure into every discussion. Mrs. Janeese writes on the chalkboard and expects the class to write down every word exactly how she writes it. Name the six major historical figures and the role each played in the battle of _____, word for word.

For her tests I've learned the more I diverge from her written lists the weaker the grade. It's only a matter of memorization, but she doesn't see it this way, and she writes so much on the chalkboard and so quickly I'm stunned every day. Blocks of information slide into the pipes, none of it retainable well without a memory like my own. Most of the time it's like I have to type term papers weekly in her class.

My computer doesn't have the battery life and there are very few electrical outlets in her classroom so I'm forced to scratch her patter and bilge into my history notebook the old-fashioned way with a Bic. As I glance around the room all are bowing their heads in time, writing down the same words as Mrs. Janeese writes them. There isn't time to have discussions about the importance of the events. Education by spew is what I call it and Mrs. Janeese vomits out this information daily. A wonderful inspiring teacher the school should be proud of: Ha! At least the interminable minutes of her class distract me from the run-in with the three stooges and Ellis. It's hard to run away in a crowded hallway and I wonder if they'll just forget about me; I vow to try to be as forgettable as possible.

* * *

Maddy parks in the staff parking lot and walks swiftly into the English Department building. Her office is on the third floor and she punches the button to start the ancient elevator. The doors creak, then part, and Maddy rushes in before they even open all the way. Then she has to wait what seems an eternity before the doors close again. The elevator is, like every elevator on campus, vandalized past the point of being embarrassing; it only makes Maddy sad. People Are Pigs! She wants to add this graffiti to the mess of signs, runes, and sigils covering the brown metal walls. She's in her office before the elevator makes its slow journey back to ground level.

Along with the political messages for Montana's Ballot measures—swing this way, please, voter! Fight noxious weeds! We need your funding. Extend term limits for legislators—never happen. My mom's a cynic when it comes to the Big Sky political establishment. Once you're in, you're in for life. A poster with a stick mom and dad and two stick children simply explaining how righteous Montana folk need to preserve the family unit: a ballot measure to provide that only marriage between a man and a woman may be valid. This will pass with flying colors. I know it will. I don't think my parents will vote yes on that one, but there's a chance. (Did my father just laugh at a gay joke? Yes!) Family values aren't high up on dinner-table conversations. Increase tobacco taxes. Yep. That's the ticket to a bigger, better, and less smoggy Montana—there are two posted messages on my mother's door attached to her bulletin board by pushpins. The first message is from the department director asking for progress on the English Department's bid to fold the Creative Writing Program into the mother hive. Maddy gets so angry at the idea, which came from the bureaucrats and pencil-pushing administrators in the English Department, and vows to fight for her small department's autonomy.

The college in Middleton is home to one of the very first writing programs in the nation (sixth or seventh), established in 1926. It breathes history and good writing and Maddy chose to teach here based on the poetry of Richard Hugo, who was the greatest of Montana poets. His work spoke of the underside of the physical world, the struggle and hardship of life. Maddy doesn't want to start her workday angry so she shelves the note and tells herself not to explode. Maybe the stress of the attempted coup in her department caused her physical collapse of the night before.

Maddy is a tenured professor in the Creative Writing Program; she was hired as an adjunct professor based on her published work and her degrees. Her career is, and always has been, promising. She continues to publish in the smaller poetry and prose journals and magazines across the Western region, but, nationally, she hasn't acquired an audience yet. It's hard to be known and then not known enough; it stays an uphill struggle. Her new novel dispenses with her poetic touches. It's based loosely on the life of the people she's known for years, her younger sister, Rhea, to be exact, and her two children, something she'll deny, something she'll never reveal to her family—she figures they'll know soon enough and hopefully forgive her for any misdirection and playfulness. Maddy can already imagine the disclaimer at the front of the book informing the reader no character you're about to read about is based on anyone in real life. Ha ha ha ha! She models what her writing teachers taught her long ago into a mantra: Write what you know! The remainder is like choosing the most delicate and filling dessert from the silver tray. You're handed the keys to the most honest work.

The second message is from Travis. He's left her a note saying she missed a good night of fun but doesn't explain 'fun' and he'll try to make it to her office hours. She doesn't have time to think about this boy. What could she possibly read between the lines he left for her to find?

She takes out her yellow legal tablets and places all but one to the side of her desktop. Maddy writes longhand with ballpoint pens—no laptop for her until the final stages. She always thinks before she begins writing, with an internal editor sharpened to cut away the chaff. She slivers her writing down to the essentials and usually her sentences remain direct and short. There are people who like this style of writing. The first chapter of her novel describes in horrifyingly precise medical detail how the youngest child of three in her made-up family dies unexpectedly when stung by a bee and can't be revived in time at the local hospital. Her book begins in the fall season when the bees of the West are out in full force hovering, searching for food and sugar before the winter cold closes in. The boy grasps a tennis ball he wants to throw for his dog. The bee rests on the side of the ball. The bee stings him in the center of his palm. The boy shrieks and flails and trips while crying. The dog, Rosie, an always-happy Irish Setter, licks the child on the face while the mother rushes outside to see what made her child scream. Rosie eats the dead bee carcass when it falls out of the child's hand. The boy gasps for air as his throat swells. He sounds raspy. His mother rushes with her child to the hospital but he doesn't breathe when she gets there and the doctors can't revive him.

Maddy guides her parents through all the stages of grief and acceptance and doubt—and their troubles mirror her own. How were they to know? What about the dead brother and the two brothers who still live? What will happen to them? Will their roles change? The middle child now becomes the youngest and he's always been the child who needed the most attention anyway. Maddy has all of the characters and their traits spliced and sorted into cubbyholes. She tells everyone she writes more for fun than to sell anything, really. Her yearning hidden deep, Maddy never takes it out to explore; what would she do if her book really made it and people in the thousands read her words? The other mantra that repeats over and over from time to time is to never change if this success happens. Always present, there's the pressure from the college to publish. Maddy hasn't reached the plateau her colleagues set for her; she feels frozen much of the time as if her move to the West disrupts the connection she reveled in while spewing flowery words across the page back in the Midwest. She's regionally famous, in poetry circles—one step, Maddy grimaces, from the cowboy poetry circuit where she would drive to one podunk Western dustbowl after another, following a trail set by the pioneers, reciting her poetry at a clip, entertaining the prairie dogs from Pocatello, Idaho, to Elko, Nevada—the occasional snippet of verse, angry at the latest political quandary, an ode to the loss of a speed limit and how, even though this lack of control is good, how psychologically the people yearn to be roped in and made to toe the line. Montana has become her muse and Maddy doesn't know if it's for the better. Again, psychobabble reinforces a collegiate propensity for feeling morose: fear of success and failure mingling well.

Maddy has barely written a page before she realizes she'll be late for the departmental meeting. Maddy can't believe she has to spend an hour listening to her colleagues scratch and crawl through the mess. There's no time to think. The pressure of productivity, publish or perish, all the many "P" words, strung together to make her think she'll be punished sooner than later. When Maddy writes, the feeling of failure haunts her, and the feeling of success does the same. She's living an intellectual dichotomy so intangible it will drive her crazy if she gives in. In the back of her mind the words of her undergraduate professor reverberate with self-importance: Figure out why you want to write and if you ever do figure it out put away your pen and paper; you won't have the drive to write anymore. All she knows, all these years, is she needs to write. And the obstacles and distractions keep looming larger, crossing her path with more urgency and frequency.

Maddy darts off to the meeting without more than a thought about her family. As she once again waits for the elevator, the feeling Geoff isn't doing everything he should be doing grows stronger.

* * *

Geoffrey sits in the home office staring out at the darkening sky and beating himself up. His limbs feel heavy and he promises for the hundredth time to walk down to the river and finally follow his pathway to the beautiful sound of trickling water so distant, stare at the trees on the far shore, their darkly-mirrored reflections in the stillness before the approaching storm. He changes his mind when he hears a car coming up the driveway. It's not a familiar sound in the middle of the day; there's something wrong with the car's transmission and then he remembers and frowns. The car belongs to Deepika.

* * *

There's a break before lunch, barely enough time to stretch and relax, regroup before English, Algebra, and French classes take over my afternoon. I almost wish my day started in reverse so I could end with gym and cut loose a bit sooner. My day, as it is, saps my energy in waves.

I find out my father doesn't have a job because Amos Morataki passes me in the cafeteria. Amos Morataki, a kid from Hawaii whose father works in the same law firm, walks back to my empty table and sits down without an invitation. He isn't acting sheepish enough. He's only fifteen after all and has an ego large enough to power the school generator for months. What a power source: teen ego.

"Sorry to hear about your dad," Amos says. Amos tries to sound sincere, innocent, anything but a button pusher.

I'm immediately on the defensive. Anyone out of the loop should play it cool and stay on defense. "What do you mean?"

"Losing his job and all," Amos says, as if I haven't heard the latest, which I haven't, and I'm stumped but also very good at not letting anything show. I hold my ground and ignore the tone of mirth coming from Amos.

Amos wants to know if my dad is cracking up. Should I tell him all the gory details? I'm not privy to much information at the house. Amos will be bored by the fact my father doesn't move from his office at all. I'm amazed how my mother hasn't really noticed either. I remain silent and rip into an overripe apple. This apple I didn't cut up at home—my teeth are still tender from the braces the orthodontist took off at the end of summer two months ago—the mushier the better.

Amos opens his brown bag and pulls out a bologna sandwich and Fritos. He arranges his meal just so in front of him, squarely and precisely centered in the middle. Then he continues: "Can't believe all this shit going on here either."

I stifle a laugh. Amos speaks with a clipped accent that makes the word shit sound foreign and like the word sheet. Oh well, I think, I'm not going to let him get to me. "Like what?" I ask.

"All the homework we have to do."

"Did your Algebra teacher pile on the homework?" With two separate Algebra teachers for the entire freshman class the odds Amos has the same teacher as I do, the happy Mr. Roffiger, are fifty-fifty.

"Doesn't he always? But you have Mr. Roffiger, the best teacher. I tried to get into your class but it was full when my name was pulled to register. Next semester I go second. I'll get all the classes I want with all the best teachers at this dump." Amos eats some Fritos, licks his lips, and burps softly, says, "Excuse me."

"Good for you." I want to know how the test was. I want to know how Amos heard about my father and what he's heard, but I can't even begin to gather the energy. What good can it possibly do? I don't gossip about my family. I don't gossip about anyone in high school and I realize I'm as boring as everyone around me thinks I am. It's the shell I've made.

Amos says, "I don't have tests until Friday. Our teacher wants us to relax on the weekends. Never gives us tests until Friday. What a crock. No tests but lots of homework. Too much."

At least I've taken Amos's mind off the problems my father has created. I want to ask Amos about my dad, but I won't. My father didn't look so hot last night. At least I'm safe in Amos's company. I never even noticed the toughs until I tripped into them earlier and part of me believes I'll never run into them again. Keep telling myself that. (I know better, and I don't know if I'd warn myself if I had that ability. My fate is sealed.)

"Listen," I say, and then open my Algebra book, "I've really got to study for this test." I sound so fake.

"What chapter are you on?"

Amos sounds curious, slightly, but in a competitive way. He isn't in the best sections and he doesn't have many friends, and he's only talking to me because our parents know each other. There isn't any other reason for him to sit next to me besides loneliness and Amos isn't my type. I picture Ellis walking by. I start to space out. Lunch is almost over and Amos won't take a hint and leave.

Then, for real, Ellis enters the picture. He approaches my table and asks, politely, if he can join us. He places his Algebra book on the surface and I ask if he knows Amos. My mouth goes instantly dry. I need water. I wonder if my face is red with embarrassment. I want to ask where his new friends are and what drugs they sold him. As Ellis sits down I see him without his shirt on strung out on meth in a dark room with his buddies.

"Hey," he says to Amos.

"Hey, dude, you two in the same class?"

"Sorry I need to ask. Chris, right?" It's unbelievable to me that he doesn't remember just two hours ago seeing me in the hallway with his burnout friends, but I nod, numb to whatever happens. I still haven't spoken a word as I watch the two people sitting at my table. I'm holding my breath for too long. I'm in the early stages of a different kind of excitement and the wish fulfillment of having Ellis appear only makes me ache. We're teenagers after all and the girls surrounding us, posing at the neighboring tables, the wannabes who skip around like teen pop stars in low-cut jeans with bellybuttons pierced, give anyone with horn dog lust an easy excuse to leer.

"Chris?"

"Ummm. Right."

Amos looks between Ellis and I and doesn't know what to think. Friends? All of a sudden I don't want Amos to leave. It'll be too obvious to everyone around us. My expression is too needy and I think about the math test I have to prepare for and the silliness of wanting to get to know the popular new kid so much. Like a toady, someone like me doesn't stand a chance of being anything but the chic kid's geek pawn. The one who helps the handsome kid pass the test but never shares an outside moment. Let's hang. I can never picture a time when Ellis will say this to me. I'll happily settle for a weak friendship.

"Can I study with you?"

Amos begins to pack up his trash, the empty sandwich bag, and I finally speak: "Sure. Amos, don't leave. Just hang out." He turns back to us and as an excuse, I add, "Amos probably knows more about Algebra than the teachers. He's also on the math team." My explanation seems to work on both of them.

"What's the test cover?" Now Amos takes over and I'm content to let him. My teenage lust subsides even though the object of my lust is right in front of me. It isn't easy to divert my mind. The power some people don't even realize they wield. Besides, I really need to pass this test, too, and there's no time.

There are ten minutes left in the lunch period and Ellis asks Amos to go over the chapter summary and we sit and listen to Amos simply explain the concept and the surprising thing is I get it, and laugh because I knew the solution but it was clouded—I can sabotage myself. It's like a light blinking on in my head completing a circuit. Ellis gets it, too, and by the time the bell rings there's a sense of relief in all three of us. Amos is happy he sat at my table and wishes us luck on the test, then departs with a carefree, "See ya 'round," and a wave.

I notice the girls circling Ellis. The cute ones who need lots more help with their schoolwork than Ellis and I ever will. The ones who wear too much makeup and swivel their hips as they walk for a certain kind of attention, the most brazen like video strumpets. A lot of the girls stare at Ellis behind his back and one of them finally screws up enough courage to ask him if he's going to play in the school's charity co-ed soccer match.

He turns to face the girl and he's kind and polite and handsome and the girl thinks she's won points. She and Ellis share a class I'm not in and it's a wonder the crush she so obviously has on Ellis allows her to function whenever he blinks out of her orbiting pattern.

"Do you want to walk to class?" the girl says.

"Sure. I just have to stop at my locker. Hold on." Ellis stands when I do and I'll be damned if I ever behave like this girl. I keep my face a blank slate and try to act as if the cram session we just took part in didn't matter in the slightest.

Ellis says to me, "Thanks a lot. I really needed the help."

"Same here."

"Are you gonna go to the extra math session after school?" Ellis asks this and I can't tell if he really wants me to be there or not.

"The math team meets at the same time. I'll see how the test goes." I hear myself and think: who cares?

"Yeah. I think I'll go anyway." The girl waits but in strained silence. She doesn't understand why Ellis would even speak to someone like me, someone picked last for basketball, someone who doesn't rate a call for the freshman float committee even though I'm an ace at the art stuff, someone she could never in a million years imagine laying naked next to Ellis because it would make her nauseous: "Look,"—she'd say, and spread it all over school within the first minutes of homeroom—"They're doing the thing that makes Jesus puke!" I'm far from unattractive but I don't stand out in any distinctive way. I want to yell at her: You don't make a good impression either. How gay is that?

She pulls Ellis away as her greedy need, an invisible cloud, surrounds them. She links her string-bean-thin arm under his and they walk among a sea of bodies as the bell rings. I walk off to my English class. I'll see Ellis in fifty minutes for the algebra test. He'll come and go throughout the day and my negativity will fade with each sighting. I'm at a crossroads; at least Ellis's appearance stymied Amos from probing about what's happening with my father. There's something else to talk about at the dinner table. I'm on my way to my locker. I pass through another hamster tunnel and witness a bolt of lightning crack like a passing thought across the horizon and imagine it touching down on the far football field, burning a hole into the ground where someone plants the ball for kickoff.

It begins to rain in a steady sheet and the gray sky opens up with booming thunder, blasphemous in its grandness. The hallway dims. English, Algebra, and French class to go and I picture my father at home, still sitting in his office chair staring out the window, the thunderclaps making him jump. I take all my books, all the homework I have for tomorrow and stuff the lot of it into my backpack with the laptop. I walk to the front entrance of the high school as the final bell rings out. I hang back in the dry part under the large overhang of the school entryway; the rain is so heavy I almost talk myself out of going but I get my legs started. I shoot one glance behind me at an office assistant who stares back with a perplexed expression, hands on her hips Old West shoot-out style. She doesn't yell but I know she's caught me, slow to figure out my intention. I watch her right arm come up and one of her long fingers with a red nail beckons me back to the school building. And I'm off, running away from the school, across the school bus lanes where the afternoon buses are already lining up, kindergarten drop-off finished, even though there are three more class periods to go. She can't possibly know who I was in my rain hood; I've only laid eyes on her for the first time right there; she won't know who runs away from her until the absence lists are turned in and cross-referenced; she'll enjoy spilling the beans and my escape will be dealt with harshly tomorrow (not going to happen) after a call home to insure the parents know about my insolent skipping.

The rain pounds onto my head and even with a hood my hair plasters itself into a bowl on my scalp. Lightning brightens my step and I'm soaked in less than a minute. It's a little over a mile to home and no one chases me from the school. I'll miss everything and more by going home. I'll have to retake the algebra test; I know Mr. Roffiger will let me take a make-up but he'll also be forced to give out a couple demerits. I'll be surprised if I don't rack up more than one week's detention with this skipping school stunt, but I have to get home. There's urgency, something I can't articulate, in my mind. I have to speak to my father right now. He'll be home. Where else would he be?

* * *

After Maddy teaches her senior Creative Fiction and Poetry class she wants to head back home to write. The rain keeps her in the Hopman Building leaning against the doorframe. She forgot her umbrella in her office and she wears the wrong kind of shoe to brave the splashes if she runs for it. She decides to wait it out.

* * *

An hour ago, in her class, Maddy braced herself for another tug-of-war at a different large table in a similar classroom. She let the students rip another self-important piece of drivel apart. The writing only felt worse over time and Maddy grimaced because this particular student had fooled her. Maddy chose who could be in her class based on a writing sample. Stick to the point. Poems and short stories, you'll have to write both. Submit three pieces during the term plus the end of chapter assignments. Make copies for everyone a week before your story or poem comes up for discussion. The story this particular student had submitted to get into her course was rough but it rang true. The ache of growing up in a cooped-up house with too many people and letting the failing neighborhood streets take over the character's life: drugs, guns, and the other side to a new West Side Story. It wasn't a great piece; it didn't have to be, it just had to be honest and Maddy fell for it.

The student never shows Maddy any respect. He always places an angry scowl on his face and the poem he turned in for today's workshop was really a song lyric, another in a long line of song lyrics he'd turned in for every assignment she'd given. She allowed him to read the song, which, when he read it, turned out to be a rap song. All about his hood, the bitch he beat to a pulp because she looked at the guy on the corner, wanted more than a blunt from the guy. Had to put her in her place and Maddy wondered if the writer really believed this. In the middle of Montana Maddy had a hard time believing in the honesty of the piece; it didn't ring true. Was Maddy racist? He told the class he loved to write rap lyrics and he was starting a band and trying out his new songs—he called them poetry—here first.

"What do you think of this song?" Maddy started the discussion with this question.

No one responded until Maddy asked the writer directly: "Do you think this piece is poetry or prose?"

He crossed his arms and held them against his chest tightly and said, "It qualifies as a poem."

"Yes. A lyric poem."

Another girl across from the rap artist spoke up, but softly, "I think it's an angry piece. Not very kind to women in general and, uh, the rhymes don't really work."

Inside, Maddy was grateful. She could always count on Cassie to make an insightful comment.

"Why, Cassie?"

"If it's a poem there's no structure to it. If it's free verse why does the author try to rhyme part of the time? If it's a prose story it doesn't work because there's no plot other than a man beating up his girlfriend for making eyes at a corner drug dealer. It's too misogynistic without a point for me to even care about any of the characters. Although I do wish I could warn the girl to stay away from the guy."

"Okay," Maddy said, "does anyone else agree or disagree with Cassie's assessment?"

Soft spoken, a junior in the back said he thought it was too easy. "There's a heavy stereotype in the piece. How many times do we have to hear about the abusive black man and his life, feel sorry for him because he's poor and violent? I'm sick of it to tell you the truth. And maybe it's because I'm black, too. So what? The writer didn't grow up on the corner in his story; he grew up in my neighborhood, my crib, in Seattle, a nice middle-class upbringing. The writer didn't make me believe his character is alive, raw, real, whatever . . . whether the author grew up there or not."

Now the writer seethed in his chair. He felt betrayed, defensive, maybe rightly so, and he steeled himself for more criticism by holding his body even more rigidly.

"No one says rap lyrics have to be true. Do they?" Maddy asked.

The rest of the students stayed silent. They were afraid to enter into a situation where race was the subject.

"So what else? Is it a poem or a short story? Let's go back to the first question."

"It's a song!" The writer said this so loudly Maddy almost jumped from her chair and she realized she had to diffuse the situation, close the discussion. She'd seen this shit before when a student's anger took over her class. It never ended well.

"Okay. Everyone," Maddy's voice rose, "Remember the three stories to read for next week and we're meeting in the basement. Roger,"—Maddy spoke only to him—"can you stay after for a second?"

The writer, Roger, wouldn't even acknowledge Maddy's question as the class picked up and filed out the door. No one wanted to be in her shoes.

"Roger. The class was a bit harsh with you." Maddy held onto her pen but didn't write on the yellow pad in front of her. The pen just hovered over the paper.

He's so proud, Maddy thought. He wouldn't relax around her; he'd put her in the enemy camp and Maddy was hurt even if it wasn't true. Maybe it was guilt.

"We're only six weeks into the term, your midterm

project is due in two weeks and I want to give you some advice. Please. This isn't easy for me." Try to be a friend, mentor him, and admit weakness. Be kind first.

"What do you know about my life?"

Maddy could tell he wanted to enlighten her but she wouldn't let him. She said, "Your life is your own. You can do what you want to with it. But you have to follow basic rules. This isn't a music class." Maddy knew this last bit was unkind, but couldn't help saying it out loud.

"It's what I write."

"You turned in a story at the beginning of the term. You used language that was raw, a bit unfocused, but you got your idea across. That piece wasn't a rap song."

"I turned that story into one."

Roger started to ease up and he unfolded his arm and placed them on the table in front of him.

"There are simple guidelines in my class. You can write whatever you want outside on your own time, and I will be happy to read this. It sounds to me like you want to be a rap artist. That's an admirable goal. You already have a band?"

"Group."

"Right."

"You call it a rap group."

"You told me you took this same level Creative Writing class last year?"

"With Mr. Abrassini." From Roger's pronunciation Maddy knew he was calling Mr. Abrassini an ass. Maddy wanted to agree with Roger; Mr. Abrassini constantly played the smug professor in her presence and flaunted his snobbish intelligence whenever the creative writing program forced the professors to mingle. She didn't want to be an ass to Roger, follow in Mr. Abrassini's footsteps.

"You got a D in his class?"

"You know I did."

"If you get a better grade in my class this grade will replace the D you got in Mr. Abrassini's. I want to warn you now, early enough in the term: If you continue to turn in rap lyrics for my writing assignments you'll get a D or worse in this class. If you want me to look at your songs on the side I'm willing to do that. This particular song doesn't work for me. Cassie hit the nail on the head when she said the rhyme structure doesn't quite fit."

"It works when I sing it."

"Just stick to the book. How are your other projects doing?" After each chapter in her textbook the students chose one topic to write about. They were currently stuck on the second part of the point-of-view chapter.

"Everything else is fine. Look, I have to go."

"If you need any help stop by my office. You can write, Roger. You know this is just a pose and I know it."

"You don't know anything." Roger screamed this in Maddy's face from a foot away. He stormed out of the room.

Maddy trembled in her seat. This kid needs help, she thought. And he's not a kid anymore; he's a senior in college. Then: Is he dangerous? Should I be scared?

The classroom discussion and her private talk replayed in her mind. What could she have done to make his tension disappear?

She pressed into her legs by running her hands along the tops of her thighs. The feeling of numbness from the night before didn't reappear. Maddy stood and gathered her class papers and briefcase.

* * *

The day's only half over and she feels drained. Her mind races to the next stop and she only wants to go home. By the time she realizes the rain won't let her step outside the building my mother is desperate but keeps everything calm. If anyone paid any attention to her they'd say, "She's got it together!"

"Do you want to share my umbrella?"

Maddy looks up and there stands Travis. He remains dry, tall and skinny and in one of his thin hands he carries a large black umbrella. "Oh," Maddy says.

"Where may I escort you?" Travis asks, gives her a grin.

"It's letting up isn't it?" What else can Maddy say feeling the way she does and reprimanding herself over and over again within? She can't seem to get the image of Roger storming from her classroom out of her head. Here's this attractive boy acting like a puppy who's aced all his training. Maddy scolds: he's being nice, she wants to yell—Stop It—at the top of her lungs and she almost starts to laugh.

"I'm headed over to the English Department anyway."

"Are you stalking me, Travis?" Maddy can't hold it in anymore and she laughs and Travis somehow knows she's joking even though he really doesn't get why but he cracks a smile.

"Only if you'll let me."

"Oh. A polite stalker."

"Yes, Ma'am."

The most dangerous kind, and don't call me Ma'am.

"Shall we?" Maddy asks, and then takes his arm as they enter the rain under the large umbrella.

* * *

I rethink skipping school ten times by the time I'm halfway home, but it's too late to turn back now. I drip water. The sky darkens more and I hope my laptop is safe from the deluge. The salesman who sold me the computer bag smiled like I was an idiot when I asked about the bag's waterproof skin. In twenty-five minutes I jog down my driveway and stop when I see the strange car parked in front of the garage. It's an old Saab, two-door, swoop-hipped and faded green, foreign and like a bathtub nonetheless. The sound of the storm hides the wet sounds I make as I enter the kitchen, water puddles at my feet. I don't hear anything and I'm so wet all I can do is grab a dish towel from the small side drawer under the microwave and start to dry off.

The first floor of the house is quiet. My dad hasn't heard me down here. I notice the answering machine light blinking again. The lights in the kitchen aren't on so the red blink is bright in the gloom. At least the power isn't off. Usually it only takes one bang of thunder for the power to go off out here in the high school area of Middleton.

Then I hear a mumbling from outside the kitchen. The whispering rises.

My father has hold of her forearm near her wrist when they stumble into the kitchen. Of course I know her, remember who she is, and I put it all together as quickly as if I was suddenly hit by a car and thrown into a ditch. She sees me first and yelps: surprise. Her name's Deepika. She arrived a year ago. She's a visiting creative writing teacher in my mother's program. Mom tells Geoffrey Deepika's two-year teaching commitment will not be extended after the winter term finishes. Now, the affair, I realize, is the reason for this, but I'm not shocked by the affair anymore; that feels so long ago. It's her very round, pregnant belly. This is what she's doing here. I remember a year ago, fall, how I met her here at the house in this same kitchen when my parents threw a party, just an informal get-together for the new staff and Marilyn, the program director's secretary.

When my mother first introduced them, Deepika said: "You can call me Deep." She laughed, a sparkling sound and I was captivated. My father, obviously, had been captivated, too.

Deep. I liked that and still do. What a cool name for a writer. Deep told me she was from a small town, really a village, from the upper Northwestern coast of India. Her parents sent her and Deepika's brother, Ananda, to America when they were teenagers to give them the best education. Deepika and Ananda never left. The schools were private and very strict and she blossomed under the American way of making a life.

In college she wrote one story lucky enough to be picked up by a national magazine. Then three years passed and her second story sold to a respected journal and her first book of short stories hit with a midsize publishing house. She took teaching positions at several writing programs across the country, traveling from place to place, saving money, writing, attending Writers' Conferences. It was a good life. Since the first book, she'd written three more collections, each one praised more highly than the last, she'd been writing her fifth collection over the past three years and took the job at Big Sky College to take the time to finish them.

The creative writing program patted itself on the back and counted its lucky blessings. Another feather in the department's cap, Deepika taught the first year of her two-year commitment, second fall semester off, and left town for the summer. She came back to finish her stories, quit her commitment to the college, and pack up her rental house before heading to Boston to be close to her brother and his family for the birth. I met Deepika a year ago and I never called her Deep even though invited to do so; it wouldn't be right.

Deepika isn't married and her parents, along with assorted siblings who stayed closer to home, and their children, visit her almost every year, wherever she is, from the family home on the coastal city of Veraval on the Arabian Sea. There are always family relations visiting her and the small town of Middleton had a growing Indian population just because of Deepika's family. Deepika's brother, Ananda, and his wife, Mira, and their children are usually too busy to take vacation time to visit her, so Deepika tries to get to Boston once or twice a year, play auntie to her nephew and niece.

My father releases Deepika's forearm and I stare at the red impression his grip leaves on her golden skin. "Chris?" my father sputters out my name.

I fumble forward and push my way past both of them with my hands held high, palms up in surrender. Then I race up the stairs and into my room with the door slamming behind me.

* * *

A true gentleman, Travis escorts my mother to her office.

DEAD

DEEPIKA LEAVES without another word. Her black hair clings to her scalp and she's soaked from the storm within seconds as she scurries to her Saab. She's never imagined the scope of Geoffrey's failure—in any other way besides the love and obey vow he once took. She's an optimist, a free spirit in a culture that indulges freedom, not to mention equality, and Deepika indulges because she's still acting out and can never believe she will ever enjoy to the fullest the freedom she has to do exactly what she wants to do—and fall to the same caveman ethics men and some of the ancient women back in her home country of India use to trap and coerce the available and unavailable girls; they choose the worst nature too easily. She starts her Saab, and her breath comes out in a rush. Deepika drove over to see Geoffrey after calling his law firm. The chirpy voice saying, "He's been let go." She hasn't seen him in over five months and she's determined to move on with her future. She doesn't want him to be a part of it either. He can't help but notice. She's come for his first reaction and the look of shock on his face. She's come to tell him her life in the present is what the situation is, and, after seeing him, she can't get away fast enough. She almost lasts an hour in his presence. She's now five, going on five and a half, months pregnant.

What is she thinking? Did he even realize how much she wants him to stand up and be a man? For himself. That's not what she plans anyway. She's taking care of it; she's made up her mind to keep her child—yes, her child—proprietary rights; after today she realizes her baby will never be his; she'll protect her child from that fate.

He fools her, and look at her now. The Saab engine stalls

and she hits the steering wheel just like a former boy her parents arranged for her to meet in their cluttered sitting room, hit hard with a flat palm, barely old enough to grow facial hair, set to date her and then marry her, with the blessing of her saintly parents. He was an angelic-featured, easily angered brute who somehow learned to enjoy dealing out pain. She remembers telling her mother: He's not suitable for marriage. Her mother calculated her response.

"It's been arranged." The persistent tone of her mother's voice lacked finality. The sky above them shimmered in the horrid summer heat and coastal humidity. Deepika couldn't respond immediately. She pressed a cool, wet glass of tea against her forehead and sighed. Her writing had been published in an obscure journal in a small university town and her plans for escape began when her mother, with a steady enthusiasm emanating only from her premeditating eyes, told her a boy, a nice boy with a respectable heritage—he wants to be a doctor just like his father—will arrive in two hours to escort her to a garden house. Deepika endured the date and he gave her some time away from the house but he had problems she saw in every man who pursued her. All they wanted was sex but couldn't get it from polished, smart women. All she wanted was sex and she couldn't get it from men because she had to marry them first. She told her mother no and the years passed.

One of her mother's daily emails told of the troubles the young (abusive in secretive, scary ways) doctor-to-be faced in medical school when he was caught with over a thousand dollars in stolen high-end dimmers and lighting equipment—a felony—hidden behind an air conditioning grill in his apartment in Boston, the police brandishing the search warrant and almost giving up, ready to apologize to the smug bastard, who sat preening on a ratty orange couch, a reject from one of the dorm lounges. Finally, they checked behind the heating-unit grate, all the stolen goods were there, and the law promptly arrested him. "The poor family," said her mother. The boy drove a BMW convertible, a red one he kept spotless, and he laughed guardedly with different shiftless, will-less American girls revolving in the passenger seat.

Deepika never replied: "This is the boy you wanted me

to end up with? Great marriage material, Mom."

The apartment the boy had stolen from was three floors below his economical one-bedroom flat and his actions made the owner so angry he told the arriving officer he wanted to press charges to the fullest—I won't accept a plea bargain for this one—even though the police officer said the courts preferred to plea down. The father of the boy begged the apartment owner, the victim of the crime, not to ruin his son's chances in medical school, begged the owner to drop the charges, please, this summer we will send him back to his home in India where he'll be dealt with under strict family law—whatever that meant, right?

Deepika almost laughs when her mother wrote this last part. A slap on the wrist and the thieving boy would be sitting pretty once more finishing out his residency and years later helping anesthetize patients undergoing hip-replacement surgeries in a hospital in the Southwest far from the scene of his former crimes.

"What did he steal?" Deepika asked.

"Lighting fixtures and high-end automatic dimmers. Puzzling beyond belief to me. High tech gadgets from mail order and Home Depot supplies available readily down the street for a pittance of his monthly allowance." He was crying out, Deepika thought, and then wondered if any of the girls he paraded around suffered from his sparking cruelty.

Deepika's never been physically demonstrative before—a hugger—Geoff actually hurts her. She feels the pain in her forearm and realizes his grip will leave a small bruise along her underarm. Then his son appears like a phantom and scares him into releasing her. Great timing. She should've turned around the second he'd opened the door, a pale ghost within the dark house. What a family. No wonder Madison became a writer if she allows herself to be surrounded by such gothic atmosphere and despair. Stupid, Deepika, Deep, how stupid, stupid, stupid; how could she descend into such stupidity? She smiles and shakes her head. Her fingernails are long and smooth with a soft rusty red applied meticulously the night before. She stares at her fingers gripping the steering wheel and the juxtaposition of how she appears outside with what she feels inside rips into her and she barks out a short laugh. One of her hands quickly covers her small mouth, hides her laughter, instinctively, and she presses harder until her laughter stops.

The Saab engine finally catches and Deepika's on the verge of tears when she places the car in reverse and floors it. The gravel rockets and flies away behind her and she thinks she's free. She doesn't have to do anything with this man, father of her child or not, ever again. She pictures her future: Her latest short story collection, all interconnected this time, the most novel-like, with recurring characters, two or three more revisions, is finishing itself, as if a phantom completes the chore, a couple more long writing sessions to go and she'll be free to take off after she wraps up her rental agreement. She'll say goodbye to her few contacts at the college. There's nothing else holding her here in Middleton. Maybe she'll leave Montana earlier and only look back when she's writing about her scandalous life in fictional terms, give it some time to sink in. No one knows. No one in the creative writing program has seen her all summer after she left for Boston in June. They thought she was writing, and traveling, finishing up her book and most of her peers were happy for her if not a bit jealous of her freedom and promise in the literary realm. She'll get out of this small city on the Western side of Montana. Deepika's hand still covers her mouth until she reaches the highway a mile away.

* * *

Geoffrey stands behind the kitchen window and watches Deepika leave. Her belly's grown large but she remains thin everywhere else. He remembers Maddy's pregnancy and how her body grew heavy, burdensome, all over, even around her wrists. Then he grows dizzy with nausea. He's aware of the awful picture from a moment ago as he gripped Deepika's tiny forearm. *The look on my face and how I brushed by them both at the kitchen door, raced up the stairs. The slamming of my bedroom door hasn't registered* yet. He's stuck in the branching web of problems in his mind.

I came home to confront my father about his job, came home to find out why my father had been lying to his family for so long now and I get another peg filled in, a huge splintered peg. Deepika looks large, over halfway through.

I take out my calendar and check the dates; it must've been early May. Mom was finishing up at the college for the year and she kicked dad out of the house for the second time (that I remember, anyway), this time for good.

Get out. How could you?

Slamming doors.

What were you thinking? You weren't thinking. I said this was the last time I'd put up with this.

Nothing Geoffrey could say in return. He left the family home and headed for Deepika's consolation hut—put a nickel in the psychological counseling booth—and received the warmth of a woman who played her part well but a little too calculatingly. Deepika didn't look scared enough; she looked angry when I appeared in the room.

Geoffrey paces the kitchen with quick steps, methodically going back and forth. Was I really going to hurt her? She hadn't told him she was pregnant until today. She'd left to visit her family for the summer season. Is it even his? Geoffrey's past year becomes a blur. With Deepika out of sight all summer and early fall—why did she have to show up at all; she's done teaching here, (and soon would be, officially) another example of Geoffrey being wrong, assuming things—he found it easier to get back into Maddy's good graces, even if she acted like she was shielding some big secret of her own from him most of the time. Let her seek some little revenge.

Geoffrey finally wonders why in the hell I'm not in school, why he's been caught out by me anyway and starts to fume with enough resentment to paint the house a different color. He turns and rushes up the stairs, his green-and-blue tie flaps against his chest. He's convinced himself instantly I'm in the wrong—being a witness to his predilection—he charges up to my door to put me in my place. My father is only thinking of himself at this point, how he himself came home early one day, so long ago in his own past (this moment from my father's history is there in the blackness with me), and this makes him even more squirrelly. He hasn't yelled at me in years and I'm glad I'm not in my room when the door bursts open. Geoffrey pants ragged breaths and his hair spirals askew.

I picture my father as Jack Torrance, the insane caretaker turning ever so slowly to madness in Stephen King's *The Shining*. It's my favorite scary book and I try to read it every single gray Montana winter. Three times through it now and I'm onto other things.

"Where are you?" Geoffrey calls out, his voice a rasp. He checks the bathroom, even pulls back the shower curtain like Norman Bates, hungry, a pattern now in my thinking: my father as every shocking movie villain. Of course I'm not there. He knew I'd gone up the stairs and he thinks I'm hiding somewhere like a little kid playing games. My father's mind isn't all there but I'm not around to figure him out or try to calm him down. As soon as I got to the top of the stairs and threw my soaked backpack against the side of my bed I quickly changed clothes, shirt, pants, and a sweatshirt with a hood. I fled out the window over the front porch. My laptop made a cracked shriek as it hit the floor; my backpack isn't made to cushion anything. The phrase, Oh Hell, repeats itself over and again in my mind, and then, shite, the Irish version, accent and everything, my favorite of all curse words.

"Chris? I want to speak to you. Please." Finally, the hint of desperation and neediness worms into my father's voice. He checks the hall linen closet when I weigh my leap down to the lawn next to the asphalt driveway. When I stand on the top of the front porch the shingles give way a bit, a slippery mess. I also catch sight of Deepika pulling away, revving speed, down the slick road and I'm ready for the chase.

Then, I jump.
And I'm off.
In pursuit.

* * *

Maddy sighs with relief. The rain lessens but she feels it's only going to be a brief respite before the clouds deliver more of the same. One of her office mates gleefully spews weather details like bullets, fast and can you believe it? This rain might turn to snow and then what will the roads be like, the first snow in October—rarely happens. I so wanted to get my winter tires on my Jetta before snow hit us—remember that one year it snowed here in September? Maddy listens to Angela continue her chipper monologue of inanity. Angela finishes by saying, "Do you want anything from the coffee shop?"

"Uh, no. Thanks anyway." Today at least Maddy's distracted enough to be polite. Angela bounces out the door to the communal office suite. Maddy's hit with a pang of jealousy—to be so free, loose, how would it feel—and doesn't trust her own thoughts. Angela shouts out a hello to Arnold and Tabby, first year adjunct professors, and asks if they want coffee. She also must need to overcompensate for some catastrophic past event and Maddy wonders what this could be and writes on her legal pad a sketch of a new scene. She won't censor herself and believes her writing can be read by anyone at any time, but she changes Angela's name just the same, to just a capital A; Angela always snoops around the office; an unsurprising day will come when Maddy limps, cane in hand—a prop—into the office. Angela has finished reading every memo and laundry list under every file name in her computer—protective security passwords be damned. The whole game in her head almost makes Maddy laugh picturing Angela as a super-stealth-mole spy set down in the creative writing program, hired by the evil, dystopian-loving, English Department to get to the undermining condemnatory truth: cut the fat and bring us the heads of all condescending writers.

Her clothes are still a bit damp from the short run to her office and Travis, to his word, remains a true gentleman. She watches his skinny fingers grasp his umbrella, chalk white, blue veins. He's sure she didn't get too wet and they both laugh when they arrive under the eave. She feels like a teenager again and has a sense of wistfulness, ruined shoes and all. She wonders if Travis recognizes this, understands her feeling.

Still, she stays strict with him, serious and shallow, and downplays her responses, especially when he follows Maddy into her office. Angela comes back with a double tall, skim, peppermint latte and flits about with a sheaf of copy paper clutched in her fist. Students linger in the office so Travis isn't unusual and Maddy hopes to keep it that way; hate to get a reputation.

"Did you have any questions about your paper?" Maddy asks as she sits down behind her desk.

"No. I'm thinking about writing about humor in poetry." Maddy realizes Travis seeks her approval, and wonders if it's a maternal thing, and then goes to the next image and feels distaste. She first met Travis when he appeared, wet, skinny as ever, in her English Literature class last year. It was his first year of grad school, and he yearned for serious conversations, polite arguments, and a secret key to Maddy's heart—that's what Maddy decided right then. In August, he signed up for her Modern Poetry class and she gave in when Travis begged her to allow him to enter her undergraduate, though senior level, Creative Writing class. He had to prove he could write first and Maddy was surprised how well he wrote fiction. Very surprised. She can tell Travis thinks he knows her better than most of the other students, but he can't grasp that she loathes his clutching neediness.

Maddy looks Travis in the eye to be polite. She hasn't always been a good listener and makes an attempt with strong, attentive, eye contact.

She notices the need-to-please tone of Travis's voice and scolds herself. He really tries too hard to be liked by her. That's all he wants. There's nothing else hidden. He's like a puppy, she muses. Maddy finds his attention flattering; how many times in the past couple years has anyone shown any interest in her or her opinions, including her wayward husband? Students in her classes did it all the time, to curry favor, to help with the grades and the mysterious wonderment of years facing arbitrary judgment from overly subjective teachers.

"You know why humor makes a difference in poetry?" Maddy asks, keeping a smile on her face as she watches Travis fiddle in his shoulder pack.

"That's a rhetorical question."

"Pretend that it's not? Try this." Maddy takes out her Norton Anthology and flips to the contents page, which list all of the hundreds of poets collected into its encyclopedic depths. Travis retrieves his book and follows along.

"I love poetry but I hate this book." Travis grimaces. He sits across from Maddy and balances his book on his right thigh.

"Go through the list here and come up with a poem or poet who strikes you as the least bit funny. Humor is the hardest to sense in a poet's hands especially if your hypothesis is taking the poem seriously or giving it a certain academic weight. Should you place Oscar Wilde's poems next to Shakespeare's sonnets? If a Robert Service line makes you laugh is it still of merit? Or does it compare to what passes on the idiot box every day—or the multiplex, for that matter? Go through this book and any other you may find in the library and come up with a thesis about humor and merit in the literary community."

Travis keeps silent for a moment too long, thinking. He hadn't planned out his paper topic and Maddy's wandering thoughts intimidate him. All he wants to do is make her laugh. She's too serious. This poetry class is the second subject he's taken with Maddy as a teacher and he's come to feel a bit protective around her. He hopes she'll never realize this fact. "Humor, the work of a comedic poet, ties into how the poet will be remembered—and, usually, the poet won't be taken seriously as a true artist."

"Yes."

Maddy watches Travis as he tightens his brow in concentration. She feels his struggle. What did he expect? He's an adult. Humor and poetry? She doesn't want to receive a twenty-page paper on a ribald subject discussing how important the dirty Irish limerick is to world literature. She refuses to put it past him now and sets this boundary automatically. A rebuttal attorney objects—She's leading the witness, Your Honor! Wow, Maddy thinks, as she realizes she's trying to set up a protective wall between Travis and herself, public and private. Why would it be so wrong to give in and crack just once? Geoffrey shouldn't be the only one allowed to play the game.

There's a small window to Maddy's left and she notices the rain petering out. Will it turn to snow? The drops fall slowly and less pock noise from the leaking gutter escape to blink against the cloudy glass.

"You were saying?" Maddy asks, knowing Travis hasn't uttered another word in response.

"Can I get back to you? You've given me a lot to think about." In Travis's mind an intellectual cloud forms. He hasn't seen the essence of what he wants to do and Maddy has led his thoughts in a new direction. He likes and then instantly dislikes the way he feels. He doesn't want to feel manipulated into any choice. He wants to show Maddy he's capable of doing his best work, creating his own thesis, without guidance. His pride percolates strongly now because he senses, for the first time, a bit of condescension in her tone.

"Sure," Maddy replies, with a smile, a slant he doesn't know how to read, positive, negative, sarcastic, weary. The rain stops. The sky outside stays a brutal gray and Maddy tries not to stare out the window; she focuses her gaze on Travis and wonders again why he's still in her office.

Travis mumbles, "I've got to get to my next class."

"Okay. Good luck on the search." Travis puts his book back and fumbles with the zipper on his pack.

"It looks like the rain's going to stop for a while."

Travis follows Maddy's look out the window and says, "Yeah. I hope so. I'm soaked from our run."

"Thanks for the assist, and, Travis, don't beat up on yourself too much over the paper. Go with it and enjoy the process. You've known me long enough after two classes to realize I like to struggle with issues out loud. You do the same and come up with your own hypothesis."

He appreciates Maddy's words. She seems to know just what to say and still see right through him. He imagines himself naked in front of her, taking a scolding. He winces and stands, still fumbling with his belongings; finally, he moves to the doorway clutching his umbrella in his tight hands.

"See you in writing class tomorrow."

The next second Travis is gone and Maddy lets out a deep sigh as if she's been holding her breath for minutes. What's she thinking? She laughs shortly, shakes her head at her own hubris.

* * *

The rain ends, peters completely out, and the roads are slick. School isn't finished for the day but will end soon and the last bell will release everyone. The algebra test's now in the past and I'm not the least bit upset by having missed it. I have a mission now.

Last fall Maddy took Geoff and me along to a faculty party at the beginning of the term. Everyone was new and still happy. 9/11 was two years in the past and no one talked about it anymore except to say the numbers for the date, which became an emblem—never forget—and make people think.

The College cycled itself into action, meeting and greeting the new professors in the department. The anti-war protestors brayed loudly against the ominous government. Always the case on a social college campus, but a couple years later, 2004, the protestors dwindled into desperate groups trying to use death and destruction as election year props. When Deepika arrived as the new Visiting Writer-In-Residence, she threw a party for the creative writing department. A potluck. But she made a stipulation: everyone must bring the one dish he or she felt was the pinnacle of cooking prowess. She called it Gourmet Potluck. Maddy made a simple spinach salad with her mother's famous citrus dressing with roasted pumpkin seeds.

Deepika made *patrani machi* with a flaky white fish wrapped in lettuce leaves and a mild coconut and cilantro chutney inserted skillfully between everything. It was difficult for Deepika to find the right ingredients for this delicate taste. The spices were all wrong, but she adjusted the cumin and cilantro until satisfied. The lettuce wilted and I wondered if the vegetables in India remained perpetually steamed to death. I also remembered my father going back for seconds and complimenting Deepika to an almost embarrassing length.

I'll never forget my interactions with her. This was the second time Geoffrey and I had met Deepika; Maddy's own house was used for that first staff get-together, fall 2003. And it was so obvious to me what happened, and then the country was thrown into official lies and war cover-ups and intrigue and the election grew more heated because of it and personal relationships mimicked the nation's struggle; another battleground put in dozens of State constitutions that marriage is a right that should be reserved for only a man and a woman and I shrunk every single time someone uttered the word gay. After the party and the fall into winter, people didn't come together on campus anymore without bitterness and anger heavy across their faces. A war to make everyone happy and set things straight started by a man of the West so he could proclaim himself a war president. There were no more parties. Maddy became quieter at home. Geoffrey became quiet in a different way and slowly withdrew from any interaction.

It's now October 2004, a year later, and Deepika somehow is back, and she's not going to ever throw another gourmet potluck. I guess it isn't at all necessary. No one knows Deepika's even in town. She's kept a very low profile. Came back to tie up her loose ends. Quit the winter term, her last final finger up. Use Middleton, its people, for her fiction, and then leave before people get steaming mad.

I thought about taking my bicycle in the drizzle but nixed the idea and now my legs feel numb. They keep moving and it's a wonder. I think about all of the relationships I'm not privy to. There isn't anyone I can call. I don't drive yet and this realization of transportation out of reach tantalizes me. There are two cars at home and I think of the year ahead when I turn sixteen in the summer and bug my parents for the driving permit. Maddy will be the one who lets me practice, but with reservations, always serious reservations. Geoffrey will be the one who winks and gives me the keys anytime I want them: "Go by yourself, Kid. I trust you." Only because I've never done anything wrong—ever, until now—and I feel humiliation seeping in. Why did everything my father say, even if he means well—Hey, Kid, I'm trying to relate—have hidden depths, words that puncture and rip through any optimism but only later when the definition is finally, if ever, clearly revealed.

As I walk the last mile through Middleton's downtown I don't pass anyone else walking on the streets. The cars *whoosh* by and stir the puddles at the edge of the road into great waves of splash. The cuffs of my jeans and hiking boots are soaked even more. I remember changing in my room and the nexus of feelings directing my actions. Deepika down in the kitchen struggles to tear her arm from my father's possessive grasp slapping me right in the face. Snap out of it. Wake up! What am I thinking now?

She's been home for almost forty-five minutes. I turn onto Hubbard Street leading to the small subdivision where she's leased a house for two years—always thinking ahead, tying up loose ends, always planning. I wonder if she planned everything and if the baby she carries is part of her planning.

There aren't any sidewalks in her subdivision and the sign, Lookout Ridge, is just plain silly. There aren't any hills here in this part of Middleton although you can see them through the haze of pollution on sunny days, and fire smoke in fall when fires are terrible (they're getting worse each year), and imagine being surrounded by them. Maybe the person who named the place long ago was chased up a tree by a grizzly bear. The side of the road is puddle, rock, pebble, and uneven under my feet. The trees aren't very mature, not over thirty years old and I crack up again with the image of a contractor clutching his blueprints caught up high and scared, his hardhat falling off his head and a large angry bear leaning against the young trunk of the pine tree, snarling with hunger. Serve him right. The bear takes the hat and bends it in two and someone in the next tree yells: Lookout!

Someone has raked all the fall leaves and piled them into large black garbage bags at the front of Deepika's driveway. I feel like ripping and tearing the bags apart and scattering the mucky leaves: Serve her right. The green Saab sits nestled up closely to her one garage bay, and I wonder why she didn't drive it inside the garage, what she's hiding there that takes up so much room. It's a tiny bungalow of a house and smoke wafts from the river stone chimney. The place looks a lot cozier than our house ever will be. The windows are shuttered from within by a dark wood, maybe a mahogany and they slant open just a crack; there's a shadowy movement from behind them and I wonder if Deepika watches me approach. I notice the red door contrasting with the dark swampy wood color of the house and it starts to blend in the more I look at it.

I stand on the front porch under a dimly glowing Greene and Greene lantern. I stand there for ten minutes just staring at the front door, talking myself into knocking or pressing the lit doorbell. I fail. What will I say anyway? I'm sure she hates my family, my father in a big way after what I witnessed, my mother because my father's still married to her and won't leave her and me because my father stayed with my mother when he got her pregnant. All the soap stories, the relationships tempered by melodrama, sift in. Does she hate anyone? She never seemed the type to wear such anger on her sleeve. When I met her the first couple of times, I felt happy in her presence. She seemed so light, and not just because she was born in a different, unique, country.

I turn around to leave, just a step from the end of the porch down to the path leading off to the left and the driveway, when Deepika opens the door, and says, "I was wondering how long you were going to lurk out here." She doesn't smile but there's a hint of humor in her tone. I can't believe she finds the situation humorous.

"Won't you come in?" Her tone is instantly serious again yet irritatingly calm; is the humor still there? How complex everyone appears to be. She tries to hide the main thought in her head, but it's somehow revealed to me now as I filter through my past—she thinks: Like father, like son. How pitiful I must look to her—following my father to her doorstep, my father knocking on the same door last spring, hurting inside, but reaching for words to disguise his base desire, Deepika taking him into her home. Did she offer him tea? Did he kiss her gently at first? What was he thinking? I picture him holding Deepika against him, whispering, lying, and talking to her as if she didn't have a choice to make. How she went to sleep, easily, after they made love, after she didn't really answer him when he asked if she used birth control, telling him not to worry—do you? And how she and my father could create a child together and how she could keep this from him for so long—again seeking solace and a right to quench the deceit.

I cannot respond vocally. I head into her simply decorated rental house and Deepika softly asks me to remove my shoes. I sit on an antique bench in the front foyer and place my shoes on the mat near the front door. Water puddles around them. I have no idea what compels me to travel such a distance. I panic. I should've spoken to my father first and let the information take hold less impulsively.

"Would you like some tea?" Deepika asks while heading into the living room. I watch her every move. She's carrying my father's baby but you'd never know it from behind. She walks effortlessly, almost glides across the hardwood floor and the area rugs she brought from home across the ocean. She doesn't wait for me to answer knowing I somehow can't find a simple vocabulary. "I'll be right back. Why don't you take a seat near the fire?"

The fireplace blazes and sparks and I watch the flames. I always love the flickering of a fire on a dreary day. One of my chores at home is stocking the wood on the woodpile and making sure the two fireplaces in the house are always ready to light.

After fiddling with the end of my soaked jeans I finally roll the bottom of them into a cuff. I hear sounds from the kitchen, water running from a faucet, the tinny sound of a kettle being filled, the door of a humming refrigerator opening and closing but I don't hear Deepika moving around the kitchen. There's a quality of ghostliness about the house and listening, if I close my eyes, makes this feeling even more apparent. I could be alone in a stranger's house with the ghost of my father's mistress plotting revenge with all the culinary knives and head-bashing cast-iron skillets that lay about. If Deepika comes back with her hands hidden behind her I'll start running again. The gloom of the day quickens my heart and I realize it's getting late. The days shrink and approach the set-your-clocks-back deadline and soon it will be dark as night by four o'clock. School's been over now for an hour and Mr. Roffiger's math team jam session's almost over. I seldom break the rules, the really important ones, and skipping school today must rank up there as the largest infraction so far.

    I picture Ellis listening, almost sweating the mathematical formulas, while Mr. Roffiger, as patient as a tollbooth operator, if not as bored, reviews this week's lesson for those who just don't get it the first time. I'd be right in there with my brow tight and my questions just fussy enough to seem appropriate on the other side of the room where the mathletes compete. There's no reason I should've left school and I can't go back now. I miss the math test as well as English and French classes. I rarely participate in English, something to do with the teacher being effusively hyper, more than I can stomach most of the time but French is where I shine and I can see the regret on the teacher's face as she fills out her demerit slip tomorrow. She and Mr. Roffiger will forever remember their disappointment with my behavior and whenever my name comes up they'll know I can't be relied upon for much—don't give him any responsibilities—except erasing the chalk off the board at the end of class. It's all Amos's fault anyway. Not mine.

    If Amos hadn't let the news slip out about my father's all-important job—no wait—no job. What did I do? I end up trying to grab some attention by skipping class and running home to confront Geoffrey the Great, icon, son of a genius, and father to a chip off the old block. So he has an affair and the time frame fits so well with the moods of mom, Maddy the Cuckold, silent sufferer of the stern countenance. And then it hits me. I'm here to ask Deepika if my mother knows. When did it start? Even though I already figured that part out I want to hear her reply. She's still in the kitchen silently opening cupboards, taking mugs out, clinking china plates and silverware. I want to run away again, take off and not confront Deepika at all. She greets me so formally and nicely and I can see why my dad fell for her. I push this thought away. Another question on my list: Are you still in love? The problem with this last question is Deepika was never in love with my father.

* * *

The teapot whistles on the hot plate plugged into the ancient wall socket and Maddy turns in her chair to lift the vessel off the burner. She fills her mug with scalding water and begins to steep rich black tea. She wants to get up and go back home but realizes it's too early and remembers she's promised to bring home Chinese dinner. Another chore to do and she scolds herself for her ungratefulness when the telephone rings.
"Hello?" she answers.
"Maddy?"
"Lance? Is that you?"
"You always know my voice." Maddy's instantly defensive. Why is Lance calling her? It's a rare occurrence; usually it's Sheila calling her. Lance calls Geoffrey, it's just how their relationship works, asking how the family is and when we're all going to get our butts in the same place.
"How's Sheila doing?"
"She's fine."
"Are you guys coming out soon?" Maddy wants to keep talking; she pictures Lance back in Ann Arbor, what time is it there? Oh yeah, two hours difference. They usually plan to be together on the New Year's Eve, missing only a few in the past ten years.
"No," Lance says, "but I wanted to speak to you. I've been calling Geoff."
"Are you at home? Just trying to figure things out," Maddy interrupts, already sounding scatterbrained; she wants to know the logistics. Something isn't right.
"I'm just about to leave the office but the weather's not

too nice right now and I thought I'd give you a call."

"It's been awful here all week. Raining like the second flood was forecast. I almost got caught in it."

"Sounds familiar. We live in gray states."

"No. You live in a blue state. The red of Montana is a joy to live with every day."

Lance laughs and silence fills the line.

"What's on your mind, Lance?" Finally she's ready enough to ask; she's taken the time, rid herself of pleasantry. Lance never really speaks to her, never initiates long distance phone calls with her, anyway; he's always been Geoffrey's old law school buddy and when they both married the dynamics changed. There's a tension between them and Maddy always believes it's her fault and wonders if Lance blames her for taking Geoffrey away from the Midwest. Tough. He's calling her up like they had calm, gossipy, chats every day of the week.

"Like I said. I'm calling because I'm worried."

"Worried about what?" Maddy asks with a hint of anger in her voice. How much does Lance know? Has Geoffrey been keeping Lance informed about every little aspect of their marriage like he used to do? She tried to put a stop to his confiding in Lance—out of embarrassment, really, how do you confess serial adultery to an old buddy?

"Geoffrey's been working on a case. Calston and Meyers."

"Get to the point, Lance. Please."

"Maddy. There's no need to get short with me. I'm calling because I'm concerned."

"Lance. I'm sorry. I just know you're going to tell me something I think I should've been able to guess on my own. Like all the other times."

"You don't know?"

"Okay. You tell me." Maddy's now the one who is embarrassed. She hasn't known her husband in a long time. What is Lance talking about?

"He's not handling the case anymore. Calston and Meyers pulled out and went to another firm. They used to be a big client who needed our services sorting out issues dealing with land trusts out West. That's why we went to

Geoffrey in the first place. He didn't tell me any of this. He quit the law firm three weeks ago, just walked out from what I can gather."

More than anything else, the secrets Geoffrey feels he needs to conceal, ever more secrets, always more and more and Maddy's left looking stupidly insufficient and out of the loop. Or worse: to blame.

"I want to come out there. Sheila, too. We have some vacation time saved up."

"Lance. I'm not sure what's happening. You don't have to drop everything and fly out here."

"I'm not giving you a choice. It sounds like you didn't even know Geoffrey left his law firm?" Maddy remembers the other day, bumping into Glynnis, who furtively wanted to duck out of the way without contact or nicety or the slightest communication as if wary to catch something, some made up flu. Maddy now realizes Glynnis feels sorry for Maddy, and Geoffrey never thought it important enough for his wife or his son to know. Maddy imagines her parents telling her: We told you so. And worse.

"I didn't know. The lie Geoffrey told me . . . he was working out of the home office."

"What's going on, Maddy?"

"I'll find out tonight. Please, Lance. I'll talk to Geoff tonight and call you tomorrow morning."

"I'll be at the office."

"Sheila knows?"

"Yes." Lance and Sheila communicate in a healthy way. Goody for them. She pictures them at the breakfast table—Sheila and Lance, brows furrowed over morning lattes flavored with Valencia, discussing Geoff's escape—just this morning; she compares the scene to her own morning with Geoffrey; so willing-to-please, make her breakfast and try so hard to keep his lie asleep. Maddy's anger at Geoffrey inflates. The last thing she wants is Lance and Sheila flying out for an intervention.

"Lance." Maddy pauses to gather strength.

"Yeah?"

"Don't come out here. I mean it. Let me handle it." There's an edge to her voice, her anger approaching extreme heights.

"He's my best friend," replies Lance in an equally sharp tone. He's perplexed by Maddy's behavior and the way she's conducting the conversation.

"I know that. Do you think I've had it easy living with poor Geoffrey this last year? There's a lot more going on than Geoff losing his job."

"He told me about his affair months ago."

"Again, it looks like you're always the first to know, and I'm the last."

"I'm willing to help. That's all."

"And we handled that so we can handle this." Maddy relents. Lance really cares and his tone of voice is soft and not as strident as hers. Maddy also gets it that Lance knows she kicked Geoff out of the house and wouldn't let him back until midsummer. Why wouldn't he know? Did he also know that Geoffrey walked up to the front door and begged for her forgiveness and she acquiesced too easily in hindsight? Maddy says, "I'm sorry, Lance. I'm really sorry."

Maddy also realizes she's speaking too loudly and getting a lot of stares and studious paper shuffling from the other people in the office outside her open door. Fuck you, she wants to shout, really stir up the gossip pool.

"Listen. Go home. Talk to Geoff, and call me at home tonight if you need to but let me know tomorrow what's up. You can count on me, Maddy. I've known Geoffrey a long time and I've seen him at his lowest before. As have you."

"I'll call you. I promise."

* * *

I force myself not to say thanks when Deepika hands me a mug of steaming hot tea. It's ingrained, to mind my manners. Thanks, Mom. An anomaly: a polite teenager.

"This tea is a favorite. My parents send me care packages and this tea, it's an old leaf from the town I grew up in."

"It smells like lemons. Thank you." (whoops . . . couldn't help it.)

I, Chris (I remember doing this), study how Deepika holds her steaming cup with slow, careful movement, elegant, her wrist so small I don't believe she's strong enough to raise her saucer as she adds milk to the lemony mix.

Deepika acts relaxed and secure. I'm not comfortable with her act. This is the woman my father moved out of the house for, left my mother for and she drifts out of her kitchen carrying a delicate tray full of tea, and a bowl of red grapes she rinsed at the sink. They look beautiful in the green bowl.

"This is how most take their tea back home, sugar and milk to fill the cup. Hot and rich."

I listen to Deepika's voice and sink into the puffed cushions of the couch. The log on the fire burns halfway down and the flames flicker less, not as frenetic. I can watch it forever.

"I don't know why I came here." Let her believe that.

Deepika murmurs, almost a laugh, but soft, and then says, "I find that hard to believe."

"I guess."

"Listen," Deepika says, "what you saw wasn't what you thought."

"My father was hurting you. How clear does that have to be?"

"Yes. What do you think happened?"

"Why did you come to my house?" I watch myself shout these words, this wet, surly Chris. The loudness of my (his) voice in the small room echoes and I picture the china shattering; I resist the urge to throw the dishes into the fireplace.

Deepika doesn't even react to the outburst. She calmly says, "I wanted to tell your father he's about to have another child. To clean the slate, so to speak. I'm moving away and I felt he had a right to know. Now I can leave."

"He didn't know until this afternoon?"

"No. But he became angry, confused."

"Aren't we all?" Every member of the Bullet family is so easily angered.

"Listen," Deepika says, "I didn't go to your house to split

up your family, or trap him into coming with me. I came to your house to release him from any responsibility."

"What?" Her dark brown eyes stare into mine but I don't understand her words.

"I'm obviously far along. The baby is due in less than four months. I won't teach the winter term, the last in my contract. I already spoke to the Department and they have enough advance time to find a good replacement. It would be awkward, besides. I'm keeping my child. It's my decision after all. And your father didn't realize I was even carrying his child; how could he; I left at the beginning of the summer."

"That's when my father moved back into the house."

"Yes. I told him to go. He still loves your mother very much."

"And if he didn't?"

"I imagine we'd still be here having the same conversation."

"You didn't tell him you were pregnant?"

"Belief. It's so hard to tell someone to have faith in another person. I can't believe you haven't spoken with your parents about the past year. You don't really know any of this. I didn't know I was pregnant until I was back on the East coast. I took one of those pharmacy pregnancy tests. And I passed."

"Where did you go?"

"Boston. To be with my brother and his family for the summer. I was supposed to come back here in the fall to finish my book, but I'm going to pack up and leave by the end of the month, before winter begins."

I'm silent for a minute. Her words make me even more tired, angrier. There's so much anger beneath the surface. I should be upset at my father, my mother's coldness, this mistress who has the composure to sit in front of me discussing my family as if it's ever so normal, refined.

"I told your father so I could move on. That sounds selfish but I never had any intention of being with your father, making a new family with him. Sorry."

It's weird. The words this woman speaks. I naively believe people have babies and both parents share responsibilities.

"I've released your father."

"I see how well that worked," and my tone is snide. I glance at the spot my father grasped and the bruise and Deepika turns her arm over and tries to catch my eye. There's a dim purplish mark but it's not swelling.

"I don't think he meant to hurt me at all."

"Aren't you the forgiving one?"

"Life is a complex animal."

"Is that stitched on a pillow somewhere?"

"Probably. Life is a continual cycle; everything repeats."

I didn't come here to banter philosophy with Geoffrey's mistress. I stare at the floor. She'll never be my father's mistress. She never was. She was using him for her own ends. I believe every word she says. And it hits me. I look at Deepika's face without any curiosity. She's a strong woman. Like and unlike my mother who hides her strength behind cold, tense, stern expressions even when she says she's happy, in a cheerful mood.

"This child you're going to have."

Deepika lets me speak, tilts her head until it leans on her palm. Her belly's so large in front of me.

"This child is going to be my brother or sister, right?"

"Half-brother or half-sister." Deepika replies as if she's just been thinking of this fact for the first time also. "The life I choose need not have any effect on you or your family anymore. That's what I told your father."

"What if it's not that simple?"

"Life never is. Your father said the same thing before he tried to—reason—with me."

I should feel sorry for her? Oh shite. She's cryptic and circular and has an answer that's more disruptive than the last, as if she's trying to bait me. The whole earth breaks, all I do is stay immovable and immobile.

* * *

Maddy sits in her office, still and silent. She doesn't touch her pens, the pile of In-box letters to answer, poetry reading requests, could she speak to the Ladies-Who-Lunch crowd, wear a smart hat and pretend the tea-drinking, local-mall-suit-wearing, nose-in-the-air, snobby wives of the faculty have any interest in her words. She's done it before and swore she'd have to remember to stock comfort bags in her briefcase if ever forced—politics—to give lectures to the covetous college world at large. Maddy once attended a Writers' Conference in Spokane. Close enough to drive herself, but far enough to make it seem like a vacation, alone in a bed and breakfast, quaintly chosen because writers are supposed to love the antiques, the gated seclusion and forced communal attributes of the inns. Let's have all the visiting writers stay together and break bread around a rickety surface!

She meets everyone and wonders what she's doing there. The conference sent an ambassador, a high school student with a big smile and fervent dreams that coming so close to a published writer will rub off on him, to ferry her around to the city's hot spots, preferable coffee shop, this is what it feels like to observe the world and write about it, and Maddy takes all of this in stride, and can use it, perhaps, and she'll take to the lecture tent, hot and humid in the summer. She'll feel a beginning stickiness on her skin and hope the hour passes quickly. Maddy stands at the podium with her sheaf of papers, a slim volume of her fourth book of collected poems, and a cappuccino—make it a triple—with organic skim milk, please, and smiles tightly at everyone. She's stiff in her walk up the stairs and she knows the audience watches her stiffness and wonders about it. Most of them don't know about the car accident and she's only written about it in passing phrasing; most of them have never heard of her before, she's the lone poet amongst the group of fiction writers. The woman who introduces her says Madison Dakota is—finally, implied—working on her first novel—as if to confirm a future reverence writers of prose receive once they give up their fanciful poetic dreams. Now, she wonders about this fact. The audience views her from far away. Maddy equally views them all as sitting so far away from her, and she's the one who has to move them closer to her with her words. They're all so neat and skeptical and awash with a hope for greatness, for entertainment. Yet, Maddy stays so physically stiff in her manner it tends to push people away. She reads her words, not as a poetic spokesperson but as an actor, and this mindset helps her relax and enjoy the words excavated from her long ago. By the end she's looser and the audience pulls closer and she has them with the finest of metaphors, the phrases duplicating the simplest shades of life's puzzlement.

Maddy remembers the feeling she gets when she finishes a reading. The applause and the smiling wonder. Then the faces in the audience become clear, someone thanks her as if from a great distance—would anyone like to ask a question of our poet? Always, there's a pause as the clapping dies abruptly and an older woman in a patterned shirt, flannel, it must be, raises her arm and asks: Is there anything behind the anger in your work?

Life is about caging anger. Disappointment.

Maddy feels compelled to complement the questioner: "That's a very interesting observation. I can honestly say I've always been propelled and repelled by conflict. It's my job to find a way to describe the human experience, the universality we share." Blah. Blah. Blah.

The next question makes Maddy think of the comfort bag again. Oh, excuse me, folks, I'll be right back, and she ducks beneath the podium and vomits into her imagination, the scene makes her hide her thoughts with a plastic smile and a nod and a sip of the coffee, now cold at the bottom of her cup, and bitter. All these people in attendance aren't writers or poets or anything close; they're mostly readers, flush enough to afford the high ticket price for the conference, and their wants and needs show this so clearly to Maddy she's on the verge of laughter. She's not laughing at them either; it's more than this; it's the moment she vows never to repeat. The people pay a fee to attend and she imagines them coming year after year, sitting in the same seat under the same tent now yellowing with age, the hands holding the interchanging programs wrinkling, the questions about inspiration no longer filtering out their desperation and Maddy smiles widely and thanks everyone and moves where she's directed and finds herself in a bar three doors down from the bed and breakfast with three other writers who accepted the chance to run workshops for the beginner and in two hours all four of them are plowed.

"Why do you think we drag ourselves out of our rigidly constructed lives?" asks one of the novelists who thinks he's on the same wavelength as Maddy. He's been inching his way ever closer to her, imperceptibly to no one, and Maddy loves the attention, even if he happens to be the largest, most pompous, slob she's been around in quite some time. After one of his exclamations Maddy asks the group: "Is pompoussistic a word?"

Everyone at the table laughs and another says, "It should be."

The inching author says, gamely, "Pompoussistic: the state of being a narcissistic, overbearing ass."

"No," someone else interrupts, "the state of being so full with the awe and wonder of yourself you have to vomit every detail of every act to anyone who will listen."

"As if your purpose in life, as a writer, is to instruct the masses on how greatly their lives are enhanced by your written word."

"Teach them a damn lesson."

"The word's close to pedantic."

"See? You just said a pompoussistic thing!"

Maddy laughs even harder. She knows she's drunker than she's been in quite a long, long time, and wonders if she's slurring her words. The inching novelist now rests his hand next to hers and Maddy lifts her martini glass, Sapphire gimlet, up, very cold, with flecks of ice still floating, and finishes the last three sips.

"I now see how we all get through these things." Maddy glances at her watch and rises from the table, tipping slightly to the left, into the grinning man, but only because she's had too many gimlets, not because she's at all contemplating sleeping with the letch. He's a good writer, but please. She can get even with Geoffrey, she instantly realizes, through the gin haze. She says goodnight to the three authors and they all wish her well and tell her they'll see her at the breakfast table, which almost makes her gag to think of omelets and buttery French toast. Nice people—regardless of desire. Walking back to her room the sky's brilliant with stars and Maddy feels a pang of loss. With affection she thinks about Geoffrey back in Montana taking care of me and she longs for a night of romance, not drunken romance either, but something seemingly lost to her and Geoffrey.

Nearing the end of the workday the office ticks and shifts down. Maddy takes out the new Chinese restaurant flier and calls up for mu shoo shrimp, tangerine chicken, and Szechwan pork green beans, three egg rolls and enough hot and sour soup and fried rice. She and Geoffrey always judge Chinese restaurants by the quality of their hot and sour soup. Around Middleton, the ethnic restaurants are few and far between and they settle for the lowest common denominator. She's heard the food is good yet reasonably priced, which is the first warning sign when she listens to Angela go on and on about her tangerine chicken feast. Maddy wants to remain calm and normal and unthreatening to Geoffrey; she plans to drive home with the promised dinner, act like her day was spent worrying over a student with promise but who seriously lacks funding, then talk about the state of education in Montana and get into a circular discussion leading to the kicker: Where the fuck have you been spending your empty days? What do you think you're doing? Why are you lying to us? Are you trying to ruin this family? Too late!

Maddy pictures herself yelling so loudly all the windows in the house shatter all at once, the Chinese food so ornately prepared, boxed, scooped onto plates and set on the table then flying through the air following the broken glass and staining the walls. She's been through tough times before with Geoffrey and thinks she can handle another episode, could this be the end? She hears, Rhea, her sister, say, "Well, Madison, we all had our reservations but we couldn't say anything; you said you were deeply in love and what can anyone do but accept your decision?"

By the time Maddy gathers her coat and briefcase she's worked herself into a state of determination. She contemplates her options and how drastic she's willing to become. Geoffrey, his behavior, is far from normal. She worries about his ability to function in a normal world. She scolds herself. She's been a witness to his breakdowns and withdrawals well before she married him, before she even gave birth, but she comes back to thoughts about love and the ups and downs and many more platitudes of saving the fallen.

As she walks down the hallway to the elevator she sees someone waiting for the lift and decides she feels too raw to make nice in a confined space, even for the short flight down three floors. She'll take the stairs; the walk will be her workout for the day—remember wanting to exercise more? Maddy moves through the exit doorway with a clank of the push bar. Geoffrey waits at home, waits for his next performance. Off the first stair, Maddy feels as if she's stepped on the hardest of marbles, an obstacle under her footing as she takes the first step down, and it's so unexpected, this feeling at the bottom of her right foot, that she's falling swiftly before she can react. Her balance goes away and in the blink of an eye she teeters and her arms pinwheel and fly out, her hand lets go of her stuffed briefcase and she crashes into the metal railing on her left almost sideways. She barely comprehends that she's falling.

* * *

"I don't understand."
"Maybe understanding isn't as important as you think," Deepika says with the same enigmatic emphasis.
I need to get out of her house. I stand to leave.
"Let me drive you home," Deepika says, switching to a careful, honest tone. I can't call it fake; she's been up front with me—yeah, an honest deceiver.
"I'd rather walk."
"You have a lot to take in. If you want—please, come back to see me and we can speak—" Deepika doesn't have any intention right then to be in Middleton for very much longer.
"Do you realize how horrible my parents have been? And knowing you've been a part of the last year's—"
I can't go on and I feel the anger twisting my stomach into knots. I study Deepika's face—as if I believe I'll never

ever see it again—as she grows alarmed, concerned for me, my state of mind. I quickly put on my shoes without bothering to lace them in her presence. I shut her front door and enter the darkness of the coming night. I don't know where I'm heading, but it's far too late to change paths; my anger propels me.

* * *

The fall down the third floor stairs is stopped when Maddy panics even more and flings her left arm out to grab onto the railing just as she's about to lose her footing and go down hard. She catches herself and realizes she's sweating again, profusely, a full, instant, sheen. She wiggles her feet one by one and breathes a sigh of relief. Shortly her heart calms its racing and she glances at the top of the stairs and looks for a pebble, some stone, something she's tripped over, but finds nothing there.

Maddy remembers the episode in her classroom, sitting without making a cry. Something's wrong; she can't control her body. Twice now in one week she's been startled by the immobility, the numbness in her extremities, and thinks about the cause. She blames Geoffrey, his wallowing act, and secretive nature causing her system to stress and crash. Then she remembers another similar tripping episode almost a month ago on the front steps of the Union Café. She laughed it off. Silly. (I wish I could comfort my mother here and tell her she's going to be okay. No one knew. She didn't tell us.)

She sits on the top step and hangs her head. Her hair falls in front of her face, limp, at the end of the day and she stares at her briefcase at the bottom flight of steps. Nothing bursts out of the seams and she's grateful for that. The panic in her mind continues to take shape and she wants to call her best friend, Nadine Gosling, on her cell and let Nadine take her to the hospital. She doesn't tell Nadine everything but knows she can count on her. She's the first friend Maddy made when they moved to Middleton, a working mother of two grown children, who has no connection to the college.

Cancer? Is something dark growing within her? Is she starting to show symptoms? She goes to grim places in her mind. Maddy can't remember the last time she's had a medical checkup and scolds herself anew, this time letting out a curse. How reckless can she be? It's been a tough year. She argues with herself.

Nadine will help, but then Nadine's husband, Bernard—Bernie to everyone—will also know; they tell each other everything. All couples should. Nothing to hide, really! She starts to focus her anger. Her breathing calms even more and she wants to keep it that way. The railing's there for her weak grip.

Maddy stands and stretches her left ankle, then stretches the right. There's no pain and she feels a sense of déjà vu. Her feet are working the way they should but she remains tense as she makes her way to the landing and gathers up her briefcase. She takes out her cell and punches the speed dial button for Nadine. It rings and rings once again before Nadine's voice comes on with the artificial cheer of a recording. Maddy hangs up without leaving a message.

From the College Maddy will pick up several take-out cartons from the Chinese restaurant. Then she'll drive home; she'll set the table and call Geoffrey down from his office, and me from my bedroom. I won't be home but all the same she'll think I am—my room lights are on—and she won't brave the steps to go upstairs and check. She'll think I'm listening to my music or a language tape with my headphones blocking her voice but she'll be wrong. She'll assume Geoffrey is in his office but he's in the bathroom. She won't think of anything except her body's failing operating instructions, her fall. She'll think so much about her own physical problems she'll never realize she has the house to herself. Geoffrey won't answer her. How can he when he lays on the floor of the bathtub unconscious and for all Maddy knows—when her impatience and unraveling fury get the best of her and she rushes up the stairs and flings open my bedroom door first and finds me gone—dead?

DARKNESS

MADDY SEETHES with the constant images of Geoffrey lying, hiding at home and pretending he still has a job. Her pulse races, her body responds loudly to the rush up the stairs. I'm falling apart. No. My family's falling apart. She pushes my bedroom door farther open, her first glance inside my room makes her do a double take. All the lights are on upstairs; she noticed this as she drove up the driveway and her brightly lit home led her to believe everyone was inside. The house blazes with the glare; this confounds and confuses Maddy. Where is Chris? (Where am I?) Maddy thinks this with a mother's dread. It's raining steadily again and the situation heightens her imagination into designing the worst scenarios. I'm an only child and even though I've been fairly self-sufficient this past year my mother's always kept tabs on my whereabouts. The smothering of an only child and all the positive and negative characteristics linked drives her response. As she enters my room to give it a steady once over she starts to believe I'm in the most horrible mess. She just doesn't know how awful as her nervy intuition takes hold.

In the midst of her confusion Maddy feels she's acting out a play, in the throes of a panoramic study on the struggle of a dying family dynamic. Pity the poor, small humans onstage. Take a lesson from all this angst and consider yourself lucky. It's funny what goes through one's mind when trying to figure out what remains hidden.

After searching my room she walks down the hall to Geoffrey's office. He has to have heard her calling. What's he doing? The selfish shit. At the forefront of her thoughts now. Maddy doesn't even want to face him but she's grown so worried about my whereabouts she promises to calm down and not address Geoffrey with an angry tone. She promises this to herself and repeats: Don't get mad. Stay calm. Don't get mad. Stay calm. She takes a deep breath and opens the office door and finds this room also empty. Then she's stumped. Truly. Has Geoffrey taken me somewhere? No, the Cadillac's in the garage.

Maddy steps into Geoffrey's office with a new, curious lack of energy as if she's spent it all in the search. She walks to the little closet and opens the bi-fold door. It's jammed with boxes of old client files and copy paper and more rolls of fax paper than anyone could ever need, bought by the handful at Costco. There's no way a person could fit in the closet so why open the door at all? Just being thorough. She's resigned and exhaustion creeps in. She has a stray thought about the Chinese food in the little white cartons now resting on the kitchen island below and how she'll have to wait to eat and her stomach growls and she allows her anger to simmer on low once more. Geoffrey's desk is piled with stacks of file folders and loose sheets of paper and post-it notes and memos and bills tucked in a black plastic tray. She notices most of the bills are unopened. She picks up envelope after envelope. The cable bill, the electric bill, home insurance, the cell phone bill, the regular telephone bill, the garbage bill, the many calls to renew all the magazines, the alumni notices asking for more donations, an old gas bill, the American Express bill—some recent but some going back more than a month—and Maddy becomes even more worried. This is your second, third, notice—a couple of the bills have this printed at the top in red. You must pay before the 15th of the month or we turn off...

The house sits in silence. Her shoulder aches from gripping the railing when she stopped her fall down the stairs and she wonders if she's sprained anything, bruised a rib. "Stop thinking about yourself," she mutters this out loud.

Then she lifts the top sheet of paper and scans the contents. Something about a case but the date reads three months ago. The files are yellowing, from the past summer, and she quickly understands they were there for show—

placed on the desk to fool her—so she'll go on thinking her tidy little family drama is balanced. The duplicity in her husband isn't as shocking after his betrayal during the past year and she seriously considers sitting down right then at Geoffrey's desk and calling the divorce attorney from his old law office. That would get him. Right now. Get the ball rolling like she should've long ago. How could she've been so foolish? She scolds herself for being so self-absorbed. She doesn't even know her child well enough to know where I am. Where are the signs—the guideposts?

Maddy presses her palms against the desktop and stands. After turning off the office light, she walks into the hall feeling numb. Her mind resigns itself to failure and she wants to take all of it on: Where the hell is my lying, dysfunctional, betrayed family?

When she enters the master bedroom she also finds the room empty, which is no longer a surprise. No one is home. She scans the room anyway and checks in the master bathroom. Why are all the lights in the house on? That should've been her first clue that something was wrong and Maddy calls herself an idiot, and again, out loud: You're Such An Idiot!

She sits on the bed and takes her shoes off. If Geoffrey chose that moment to walk into the room startling her like he had that very morning, Maddy doesn't know what she'd hit him with first. She imagines picking up the bedside alarm clock, the heavy brass box, and flinging it at his head and following that with the small bud vase, a contemporary glass shaped like a raindrop, and watch it shatter against the wall. Maddy feels like throwing the vase anyway.

By this point she starts to worry not just about my whereabouts but Geoffrey's too and she can't help it. There was a time in late June, before Geoffrey asked, begged Maddy to take him back, when she'd spent all her anger and embarrassment and the silent house didn't hold much comfort after she had nothing left to give. She'd have conversations with me in a tone of voice as if I needed to be held by the hand and would break if offered all the salacious details. She said, "Your father and I are going through something very difficult, Chris. We're working things out." And my mother honestly believed this. She wanted to for my sake. And why wouldn't she? But she never really told me the truth, all the gory details—kept silent so as not to make me think anything was out of the ordinary—because I was still that little kid in her eyes, the only child, strapped back in that car seat too short to see clearly out the window, someone to protect from harm.

Well, in hindsight, Geoffrey's moods have startled her before. Maddy rests on the bed and covers her eyes with her left forearm, letting her fingers hang limply. She remembers the months before Geoffrey asked Maddy to marry him. Romantic and pastoral in the Ann Arbor woods walking along the forest pathways in the fall. Geoffrey held her hand. They circled the reservoir along a leaf-strewn path and stopped to watch the University of Michigan Crew Sculls, The Eights, turn at the end of a practice run, the port oars staying dipped in the water as the boats gently turned. Geoffrey told Maddy he'd always wanted to learn how to row. Maddy watched the men in the thin boats dip their shoulders in unison. The crew coach stayed beside his team in a small, motored boat. He lifted a bullhorn pressed to his lips and his raspy voice barked instructions. He sounded a bit surly and disappointed with the day's performance. She remembers the coach yelling at his team: "We'll run this drill until we get it right, you pussies." Geoffrey and Maddy laughed loudly. Maddy said, "Keep your day job, Geoff. Your boss isn't that bad. I wonder if he's the women's coach, too, and if he dares use that word."

In the months ahead of them Maddy teased Geoffrey by saying, "Hey, Puss, do you want to meet for dinner?"

"Sure, Pussy," he'd respond, but this time in his Connery as James Bond as crew-coach voice, and it became their little joke.

Not now. Maddy doesn't remember the last time she and Geoffrey laughed about the past and teased each other with ease. Hey, Puss, why did you cheat on me again?

I don't know, Pussy. The feeling just came over me one day. I met Deepika in a bookstore, we chatted, and then she left. I followed her back to her charming little rental cottage and we fucked our brains out.

Hey, Puss, why did I take you back?

Because you know it didn't mean anything and I love you and I'm so so so so so very very sorry and I'll never do it again and I'll never let you down again, Pussy.

Maddy feels like one big rube as she weighs the meandering steps leading to her present situation. Her stomach growls again. Her shoulder still aches, her feet feel normal and her legs aren't giving her strange signals. She stands once more and reties her hair into a ponytail. She takes off her work clothes and lets them fall on the floor next to the bed. When she enters her closet she's disturbed by the empty silence of the house around her and she pushes to keep a creeping paranoia at bay. Where's Chris? Where did Geoffrey go? But she's not worried yet about our safety. For all she knows we're enjoying a trip to Blockbuster to get the latest movie release, something they could all watch as a family. But, again, in what car? Where are they? She laughs and disregards the notion that we're out doing anything together. Geoff's not capable—even this morning's performance, the breakfast display, doesn't convince Maddy—and thinking so negatively makes her dress faster in blue jeans, a white Big Sky College t-shirt and a worn, black Nike sweatshirt she wears to work out in.

Maddy feels a sense of melancholy, of being so alone she imagines a future devoid of anyone living with her, around her, something she's grown to fear as she ages, something she's never admitted to; it's one of the solid factors keeping her tied to Geoffrey, but this factor remains buried deep. She's such a coward. She'll dwell on this scenario from time to time: being alone in her office and writing her poetic lines hour after hour, stretching her arms, turning her neck left to right, never noticing how empty her office has become, an empty life. When she's wallowing in her loneliness Maddy usually calls Nadine but she hates using Nadine as a crutch.

Me—she thinks about her son—before entering my teenage years, always kept company with Maddy. After school I'd ride my bike over to campus and do my homework on the battered and graffiti-riddled desk Maddy confiscated from the janitorial office and placed against the pale-blue painted walls. She even found an old wooden office chair with working wheels. I loved to take the chair, hard and uncomfortable as it looked, for a spin around the office, constantly chatting about my teachers and the gossip about who was offended that day by those who wanted more. I was one of her bright lights, always informative, and full of humor, her type of humor. Maddy realizes it's been over a year since I visited her office to study after school and unwind in the details. It's a realization that keeps repeating itself in her mind again and again as the days to come pass. He's a teenager now, with teenage secrets a mother shouldn't be privy to; Maddy brushes my distance and behavior off as normal teenage dilemma and crisis.

The hall bathroom door slants half open and the weak light over the sink shines out in Maddy's peripheral vision as she approaches the doorway. This is the bathroom I share with my father, the one he runs to from his office. Maddy almost walks past the door again but her growing unease pulses in the silence. She doesn't scream when she pushes the bathroom door open and flicks the dimmer switch to make the room brighter; she's not even shocked or terrified to find Geoffrey reclining in the bathtub. He's fully dressed in the suit he changed into that very morning and his tie is askew making the horizontal lines, blue and white, thin, appear crazed like the stuttering background of a television on the fritz.

He's dead, Maddy thinks. Rationally. She moves to the side of the white tub, one of the current Jacuzzi models with two jets placed on the sides to stir hot water around aches and pains. Geoffrey's head tilts downward and Maddy has to stoop to gaze at his face. His eyes are closed and she just now feels flush, a rising color and warmth, on her face, in her chest, panicky warmth.

Call 911!

Maddy stretches her arm out and presses the fingers of her hand against Geoffrey's neck. She can't find anything and believes there's no pulse. She touches his pale cheek and it remains warm but Maddy believes it could be cooling and she wants to run and discard her feeling that this tableau is normal, that there isn't anything to worry about. She picks up Geoffrey's left wrist, checks for a pulse, fails to find one, and raises his arm a foot in the air and then lets it drop quickly and limply. She notices the generic bottle of acetaminophen resting on the rim of the far side of the tub and an empty half-liter bottle of water, oh, and there's the fancy bottle of vodka just beneath the large rectangular window overlooking the backyard, a window Maddy insisted be installed when they remodeled the house. No one's ever going to peep in way out here and the window lets the light into such a dark little room—plus she knows it will make me happy, a bathroom with a view to the nonexistent river beyond the trees. I never tell my mother I always imagine people in the woods staring at me when I shower; even though the window is at a height starting at my chest the sense of exhibitionism makes me rush to finish showering quickly.

Call 911. This thought blinks for the second time.

Then her crystallizing panic takes hold and Maddy is almost sick. She picks up the closed toilet seat to let loose but controls her nausea with every ounce of effort. This can't be happening. She tightly presses her right palm against her mouth. This can't be happening. Maddy stumbles out of the bathroom, stops, rests, leans over, hands on her knees in the bright upstairs hallway. Why didn't I look in the bathroom first? What if Geoffrey was still alive ten minutes ago and I could've acted in time? You don't know if he's dead.

Maddy's on her way to the top of the stairwell to run down them without a hitch—to make hay—to get to the kitchen telephone when she realizes there's a flashing blue light patterning the stairwell. Somehow the police have been called; did Geoff do it before he took the pills? A last cry for help? They've arrived in the nick of time. Maddy thinks this because it's what happens on TV all the time and why not in real life? Everything's going to be okay, everything's normal. Maybe Geoff's just fooling her again, trying to gain sympathy for all his selfish actions. Then Maddy's down the stairs heading to the front door as the doorbell chimes. She sees two flitting shadows through the opaque glass bordering the doorframe.

Maddy opens the front door and in a panic, shouts, "You have to help. I think he's dead. My husband. Upstairs.

Please, you've got to help him."

Maddy doesn't notice their puzzled faces. The two police officers, wearing Middleton's finest blue uniforms with all the bell-and-whistle gadgets hooked to their belts and strung around their shoulders, stare too long right into her face before they react.

"Ma'am. Calm down."

From their reaction Maddy instantly realizes they're not at her door because they know about Geoffrey up in the bathtub dying—dead—of an overdose. But she doesn't have time to listen and pulls the smaller of the two men by grasping his hand. "Please. Hurry."

"Ma'am. Calm down. Now." His voice is free of any tone except an even sternness that's somehow comforting. Maddy drops his hand.

"My husband. He's upstairs. I think he took a lot of pills."

Then the larger of the two officers leans into the front entryway and orders the other man to check it out.

"I can't go back up there," Maddy says with finality.

"You go," the officer says to his smaller partner. Then to Maddy, "Try to calm down. I'll call for an ambulance."

Maddy understands why the two men separate: they don't trust her. How could they? They come to her house with their lights revolving—for some other reason—and are greeted by a manic woman with stringy hair: definitely a nutcase. Let's call it in.

"Who called you?" Maddy asks, and then she yells up the stairs, "the bathroom is the second doorway on the right," to the officer who is halfway up. He's not running yet; he's cautious; at least he doesn't pull his gun out. Isn't that procedure? You'll be running soon.

"I think it would be better if you sat down, Ma'am." The larger officer, Maddy notices his nametag, Officer Purdue, motions her towards the living area to the left of the entryway. As orderly as clutter can be, the cushions are large and upholstered in earth tones; the end tables piled with old *New Yorker* magazines and alumni catalogs. Maddy wants to move along the room and pick up all the detritus, the stack of old books she's never had time to read, the games for the Nintendo Gamecube, put them away or throw them out, this one always directed at me, give the books to the local charity, take a tax write-off—give Geoffrey's favorite chair away, open the space up—and start cleaning house.

"Why? My husband is dead. He's in the bathroom. I was coming down the stairs to call you." This almost makes Maddy let out a wry laugh.

Officer Purdue speaks into his shoulder walkie-talkie-thing and asks, in police jargon, for an ambulance to be sent to our address. The other officer leans over the second-floor railing and yells out: "I think I found a pulse. Get them here quick."

Maddy sits on her sofa. She's still making renovations to her living room. She'll finally ship her grandmother's ancient mahjongg table, discolored bone tiles, to her sister, make her wonder why she's all-of-a-sudden being so nice and giving. This isn't your nature, she can hear her sister say with a laugh, but thanks, you know I've always loved it. Her sister hasn't taken the time to learn how to play the game, a game of patience and skill, cunning. A game no one has used for two generations. Her sister won't know what to do with it. Maddy stopped playing mahjongg when she left Ann Arbor long ago—another pastime she'd forgotten about. Give it all away.

The bookshelves she'll paint black. She hears Angela's voice at the office chiming in that black is now so in, while cracked, off-white furniture is so five minutes ago. Also, paint the walls—the contemporary white in the room has to change—an antique plaster green to make the Stickley furniture pop. "What?" Maddy, confused, replies.

"Are you okay?"

Maddy stares at her hands; they don't tremble. Her aches diminish and she realizes there's a strong smell coming from the Chinese food containers on the kitchen counter a room away. Her stomach actually rumbles and she feels faint.

Officer Purdue places his hands on his hips, but loosely, not as if he accuses her of anything.

"I just got home and I can't find Chris."

"Chris is your son?" Did the officer's face tighten up?

"Yes."

"Ma'am."

"Please call me Maddy."

"Maddy. We came to your house because of your son."

"What?" Does this make sense? No. I—from my blackening state—never got the chance to call the police. She glances at her wristwatch and sinks into the sofa even more. There's a second where she's sure I'm the one who's dead; that's how these unannounced police visits go on television. Her husband has a pulse upstairs, the other officer is able to find one where she couldn't, but it's really not as if she tried very hard. What could she expect? Surprise.

"What are you talking about?"

"Your son was taken to the hospital. He was attacked."

"What?" Maddy's voice grows louder, almost to a wailing pitch.

"He was found by a classmate. A girl named Mary Follick."

"What?" This time Maddy screams, repeats the word again.

"Please. Try to stay calm. I'm going to take you to the hospital." He doesn't add: And your husband too.

* * *

Deepika rubs her shoulders and listens as the rain picks up again, the wind swirling it around, flicking sounds reverberate after hitting her gutters and the skylight above the kitchen island, and she briefly wonders if the rain will turn to hail. She still can't believe I would seek her out, run about in such awful weather. People in this country have the ability to surprise her more and more. To her, I look a lot like my father, and then she believes I appeared and acted with such desperation, at wit's end, itching to be as angry as an attack.

She doesn't think I wanted anything.

Besides, for the time being anyway, the point is moot.

Earlier, Geoffrey instantly said he wants to take care of her. He wants the damage he's done to go away, but Deepika doesn't think of the child she carries as damage.

She's always kept her poise even at the most challenging turn of events. Her mother says she has true grace under pressure. And Deepika misses her mother and father, her stay-near-home siblings, and wants to be with them now. She's already told them they're going to be grandparents, aunt and uncles, once more, and she'll celebrate with them again when she sees her parents at the end of November in Boston for their annual visit. The joy. Tell them they're going to be grandparents in great standing; she's created a life.

They'll be so happy and maybe not so happy about her marital status. Deepika wants to call them but it's not the right time. She wants to talk to them face-to-face. Maybe her parents will be the ones who she can reveal all her secrets to and move on. She'll take a trip back to her parents, to her small city by the water, the beautiful home, flowers rampant and too colorful along the garden edges, soon, maybe in spring, if her doctor says it's okay for her and the baby to travel.

There's a sense of worry. She's not completely without feeling for Geoffrey and the place she's now in. Deepika even gives a spare thought to Maddy and what she'll do when she finds out. It will be the scandal for quite some time in the creative writing department. Her due date is mid-February, somewhere centered on February 12th. The doctor says, "You'll give birth to an Aquarian. This is very good."

"If you believe," Deepika rebuts.

Her telephone rings and instantly disturbs her. She thinks of the interruption as a bother and decides to let her answering machine screen the call. Ding, a bell goes off, and Deepika's supposed to stop what she's in the middle of and run to the infernal noise? She seldom answers the telephone anyway and all of Deepika's complaining helps to soothe her growing concerns. She hears her serious tone on the message play on the machine: "Hello. No one is in residence. Please leave a message." She is short and to the point.

Deepika cringes. The beep comes and her mother's voice, deep, and husky, considered masculine by most, purrs forth. "Bauble, are you home?"

It must be another day back home, just getting started. Her mother must be planning her trip to Boston, now a month away.

"I guess you're not home. Your father wants to speak to you soon."

Then why isn't he the one who calls? Deepika wonders.

"I'm going to visit my sister today. She wants to cut my hair again."

The first time was a disaster, but Deepika's aunt is in classes at a local salon and wants to try again. Deepika reminds herself to get her hair done the week before she goes to her brother's house over the Thanksgiving holiday.

"Bauble . . ." Her mother sounds weary, tentative.

There's a pause as Deepika debates whether or not to pick up the receiver. She resists. Staring at the fire she listens for her mother's next word.

"There's something wrong?"

She's been calling Deepika by the Bauble nickname since she was born and soon after crawling around the house playing with her jewelry. You're in love with sparkle. Deepika waits and is glad she programmed the answering machine for long messages.

"I need to talk to you. I love you. Your brothers miss you too. Ananda tells me he's worried for you."

Damn him, Deepika thinks. Always laying it on too thick. Why did she ever confide in him? Her older brother, Ananda, took it upon himself to wind her mother up until she's worried about her welfare. Can't he leave well enough alone? He's playing the same game he's always played. When will he realize he doesn't control her decisions? Deepika is definitely glad she didn't answer the telephone now. After I, she thinks, after the boy, came and then raged out of her house, she's been sitting in front of the fire trying to calm down. The house shelters her.

"Call this weekend? Please. I'll be home all day. Love."

Her mother disconnects and Deepika sits with her tea, adrift.

Back home, in her youth, before Deepika left India for Emerson College in Boston, she'd already published a series of stories in a small magazine. Character studies based loosely on the friends and strangers she passed every day in the town, the magazine edited them with a rigid glee; the monthly received more mail and praise for Deepika's stories than they did on the tell-alls of the rich and famous who spent their holidays on the beaches.

She pinpoints the sadness, and yes, sometimes, happiness, of the people who live on the streets, beg with raised hands, sit next to the doors of the ritzy hotels, who are shooed away by the dressed liveries. They always come back.

The woman who marries someone she has to accept. The terrible choices her brothers make. How her younger sister, now long married, clung to their mother's silks, a people pleaser, pretty but not strikingly beautiful, solid, someone who listened to their mother's marital advice, and fell into that web in due course . . . with four grandchildren of her own, nieces and a nephew, finally, another prince. These she really has to fictionalize, but they know. Ananda, the sharp one, laughs at her whimsy and hubris. Still does. Make fun of me all you want. Good. Bad. I can take it if you can.

She writes a story about an American and her entourage visiting her town with the patronizing demeanor of the self-important. A royal queen descending on the town, who spends her days golfing and drinking from noon to night most days, soaking in the scent of decay mixed with the perfumes of princes, a dichotomy captured by the woman's shout, always too loud, across the way to a traveling companion three feet from her, for everyone to hear: You actually smell death here. And this is your idea of wonderful? After we visit the Taj Mahal we're out of here? Then relenting after being overheard.

Isn't this exciting?

As if visiting a zoo where the tigers are magnificent but you can't get close to the cages because of the stench of dung. Deepika writes this story from the perspective of a caged animal saddened by the observations of this visitor. What did she know?

There are too many stories to tell of the bumbling tourist. The culture shock is incredible. Most of the tourists mumbling: I could never live here. What they really meant to say being: How can these people live here, like this?

Still, Deepika misses her family and the constant companionship of the nieces and nephews. She focuses on her own child growing within her and knows she's made the right choice. In telling Geoffrey about the baby, that is—she knows her family is happily surprised and she's staved off judgment because she's keeping the baby, the grandchild, the cousin to all the rest back in India. Ananda has three children, two girls and one boy, the youngest, and he's stopped there after having his son. Her younger sister, Ritu, has four children, again three girls and a boy, the boy coming third in the order, but still made to feel as if he came first, always. Deepika couldn't care less if she has a boy or a girl because there is a living, breathing half-brother, Chris Bullet (me—my family just grew by leaps and bounds), half-cousin to all the half-cousins.

The rain pounds against the rooftop with more force and she realizes the storm has indeed turned to hail.

Deepika sits at her writing desk in the small back room of her house. The sound of the storm outside becomes white noise. She doesn't feel calm. Inside she's torn and full of energy. Her baby moves around too much and Deepika imagines the child taking on her anxiety and wills herself to stop being silly. Her chair is cushioned and sturdy and the desk is at an appropriate height. Her laptop rests on a small computer stand and her long story is nearing an ending of sorts. She takes out a pen and makes a note on the legal tablet next to her PowerBook:

- Sai is a small mountain town reporter—established earlier
- Sai's father dies suddenly back east—an accident?
- Sai's mother is alive, but disabled—not going anywhere
- Sai receives the news from his mother's friend—Gladys? Tekla?

- Sai revisits his history:
  - when he was born—what were his circumstances growing up?
  - why were his parents always consumed by bickering?
  - what were their parents like?
  - when did they come to America?
  - how was he raised by two people so unhappy in their lives?

Deepika types. She imagines a pussycat ripe with anger. The cat's owner states her case to Sai. Mrs. Plesher, a nononsense woman who sees everything in black and white, with dark secrets to keep, lays out her present while Sai daydreams about her past. She calls the town newspaper to tell her side of a dispute with the neighbors in her subdivision. The newspaper sends Sai. Begin here, Deepika thinks, where I left off. She writes (I read over her shoulder—a phantom—join me, please):

* * *

A Great Distance (excerpts from)
By
Deepika Webber

"Best to not anger The Main Puss. She'll rip you a new one without regrets or condolences." One of the cat's claws rips its way through the skin and Sai flashes on a news story about infection and how cat bites and cuts are nothing to be foolish with nor are they to be treated cavalierly. A cousin of Sai's mother, whom he never met, lost the tip of one of her fingers on her right hand from a cat bite that quickly became infected.

When Sai was younger and constantly begging for a pet

his mother told him this story, and worse, to scare the hell out of him. Cats were not Sai's mother's favorite animals. She put them up there on a forbidden shelf with rabbits, tricksters, animals that move about so easily—charlatans of good will.

Then came Sai's long ago request for a puppy, any kind, can't we please, please, please, get a mutt from the pound for gosh sake. No, Sai, then you'll ask for a horse and pony show. And I'll be the one walking the stupid animal and your father will yell and smack it into a cowering animal of yelps, crap, and unstoppable begging and mewling.

His mother and father were the dramatic ones in the family and that kernel of truth and awareness sat there stunted in his childhood; there was always a reason to say no to Sai. He dutifully accepted this with silence. If he came back later, a day or week or even a whole month later and asked for the same thing Sai learned he'd get it even harder. "Don't you ever listen to me, us, any adult, without thinking of yourself first?"

Becoming an active listener, letting people tell their stories, how they ebb and flow, their story sometimes twisting around them, was good preparation for being a journalist. Sai grew up thinking this odd way: never speak, observe, listen, and learn.

"Mrs. Plesher, can you tell me why you believe your neighbors are singling you out?"

"Because I've been here longer than any of them." Sai hears the sound of an old car stuttering up the curved driveway, the engine being turned off and the noise dying out like a wounded animal.

"That'll be Shorty."

"Your brother?"

"You have been listening."

A dour man comes into the kitchen through a side door. He carries two paper Brightman's grocery bags. His forehead shines out pale and spans the top of his head like a sail before his receding hairline catches up to it. They share the same nose, Mrs. Plesher and Shorty, but the similarity ends there. Shorty has stooped shoulders and graying teeth and a thinness bordering on brittle. His walk, because of his weak condition, is a shuffle. His lips aren't the size of frog legs.

"Shorty, say hello to our intrepid town reporter, Mr. Sai Amrashi."

"Hello." Shorty takes his own time reaching the counter with the groceries where he unloads a carton of organic milk, a loaf of wheat bread, four large glistening heirloom tomatoes and a bag of green grapes.

"You checked the fruit before you bought it?" Mrs. Plesher twists her upper body in the chair to face Shorty.

"Yes, Alice."

It's the perfect name. Sai can tell Mrs. Plesher is unhappy her first name has been spoken out loud.

"Every other time Shorty goes to the market he buys bad fruit. Oh it's not his fault. That market rips everyone off. Best produce in town my dainty foot. You buy it and it turns bad by the time you get it home. I make Shorty take it back too, save every receipt."

"A never-ending cycle," Shorty adds. "Would you like a tomato sandwich, Mr. Amrashi?"

"Oh. No, thank you. I think I have to go soon anyway. I mean this shouldn't take that long."

"Dig your own hole, reporter. Shorty. Leave the boy alone and let us finish our business." Then Alice Plesher swivels her body back and levels a wrinkled, pointer finger right at Sai and says, "And you stay there and ask me everything. No matter how long it takes."

* * *

"When did you and your brothers decide to murder your father?" The first of many questions Sai worked into his mind.

The five children sat in their sheltering fort under a canopy of aspens near the river and the four brothers listened to Alice's stories. They ran away now every chance they could get.

* * *

Of course Sai never asks Mrs. Plesher that question. He keeps his grin well hidden. If he wants to shock the scorn out of her face his fantasies wouldn't be enough to do it.

* * *

"You'll run the farm and mother and father will take care of you until they grow old."
"They die when they get old."
"I wish they'd just die now."
"Don't let me hear you say that again. Especially around the house."
"Father always has a cold. He's sick all the time."
Curtis interrupted by hitting his brother on the arm and said, "Shorty's too chicken to say anything."
"Am not." Alice understood Shorty's anger because all of them lived in fear.
The wind picked up and blew dried leaves into the enclosure. Alice thought about her life and how she'd soon get away. The schools would support her with a scholarship; she learned everything. She stared at Shorty and Forrest and told the others they had to get back. If they stayed down by the river much longer mother and father would start to worry, but only for a short time before their worry turned to punishing anger.
"We've got to get back."
"Can you tell us the rest of the story tonight?"
"If you promise to take a bath. I hate smelling you dirty from the day and thinking you fooled everyone when you lie about washing up. I hate that even more."

* * *

"Shorty," Mrs. Plesher harps, "You're dripping tomato

juice all over the floor and I won't tell you again. Get your sandwich made. Clean up your mess and go eat in the television room."

"You sound just like mom."

Mrs. Plesher's face shows her anger, the planes of her cheeks grow taught and her eyes stare at her brother until he looks away. Shorty grabs a dishrag and wipes up the tomato mess. Then he takes his snack and walks out of the kitchen letting the swinging door bang shut in a large arc, cutting off the room, pissing Mrs. Alice Plesher completely off; how can the cats run free with the kitchen door shut—a staggering pet peeve, Sai jots in his notebook, of epic proportion in this house feline.

"All of these cats. How many do you have living in the house?"

"Well I don't have any dead cats if that's what you mean. Excuse me," Mrs. Plesher says as she stands and walks briskly to the kitchen door and props it open with a rubber doorstop. She yells out, "Shorty, turn that T.V. down. Now." She returns to the table and continues, "Where were we?"

"No. I just want the story." Sai's tone of voice sounds frail, questioning, and Mrs. Plesher isn't letting him go the easy way.

"How did you end up here?" she asks.

"I wanted to take a break after college so I moved to California to get a job." Sai doesn't go into specifics since there's no need to bring up his ex-partner, Joe, but his face is there, the unhappiness similar to the expression on Mrs. Plesher's face; Sai banishes the image and keeps everything general and boring and less circular so Alice will get back to her story. He's made up his mind about her cats and her life and the sadness in the house that leaves a scent stronger than any cat box. He doesn't want to tell this woman how he had followed his first real love, Joe, to California and how they set up a wobbly house of cards that eventually blew down and how he had to get out.

"From California I drove here after another friend told me how beautiful it was here in the summer. The best season to live in Sun Valley is summer. My friend was right."

"Unless you're allergic to sage." Mrs. Plesher seemed to

be scolding Sai anew for not caring about allergy sufferers.

* * *

The fields turned brown after the fall harvest. To the horizon the earth stayed dull and without hope. All the brothers worried about Alice and when she'd be sent away. She kept telling them her made-up stories until they couldn't get enough and they knew she'd . . . Was everything always this complicated? By the time Alice left for college father would be dead and in the ground three months. A ravaging, smoker's death. Hacking. He wouldn't make it through the last summer. Forrest wouldn't make it either, a farm accident involving a thresher; so much pain and loss in one family, too much to bear; Forrest wasn't the brightest monkey in the barrel, a step below Shorty in the brains department, and mother almost stopped all the plans Alice had made; with so much death in one family, all at once, the family had to stick together. Alice preserved the green beans and stewed tomatoes in a large pot. The kitchen remained hot and with the stove working night and day the room never cooled off in the early days of that last summer. Father gone and mother wilted within her bedroom in mourning, days turning into weeks and the end of July close enough to touch.

* * *

"You killed them," Sai says to Mrs. Plesher, who sits across from him periodically pulling at her housedress or adjusting the straps of her bra, cutting into the skin of her shoulders.

"No one can prove anything anyways," Alice retorts.

"What do you mean? Then it's true? They said you bury them, against code, in your backyard along the fence line."

"Who are They? I know my rights. I can have as many cats as I want and I'm not going to let any of my new snot-nosed neighbors from California come in here and tell me anything different. I've been here longer than these hills. You just ask anyone. They say they can smell my litter boxes. Those new neighbors should just watch out if they know what's good for them."

"But they're suing you. All the neighbors are. The subdivision has its bylaws to maintain."

"Now you're on their side, too? Figures."

"What's that supposed to mean?"

"When did you move to the valley?"

"Almost a year ago." Sai closes his notebook and stares at the murderess. The big tomcat nearest the kitchen table licks its front paw, in between keeping a baleful eye on him, ready to pounce at his mistress's command.

"Not long enough to hold an opinion as far as I can see."

"There's no proof, you say."

"Darn tootin.'"

"I've counted at least eight cats since I've entered your house."

"Aren't you the number runner . . . and I suppose you're going to take their side and write about all these supposed cats in your smear article?"

* * *

"There's no proof you murdered your father and mother, and Little Forrest too for some unfathomable reason. With a slow-acting poison you found lying about the farm you got rid of the people who brought you into this world. Shorty was your accomplice. You were the brains and he followed your orders—became addicted to heirloom tomato sandwiches. Right?"

* * *

"Right what, you son-of-a-bitch?"

Sai stands up from the table grasping his notebook. "Listen. I'll talk to the others who made this decision and write up an article for next week's paper. I'll try to remain objective."

"Wipe that smirk off your face. I know what you write."

Sai is actually pleased that even this monster of a woman has read his stories.

"You wrote that piece-of-shit story about the people who rigged the duck race. Those were my friends and they didn't steal anything."

"I'm now aware of your opinion. So, if there's anything else. I do have to get back."

Before Mrs. Plesher can call her stoop-shouldered brother into the kitchen to chop Sai into pieces with a dull tomato-cutting knife he takes his leave. He's almost at the end of the curved driveway when he hears Mrs. Plesher shout to him: "Don't let them take my babies away. You can save them."

Sai keeps his back turned to Mrs. Plesher and her cathouse and faces the half-mile walk back to the bus stop. The mountains form a wall around him on this side of Elkhorn and he imagines himself in a different time when there weren't any of the homes marring the sage and pine landscape. He waits for the lumbering transport bus and Sai doesn't know what he's going to do with his stalled car when he flies home to take care of his mother. He has arrangements to make.

Once the bus drops Sai off in Ketchum he walks back to his tiny office with the glorious view of the ski mountain and writes up the story. Wasn't there something he could do for such an unhappy woman? He thought about it and decided there wasn't much. She, unfortunately, reminds Sai too much of his dead father. Sai places the story with the editor and tells his boss he has a family emergency. She has to make plans for his departure, tells Sai she doesn't know if she can pay him for too many missed days. Please, Sai says, I won't be gone that long; he wonders why he has to justify his absence. Isn't death enough? He doesn't want to beg for his job when he gets back and this is another inconvenient burr in his mind. He flees the office for home. His step is quick, and he wants time to speed up.

* * *

This next section of Deepika's story ends and Mrs. Plesher is a "thing" of the past in her head—in my state of black. Deepika moves forward thinking about Sai's new place. I hold onto this voyeuristic feeling, and it soon becomes clear to me that Deepika thinks of me, less angry, fleeing my own family, my father, unknowing it's much too early, or late, really, to find myself reaching for balance.

* * *

Maddy listens to the beeps and clicks of the machines helping me breathe. She will not leave my side, and the many doctors, nurses, and techs, in and out of the emergency room cubicle make room for her off to the side. My face is a mass of bruises and there's a tube down my throat. My nose is broken in three places. There's a fracture in my spine. Two of my fingers on the right hand are broken and my right elbow is shattered. They're very worried about brain damage and hemorrhages and the situation has everyone moving quickly. They needed to perform surgery to help relieve the pressure from the swelling in my brain, and this happens almost immediately. My mother is left alone once more.

* * *

I return to a bland hospital room, still unconscious, and the doctors are really afraid about whether or not the swelling will stop. There's a major head injury. My mother can hear the doctor whispering outside the door as she moves her chair closer and comes to sit next to the hospital bed.

She's hardly composed in the hospital room. My mind is shut off and the coma has taken complete control. If I wake up I won't remember the same scene after my mother's accident long ago with her in the bed this time and the fear of death—is she dying—am I?

It's probably the world slowing down because—again, if I wake up at all—I won't remember much about the attack but I'll have the feeling I'm partially to blame for the fight; I always stick my big fat opinion into any argument. I'll never remember leaving Deepika's house angry at her, my father, my mother, the way I leave school, the way I will have to suck up and eat crow in Algebra class tomorrow and I start to walk home during the brief respite from the rain. It's down to a drizzle and the streets glisten and I almost walk the entire distance home, a mile away, when I hear the first crash of shattering glass.

I should've turned away right then. Start running you fool. Get out. Run like you always do. Instead I make an error in judgment, an error that should never cost a life: "Hey, what are you doing? Stop!" I'm so pent up, angry, that I have to rethink my father passing that death wish trait down to me thing. I'm crazy?

I don't even know all their names but I walk right into their nest. The three older boys who cornered their prey so easily in the school hallway hours ago have broken the passenger window of a small Toyota truck and I can't help what I do next. I look like a soaked rat. I cannot believe these other kids think they'll get away with this. There are lights on in all the houses lining the street but the houses are set far back from the street and no one's come outside to see what the noise is all about. A little breaking glass isn't louder than the sounds of the rainstorm, blaring televisions. But someone must've called the police. There must be someone responsible coming soon to take charge, to take these idiot vandals by the neck and shake the snot out of them.

Bang. Like a shot. The back window of the next car parked behind the truck shatters. Glass flies into the car and shards hit the curb and scatter onto the street. No one's around and they don't notice when I approach. This is what I'll never remember because I can't recall much after I'm spotted, maybe because my brain is on fire and swelling as the doctor describes a medical process to my mom.

The deer in the headlights—that's me. Only one of the teenagers has a bat and they pass it around, egging the next boy to give another car, a rusting Honda, a good whack. And then I spot Ellis. He's hanging back. There are four of them in the group now. What's he doing with them? Oh, yeah, he left school after the math meeting. It's late in the day and he's following an invitation, orders. I open my mouth. I want to say something funny, a joke, to take away my growing anxiety. They don't think they'll be caught; there's no one around. They don't think.

Things like being beaten to a pulp by school bullies, the vision of being kicked by steel-toed work boots in the locker room, the name-calling, vitriolic spew, have all crossed my mind. I picture the scenario a hundred times. I've always tried to keep a low profile; I always try to hide myself on the fringe of every group—to fit in no matter the cost.

And it happens, unfolding in quick time. There really isn't any time for me to adjust my direction. I'm at a crisis point. I bottle up my anger and explode at Deepika and how she tricked (this is my new thought) my father and I'm interacting with the three teenagers, four if you count Ellis, who, so many short hours ago, already accosted me that very day at school—and I don't care. It's the same idiotic threesome and I show them my fear through a sputtering rage. I'm outnumbered once again and always.

I don't even remember who hits me first.

But I know that's when my fingers break.

My right arm's stretched stiffly out to defend against the swing of the bat—

Did I scream?

Did one of them yell: Faggot?

I think so.

And Ellis is behind them, quiet and stricken. I see how he eggs them on when the bat passes to the next slugger. So that he himself won't appear weak in their presence.

He gets in a shot to the elbow as I cradle my fingers and slump to the pavement. I must've been crying and begging because they turn crazy and I black out, but I won't remember any of this when I wake up, if I wake up. How is it possible to remember such trauma? It's probably all lost in the comatose state I'm locked in.

How can Ellis be there?

When I awake I won't remember I'm a part of this and it'll be a long time before I can believe it myself without shuddering. I won't remember anything. My father, my mother; the car accident long ago still unforgettably present, the way the rain smells oily on the road, the sky pouring out a deluge. I won't have amnesia; that would be too perfect and very welcome, but my mind won't be able to process the current situation. It will have to be told to me again and again like a fairytale for the young and impressionable, something so fantastic it has to be based on fact—a myth made real.

It will all come together later when Deepika sneaks, deftly steps, past security, in for a visit and appears at my bedside as big as a couch around the middle and takes my hand and wishes she drove me home the night I ran from her house. Another thing I will never recall; it's better this way, that's what everyone says: ever going to her house at all.

And if I could cry I would.

Not in front of anyone. Never in front of anyone.

Definitely not where my parents could see, or Deepika, not the doctors who act as if they've seen it all and therefore know me intimately, or the nurses who bathe my body using warm sponges with an almost militant glee; I imagine the principal will visit and wring his hands; the police too when and if I do wake up to tell them I don't remember a thing. Make the case your own damn selves without my help. Leave me alone already. I won't picture this happening. None of them would believe me anyway and I will cry for myself and lose an inch at a time, alone. I will hope I sleep for six days as if in the midst of a real fantasy story, a central character placed between illusionary worlds.

My mother sits in the chair beside my bed, post-surgery, hours later. She stays rigid and silent. There's no one else to speak to. The doctor comes in once I'm transferred after surgery to repair the elbow, crack my fingers into splints, and cut into my skull. I'm in traction to ease the pressure on my back; the fracture in my spine will heal, the doctor says, in time, diverting his eyes. But this may not ever come to pass. It's what I want if I could only respond. Fix my elbow now, but they can't until I regain consciousness and who really knows if I'll only sleep for six days, when, if the swelling doesn't go down by the third day . . . It's just a guess, my mother's wish, and her hope.

The doctor's so vague Maddy doesn't know how to respond. Doctors must get a degree in how to say as little as possible. The fear of being sued makes them jumpy. She thinks about doing just that and how far her lawsuit will get her and what she'll be suing for if she really could, a game to pass the quiet time. She's alone, surrounded by beeps and futuristic whistles that can do little to ease her worries. The I.V. feeds me.

The police and the paramedics start the ball rolling at the house. My mother answers questions for more than an hour once she reaches the hospital. Jigsaw pieces connect and form pictures of Geoffrey and how he spent his afternoon. The emergency room doctors place Geoffrey in a trauma bay unconscious and hook him up to machines almost immediately. They force charcoal into his stomach until he retches and gets as much of the toxins out of his system. The doctor and the emergency room nurses treat his body with barely concealed contempt: for the waste. They've seen suicides and can never fathom the pain. They want to slap Geoffrey awake and scold him until his skin is red, raw and cracking from embarrassment. It's a good thing Maddy isn't in the trauma bay to witness this behavior; she'd have something to sue them for then wouldn't she?

It's how the medical staff deals with attempted suicides. Shove them into a drawer after reviving them. The charcoal mixture goes down and Geoffrey's system accommodates the fluid and then vomits everything back up. Maddy, at that time, is in an administrative cubicle filling out information on Geoffrey and asking questions about her son's whereabouts—operating room B3 for head trauma, sign here—and the administrative assistant asks her for the insurance card. Maddy passes her Blue Shield card across the desk. The police wait impatiently for Maddy so they can interview her and find out what she knows about her son. A police officer, not Purdue, a different uniformed companion, stands behind Maddy. The police have told the hospital security to be on heightened awareness, a different code. They're worried about my broken body, maybe it's drug related, gang related, and maybe there will be those who still seek my death and will want to finish the job. A bit paranoid perhaps, but part of the protocol. It's been known to happen.

Once, a man in his thirties was chased and hit by an eighteen-wheeler while trying to race from harm on his motorcycle. The man who ran him over was his father. His arm was broken, his hip, an eye hung from the socket, his legs were a shattered mess, but he's still alive and healing to this day. The father escaped, drove away, but found out his son wasn't dead. Later, the hospital security guards caught the father on the fourth floor in search of his son's room—to finish the job he started.

Over a year passed and it was the father's turn in the emergency room. Strung out from a beating so severe he almost didn't make it. The son smiling. The world turning. The nurse on duty in the O.R. thinks about this father and son when readying my I.V. and I eavesdrop, somehow. I've never believed in outer body experiences before and if I wake up I want to remember this floating...

Maddy envisions me in the operating room and tells the clerk and the police she wants to be taken to me immediately.

"We're almost finished here. I need you to sign these parental permission treatment forms. Your son needed to be taken to the O.R. before we got your signature and if you don't sign these"—the woman's voice trails off as Maddy signs the forms.

"Does your son or your husband have any allergies?"

"No."

The woman doesn't have to say: How bizarre ... two family members brought in on the same day. Two for one. How strange. But she's seen far stranger things than this. Whole families in car crashes and taking up trauma bays. Are you feeling okay? Do you want to lie down? Do you want to call anyone? Remember, no cell phones in the ICU but they're okay everywhere else in the hospital. Everything is written on the woman's face.

On the ride over in the ambulance Maddy tries to act calmly. It isn't hard for her to do. She asks the police officer questions about her son. "You said a classmate of Chris's called the police?"

"Yes. Mary Follick. She was leaving school after an extra credit study session, which ended later than usual. She saw four boys, the attack, and then the gang running away from the scene."

"Did she recognize any of these boys?"

"It's an ongoing investigation now. I probably shouldn't have said even this much."

"Did she know any of the kids who did this to my son?"

"She told us where to look."

"Good."

By the time Maddy finishes with hospital admittance questions the clerk says, "Listen, you can go see your husband in the E.R. bay now, a nurse will escort you back."

"I want to go up to the O.R. first. To see my son."

The police officer stashes this choice, Maddy's behavior, in the back of his mind. Who can blame her for wanting to be with her child first? He finds it strange Maddy doesn't want to find out if her husband is alive or not. Since she's right here, twenty steps away.

"Can someone escort me there?"

"A patient transporter will be here momentarily. She can guide you on one of her runs."

The police officer says, "May I ask you a couple questions first?"

Maddy doesn't respond. She's led to a chair across the way and the police officer with no name asks: "Do you know where your son was before he was attacked?"

"No. I was at the college. In my office. I teach there. I assumed Chris was on his way home from school, one of his after school team meetings. He's on the math team. I brought Chinese home for dinner. It's still sitting on the kitchen counter."

"Did you know your son skipped school?"

"No."

"After lunch period he left."

"Where did he go?"

"No one knows. Has your son ever, to your knowledge, taken drugs?"

"He hasn't even experimented. He'd tell me if he did. That's our arrangement. Are the other kids who did this to him involved with drugs?"

"I can't say." He's heard this before. Parents who think their kids tell them everything when it's always the exact opposite and a lot of camouflage.

"You won't say," Maddy, continues, "Chris's backpack was in his room. I searched there when I got home. Before I found Geoff—"

"So he came home at some time after leaving school. That helps."

"He told me he had an algebra test today and little else—my son is a smart kid, officer. He could be valedictorian down the line, excuse me; I'm not bragging (but a tiny part of her was, and this praise, so few and far between, I'll try not to forget). He's never been tested, but he could be at genius levels for his age—he's not the kind of kid who makes stupid choices. He needed to go to an extra math team session after school."

"He never made that either."

"What does his algebra teacher say?"

"He never saw Chris. He's worried; he led me to believe Chris wouldn't behave this way either, as if it wasn't in his character."

The police officer pauses. He's waiting for Maddy to reveal an extreme situation, something that would make her son act so perplexingly. And, he's heard people, perps, family of victims, charlatans, lie so many times right to his face, he has a policy to never trust what anyone says, and this stressed and hurting woman in front of him switches his alarm bells on full ring.

"I don't know what caused Chris to skip school, run home in the pouring rain and end up beaten to a pulp by four boys hours later, someone told me they were classmates of Chris's. They left his body on a sidewalk surrounded by broken car-window glass. I want you to catch them and lock them away. They can't—"

"We'll get them. They're being rounded up now."

Maddy nods and rises from her plastic chair.

"A couple more questions if you don't mind. I won't take much more of your time and then I'll take you up to the O.R. waiting room myself. I know this is hard.

"It seems like your son and your husband have been through something really terrible today. Your husband's in there fighting for his life."

"Are you so sure of that?" Maddy says in her singular dry voice.

The police officer doesn't ask what Maddy means and instead says, "He tried to commit suicide."

"It appears that way. That's what I meant when I said he may not be fighting all that hard for his life."

"Do you have any idea why your husband would act so desperate?"

"It's not clear to me why."

"Is there anything you can tell me?"

"You think what happened to my son and my husband . . . that there's a connection?"

"Yes."

"My husband's been depressed for quite some time."

"Has he sought help?"

From Deepika, Maddy wants to reveal, but then says, "From a professional? No."

The officer doesn't ask why not.

"He always said he could handle it. This is something we haven't dealt with before."

"But it's the first time he's tried to commit suicide?"

"That I know of."

"So he hasn't been happy for a long time."

"Listen. Right now I don't care about my husband's happiness. Excuse me if that makes me sound heartless, or irrational. I know you're trying to piece together what's happened. And I do want to help . . . I appreciate your concern but I want to be with my son now."

"Sure. We'll continue this conversation later?"

"Certainly."

The police officer and Maddy stand. Debbie, a frizzy-haired patient transporter full of union-backed slowness, finally arrives to lead Maddy to her destination. Debbie doesn't know Maddy and treats her and anyone she has to transport with an easy wisecracking familiarity.

"What you in for?" Debbie asks with an added grunt and a commiserating expression.

Maddy doesn't respond. Oblivious, Debbie keeps talking, rolling her eyes, hands flapping punctuation.

"Yep. This hospital sees everything. I've already made ten trips to X-Ray. You'd think the people who drew up the plans for this building would know how to design, go to school and everything to learn it. They put the blood lab all the way down this long, long hall. No sense of design. My feet hurt every trip I have to go there."

Maddy heads to a bank of elevators and listens to Debbie who she'd find amusing if Maddy were there for any other reason. She's detached and so disconnected she's on the verge of nervous, defensive laughter.

"This is a new hospital, and all, but you have to wait long, sometimes a really long time for the elevator. Why is that? I ask you. Anyway," Debbie allows Maddy to enter the elevator first as the doors finish opening slowly—"we'll get out on two and then we have to walk halfway down that long hallway to get to the O.R. waiting room."

"Can you tell me where the cafeteria is?" Maddy asks without any idea why because she sounds indifferent to the emergencies in her family. She hasn't eaten in hours and her stomach is jumpy with unease. Maybe she's feeling too vulnerable, making conversation with someone who obviously loves to talk no matter if anyone listens or purposely tunes her out. She feels starving. She's never eaten dinner and now and, oh, why is she thinking about food when her son is under the knife?

"Oh"—Debbie perks up—"That's on the third floor but avoid the coffee if that's what you're looking for. There's a coffee shop next to the lobby that's better even though it's generic coffee. At least it's hot."

Debbie leads Maddy down the long hallway to the O.R. waiting room. When they arrive Debbie says, "I hope things get better for you and your family."

"Thank you," Maddy replies.

Geoffrey's unconsciousness continues to be monitored by machines. The hospital admits him for the required 72 hours, on suicide watch, his mental future now depending on a psych consult when his physical system is out of danger. The doctor on staff worries about his liver and kidney functions, but only perfunctorily; he's seen worse. Geoffrey hasn't taken as many pills as they'd first thought but they've been in his system a long time now and they worry about possible organ damage. They don't tell Maddy this; she's now up in a different waiting room and there isn't a person to spare to run up and tell her Geoffrey isn't even close to expiring; he only needs to be watched closely.

* * *

Deepika prints out the pages she's just written and then rewritten. There are at least two thousand words and she likes to go over them before settling down for the evening. She remembers the past day and the confrontational attitude of both father and son and this regret she feels slivers into her fiction. She makes Sai act cavalierly with Mrs. Plesher. Deepika wishes she had stopped me from leaving in a frantic rage. Deepika's mother would tell her it was meant to be. Do not fret over unchangeable things.

Regardless, there's a note of sadness. After reading the pages Deepika corrects some phrasing that doesn't pop out at her and writes more about her central character, Sai, a man whose karma hits him hard. She wants karma to play a recurring theme throughout her collection of stories and character sketches, both real and imagined. The good, the bad, the indifferent, and how everyone's ruled by it. Sai lives in a major ski resort in Idaho, Sun Valley, a ski town where the glamour of the Hollywood past has faded only slightly, where you turn the Ketchum corner or snowboard down any run, ride the ski lifts, sitting right next to the latest famous celebrities, who want to live low-key lives where the locals treat them like everyday people and actually protect them from nosey tourists and *People* magazine reporters who want to know where Bruce Willis now lives. The ski resort owner still tries to make it in a competitive industry. Sai is a reporter for one of several small weekly mountain newspapers and he's bitter because his family abandoned him to his choices long ago—you moved so geographically far away, why should we be the ones to spend our money visiting you? They don't write or call him anymore. Sai hasn't found a mate. His friends, if he ever really had any close friends, have given up on him one at a time; none of them will visit him in Sun Valley, too far to go to see someone they never truly took the time to get to know. Sai has his shell up for a reason, and the long distance friendships deteriorate within a year or two. Sai will try to keep in touch with these friends from his past. Deepika has written his life as a complex composite of so many people she's met while living in Sun Valley for a winter season; the misfits, ski bums, fancy ladies-who-lunch specials, the bookstores that somehow make a living in the small, literary town, Ernest Hemingway's legend, the ice shows every weekend outdoors in the summer at the high-altitude ice rink, the bar scene, the righteousness of the privileged on their playground. Deepika tries to find the equivalent passion for her main character's descent into despair. She feels his path as inevitable, as simple as good and bad karma.

She doesn't know if she succeeds yet or not but at least she's writing. Her agent will tell her the truth when she's finished. She's just put her laptop away when the telephone rings.

This time she decides to answer it.

"Deepika?"

"Yes."

"Thank goodness you're still around. I know I know you told me you couldn't fulfill your teaching commitment next term, but we're at wit's end here and we couldn't think of anyone else. It's Marjolaine. You're our last hope. There's been an emergency at the College"—Deepika lets Marjolaine, the Creative Writing Program administrative assistant, breathless and quick as she's speaking, continue without interruption—"We've tried everyone else and we know you aren't teaching anymore, but we're at a loss."

Deepika always finds it odd when a person speaks as a 'We,' for the whole group, but she doesn't comment on it. She remembers Marjolaine as efficient and the brains behind the labyrinthine coordination of teacher schedules and class assignments. She's always tried to stay in her good graces.

"What's happened?"

"Madison Dakota has a family emergency." Marjolaine pauses to let this sink in.

"Marjolaine, what kind of emergency?"

"I'm not privy to specific information yet; she just called me at home from the hospital. Her son was attacked and he's in the hospital. That's all I know."

Deepika's throat tightens and her mouth dries up.

"I'm calling because Madison needs someone to teach her two classes tomorrow—it's policy to find substitutes first. There's an English Literature class. The class is reading Zora Neale Hurston. Are you familiar with her work?"

"Of course," she replies. Deepika read Hurston's hurricane of a book long ago and the images stay with her. "Of course I can substitute." Full circle Karma. The only ready Hindu concept she attaches to her direct moral actions, forming a cycle.

"The other course in the afternoon is a senior-level Creative Writing class."

"I can step right into that one."

"Thanks Deepika." Marjolaine breathes a sigh of relief at having completed her task. "I'm so grateful. We're so grateful. Just stop by my office by ten to get the building locations for the classes and the student rosters from me. I don't think Madison will be back anytime soon. I was told you're to be given your same wage rate."

Deepika wonders what they'll say when she walks into the English Department showing so much. She tendered her resignation by mail and telephone. Marjolaine will sit and hide her shock and finally, bluntly, ask who the father is, anyone I know—and by golly, you've been hiding out in the sticks. She won't have to say, no one even knew you were pregnant. She's already set up to ask Deepika to fill in for

Madison for the entire next week, possibly longer, implied, and Marjolaine still needs something from her so she'll try to contain her curiosity, remain circumspect. Her eagerness for information will win out nonetheless and by the end of the week she'll make a judgment without fact based on Deepika's apparently cavalier demeanor.

"Again. Thanks Deepika. You're a doll."

"No problem," Deepika replies.

"Let's hope everything's okay at the hospital."

The two women hang up and Deepika looks up the first hospital number in the Yellow Pages and punches in the number with a calm feeling of inevitability.

"St. George's"—a strong, deep man's voice announces the hospital. There are two hospitals and Deepika tries St. George's first because it's the closest, right downtown on West Broadway, and the one the College uses if ever there's an emergency on its grounds.

"Yes," Deepika responds, "I'm calling about the Dakota family?"

She's put on hold but Deepika can hear tapping from a computer keyboard. The man says, "There's no one by the name Dakota here."

"A teenage boy, first name Chris. He could've been there late afternoon, early evening?" Deepika's guessing now.

"No. Not a thing. Did you try the Mountain Group Hospital over on Fort Middleton?" The man's tone is heavy with disdain. Always competition, always in every instance Deepika can think of here in the States, amplified more and more, everything a contest.

"Wait. Please try Chris Bullet. Dakota is his mother's name."

"Okay. Hold on a second."

Again there's a void on the line, a slight background hum and Deepika hears other voices muted—other people trying to get through to their damaged or sick relatives and friends—and she places a hand on her belly as the child within gives a soft kick. Deepika keeps her free hand there waiting for the next.

"No Bullets admitted. Sorry. Try Mountain Group." And the man disconnects. Deepika relishes his rudeness, laughs shortly and looks up the number for the competing hospital. It's the one Deepika uses. Fort Middleton is a shorter drive from her home. She steers clear of the St. George's Big Sky College Hospital, finds a baby doctor who will see her for periodic checkups until she leaves for Boston, and this makes Deepika think about something else as the telephone rings.

"Mountain Group Hospital, how can I direct you?" A nice voice, a pleasant woman's tone, comes through the line.

"I'm looking for a patient, last name Bullet."

"We have two Bullets."

"Two Bullets?"

"Yes. Father and son." The woman catches herself as if she's done something wrong. "I cannot give out any names of children admitted. Are you a family member?"

"Please, does the adult patient have the name Geoff or Geoffrey? Spelled the old English way?"

"Yes. I guess I can tell you that much. Are you a family member?"

The woman's tone is insistent now; she wants to protect people she doesn't know from the outside world. Understandable. And she'll face much worse in the coming days, a torrent of calls.

"No, but I know both of them. Is there something—"

Deepika knows she won't get more information out of the clerk. She says, "Thank you," and disconnects.

What happened to Geoff? The question lays there in her mind. Deepika stands and paces, and, after a minute, decides to drive to the hospital. Then she thinks she's done enough and should act like nothing's happened because of her. Her karma. She knows her path, her fate, is racing beside her like a horse catching up with her. There's nothing she can do for the Bullets.

Worry. Yes. She can worry.

* * *

Tests in hospitals, even if marked STAT, are never

finished as quickly as they should be, especially in a large city hospital. The doctors continually harp on the nurses—Where's the CBC or I need those drug levels yesterday or cliché after cliché—and the nurses throw shade back to the Patient Care Coordinator in the E.R. who labels vials of blood and marks the test forms and places everything in a container ready for transport to the blood lab. It's then that the Patient Transporter sidles in and sits down, tells a joke, regardless of the bustle, and ignores a peeved nurse, impatience explosion bristling, and finally caws out to Debbie to get moving. Debbie gives the PCC her bothersome look: What's gotten into her?

It's an emergency room but the priorities all follow a pecking order and the blood sits there until Debbie daintily puts on new protective gloves—wouldn't want to spill the blood—and signs out—every footstep carefully noted—for her next trip down the long hallway to the blood lab. Before she leaves, Alma, a nurse with a slight Irish accent, begs—because she knows with Debbie she has to beg—"Please, please, please Debbie will you please transport the patient in trauma bay three to X-Ray on your way to the lab? He's ready to go and X-Ray won't hold his spot for long and I begged Arlene down there to fit him in now, please Debbie, I'll bring an extra cruller this weekend." Alma and the other rotation nurse, Katherine, always gripe and equally laugh sometimes, about the slowness in the E.R. It's full of characters. On and on. Geoffrey stays unconscious on his stretcher with fluids and charcoal fading on his lips after Katherine wipes his mouth. He never awakens during all this and his liver levels aren't back yet. Debbie transported his blood to the lab only twenty minutes prior and the hospital system quickens. The doctor at the head of the pecking order fumes.

Once the blood finds its way to the lab there are more political steps and byzantine procedures to follow; no one wants to make a mistake, God forbid anything is mislabeled from the start by the nurse or the PCC, reprimand, reprimand, but it's been known to happen. The best nurses are those who know how to multitask, deal with the cursing drunk homeless woman with the infected foot who smells like rotting fish, who really needs to be shackled to the shower and rinsed for a week while the man with his arm hanging from a chainsaw stupidity waits in shock for the doctors to realize how much pain he's really in. "Take his blood so the O.R. can type and match—this one's definitely going to need the vascular touch, who's on call tonight? My father sleeps while the labs inch toward enlightenment.

Maddy sits in the Operating Room waiting area holding a cup of tepid vending machine coffee. The room is painted faded tangerine and the seats are worn and hopefully only appear oily. There's no word on Geoffrey yet and the receptionist promises to notify Maddy first thing about where her husband will be taken. To the nut house. Maddy cringes.

It's almost an hour to midnight and Maddy rests without comfort, eyes heavy. She needs coffee to perk her up since the chairs are so uncomfortable going to sleep won't be possible even if she wished it. She's called Marjolaine and sketched a story vague, serious, unspecific enough to maintain an aura of curiosity.

I won't be in. Tomorrow.

No. My son was attacked.

Yes. It's serious—and Maddy doesn't breathe a word about Geoffrey—I'll find out more tomorrow. If you can't locate anyone just cancel my classes. I don't teach on Friday anyway so I'll know more about next week's schedule and call you.

I'm fine. Don't worry about me, a shining example of my mother being polite to a fault.

The police officer left her alone without asking another question, a relief. He'll catch up with her tomorrow—to help with clarifications, timelines. He knows where to find her.

It's a good thing they never got a dog or a cat that needs feeding. Maddy put a stop to that one since she's the one who'd be left alone to take care of that animal, too. She imagines a golden retriever, like her childhood pet, Bucky, so kind all the time. Maybe she'll get one, or a mix, save a dog at the animal shelter. She knows I've always wanted a dog, and this becomes another unfulfilled childhood milestone—too busy with their jobs the major excuse.

Maddy now imagines having a family dog all the same, and in her imaginings Maddy gets the panicky news about Geoffrey and me, forgets about the made-up pooch, and finds out later that the dog was hit by a car and was rushed to the vet's by the sorry-as-hell-but-still-going-way-too-fast driver. In a fit, Maddy'll desert me and set up a vigil in that veterinary hospital's waiting area next and cry and cry because the animal, so like her first dog, would be the only one she honestly cares about. This is my truth not my mom's. This is what I see and feel. Who really knows if my mom would care more for an imaginary pet than her crumbling family?

Maddy thinks about calling Nadine again and she really should. Tomorrow she'll sit all day with Nadine and let her take care of her for once. Is she really that selfish? Her family falls apart and she's adrift? She should call Geoffrey's sister, Nell. No, wait until she hears from the doctor about his condition. He was dead. Maddy couldn't find a pulse. It's a good thing, ha, I got beaten up, bloody and ferocious, otherwise the police wouldn't have come in time and Geoffrey would've been rub a dub dead in the tub, ha, ha, ha.

Ha, ha, ha.

Maddy reviews all that could've happened and realizes there are tears on her cheeks. She wipes them away with the back of her free hand and then sips cold coffee. The door to the waiting room opens and Maddy shifts slightly in her seat. It's an older woman with gray-streaked hair, darker gray at the roots. She wears a red Eddie Bauer winter coat, puffy with stuffing, and her eyes are just as red. Maddy realizes this other woman's been crying, too, and part of her wants to engage, sympathize with her somehow by making small talk, but she tightens up and looks away, disengages, picks up an ancient *National Geographic* with a picture of Saturn and its mysterious rings on the cover. Maddy won't make eye contact with the new woman who also waits; her colors clash with the tangerine walls and Maddy doesn't want to be in the same boat. She does nod, however, gives that much; anything less would really be rude—always be proper—brought up by parents who still try not to show favoritism. They've always been proud of her and her writing even though they secretly think it won't really get her anywhere. It moved her away from them, made her leave the Midwest, all the way out to the Montana borderland. Her sister also moving a country away to California, but her parents never connect a familial cause.

Her mother once said to Maddy, "We don't care if our children aren't successful as long as they live in nice places to visit."

"Do you really mean that?"

Her mother responded, "Of course not. Please. I was kidding."

"It's really not a funny joke." Maddy wonders if her mother teases her sister, Rhea, with the two golden grandchildren and stay-at-home motherhood, married and living in a coastal town so crazily overpopulated and fast-paced, but a very nice place to visit. What did she and Rhea ever accomplish? Rhea was a successful interior designer at one point, until the kids popped into being, and retiring, and Rhea can't help but bring up the homes in the San Diego area she created, lists her unforgettable designs at the drop of a hat. Success is a different arbiter of respect and totally within the realm of judgment. Her mother twists in some comment about Rhea and Carl and the choices her youngest made. For better. For worse. She delicately positions both her children under a microscope and dishes out her own wisdom. Dad never gets involved. He enjoys his retirement and channels his free time into the RV world. He says, "Your mother keeps a tight ship!" They do the long-distance drive once a year because Dad insists on being in control and loves to play the commander. And he's deathly fearful of being in any airplane, big or small. Mom follows along.

"Mom"—don't forget. Rhea and her family live two thousand plus miles away from you too. Not just me. We both wanted to get away. Try to see things our way for once. Maybe it's about you.

Maddy's talking herself down even more. The door (thank goodness) to the waiting room opens. The older woman in the red coat looks up expectantly but it's a nurse who asks Maddy to follow her into the hall. There's no emotion on the nurse's face to read one way or another.

A stubble-jawed surgeon, dressed in green, blood on the hem of his scrub shirt, writes on a chart at the reception desk. He flips pages and doesn't look up even when Maddy's brought to his side. The nurse waits and Maddy can tell, just that little step, the nurse has the utmost respect for the surgeon, someone who reminds Maddy of a bum. His scrubs are disheveled and he's let his middle turn to gut fat; with the unshaven beard and the hair askew he can just as easily pass for the homeless men at the supermarket who shift through trash bins. Maddy reminds herself to be charitable, keep it together. The man doesn't even begin to look up until he's finished with his chart. Maddy glances at what he writes and the last name of the patient at the top of the file isn't even her son's name.

"I think I need to sit down," Maddy says.

The surgeon looks up then. Got his attention. The nurse points to a small office and leads Maddy to a chair.

"Oh," the surgeon finally says, "Mrs. Bullet?"

"Yes." Maddy sits down with some relief. "But it's Dakota. Different last names. I didn't take my husband's name." She doesn't say: Does this really matter?

"Your son, Chris, is stable now."

Maddy knows the type: someone who has to be prodded to reveal anything of substance. "Just tell me what the situation is, please?"

"Well." The doctor can't even look her in the eye.

Maddy interrupts, firmly. "Let's start over."

The doctor then tries to act alert.

"My name is Maddy. And you are?"

He's recovering, now paying attention.

"Doctor Gapestill. Sorry. I realize this is very difficult."

She holds herself in check, resists the urge to become publicly disrespectful, yet she's ready to erupt at Doctor Gapestill's patronizing tone. Somehow, Maddy stifles her own ego and lets the doctor continue.

"The people who did this to your son almost killed him. That's the blunt truth."

This is his bedside manner? Maddy is bewildered.

"He's mending now. There are a lot of broken bones to heal. His elbow alone will take one or possibly two more operations once he wakes up. He's in traction because of the stress on his spine, but these aren't even the most serious of his injuries."

"What is?"

"Chris is in a coma."

"What does that mean?"

"Chris took a serious blow to the head, to the temple where there's little protection."

"The police told me this."

"It's natural for the body to slow down. It's a protective move. The coma is deep and there's some swelling. With head injuries we have to go slowly. I wasn't able to relieve the swelling completely. We'll know more in the next 24 hours."

"What will you know?"

"There's a chance the swelling could get worse. Lead to a brain hemorrhage." The doctor touches his fingers to the area above his right ear close to the temple, and says, repeating himself to Maddy, tries to make her understand the seriousness, that there may not be a good way out, "This is where the blow to the head did the most damage. It's a tender area and it really doesn't take much to hurt anyone there. Whoever did this lost control, but all we can do is wait."

Maddy doesn't have anything to say. She's thinking she should've been there. She should've been the one protecting her son. Here's a portrait of a mother in failure, someone who can't stop to find out what her son likes or dislikes as he grows into his teens. When's the last time she spoke to me? She starts to beat herself up. It's all her fault. She's been so involved in her own world, the disintegration of her marriage over the last year made her want to spend less and less time at home, write more at the office, and take on more College obligations, most of which are voluntary—Maddy will do it because what does she have to go home to?

"Can I see him?"

"He'll be taken over to the Pediatric Intensive Care wing, perhaps in another hour if we can get him stable enough."

Maddy looks at her watch and realizes she's been in the waiting room for more than three hours. Time flies and it's

a couple hours past midnight, the beginning of the morning. The nurse butts in and says there's a place Maddy can lie down to rest if she wants to, within the Pediatric Intensive Care Unit. When he arrives there you'll be notified.
"What about his brain? Is it damaged?"
"We don't know yet. We'll know more when he wakes up.
And that's where I am.
Adrift.
Coma.
Observation mode.
I know all of this. I've had time to sort everything out. All of Maddy Mother. All of Geoffrey Father. All of Deepika too, stronger than any of us, on her own path. Fate. I know I'm in crisis. I know everything about the last year. I know my father had an affair. I know my mother kicked him out of the house. I know Deepika doesn't love my father. I know he's adrift (caught) in another part of the hospital, waiting, depressed, depressingly unconscious from the overdose he took. I know the four boys who took part in my beating, but I only know one of their names. I remember everything and I don't remember any of it. It's all there for me to see, the past, it's there right in front of me—the present too, but not the big, curtain-falling future. I won't remember any of it if I wake up.

I'm a sage, omniscient, but only while in this state as I lay on an uncomfortable stretcher. How do I know it's uncomfortable? I'm guessing. My body doesn't feel a thing. There's no pain where my consciousness floats. All of the information I just told you I'm guessing. How can anyone really know exactly what another person feels? I put everything together and make educated guesses, roll the film. Before my brain bursts like its own alien monster I'll make more connections.

Right now I can't even tell you if my father still wants to kick the bucket, and, yes, I realize how awful my words are, makes me sound ungrateful, unlikeable even, but if my father woke up and I could say one more thing to him I'd tell him I do love him. He's downstairs, trapped in the same solitary world he's trying so hard to leave.

What does a nurse feel when she's trying to save the

life of someone who doesn't want to live? No wonder there's so much barely concealed contempt for the suicidal patient—and even this I depart from. These nurses should be ashamed.

So you've got the story so far.

I hope it'll change when I wake up. Deepika will visit me. Her nonexistent guilt will show as much as my half-sibling in her belly. Maybe she'll bump into my mother, and I imagine the shock on both of their faces, and who knows? Deepika prepares for this interaction, ready with a deft, direct apology. Bring it on. Let them sort out why they're all so miserable. Let them remember all the horrible things in their pasts, the things that embolden their pressure decisions, life-altering choices. I'll wake up for that. That's a promise. Front row seating.

Will there be a Geoffrey for Deepika to visit?

Let me know later.

My mother will sit and sit and cringe and second-guess her behavior. She tries to convince herself she didn't do anything wrong. No one ever does anything wrong. Take a pill.

I can observe the three of them, my Mother and Father spiraling out of control, separately, bound together, and unable to realize they're taking me down with them. Deepika wrapping up loose ends and moving on—the only smart one. My situation is not of their making; it's my own. I opened my big mouth and approached the bullying vandals, such a pansy word if you think about it much, stop it, stop it, stop it, and then I fall back into blackness—accepting its embrace—I spiral in and out of existence. I am failing, falling, each second a glimpse, a settling of pace, fluid, I'm in many places at once, a sliver of myself watches the inconsequential. How bright each person strives even when believing the opposite—that they're living a mundane life—this is something important, and I try to hold onto this revelation.

PART THREE

If the doors of perception were cleansed everything would appear to man as it is, infinite.

~William Blake

FRAILTY

MY FATHER'S NOT THINKING, I mean, I can no longer sense his thoughts, and there's no one wringing their hands bedside talking to him, trying to communicate with him, wake him up. He's also trapped in the void between living and dead. Deepika would say there's a name for this void, some word vaguely familiar off the tongue, lyrical and pleasing. For some, they believe the concept of yin and yang and how both appear to exchange qualities within a soul. For Catholics and the evangelical there's heaven and hell, but so many deny the existence of hell and float through life on dreams of paradise (if they can only get through this hell of reality). If you believe in angels don't think falsely of the existence of demons. The night I'm brought to the hospital in a roaring ambulance through the rainy streets of Middleton, Deepika doesn't light the candle in the corner of her house she uses for meditation. It's a gift from Liv, just for looks, and only there in case Liv notices it and asks Deepika if she likes it. Oh, yes, such a thoughtful gift. Liv, you're too good to me, a little white lie of graciousness.

The purple round candle with the scent of darkening fruit about to turn rests on a small rectangular table made of dark, rich cherry wood but Deepika doesn't light it during her meditation hour. She'd rather use the single bronze oil lamp. There's a luster to the table brought out by careful years of polishing, a small container of holy ash on the far side of the table, and a clear glass bowl filled with water in the center. Lotus flower petals float in the water but there's no scent of them in the air strong enough to even mingle with the candle. She lights a small lamp, a bronze container filled with oil, and the flame gives the enclosure a warm glow.

Deepika thinks about Geoffrey and then tries to clear her mind of his image. She wants to lose herself in her thoughts, but not of him. She will start to tremble otherwise. Her fingers shake when she lights the oil lamp and she sprays cleansing rose water into the air above her head. Always a habitual tradition, every moment is like the last and carefully repeated in her meditation chamber. There's never been a time when she's doubted the power of her faith, her belief in a world of creation; what she believes to be true is nothing to her but at once it's also everything.

The image of Madison fills her mind and she doesn't brush this picture away. She imagines Madison as she last saw her sitting alone in the campus coffee café reading a coverless book. Deepika, at the time, wanted to know what book captivated Maddy so much she could ignore the bustle of the populated cafeteria. She had total concentration, a quality Deepika admires. Then Deepika realizes Maddy was in a defensive posture, firm, rigidly aware of those who could at any moment invade her space. No judgment but enough faith in her fellow man to provide Deepika with many insights; she wishes she'd approached Maddy and crossed the line even more, but her presence would only salt wounds better left alone.

Her name means: The Light, The lighting of the lamp. Deepika.

People always ask her for a definition, a compelling curiosity she grows tired of, but she answers in her usual tone of wonder and amusement with no visible judgment showing. Her parents went to a family doctor when she was born and the doctor's wife, since the child was the first baby girl, was given the gift of naming her. What an auspicious beginning . . . many names derived from the constellations above, giving importance and depth to the naming process. Deepika always wants to ask for the definition of mundane English names. What does Susan mean? Steve? Charlie? Sean? Exotic names must have an intensity hidden from the outside world. Usually the English name their children based on the large egos of the parents, the importance of the name being the continuance of history and tradition even if Uncle Barry or poor Aunt Courtney could seldom be called superb role models.

Deepika concentrates on the meaning of her name. She stares into the lamp's flame. Earth, air, water, fire and *arash* combine to create a force field. The *arash* or ether strips away all thoughts of impurity as Deepika flees deeper into thought and beyond.

After minutes pass Deepika dips her fingertips in the ash on the table and touches the powder to her forehead. A dash appears in a line and then again and finally, once more, Deepika traces three lines above her brow. The top line of Bhasma, holy ash, is called Anava and represents her primal ignorance. The middle line stands in place for Karma, below ignorance, yet connected, and channels her actions and reactions. The bottom line, Maya, embodies all form. Everything around Deepika signifies Maya.

Deepika dreams of becoming transparent and to live like writing on water. There's nothing against her. Everything denotes Maya, Karma, Anava, and she corresponds with everything all at once—creates. The situation she has created for herself is part of the world and she believes her world is larger because of her belief—fateful.

Concentrate—study—meditate—be. After thirty minutes of sitting Deepika waves her hand above the flame and the rush of wind snuffs out the oil lamp. Not long enough but she imagines herself edging into paranoia and gossip. When this happens she doesn't stop. She stands, turns the dim lights off, and contemplates the quiet of the house. Deepika wipes her forehead with a washcloth in her tiny bathroom. The gray powder swirls down the drain. The pipes squeak and water comes out in a trickle. Tomorrow she'll call Liv, her landlord, her one true friend in Middleton, finally, and ask for a plumber to schedule a checkup; Deepika is leaving but Liv will want to get the plumbing fixed for the next tenant. Her mind fills up with battling thoughts once more and she smiles. No, she will let Liv know there's a problem with the pipes so the next renter won't complain, like duty in good faith, make it all about Liv, get things done.

In the morning she'll call the hospital and prepare to

substitute Madison's classes. There's a part of her fully at peace with the situation. Deepika wants to find out what's happened to Geoffrey and me but she waits. It won't keep her up at night as much as the kicking of her child.

* * *

Nadine enters the waiting room in a hurried and harried maelstrom. She hugs Maddy, really clutches, hugs, and doesn't release her grasp for almost a minute. They're left alone in the waiting room for the P.I.C.U. in the children's wing of the hospital. Nadine sits in another ugly chair beside my mother and keeps hold of her hand. Transferred there in the early morning hour, with my head bandaged, and in all appearance like a wrapped bowling ball boy, they tell Maddy they shaved my head completely and Maddy hopes to find this out when I awake with one weeks' growth of stubble, like fine sand, just breaking the scalp, bordering the zigzag scars. Maybe the surgical scar near my temple will stay red and angry for many weeks and I'll eventually grow my hair long to cover it up. But Nadine hasn't seen me yet and it's too early now for Maddy to do anything but allow Nadine to take her hand and collapse beside her.

"I can't believe this is happening," Nadine says with real regret. She's in a bit of a shock. Her own husband, Bernie, is asleep and she left him safe in their master bed unprepared to take on his own breakfast duties the following morning; Nadine has two begging moocher dogs to feed and one persistent cat that especially acts starved for food and meows interminably until fed. This is Nadine's chore. The ritual begins around 6am and Nadine has begun to resent the cat her husband insisted on getting for their children ten years ago. Old cat, old resentment, but she's the one who wakes every morning and feeds the damn thing regardless. Walk the dogs, Nadine wrote on a Post-It note. You can reach me on my cell. She attached the note to the bathroom mirror.

Maddy manages a wan reply: "I can't believe it either.

Nothing is sinking in."

"How's Geoffrey?"

"I don't know."

"I'll check if you want me to." Nadine rises to leave but Maddy keeps hold of her hand and Nadine sits down again.

"No. Please don't."

"Maddy."

"Do you remember the time we all drove up to Glacier together?"

"Sure."

"I've been thinking about that trip. We stayed in a small hotel in Kalispell—a couple years before you bought the summer home on Swan Lake. It was July."

Nadine interjects, "My kids hated it. Imagine." Nadine thinks of her two kids, Tony and Belinda, who she calls Bling when she's being affectionate or really stern. They still come home for Thanksgiving and Christmas out of some familial sense of duty, and as long as the airfare is picked up, but they live in the East. They made the choice to go to college in Ohio and Pennsylvania. Tony wants to be an attorney and work in family law. Nadine has made the suggestion several times to Tony: take the Montana bar exam. He hasn't responded to her prodding; his life's in Pittsburgh now and he's dating and enjoying being so far from home. He comes back less and less. Belinda Bling has another year left at Oberlin; she plays the violin and is making the rounds auditioning for symphony work. Maybe I'll play at Carnegie Hall some day, Mom. I'm so happy for you, Nadine says with true pride, but she knows Belinda won't travel home to play in the Middleton Summer Symphony anytime soon. Nadine blames herself with real sadness for her children's unhappiness like all mothers do eventually, but also refutes credit if her children are happy and does so with ingrained humility.

"They're all gone now," Maddy says, "You have the house to yourself. You and Bernie."

"A small blessing." Nadine doesn't know where her friend's going with this memory walk but she lets Maddy speak. She worries more.

"It was a little more than a year after the car accident, when Christopher had just turned seven and Tony kept telling him stories about grizzly bears. By the time we drove to Glacier for the day and parked in the lot he didn't want to get out of the car, remember?"

"Perfectly."

"What a day," Maddy exclaims. "We parked at the top of Going-to-the-Sun Road and the air was so clear, the sky so blue."

"Like infinity."

Maddy chuckles, "You always describe the sky with that word." Maddy knows Nadine uses infinity as a definition for many things and she wants her to continue.

"Yes. The largest bowl. Covering the mountains where there's no edge. It really has earned the name Crown of the Continent."

"So, do you remember talking Chris into walking up the path?"

"I told him there was a wise old man who lived in a tiny house at the top who had all his video game secrets memorized."

"Or something like that. He held onto your hand and I watched him all day with you. I could picture you as his mother," Maddy says.

"After the way my two kids sulked the entire trip I wouldn't wish that on you."

"Tony and Belinda were young."

"Even if they were sullen and spoiled, with ripening teenage complexes, you still can blame them."

"And now Chris is here. He hits his teenage years and I don't even know him or why this has happened to him."

"He's going to be okay." Nadine tries to sound reassuring.

"The police came back. They caught all four of the boys who did this. They're locked up down at the police station. Do you know one of them was in most of Chris's classes? He's the one who told the police the names of the other three. He said he was just walking home with them and Chris appeared; he said he didn't take part in it. He ran away just the same. He's separated from the other three."

"What did the other boys say?"

"Their parents and their lawyers surround them and will

try to protect them. Not in a good way. The girl, Mary, the one who called the police, she witnessed the attack, the end of the fighting. Some people heard the boys from the front porches of their houses, but it was dark and they were too far away in the rain. The detective in charge said he'd be back tomorrow after he's talked to all of them."

"Mad—I'm so sorry." Nadine grasps Maddy's hand and squeezes. Her fingers stay loose in Nadine's palm.

"There's something else," Maddy sighs.

The door to the waiting room opens and a nurse asks if she can get coffee or pillows for them. She knows they'll be spending a lot of time in this room. "Do you want to see Chris? Just for a moment?" The nurse gestures and the two women follow her into the heart of the P.I.C.U.

Nadine wonders what Maddy's going to say. She stands, takes control. She wants Maddy to lean on her. She wants to give her strength.

* * *

Geoffrey's taken to a room in the lock-up, Psychiatric Ward. It turns out he didn't ingest enough pills to cause anyone, except Maddy, to really worry about him dying—it turns out he didn't take enough pills to even destroy one of his kidneys—and in so many cases appearances can be deceiving.

If Maddy has to think about giving one of her kidneys to Geoffrey she knows she'd have trouble deciding yes or no; it's a natural progression; and she wouldn't be able to come to a definitive answer. Would I? Probably, only because I can see how weak he is, in both mind and body, but I can't speak and the point is moot. The E.R. staff pumps Geoffrey's stomach as he regains a semblance of consciousness followed by a cursory psych evaluation in the E.R. and then he's shipped upstairs to sleep the night away. They don't know why his wife couldn't find a pulse. For some unknown reason, the police drop the ball; there isn't any mention of alcohol lying about the scene, a bottle of vodka to wash the pills down, but the tox screen came back with a high alcohol content—he definitely couldn't get behind the wheel of a car. Maybe the wife panicked. It's been known to happen. He did try to kill himself but maybe he really isn't any good at it. A dozen pills and a lot of vodka isn't necessarily a suicide unless he actually was behind the wheel of a car. He's sleeping it off. The nurses aren't gentle with him and Maddy doesn't even know Geoffrey's been moved yet. One of the nurses, Katherine, says, "He'll be in for a surprise when he wakes up in the Psych Ward." The nurses aren't sorry for him either. Being firm is part of the modus operandi, an almost inhumane brusqueness with Geoffrey. They may not understand or empathize with my father's weakness, how he holds secrets.

* * *

Deepika opens her eyes from sleep, pulls her hair back and splashes water in her face, works out on her bedroom floor, small, baby sit-ups she couldn't even call exercise, just waking up, a dozen slow elbow half push-ups as she watches CNN, talks with Britain about who would be a better friend after the Presidential election, because who really believes their Prime Minister anyway, complicit in all the lying buddy-buddy behavior between the two countries, and the anchorman speaks with a gleam in the eye, sanctions, North Korea duplicity, local news, hell in a handbasket, education funding cut across the state, peace rallies on the capitol steps; Deepika breathes slowly and exerts herself more when she climbs onto her stationary bicycle for fifteen minutes of slower than slow pedaling, something she's done for years, something she has trouble giving up and longs for when she travels across the globe. Her doctor tells her a light amount of exercise will do no harm to the baby and Deepika imagines the baby within cataloguing the motion above the bicycle and years down the road taking to bicycling like a virtuoso. She's sweating by the end when she starts coffee and hops into the shower. In that specific order she begins her day. She feels alone and even though she's carrying a child and her stretching on the floor is limited, she believes she's more alone than ever. Her thoughts awaken slowly as the hot spray drenches and wakes her up even more. Because she's handling her situation on her own, and doesn't have anyone else to rely on, Deepika has been seeing a doctor at the hospital outside the college system. Deepika purchased all the recommended books on what to do while pregnant, and what not to do. Smoke, drink, cuss, spit, chew, do laugh, a lot, do cry if happy but not if you're sad, and if you do, don't beat yourself up about it.

There's a sense of calm within her home. Deepika cannot allow herself to dwell on chaos, bad choices leading to even worse outcomes. She (aren't we all?) is witness to this destruction and wonders where each tragic moment began—from a loving moment, if you go back far enough. I can't believe she and I are on the same page. I want to find out everything, figure out why.

Deepika shakes off her unrestful night spent worrying about the future. Life's but a trial, a series of choices, and most of them forgettable; no one can predict the future—she believes this strongly, before and after she meditates, concentrates on images of a bird flying away. She plans her morning and tells herself again and again to shield herself from the questions she knows are forthcoming from the department and the group at the college who consider themselves her peers. She could've just said no to Marjolaine. When she dresses in a conservative, brown full-length skirt and a very large red blouse to cover her belly, comfortable clothes to move around in, Deepika finds resolve. Fill in while Madison is gone, just this week, and then pack up and leave fast.

The drive to the faculty parking structure is a busy one with all the students rushing about. The rumors of war have long-since shriveled away and become reality—feeble protests at this point, the year of politicking so close to being over. The President proudly states, in flight suit, that the mission is accomplished almost a year past, but he's been foolish. On campus, in the air this October day, with the president of the country doing his best to instill an unwavering honesty, a folksiness in faltering debates; with his faith in God verging on fundamental, Deepika believes he comes off as a little too simple, dazed with fervor, yet still shrewd enough not to be underestimated, something she hears all the time from her relatives back home. Her mother always says Deepika lives in a country where it seems the electorate feels moved by the antics of an imagined third cousin once removed, and somehow this distant, distaff family member has come to power and taken over and flipped the family dynamics. India, as a whole, is fractured into too many separate visions to realize the same thing happens there every day. Politics are no different. Deepika always brings up Pakistan.

Oh. Are they trafficking in nuclear materials? Watch North Korea, Mom.

The weight of the proclamations made by India's high-powered decision makers—follow them.

And what were they thinking in Sri Lanka? Please, Mummy, pronounce judgments a little closer to home.

Deepika will never say any of this to her mother—keep the air light, breathable. It's too easy and predictable. She misses deep, intricate political discussion back home where people argue without fear of being categorized as strictly only being one way or the wrong way. It's more civilized somehow, even when her brothers raise their voices as if to say: Women, what do they know about world affairs. She knows her older brother will be happy if his wife stays in the kitchen all day or pushes out baby after baby; she raises them; he praises them.

If Deepika was back home sitting in her mother's living room staring out the window with a view to the back gardens, all the flowers now cultivated and some covered in the fall, the tomato stakes piled up against the garden shed, she would sip strong tea with a rich honey bought from the vendors in the center of town, the birds and monkeys chattering in the park and zoo a block away. The sisters of her mother would descend on her and make her feel like a queen. Another little baby to enter a world bent on creation and destruction. Her father wouldn't say much at all but he would understand, probably the only one in the family to really get what Deepika has done; once following a similar path long ago, a longing path. They wouldn't even contemplate casting Deepika aside. It's a different culture where all life is celebrated. So what if she's an unmarried woman with a child on the way. Deal with it and laugh and enjoy the world.

Deepika cannot wait to fly home. She's entering a parking space when the child within her gives the strongest kick yet and Deepika's car lurches forward until the front of her Saab rests against the wall. No damage but enough of a jolt for it to make Deepika wince. She wrestles herself out of the car and walks to the front to see if she's put another scratch on her bumper. Nothing.

The campus paper is strewn about the dank garage. Deepika doesn't stoop to pick one up. She can read the headline: **STREAKER DISRUPTS NEO-NAZI FORUM**. She envisions balls juggling in the air and the white supremacists' anger fomenting and the streaker with the red converse tennis shoes, the paper says he was also wearing a green scarf, possibly an early holiday ensemble, looking over his shoulder in fear as he realized maybe this wasn't such a grand idea because at least three burly bald swastika guards were chasing him in their jackboots. Campus security had to hold them back and protect the streaker and the story doesn't identify the smart aleck student. He has a Ted Kaczynski—why is this always the case in The West—beard, and he's as skinny as a refugee and the photo in the paper, only showing his upper torso, remains just grainy enough to display a tattoo on the man's upper left shoulder of a Buddhist figure seated with palms at rest but pointing to the sky, a serene expression on the face. Deepika laughs.

Big Sky College is in the throes of budget deficits and a downward trend in alumni giving. The powers that be consider raising tuition once again and cutting back on pay for the part-time teaching assistants starting the winter term. No one's happy about this but the administration continually sends the message: our hands are tied and there's nothing else to be done. God forbid the administration ever realizes a pay cut of its own. Just the suggestion brings apoplexy and sudden distrust, and a focus on the person who makes such a statement. That teacher will find no tenure and a borrowed suitcase to pack with after the next round of budget cuts.

Deepika walks into Marjolaine's cramped office a little early. Shelves overflow with books, notebooks, file folders and loose paper. There's confusion to be found in her tiny space. Papers and file folders pile up across every surface top and Marjolaine apologizes for the disaster, because she does know where everything is, another expert in efficiency, something America thrives on with a chip on the shoulder. It takes a temp three days to sort it out every time Marjolaine goes on vacation.

"Have you heard anything about Madison?" Marjolaine asks this first to subdue her growing desire to ask about Deepika's pregnancy. They've never been friends or even close acquaintances, but Deepika's exotic to her and someone who has Up-N-Coming Star Writer stamped all over her. Marjolaine curries favor with Deepika because maybe this star quality will rub off. Deepika smiles.

"No. I was going to ask you the same question."

"She's been at the hospital all night. There's been no change in her son's condition."

"Did anyone figure out what happened?" Only for a second does Deepika wonder if Marjolaine knows anything about Geoffrey and quickly realizes she doesn't know a thing. Maddy tries to keep Geoffrey separate except for the occasional staff party Geoffrey feels well enough and obligated enough to attend.

"It's in the Middleton paper. Four boys attacked him. One of them had a baseball bat. Sounds awful. A bit sketchy. Reminds me, oh, they made a movie about that poor boy from Wyoming. I saw the film on cable and it almost brought me to tears—leaving that poor boy tied to a fence." As she gives voice to them Marjolaine's thoughts run into each other with speed and less conviction. "They were breaking windows on some cars when they came across him. It sounds like they all knew each other from school. There aren't a lot of eyewitnesses. I bet the owners of the cars are really angry, too."

"Madison also."

"Yeah. Can you imagine? How stupid people are. I'm so relieved you haven't left yet. Finding a replacement next term will be terribly hard, but I'm so glad you could take over her classes. I hope you're free for the next week?" This question is stated like a demand.

"I guess so but I wouldn't want Madison to think I was taking over. And I can only commit to one week." Deepika doesn't add that she's moving away the very next day after her commitment.

"Oh. She won't think that. She's the nicest person in the department. A bit self-contained but she throws the best parties. Remember? We're lucky to have her here."

"Of course. Okay. What building is the first class in?"

"Merriam Hall. Second floor. Room 2223 in half an hour. Until then, you can hang out in her office if you'd like. She's on the third floor of the office center. Or you can hang out in the communal space in the basement. Maddy's office is great; she's one of the lucky few with an alcove office and a window. She said anyone who subs is welcome to use it; I don't think she keeps anything personal there anyway."

"Can you give me the heads up on the afternoon class?"

Deepika watches calmly as Marjolaine collects the student lists and the classroom assignments. This calmness makes Marjolaine nervous.

There's something sly and shifty about Marjolaine's movement. Her fingers slinky and uncurling from her rounded fists, purposefully guided by a basic principle: she wants the dirt on the situation and everything Deepika refuses to tell her keeps Marjolaine from getting what she wants: YOU are NOT MARRIED and you're PREGNANT! Marjolaine won't give anything else away—just the truth of her station.

"Is there anything I can do for you?" Marjolaine asks.

Deepika finally detects caring in Marjolaine's tone and she isn't faking it. Deepika, around enough to learn the ropes the first year, doesn't gossip or join in speculation about the English Department Schedule Coordinator—almost thirty years ago she was just another ranch girl from outside the Flathead Lake area who got pregnant in high school, and the boy of flash and substance would tell her he was leaving, joining the Army, going off to war, just try to get child support from me way over there, and the baby was her choice, left Marjolaine in the lurch with parents too Christian to confide in, for all appearances she could pass as a sweet Washington apple—fled across the state border for the clinical consult without the parental approval and federal intervention—and she felt so alone until her friend Belinda, the girl she sat next to on the school bus for ten years, drove her to Pullman, Washington, for the termination, and eventual denial the event had ever happened.

Deepika doesn't know any of this in the moment Marjolaine hands the class roster over the paper-strewn desktop. How could she? I'm only aware because I see this image brightly hidden within Marjolaine. It shines there. She's never told anyone about her past, but seeing Deepika pregnant brings it all up again. In darkness, I lay there with all people, all their secrets unfolding, around me, scurrying ants busy, most with a certain lack of enjoyment involved in any interaction. I know her secret. I can see people. Feel them nearby. Marjolaine's secret isn't the only one I'm privy to in my current state.

Right now at this moment there's a visitor to Middleton walking his two dogs, Myrtle and Lucille, by the river, along the popular jogging path used by the city and the college students—he's not important, this dogwalker, his dogs are cute but also unimportant. The viewpoint shifts and I don't know why this scene is crucial for me to view, but I can't ask questions. I'm brought here for only an instant unfolding. The joggers are so close to me they run like water over rocks—time speeds up. Overweight, handsome, ugly, beautiful people run and bike by, dodging. It isn't raining anymore. It's daylight now, almost eleven; the day has already begun when the owner of the two dogs lets Lucille off leash. He knows—and now I know—Lucille will only do her business in private and never near her step-dog-sister, Myrtle.

Of course the owner also knows he shouldn't be unleashing his dog in a place with signs clearly stating pet regulations. Picture the owner smiling and walking slowly toward a squirrel climbing a distant tree, a large squirrel too old and wise to be chomped to death by Lucille even though she is part Chow Chow. That squirrel sits up on a thin branch in the tree chittering down at the dog. The owner notices a Nike-dressed runner smiling at Lucille's obvious lust for the squirrel. A sudden flash of movement and it's suddenly perched on a higher branch making pithy grunts of satisfaction. Out of the blue a man nearby on the lawn, doing yoga stretches on his own dry yoga matt, stridently calls out: "Is that your dog?"

"No." The dog owner lies, but who can blame him when the tone of the yoga man is so pressing and prissy.

"Do you know your dog has to be on a leash?"

"No. I didn't know that." There's tension in his voice now but he's keeping it close. "Why don't you report me?"

"I think I will. What's your name?" The yoga man isn't giving up.

Now the petulant man's voice has turned prim with righteousness and need. He's stretching an arm around his head while grabbing his leg with the other free arm and calmly trying to control a man who is breaking the rules right in front of him for some unknowable reason.

"I think you should mind your own business." The owner of the dogs tries to sound disgusted. Lucille still keeps both her eyes on the squirrel. The squirrel watches the two dogs and the two humans engaging in a verbal joust. The Nike runner smirks at the situation and continues to do his own stretches as he waits for his running companions. He can't wait to tell them about the dogs, the squirrel, and the yoga prick.

"Are you ashamed of your own name? Why won't you tell me your name?"

"Lucille. Lucille. Come here." The dog owner calls Lucille back because she's ambling closer to the yoga man to sniff and is within two feet of the man who, if the dog came any closer, would've slapped her nose so hard she'd cry like a stuck pig. Lucille trots back and the owner snaps the coupler leash on. The dog owner remains flustered by his actions and the superiority in the yoga man's voice.

"Good girls. Don't listen to the nasty man," the owner

says. He's thinking of what to say to the man, ordering his words.

"You must be ashamed of your own name if you won't tell it to me."

"No. I'm just amazed at your logic. Your behavior shocks me; your basic idiocy; you've got a large, festering, bitter suppository shoved so far up your ass you can't enjoy what's left of your life. It must rub you so raw, the wrong way, that you can't control anyone else."

"I'm going to call the police if you don't stop badgering me and if you don't keep your dog on a leash. You're verbally assaulting me."

No one but I can see the yoga man's death coming in less than fifteen years, and only three years into a forced retirement where he's alone, a widower of five years, a retired therapist in Palm Desert, in a nice condo with two bedrooms, one for guests who never come, and a rattling air conditioning system he can never fix properly. He never had a pet. He never had children. He's alone and stifled and watches this dog owner get away with it. The law says he has to keep his stinking dogs on a leash and pick up after them—shovel the shit. He's the loser who thinks rules don't apply to him. And the yoga man is right for he has good intentions. The dog owner also has good intentions even if he does bend rules to satisfy himself—selfish bastard.

The dog owner leaves because he realizes the man is more than a step away from acting crazy with indignation and he wants to dissolve this confrontation. It doesn't do any good to challenge him, pick a fight; he's just a sad, old man.

The Nike runner shakes his head but keeps a smart-alec smirk on his face. He's handsome and oblivious and a college student headed for great things; he studies economics and wants to go to business school, become a stock broker, juggle the numbers and follow in his father's footsteps—he's young, rugged, handsome, and people turn their heads to look at him as he runs by—he has a future and he stays uninvolved with the tableau of conflict in front of him.

The yoga man finishes his stretching and rolls up his

yoga mat—he jogs to his car twenty feet away in the adjacent parking lot and places the mat in the trunk of his new 2004 Prius Hybrid. He thinks he told that scofflaw a thing or two. He can't believe he caught someone breaking the leash law so blatantly in front of him, a law so important to him because he runs the paths daily and it's almost physically hurtful for him to see dogs running off leash doing their business and the owners never picking up after them. He waves to his friend, an old woman retired from the hospital, who finally arrives to run the loop with him and he tells her the whole story. After three miles, he says, "Can you believe how inconsiderate people are today?"

The retired woman only tut, tut, tuts under her breath because she's heard it all before and wonders why she even spends her days running with such an unhappy influence. He does most of the talking, and it isn't the first time someone doesn't live up to his high standards. Lighten up! She wants to scream. You carry such shit around in your head all the time it makes me want to vomit. How can you stand it? Let it go. But she remains silent, nodding, works out and then departs.

The dog owner meets up with his partner, another man a few years older but still in his late thirties, both are visitors to Middleton—let's be gay in Middleton, let's give it a try, it seems like a nice town—can you believe it, and tells him the whole story minus the part about Lucille being aggressive towards the squirrel. "Can you believe how asinine people are today?"

"You did have Lucille off her leash."

"Yeah, but well within voice control. Lucille never runs away from us and you know it. That Cindy Brady tattler just has to feel like she's in control of every situation. She acted like such a jerk."

"Take it easy."

"Why do you always take the other side?"

No one else can see all of this—entertainment—from my hospital room. I drift, my mind drifts, as my mother sits near my bed wringing her stiff hands. Nadine sits next to Maddy and she's thinking about her youngest child who hasn't called home in three weeks. She won't give in, and she won't be the first to call her. She's not thinking of me. She can't even look at my bandaged face. Her own children have ruined her, but, unlike me, they can't see her point of view and wouldn't want to open up to it even if they allowed themselves to.

Deepika has almost half an hour free so she heads to Maddy's office after wishing Marjolaine a good day. She doesn't give away anything about her situation. She thinks her behavior is part of a game and she has fun with it. That is fiction. It's what she is good at creating.

* * *

I remain so still Maddy once more believes, like Geoffrey in the bathtub, that I'm not breathing and she starts to shiver. My mother and Nadine are now next to the side of my bed. Nadine holds onto Maddy and supports her shoulders. "It's okay," Nadine whispers. Maddy then stares at the machines helping me breathe and the bleep of the I.V. and she has to move to the wooden chair to sit. She feels like she doesn't have use of her legs again and thinks of her near fall down the stairs. It isn't time to reveal to anyone she's a little concerned about her own failing health and she grows paranoid about becoming a hypochondriac just to fit into the hospital system, become friends with all the doctors, nurses, build up a new life, supply a new world of pain and sickness.

"He'll wake up," Nadine says. "You know he will. Very soon." Maddy can only laugh the moment her friend utters those words. Comfort comes from a woman who predicted all of this would happen two summers ago with an 'it's fun' reading from an ancient deck of tarot cards Nadine has always fooled with.

Up in Nadine's cabin on Swan Lake, in the screen porch, protected from the mosquitos. "Let's try it, Maddy. You'll get a kick out of it. Just think of a question you want to ask but don't tell me what the question is."

The husbands were out fishing and drinking beer in the

haze of summer and Nadine and Maddy shared a bottle of ice-cold Pinot Grigio and complained about their children. I was reading the latest Koontz thriller, solitary, lakeside, after being sprayed head to toe with insect repellant. Maddy knows all of this now. Maddy only wanted me to be happy but I kept to myself so much my mother believed I must be lonely, and, the best of intentions aside, she wanted to change this somehow.

"Just wait," Nadine responded, "when the girls start calling and you lose him forever. Like I did with my kids."

"You haven't lost them. They'll come back to you. We all went through this ourselves with our own parents. I'm much closer to my parents now that I'm an adult. I inherited all of my mother's traits. I keep so much inside. You know I don't like being emotional."

"Yeah. You're like The Terminator without the Austrian accent. I can't believe you're confiding in me at all, you old stone."

"Don't make me laugh."

"I didn't know you could do that, ha ha. We do tend to wallow in our own messes," Nadine said with a hint of whimsy. "A psychic, a palm reader told me to buy this book on the astrology of relationships and I looked up my mom and me based on our birthdates and you know what it said?"

"What?"

"We'd be mortal enemies throughout childhood."

"From what you told me the book was right."

"Yes, but, it won't be until later, when we're adults that we'll make a connection and become friends, that we'll really understand each other."

"You and your mother seem to get along famously."

"Now we do."

"So astrology really is a science?" Maddy asked this with one eyebrow raised.

"Don't tease. It's just a game."

"Nadine, it's a game you play a lot. If you told me—that when I was born the stars up above me in the sky at that very moment, above the hospital, would have an effect and guide every aspect of my life I'd have to say you're nuts."

"But?"

"But I'm not so sure anymore because you do have a belief system. Unlike me."

"You tend to discard religious theory out of spite. And so what if I want to believe in something even if it's closer to the supernatural? You do make me happy."

"Ha ha. All this astrology hooey comes from a registered Episcopalian. "

"Amen. Really. Well don't get so superior. Okay?" said Nadine as she handed a newer deck of tarot cards to Maddy, each one larger than her hand, and very difficult to shuffle without placing them on the table to straighten the edges together. "These are so unused they still have a slick plastic feel."

"I can barely get them separated," Maddy said, "Maybe it would help if I filled my wine glass. There."

"Just spread the cards around in a big pile until they feel right."

"Nadine, how long have you been doing this?"

"Not professional enough for you, Dearie?"

"Ha. Do you have time for me to go buy you a gypsy shawl, gold hoop earrings and a peasant skirt?" Laughing once again, then, "Next you'll be buying aura machines and telling me my yellow color is boosting my creativity but the window's almost shut." The two women laughed and took sips of their wine.

"I haven't done this since my college days," Nadine admitted.

"When you were a hippie living in a commune in Southern Oregon?"

"I was renamed Rosemary Rain and proud of it."

"You never told me that."

"Well. I don't like to dwell on the past. This particular tarot deck is supposed to be a good one, meaning positive. I have several different decks. Do you see the pictures of the English knights of old? I read the pamphlet and the tarot artist lives in Sedona and she believes only in the positive vibrations of the cards and doesn't want me to read them in reverse. I bought them in a small New Age bookstore when we drove down to Laguna last spring break. No one would let me do a reading."

"Imagine that."

"Cut the sarcasm or it won't work," Nadine said. She faked being cross well.

"So. No negativity from the get-go. If you have to turn a card out of the reverse position isn't that cheating?"

"Maybe. But if I don't follow the instructions we won't have a positive experience."

"And it's all about feeling good isn't it? Do you have more hooch we can bring to the table before we start?"

"Don't laugh, Maddy. Let me pretend I know what I'm doing."

"Okay, Rosemary Rain Crowley, I think the cards are just about right." Maddy slapped the deck onto the table in front of Nadine.

"Keep shuffling until they feel absolutely right."

"Just a figure of speech. They're so right they're almost glowing."

"The boys forgot sunscreen," Nadine said.

"Did they?"

"They're going to be burnt lobsters when they get off the water."

There was a buzz of logging trucks from a distance across the water where there weren't any homes. Maddy always felt the noise was intrusive and ruined the pristine setting of the log cabin. One day the rich would rise up and form a committee and appoint an overseer to steer the logging road away from the lake and all would be well again. But when Maddy and Nadine were lazing about the screened-in sun porch Nadine always had NPR playing in the background to cut the truck engine noise.

"It's not like we didn't warn them. Enough shuffling. Now what, Miss Guru?"

"Hand them over." Nadine opened her tarot handbook and proceeded to sort the deck into three stacks and said, "Now take each of these smaller piles and shuffle until they feel right to you."

"You didn't tell me there would be this much shuffling. How many rights make a wrong? I think I'm going to need more munchies, too."

"Just keep your mind open."

* * *

When Geoffrey finally opens his eyes he doesn't remember anything about the previous evening. His throat feels raw and sore and burning and he can't move his arms or legs. He closes his eyes and takes in a deep breath before a stuttering cough convulses his body. It takes him a little longer to realize he's strapped to a bed and the room isn't his own.

He's tied down in a dismal gray-tiled room with fluorescent lighting and a dropped-ceiling. He wakes up alone and scared, but at least he wakes up.

Geoffrey can't even scratch an itch along his scalp. "Help," he shouts out.

The door to the room unlocks, opens, and a nurse in light blue scrubs strolls in. He's a large white man who wears black boots the size of shoeboxes. His fingers aren't long but they appear strong and his expression brims with disdain.

"Good morning, Mr. Bullet."

"Where am I?"

"You are a guest of the hospital's psychiatric evaluation unit. My name is Harry." Harry lets his words speak for him in the silence that follows. He imagines Mr. Bullet taking his own life and saving him the trouble of bathing his body with a sponge. Alcohol and pills, another one who couldn't get it right the first time, another cry for the help Harry's paid to give. The sour smell of alcohol-mixed-with-charcoal bad breath fills the room and Harry's first task of the day shift is to clean Geoffrey up, brush his teeth for him if it comes to that.

"Why am I here?"

"You don't remember?"

"Just save the bullshit and tell me what I'm doing strapped to a hospital bed."

"You tried to kill yourself last night."

"I did not," Geoffrey says with utter conviction.

"Okay. The doctor will be in shortly. It's my job to get you presentable and smelling like a rose."

"Don't touch me. You have no right. Where's my wife?"

This question stops Harry because there isn't any mention of a wife or relative waiting to see Mr. Bullet. When the night shift logged out there had been only two new admits. Mr. Geoffrey Bullet, attempted suicide by O.D. and a Miss Valeria Brandow who was found naked riding a horse through downtown Middleton at midnight. She told the police to call her Lady Godiva and brandished a long steak knife. It took four patrol cars to stop the skittish horse and by then there were a lot of bar patrons surrounding the scene, a lot of catcalls and whistles and even a few video cameras rolling to make sure the police did everything by the book. Some of the footage appeared on the Montana news that morning, as a side-note to my brutal story, and by noon it was a small blip on CNN Headline news and the morning's *USA Today* Nationline column.
    But no one waits to see either of them. Valeria Brandow didn't have alcohol in her system when she was brought in; the psych resident on-call was familiar with Valeria's long history and called in a specialist who's taken care of her before. Valeria was harmless in the horse incident and most people who witnessed her display laughed uncontrollably and hooted and whistled but Valeria, without reason, could harm others and herself because of her lack of common sense and the inability to distinguish between fantasy and reality. Not scientific enough for Harry, but the end result: Valeria Brandow stopped taking her medication and she fell into an imaginary episode where she believed she was someone else, someone hunted, she grew paranoid and discomfort wiggled its way into her mind. She threw the pills that kept her in a docile fugue state into the trashcan beneath her kitchen sink.
    Her sister, Nancy Followatta, a dental hygienist, contacts the hospital, and, with doctor in tow, brings in the medication. She pleads with Valeria to start taking them again. Valeria will be given the same battery of tests she's always been given by every doctor. The main doctor she'll continue with ups one of her medications and discontinues another in a spiraling game of prescription bingo. Then the hospital releases Valeria into her sister's care with a strict warning.

Harry explains to Geoffrey how he's only going to wash his arms and face and get him presentable. He fills a small plastic bowl with warm soapy water, squeezes a sponge, and warns Geoffrey not to give him any trouble or things could get worse.

"May I brush my teeth?"

"I'll do that too."

"When can I get these straps off?"

"That depends on you and what the doctor says."

"Can I make a telephone call?"

"After the doctor sees you."

"Please." Geoffrey feels like shouting out, crying, throwing a childish tantrum, but somehow knows such a display will have no effect on Harry.

"You really don't know why you're here?"

"I don't remember anything. My head aches."

"You drank a lot of vodka and took some pills. Then you fell into the bathtub and bumped your head slightly but not seriously. The E.R. doctors checked that out thoroughly, pumped your stomach, and sent you up here for evaluation. If all goes well you'll be out of here as soon as you come clean about why you took all those pills with the alcohol."

"I tried to kill myself?" It's as if Geoffrey's trying to talk himself into believing it for himself.

"If you have to ask me that question you might be in here longer than you think."

Geoffrey turns his head to stare at the far wall of the bleak room. His shirtsleeve brushes against his skin as Harry roles it up to his shoulders. The sponge bath begins and Geoffrey realizes Harry is being gentle, thorough, and the situation he's in could be a horrible misunderstanding. He could get out of this one if he plays along. He convinces himself of this as Harry finishes.

"Thanks," Geoffrey says.

"You're welcome."

"Is there any way you can check to see where my wife is?"

"I'll ask the front desk staff and check the log-in sheets for visitor requests."

"I'd appreciate it. I'd also like time to call my lawyer."

Geoffrey notices how Harry visibly shivers, just a jolt, at the word lawyer. People must threaten him all the time in here, with physical—even though Harry's such a big guy, imposing—and emotional manipulation.

"That will have to wait till later, after you've seen your doctors."

Geoffrey, for the first time, wishes Maddy was beside him right now holding his hand and telling him everything will be all right.

* * *

Soon, like the most devious voyeur phantom in the world, I hover and watch Deepika take attendance in the senior Creative Writing class. She sits in the middle of a long conference table and takes a deep, silent breath.

The students show her nothing. They aren't even fiddling with their backpacks. But, inevitably, a flip-phone rings and a girl with long brown hair and a lot of dark eye makeup blushes, plunges her hand into her purse to retrieve the cell to turn off the ringing. At least she doesn't answer and start talking.

"Sorry," she mumbles.

"Okay," Deepika says. She smiles. "Some of you may not know me." Last year Deepika taught an upper level graduate Writing class and she recognizes one of the boys sitting to her left. This boy must eat writing classes for lunch, attends as many as he can, even if they're beneath his education level. It's not Deepika's concern. She continues: "I'm subbing for Madison Dakota today." She then remembers the student as a needling presence in her class, and wonders what he's doing taking an undergraduate Writing Class as a graduate student. She will remain wary of him.

"Is she all right?"

"Of course. Travis, right?" Deepika calls forth his name.

"Yes. We heard she was in the hospital."

"Well she's there because of her family but she's perfectly okay."

"That's a relief," says Travis, whose bearded face hides what could be the saddest expression ever.

Deepika isn't going to be drawn into a conversation about Madison. No one knows anything and the department gossip and rumor squads have been spreading stories like the best military propagandists.

"We heard her son was beaten up because he's gay. That he's in a coma."

Deepika's startled now by these words. She remembers me leaving in a fit of sadness and grief and anger, slamming the door—but with such force; she's surprised by the girl's statement about me being gay. It isn't (and wasn't) obvious to her. And she married and then divorced someone who turned out to be gay. He thought she would save him and she did by helping him come out of his own closet, he remains one of her distant but close, longtime friends.

"Fiction or nonfiction?" Deepika asks with an upturned curiosity. And calls on a slight, handsome skinny boy.

"What do you mean?"

"What we're talking about. Is this good fiction? Does gossip have to be bad? Avoided?"

"Well, we're talking about our teacher."

"But, do you know her outside this classroom? Do you know her family?"

No one responds but they're on their toes now ready to jump into the round table discussion. Deepika wants to wind it down and stop it but the rumor mill has taken hold.

"Do you think Madison would like to hear her class discuss her personal life?"

"Of course not."

"But?"

"But we care about what happens to her."

Deepika says, "I know. But I really think we should start to talk about the story Camille passed out at the last class. The office assistant gave me a copy and I read it through this morning. How are you used to discussing a proffered piece of fiction?"

Travis answers, "We usually begin with the author."

"Okay then, Camille, is there anything you want to say before the group begins to critique your short story? What gave you the idea?"

"I was up late two weeks ago and locked out of my dorm room and I wrote this about that experience."

"So it's nonfiction?" A good-looking, brown-haired boy says this. He's a bit snarky and Deepika stares at him and he glances away. No one's laughing.

"No. I changed a lot of the details and made up some of the characters."

"I would hope so," says a girl with mousy brown unevenly cut hair, "since the main character ends up getting raped in the abandoned dorm cafeteria."

A boy wearing a green Polo short sleeve shirt introduces himself as Charlie and contributes: "I didn't believe a word of it. The author didn't make me believe it."

"Why not?" Deepika asks the class.

"We're thrown into the story at the beginning of the evening. She's leaving her friends at the library—"

"It's not me," Camille interrupts, "this is fiction class!"

Deepika quickly says, "Yes. Of course."

"Well why does Charlie keep staring at me when he's talking about the story."

"Oh please. You're being a bit sensitive." Charlie says as he crosses his arms in front of him and stops talking as if it's a lost cause.

"Please calm down," Deepika says with a chuckle. Deepika's bewildered by the class and the different personalities warring against one another. It happens in every class where negative criticism takes over, and it's encouraged, seen as a good thing. The slam. How to slam other writers until there's nothing left; the workshop system. Deepika knows there's good that comes out of it also.

"Let's remain on target. Okay? Camille, everyone, should an author ever defend his or her work?"

The silence in the room interests Deepika because she firmly believes the written work, her own fiction, should never be defended, especially when offered up to the public. It's out there. Let it go. Deepika steers the conversation back to the story of the poor fictional character locked out of her dorm room who falls prey to the wilder boys on the bottom floor.

In the back of her mind she can't stop from thinking about what the student said about me. That isn't the important thing really, the being gay part; Deepika gets this and she feels concerned because she hopes I will be all right. The next day's paper will be a banner headline front-page story loudly and righteously proclaiming a hate crime rocks Middleton and the star will be Geoffrey's son, me, but since I'm a minor, my name won't be available for the press to use until my parents give the okay. The police will seal up the file as tightly as possible but the media do everything sneaky to find out by leakage and start to hound the hospital. Then the spinning of lives into media-frenzied stories continues. In this day and age it's simpler to find someone willing to speak on the record, find a sliver of fame.

The reporters for the Middleton newspaper will try to find out the names of the four boys who assaulted a defenseless gay teenager but won't get any cooperation. I will be outed in the city paper, and I'm too young to be outed. I'm in the closet for a reason. There's really no proof that I'm gay. I've never told anyone about my sexual yearnings. I wouldn't tell anyone stuff like that. I've been hiding it well, and it's been quite easy to do. I act normal, meaning, straight (and even this makes me sweat—why should I have to act straight?), I'm fairly bright, I'm male, I keep to myself and try to fit in, not make waves, I'm not too effeminate even though I'm sensitive to a fault and overanalyze everything, and I speak up when injustice happens right in front of me. Only a few girls have shown any interest in being my friend or more than friends and I always ran away from them, ducked.

One girl, Mary Follick, who has quickly fashioned herself the star witness, who hasn't pursued me greatly since the seventh-grade dance when I bluntly, rudely, told her to leave me alone and said I didn't want to go out with her—I meant, I'm only thirteen-years-old, and a girl wants me to dance with her? Not interested. Go figure. I knew, in the back of my mind, wriggling, I knew I wasn't attracted to girls—I knew this back when I was learning how to swim at the swimming pool, before the car crash, when I was five, paddling around—I wasn't staring at the girls. I took my cue on how to treat aggressive girls from my classmates: be blunt (and almost mean, sadly, to keep them from wanting to pursue you more) and I feel some guilt when I behave this way. I hurt so much so why do I purposely hurt others? At that time I could've been straight because none of my classmates wanted to go out with any of the girls; they just wanted to use them. Another girl chased me around the playground in third grade bent on kissing me on the lips and she dropped out of high school a month before my hospitalization here because some boy got her pregnant. If I could fast-forward to a reunion ten years in the future I'd find out she's raising a capable, sweet-natured child, actually married the father, has two other children, and runs a computer technical assistance business, one of the better ones in Middleton. But here I am in the hospital unable to think and prognosticate while sleeping and trying to build up strength.

* * *

I can't hear my mother talking to me while Nadine sits in the backbreaking wooden-armed, barely padded chair next to her. They speak to each other in a whisper. Nadine prods Maddy to go check on Geoffrey and asks from time to time if she should go find out herself but she doesn't want to let Maddy down. She considers herself Maddy's friend, not Geoffrey's. She's already taken sides after all she's been privy to in secret: the tarot reading foretold Geoffrey's affair and big change, a storm of a change. Everything's out in the open now, but she wants to do the just thing and make sure Geoffrey is okay. There's been no word.

Another doctor enters the room and encourages Maddy and Nadine to converse, one-sidedly, with me. Maybe I can hear you. Maybe your words will bring me out of my sleep as if in some fairytale: wake the fairy. Maddy is clueless about what the four boys said to me when they went ballistic on my ass. The police haven't revealed that much yet and Maddy only wants me awake, smiling, involved again.

Nadine listens to Maddy share memories about her parents and Nadine chimes in. She called them several hours ago and they planned to put the pedal to the floor and drive all night and day to get home to Ohio, put the R.V. away, and—despite her father's fear of airplanes—fly out to Middleton on the next available flight. They said they'd be there soon if all goes well. They can't believe what Nadine's told them; they don't even ask about Geoffrey. No one knows anything about him and Nadine stretches and says: "Maddy?"

"What?"

"Sorry to interrupt, but I think I'll go ask where Geoffrey ended up."

"You do what you have to."

"Don't be mad at me. Please—I've called everyone in your family and his family needs to know what's happened also."

"That makes sense."

"What then?"

"I just can't bring myself to care what happens to Geoffrey right now. If I'm a monster, so be it."

"Oh, Honey, no. Just let me handle this part."

"I still need to finish talking to you about that summer out on your screen porch."

"The tarot cards again?" Nadine wants to tell Maddy to just drop it, just stop obsessing about what the cards revealed. Maddy knew from the get-go the real meaning of the cards while Nadine had only a feeling about Geoffrey's infidelities, and somehow, the topic had always been changed; they didn't need the cards to tell them this fact.

"Yes."

"Do you know I threw them away the next morning?"

"They scared you, too, huh? You never let me forget how potent your powers of intuition are."

"Well, you have to admit the reading was kind of prescient, and, I admit, scary too. With all that's happened and all that is happening. Major change. I thought you didn't believe in it? That it was only a game."

Nadine once again remembers sitting across from Maddy at the shore-side cabin on Swan Lake, in the shade, getting tipsy late afternoon with her best friend. She takes the cards, completely shuffles time and time again, and turns over the first card. She remembers the card is a high sword number, a sign of hidden conflict. Then she can't remember anything except the overall message of the reading: You will face great challenges ahead and major change in your life and the lives of your family, but not in a positive way; the message is so negative Nadine shakes it off, makes her dwell on Maddy and what the future holds for her friend.

Maddy says, "Remember? That deck was really supposed to only show good things. Don't reverse the cards and all that, you said."

"I gave up reading tarot cards for the rest of my life."

"Very melodramatic of you. You said the cards only touched on the positive."

"All I can think is the positive will arrive after all the negative shit has run its course."

"And I'm in the thick of it," Maddy says.

"I know you'll get through this."

"Geoffrey had an affair."

Nadine never lets on that she knows this already; she was waiting for Maddy to tell her.

"You probably already know. We tried to keep it our little secret but somehow it's come back to haunt us and I guess it always will. He's had several affairs. All the way back to just before we were married and in the getting to know each other phase—boy, he kept that part hidden and it was bound to boil over at some point; when I sat petrified at the side of the road with Chris in his child carrier so long ago. I knew Geoffrey had a roving eye, that he needed something more, that there was also something dark inside of him. The cards didn't tell me anything I didn't already know but they made me worry about it more. I closed up a lot after that and I blame myself."

Nadine grasps Maddy's hand to reassure her that she understands, and says, "No, don't do that. You had nothing to do with Geoffrey's choices. He's the selfish one. He'll probably blame you for his serial adultery, men always do—bastards—and they so easily want to make us the bad ones when they're weak."

"What about Chris?" There's a long pause and both women stare at the wall in front of them. Finally, Maddy says, "See? You know too much to think I shouldn't blame myself. You blame me too."

"Oh, no, Maddy. How could I do that?"

"Go. Nadine. Find out where Geoffrey is and call his sister. His own mother's dead."

"I remember."

"Geoffrey's father hasn't been in touch in years. I don't even know how to reach him."

"The Chess King?"

"That's what Geoff calls him. Geoff says Chris inherited The Chess King's prowess for the game, and maybe his smarts."

"He's traveled the world alone ever since his wife, Geoffrey's mother, died?"

"He traveled alone most of his life, even when married, since way before that because it seems The Chess King gave Geoffrey everything, including his ability to pick up women from time to time, like trip souvenirs."

"Who'd have thought chess players had such magnetic personalities." Nadine tries to lighten the atmosphere.

"Geoffrey's father is a cantankerous, egotistical troll of a man who has only cared about himself most of his life."

"I don't think I ever met him."

"You wouldn't have since he's never visited us here in Montana. Geoff wouldn't allow it."

"Well. At least that's one telephone call I won't have to make. What about his sister?"

"Nell. She's a piece of work, too. A lot older than Geoffrey with a whole different mind set. At one time Geoffrey called me his life buoy. He says I saved him from his family. Why does everyone's family have to be so dysfunctional?"

"Doesn't sound like the most conventional, by no means."

"Nadine, I'm surprised you don't already know this. Didn't we get drunk on cosmopolitans once and go over Geoffrey's family?"

"I vaguely recall."

"Geoffrey doesn't sit around talking about his parents with me. Or his sister, either. She's nice enough. Loved her mother to death. Idolized her really. It was Nell and Geoffrey choosing between their parents and realizing too late the father lived by a different creed."

"But Geoffrey's father and mother got married, had two kids, and they remained together, until she died."

"When The Chess King met his wife, Geoffrey's mother, in the late '40s he traveled the world selling optical glass to laboratories. He had schemes he followed, connections to mines, and lots of chutzpah. He hired her to be his secretary when he stayed in London and they had a long working relationship. He traveled for his work six months a year and asked for her hand in marriage in 1949. Nell was born the next year. I remember this because Geoffrey and Nell are eight years apart."

"I can't believe I never knew about Nell."

"There's always family people don't want to talk about. But the one deal breaker, the most important thing to him, The Chess King did, before asking Geoffrey's mother if she'd marry him, was he laid out how third parties would be involved."

"Affairs?"

"Yes. He was up front about it and wanted her to know that since he traveled six months out of the year he couldn't possibly remain faithful, sexually, to her. He didn't believe in monogamy."

"A lot of young people today don't either. Imagine. An unorthodox sexual pioneer cut loose in the '50s."

"The Chess King didn't expect his wife-to-be to just wait for him either. They talked it all out and she could seek what she needed also."

"How big of him."

"So, you see, Geoffrey learned this behavior from his parents."

"Again and again. Pass the comfort bag, please."

"Geoffrey and I didn't have a contract, an understanding, like his parents. He probably grew up thinking it was a silent understanding."

"It is kind of wild if you think about it."

"A total difference in time. Geoffrey's parents would be good fodder for an entire trilogy."

"Write it then. Geoffrey's parents were probably the early prototype of the swingers who came later in the '60s."

"Geoffrey's mother married The Chess King."

"Why do you call him that?" Nadine asks.

"Because that's what he is. He'll tell you he's the best chess player in the world, smarter than all the computers programmed to beat Kasparov. He says he has an I.Q. of 174, that he's a genius."

"A genius troll? What bridge does he haunt lately? I sense you've never believed the biography of Geoffrey's father."

"I don't think Geoffrey ever spoke the truth to me where his family is concerned, if he ever did about anything."

Both women stir their conversation at my bedside. I can't react to any of this information. Maybe the doctors and nurses are right: keep speaking to me because I can hear you and maybe your words will bring me out of my relentless sleep. I want to remember what my mother says about my grandparents; I don't remember them at all and they sound like they can fill in holes of unspoken yearning.

Maddy continues, "The Chess King still travels the world playing chess with all the rest of his cronies, and yes, I guess quite a few of them are still alive, but most of them have died and he plays with a younger chess crowd and still beats them—that's just a guess at this point but I like to think of Geoffrey's father as winning."

"How old is he?"

"He must be in his eighties, a fit, vitamin-popping octogenarian, but Geoffrey forbids speaking about him and hasn't for a long time. Nell doesn't even dare bring him up in conversation. She wants Geoffrey to reconcile, and that's not going to happen."

"So there's no way to reach him."

"Maybe Nell has his number."

"Do you want me to call Nell? I can ask her just as easily as you can."

"She won't understand why I'm not calling myself and give you grief about it."

"Just leave that worry to me."

"You, fortunately, have never met Nell."

"That bad?"

"Worse."

"But you're biased beyond belief. No one gets along one hundred per cent with the in-laws and if you show me someone who does I'll introduce you to a liar."

"Let me make a prediction—you'll call and Nell will act all concerned; her heart is in the right place, but she won't care about what's happened to Chris, her nephew; one of the main reasons I'm not ready to call Nell is because I'd have to tell her what Geoffrey did and that he's on death's door with people all around him who just can't wait to scold him for taking pills. If he were here I'd scold him for not taking enough of them."

"You don't mean that."

"Right now I most certainly do."

It's very early in the morning and Nadine stands up, stretches the stiffness away, and says, "I'll handle Nell. Be my usual sourly optimistic self; and afterwards I'll check on Geoffrey, see if he needs anything and then I'll be right back with cafeteria coffee." She leaves the room as Maddy takes my limp hand in her own and then rests her head gently against the side of the bed. "You're going to be all right," she whispers. She can feel her own limbs going numb. She doesn't register this fact and no one can help her. The machines pumping and blinking and bleeping next to me are the only things keeping me asleep.

COMPLICATIONS

DESPITE HER EARLIER meditation session and the head-clearing lighting of the lamp and the peace-offering ashes swept across the table in her orange and red meditation chamber Deepika couldn't get me out of her thoughts. She will never understand why, I, the boy, she calls me, in her thoughts anyway, followed her home in the middle of a rainstorm. Why I left so angry she understands (she didn't see me as angry... only uninformed, frustrated), but, nonetheless, look where anger brought me; she will not allow sadness to overwhelm her.

At the end of subbing for Maddy, Deepika feels exhausted by the back and forth clinical negation of the impulse of the writers in the class. The spark is there but what if it doesn't ignite anything but shite?

Travis follows Deepika out of the room asking about Maddy and she cuts him off and acts as if all information is a state secret. She doesn't like giving Travis the brush-off but by spending only one hour with the boy she knows he's the type who takes and takes and takes up all the energy around him without any concern for the people within his sphere who then suffocate. He's left stunned by her abrupt departure.

Deepika throws her book stack onto the backseat of her Saab. She sits in the car grasping the steering wheel until her fingers pale. She makes her mind up, puts the car in drive, and backs out of the parking space. She drives to the hospital and parks in another parking garage, generic, and somehow unwelcoming. She tries to compose herself and what she's going to say. Her actions are for once not totally of her own design. They aren't overly calculated. Her hair's a mess of wispy strands. She rarely leaves the house without any lipstick and her face is drawn and needs a touch-up. How can I look pale? Got to get the Montana sun to shine once more before winter starts like a demon.

Should I do this? Deepika asks herself this question again and again, plays it over in her mind. Go see what happened to Geoffrey and her unborn child's half-brother.

She doesn't know what she'll do if she bumps into Madison. Last spring they avoided contact with each other as best as they could. No one knew the real reason except Geoffrey, Madison, Deepika, Nadine, and now me.

As Deepika struggles out of her car and shuts her door, the sound, distorting and loud, makes her shiver. It's late in the day and the structure remains shadowy and dim and barely lit by the orange safety sconces placed high up on the concrete pillars. Get moving. No one could feel her wariness. No one knows how she struggles with all that has come before. The way I stormed out of her little bungalow. How could she meditate after that? Yet somehow she did, little knowing I was approaching my fateful doom. Deepika wishes she had known me before. She wishes I had taken an interest before, that we could even be friends; she seems to lack the gene that makes so many others pass judgment upon the actions of others. This pregnant woman from Northern India, a bustling fishing city on the coast embroiled in poverty issues and the class struggle of the wealthy and the very, very poor and the warring politics so close to Kashmir, is the woman with whom my father sought solace and redemption and a cure for his depressing mindset.

Deepika presses her palms together and then folds her fingers into one ball at the end of her brown wrists. Her winter coat is tan, puffy a bit. She's not used to the chill. The coat doesn't close around her stomach. She walks into the hospital and heads straight to the admittance desk.

"Excuse me," Deepika says to a pink-jacketed admissions receptionist, an elderly woman with short, pure white, eagle-feathered hair.

"I'll be with you in a moment," the woman replies with a winning tone of sympathy as if she's been holding people at bay for decades. She has it down pat. "Sorry about that. It seems so busy now with all the media—I just call them a bunch of sneaks—you must've heard." The receptionist is breathless, the nervous type, picking imaginary lint from her smock, smoothing her feathery hair to a slick bowl along her forehead.

"No."

"I shouldn't be saying anything anyway." To Deepika's surprise the woman becomes businesslike, instantly efficient as if a switch has been thrown. "What can I do for you? You're not with the press are you? You have to tell me if you are. I guess it's a law."

Deepika resists laughing. "No. I'm not with the press."

"I didn't think so. Are you looking for OB/GYN? That's the far entrance on the other side of the neighboring building, but you can get there from here if you use the tunnel."

Mesmerized by Deepika's growing belly, as Deepika continues rubbing in a slow circular motion, the woman will display another personality if Deepika sticks around and hypnotizes her into acting like a chicken. "I'm searching for information about a Geoffrey Bullet, spelled with a 'G' the old English way."

"Let me check." The woman's head ducks bird-like as she taps the name into her computer console. Her head pops back up. "I don't have a patient here registered with that name."

"Are you sure?" Deepika knows the woman is lying to her. She's not good at it. Her cheeks brighten redly and she can't keep eye contact.

"Positively," the woman says with forced cheer. "Are you a family member?"

"His family is here, too. I'm a close friend from the College."

"I can't help you."

The woman clams up and crosses her spindly arms across her chest. She's very suspicious now and always is; it comes with the job. She'll let her friends walk right by her desk without a question but someone comes in searching for the ill or abused or damaged and, without that family link, will not gain admittance unless permitted to do so.

"Thank you for checking," Deepika manages.

The woman picks up her telephone.

Deepika walks back to her Saab as the receptionist alerts security about the heavily pregnant Indian woman asking about The Family.

"I don't know," the receptionist says to the security guard who arrives five minutes later—after Deepika left the parking lot, too late—"She seemed strange to me, and not because she was from India either; she seemed to know something about the family with the boy in the coma."

"Did you get her name?"

"She didn't tell me that."

The guard is officious now filled with the realization he's not getting any information he can use for any purpose, but he keeps talking just to keep talking. Everyone in the hospital is jumpy, paranoid, and these cry-wolf calls are starting to bug him. The administrative receptionist feels important and she almost glows; she's only doing her job.

"How's the main hospital entrance? Overrun?"

The guard replies, "We got a good handle on the situation."

"I bet you never expected this much commotion when you came to work this morning."

"What's your full name? For my report."

"Joan. Joan Buckster."

"When did the woman, the woman from India, you say," the man pauses.

"Well she spoke with a slight accent. She also seemed very sharp. Smart."

"When did she come up to your desk?"

"Five, ten minutes ago now and I got a strange feeling about her. She was very pregnant and maybe that threw me off because: How many reporters are still up doing their job in their second trimester?" She asks the question like anyone who's been hanging around the medical profession would, as if the knowledge has sunk in through close proximity.

"I think we'll have to set up additional security down here at the Emergency entrance. I thought Jerome and Harrison could handle it but they probably don't have a clue about the woman you met. One nut from the local channel tried to get past Danny upstairs. He kept lying and lying about knowing someone, a doctor, a nurse, a patient care coordinator, and wouldn't stop until we escorted the bum outside . . . the nerve of the altruistic press, lying for the story."

"Makes you wonder if what they write isn't all just a bunch of lies, too, if they do it so easily."

* * *

Maddy rests her head next to my body on the bed. Nadine hasn't come back from her telephone call duty. The air smells stale in the small room with the curtain pulled across the middle dividing the space into two distinct areas. The doctors decide to move me to a very private room later in the day, when I'm even more stable. For now, there's another bed three, four feet away, empty, but I can't complain about a roommate even if I wanted to. The doctor hasn't been back in a while but the machines bleep and sound out an almost syncopated electronic trance.

Maddy wants to cry, and she would if she didn't feel so drained. She knows all of this but there isn't anyone who can reassure her and tell her everything is going to be all right. It's so bizarre. And the tableau is even more bizarre when Maddy realizes she can no longer move her legs, once again. They stop working like the episode in the classroom two nights ago, and she grows flustered, frustrated, and scared like she hasn't been since she was a little girl lost in the woods behind her parents' farm for an hour, and she can't move and I sleep in front of her with a ragged bandage covering the side of my face and most of my bowling ball head. I'm paler and weaker and not about to form audible questions.

Maddy thinks about Geoffrey then and wonders what's become of him and actually wishes he was right there beside her so he could help her stand. She figures he owes her more than he can ever repay her. They haven't been communicating well for weeks, and months before, until a good patch, when he showed up at the house and begged her to consider letting him come back. Why was I never around for his display? Why hide the reconciliation from your own son? Why ease Geoffrey back into the house without a word; without a warning, there he is when I get back from the library in late June, the hot humid week before the 4th celebration.

All he says at the first meeting in the kitchen, "Hi."

And that one word, despite every movie cliché, doesn't speak volumes. Life just goes on, as before, as if Geoffrey has only been away on vacation and no one wants to risk getting bored by flipping through the three thousand slides of his trip. So why ask anything about his time away?

Maddy finally ends up calling for a nurse with the bedside assistance button.

A young woman with long curly brown hair and a pinched face beneath the locks opens the door and whisks in as if expecting a short visit before heading back to the break room for coffee and laughter with the other nurses. She wears a nametag: Minnie.

"What seems to be the problem?" She gives me the once over, checks the machines with her eye on any buzz or blip that may be off, presses my wrist to find a pulse.

Maddy says, "I'm afraid it's me. I need help. I can't move my legs."

Now Minnie stops moving and recalibrates. She's aware of procedure and her strong efficiency has always given her the highest quarterly evaluation marks. She has to take care of me first though, and says, "Any changes in Chris's condition?"

"He hasn't even blinked involuntarily. I'm being serious here. I don't think comas are catching but I can't seem to stand."

Minnie kneels down next to Maddy and with curiosity blazing across her features rests a palm on my mother's thigh above her knee. "Can you feel my hand against your leg?"

"No."

"What about on your calf, here? Any tenderness?"

"Nothing. Not even a tingle."

"Has this lack of feeling in your legs ever happened before?"

Maddy lets it all out. She says, "About two months ago I noticed a tingling in my feet, but it went away and I didn't think about it again. They went to sleep for longer than ever before, and the normal tingling happened and nothing like that for another month. Three other times, more recently, something went off in my legs and feet. I almost tripped down the stairs the other day but nothing like two days ago. I couldn't move my legs for two or three hours at school. I've been under a lot of stress, emotionally"—and again she wants to curse Geoffrey, she wonders if she's babbling, repeating herself, something she always does when she's nervous.

After the car accident she resists going to doctors, can't stand spending time in their presence, checks the internet, self-evaluates and lives—"I thought about getting checked by my own doctor but with what's been happening I never got around to it." Something else always gets in the way—and she understands she's being selfish, instantly regrets her tone of voice, the sharpness she uses to answer the nurse—and Maddy continues, "I'm sorry."

The nurse doesn't give Maddy's apology another thought. Minnie can tell from Maddy's tone of voice that she's scared and doesn't want to cause her to slip into a panic. By the numbers, Minnie. She can better assess the patient—she doesn't say: this poor family—if she moves her onto a stretcher and escorts her down and over to the adult E.R. That's procedure. Anyone who becomes hurt or injured or sick within the hospital itself must be brought to the E.R. for assessment.

"Okay, Madison? Right?"

"Maddy."

"I'm going to get the other nurses and we're going to take you to a doctor right away. She doesn't say: Don't move, I'll be right back. Minnie leaves to go round up a couple nurses to help transfer Maddy to a stretcher.

The door opens and three people, Minnie and two other nurses, a man with a goatee neatly trimmed to a point, and a heavyset woman with dyed blonde hair bustle in rolling a stretcher. All of them move efficiently; all of them show professional concern.

Minnie says, "Nick, would you get vitals? I've started a chart."

"Sure," Nick replies as soon as Maddy's lifted carefully onto the stretcher without any feeling in her lower extremities. He tightens the cuff around her arm and takes her blood pressure. Maddy stares at me. This isn't your fault, she thinks. You fight this, Christopher. You wake up.

"My friend, Nadine, will be right back."

"We'll send her over to the E.R."

"Can someone get her? Please. She's making calls to my family."

"I'll check the waiting room and see if I can find her."

"Thank you," Maddy says with some relief; she's not even worried about this turn of events. It's not as if this lack of feeling in her legs hasn't happened before; it's not as if she wants to get used to it either but with me unconscious on the bed in front of her trying to heal from the beating it's not as if she's had anything else to take her mind away from my situation, not that she needs anything to take her mind off my situation.

The room empties of everyone and the door shuts soundlessly. I stay, in the quietly beeping room, alone. There are no more family members who will sit by my side. There are no family members to sit beside my mother. Good thing she has Nadine.

* * *

I shift time once again and concentrate on another doctor's voice: "We need a contract from you." It's early in the morning and my father feels hunger as his stomach turns. He hasn't eaten much and his stomach is in revolt, but he feels hungry.

"What kind of contract?" Geoffrey, dressed in hospital scrubs, sits in an office overlooking the parking structure. Steam flows from rooftop vents. The sky remains gray and forbidding.

"Well," the appointed doctor says, "that depends on you."

Geoffrey wonders at the use of the word contract and how similar the legal and medical professions try to be. He grows bored, and his mind starts philosophizing. He barely makes eye contact with the doctor in the industrial office. He imagines himself in a cold Siberian prison interrogation room, just for a second, and then he drifts back to contracts again and how he and all people make them and break them day after day. He's sick and tired of people depending on him; his actions are reprehensible and people shouldn't depend on him anymore. Geoffrey knows Maddy won't be depending on him any time in his near future, as last straws go. The medical staff hasn't told Geoffrey yet about me, asleep and barely healing three buildings over and alone again. They have to ascertain his state of mind, the fragility of the depressive, whether he's harmful to himself or not and whether or not that's controllable through substances.

If I hadn't met up with Ellis and his three cohorts, twice in one day, I'd be home answering the telephone and telling people my dad has gone nuts. Even Lance would get the cold shoulder from me but the truth would weigh in and I would let him have it. His father's best man standing up so long ago and taking his time relishing his own sense of self-importance, his time in the spotlight. Lance, good buddy—call me Uncle Lance, please, Chris—your best friend from ages ago has split the sheets, he's insanely depressed and there's nothing you can do about it so don't even think of flying out here to save the day.

"I'm tired," Geoffrey says to the doctor. "And I'm hungry."

"I'll let you go back to your room in a few minutes. Lunch is in an hour. As I was saying, you were brought to us because you took too many pills and drank too much alcohol in combination."

"I had a bad day." Geoffrey can't believe he's trying to justify his actions; he wrestles with the issue himself: I've had a bad year.

"Bad days tend to multiply."

"Are you speaking from experience?"

The doctor has a face weathered by too many Montana winters, and he adjusts the file of paper in front of him and smiles, wrinkles deepening. This smile of his doesn't look natural. He doesn't do it much and it looks like it pains him. "Let's just say there aren't any easy answers. I was telling you about the next step: getting a contract from you."

Geoffrey remains silent and slouches down in the overstuffed chair across from the doctor's desk. He hates it when I slouch and he always tells me to sit up in my chair, couch, back seat of the car, as if I've caught some type of slacker syndrome. If he only knew.

"A contract. Not just between you and me but between everyone on the floor. I can accept a verbal contract from you. Really what I'm asking for is some type of agreement stating you won't try and hurt yourself again."

"What if a verbal agreement won't do?"

"That's where my title comes in. I get to decide whether or not your word is good. You have to prove it to me."

"How enlightening."

"It's for your own safety and the safety of the other doctors, nurses, orderlies, and patients."

"Everyone here has to sign a contract?"

"Just the people conscious enough to realize they've tried to hurt themselves. Sometimes, in some people, this contract is broken rather quickly."

"I'm not going to hurt myself." Geoffrey says this as if the idea is preposterous.

"I'm glad to hear it."

"Or anyone else. I've done a good job of that already."

"Mr. Bullet, have you ever been in therapy?"

"No."

"Why do you think you took the pills last night?"

"I couldn't get out."

The doctor takes a paper cup from a stack on the file cabinet behind him and pours water from a pitcher. "Here," he says, and hands Geoffrey the glass.

"Do you still feel like you can't get out?"

"Yes. The light of day doesn't change that but I'm not going to hurt myself. How long do I have to stay here?"

"A minimum of 72 hours."

"What? Three days? That's absurd. Three days." Geoffrey says the last as a statement he can't wrap his head around.

"Yes."

"Or? Is there another option here?"

"Or until you feel up to it."

The doctor changed his line of questioning, "Do you know who brought you to the hospital?"

"No. I don't really remember much."

"What do you remember?"

"I was alone in the house. Chris, my son, had come home early from school."

"Do you know why?"

"Do I know why he came home early? No. We didn't say a word to each other, but he was angry with me. I can't believe—"

"What?"

"That I'm here."

The doctor got into the business because he'd started going to therapy in high school after his well-to-do father abandoned him, his mother, and two sisters after making bad real estate deals. There wasn't any money to pay for his hour talk each week for two years. The therapist was a family friend of his father and guilt played a huge factor in the arrangement. When he graduated from the University of Washington he paid back every dime. Of course the therapist didn't want to accept payment, but he did because it was important, and he then gave the money to a charitable foundation for kids. Dr. Minogue had his own clients and an office in downtown Middleton: enter the building, take the elevator to the fifth floor, turn right, go past four other plain walnut office doors, find the door with the plaque reading Dr. Minogue. The doctor had hours yet to fulfill his obligation, the debt so large he'd never stop volunteering for duty at the hospital's psychiatric wing. He needed to help other people in order to pay back his debt.

Dr. Minogue tells Geoffrey to relax and remain silent for a moment. Take a deep breath. He's witnessed too much depression not to realize this man in front of him aches for someone to wave a magic wand in front of him and heal his pain. Make all of the unpleasantness go away. A time machine couldn't do it.

"Do you know what a psych evaluation is?" Dr. Minogue asks after another minute of silence.

"It sounds sterile, boring."

"Well, yes. The questions are fairly generic but there are quite a few of them." Dr. Minogue lifts the stack of papers. "Let's accomplish the first step."

"The contract."

"Yes."

"Where do I sign?"

"Right here. This is a form stating you won't try to hurt yourself or anyone else."

"I'd like to call my lawyer. Did Harry tell you I want to speak to my lawyer?"

"Yes. You can make a call to your lawyer after we get the contract from you."

"What if he needs to read the contract first?"

"This isn't the difficult part, Mr. Bullet."

"Call me Geoffrey. O.K. As long as you hear me."

"Everything is going to get better for you." A platitude so meaningless at this moment in Geoffrey's life it almost makes him cackle, but then they would think he's crazy.

"I'm sure you're right. Doctors always are."

"Let's get through this. Now. Where were you born?"

"Connecticut."

"Do you have any siblings?"

"One sister. Nell. She's eight years older. We're not what you'd call close."

"Where does she live?"

"Southern California. Palm Springs."

"You don't have a close relationship with Nell?"

"Let's just say I don't think she's any happier than I am but somehow she thrives and perseveres."

"What about your parents?"

"My mother died more than ten years ago. My father's still alive, as far as I know."

"You don't know for sure?"

"He and I haven't spoken since before my mother died.

Nell would let me know if anything happened to my father." Geoffrey repeats the phrase Psychobabble Horseshit over and over again in his mind. How will this possibly help? He continues to think of his life as one straight line heading into a blank future without options.

Geoffrey's tone of voice makes it clear to the doctor not to discuss his father. Dr. Minogue catalogues this fact and continues with the next question.

* * *

Now mid-morning, Maddy lays prone on a stretcher in a private cubicle of a room in the E.R. and answers her own set of questions from a resident, Doctor Fusil, who appears to have just graduated from medical school. Doctor Fusil, a vibrant, youthful woman with long, straight, red hair tests Maddy's reflexes with a small triangle-shaped rubber mallet. Maddy watches closely as Doctor Fusil smiles beatifically, the angles and planes of her face shining, coltish and enthusiastic, making little adjustments with her equipment. Maddy immediately takes to her bedside manner. She thinks, what other choice do I have? In for a penny.

"I can't move my legs."

"Is that the same as feeling your legs?"

Maddy seems puzzled by the doctor's question; she's at a loss. She wants to answer correctly as if there really is only one perfect response.

"When I press on the underside of your foot what do you feel?"

"Barely anything."

There are two emergency room nurses working busily around Maddy's stretcher as Doctor Fusil examines Maddy's body. One of them takes blood from her left arm, fills four tiny vials with different colored caps and labels them with stickers. The nurse asks the doctor what tests she should mark on the forms and leaves to give the blood to a patient transporter to take to the blood lab way down the hall, the beginning of the slow journey. One of the nurses, stressing with a bit of crankiness, says, "The tests should arrive in thirty minutes, quicker if the transporter doesn't dawdle and gossip with the x-ray techs on her way."

"We'll need to get films," says the doctor. Maddy feels relieved the questions have come to an end and asks if Nadine can stay by her side. One of the nurses leaves and brings Nadine in from the waiting room. There's no one else to sit by; there's no one up keeping watch next to me, and Maddy almost bursts into tears. She has plenty of practice keeping them at bay; there's no one upstairs talking sense into her husband; Maddy finally realizes there's no miracle left to wish for yet still she refuses to let one tear escape. She thinks, with futility, how each member of her family is being treated in this hospital, a horrible coincidence, and a similarity that unsettles her more and more as each minute passes.

Nadine grabs her hand. Watching her best friend's family fall apart makes her act without thinking, fast and jerky. She says softly to Maddy, "Everything's going to be okay." She knows she's talking just to be talking. "Did the doctor say anything?"

"They're at the start of their testing phase. They don't have a clue yet."

"It'll be okay. You're just stressed out. No one could blame you."

Maddy doesn't say: Yes, they could.

"Did you reach my parents?'

"Your dad and mom are probably close to home by now but I didn't reach them. I left a message on their answering machine to call your cell, which I'll keep for you. If they leave a message I'll go outside and call them back."

"They should've been home by now. I worried about my dad driving all night. They'll be exhausted once they get here."

"Your sister, on the other hand, was home. What a piece of work."

"Rhea's not that bad."

"You won't be able to convince me of that. Anyway, I could tell by her reaction she thinks there's some ulterior motive to what's going on."

"She didn't say she'd be coming right away?"

"What do you think? You and Rhea never got along. From what you told me about your childhood you're lucky she didn't bury you in the backyard garden."

"That's why you love me." Nadine's trying to keep her mind off her legs, her immobility, and me; Maddy doesn't want to keep her mind off me. We've both been in the hospital at the same time before and she remembers this. She wants to keep my image in the forefront. Nadine's the only person she allows to malign her family; she's met them and somehow kept a straight face at the dinner table when Rhea's criticisms and little judgmental jabs littered the conversation.

"My sister and I are more like stepsisters," Maddy says, "but that doesn't mean I don't love her."

"She always struck me as a very competitive wench if you ask me."

"I didn't ask, but don't hold back on my account," Maddy says, sighing once again. She thinks about how she and her sister get along because of their parents. Why can't you two girls be nice to each other? Maddy remembers what her mother always had to say to them growing up. You're the only family you've got. Rhea's jealous of how strong Maddy always appears to be, how doors open for her, how liked Maddy is, how teachers always compared her to Maddy in a way that made Rhea think she was the ill-favored one, that she somehow was less solid. Maddy's jealous of the constant fawning attention her younger sister gets from her parents. She went away to college and Rhea started 8th grade, braces off finally, hair large with a brassy curly perm, and an attitude. Mom just rolled her eyes after having survived the trials of Maddy's high school years, the tug of war, the struggle of wills, the constant whining and fighting; Maddy's mother knew what to expect and somehow that helped. Rhea, whenever picking a petulant fight with Mom, hated it most of all when her mother said: I went through the same thing with your sister so don't think I've changed my mind now that you're starting to date. The answer is no—but Mom— and the answer will still be no in the morning. There's no way you can stay out any longer on a school night."

"So—Rhea isn't coming. That's actually a relief."

"Oh, I didn't say that. She's going to wait until she speaks to your parents."

"That sounds just like what Rhea would do."

"Nell, on the other hand, is booking the first flight out of Palm Springs and should be arriving in a matter of hours, probably by late afternoon. Fasten your seatbelts."

"Great."

"Did I ever tell you sarcasm is your finest trait?"

"What did she say?"

"Nell imperiously demanded to know why I, just a friend of yours, was making the telephone call. When I told her you were also being treated in the E.R., she scoffed and asked who was taking care of her brother."

"Did she ask about Chris?"

"No."

"That's a good aunt for you."

"You have Rhea, and Geoffrey has Nell. Maybe they can share a hotel room?"

"In better days Geoffrey and I often tried to figure out which sister-in-law was the worst growing up and who would win if both of them were put in a boxing ring. At least Rhea never stuffed me into a rolled-up sofa bed like Nell did to Geoffrey. She left him there for hours. He loves to remind Nell of that babysitting experience. She opted out of the parenting thing. Imagine."

"In the ring, it would go several rounds and end up a draw."

"Nell's probably miffed because she's the official hypochondriac of the family—any new finding in the medical field and she's on the phone to her doctors. She'll fly in and take over the role as expert in the field. She has to be the center of attention. God forbid someone die before her. That was mean. I'm just venting. I don't mean it."

"Yes, you do, and it's okay. Well, at least she's flying in without waiting for parental permission."

"Geoffrey, remember, doesn't even know if his father is still alive."

"Why does The Chess King always pop up in

conversations about Geoffrey?"

"He never told me why there's this rift. Not really."

Nadine wants to keep Maddy's mind occupied, diverted, and she says: "I knew there's more to tell."

"Why do you care about him?"

"I just find his life story interesting. There's no one in my family history who can come close to his exploits."

"The short but colorful biography of Geoffrey's father—all I've gathered after so many years is that his father, now keep in mind I've never met the man, has a genius-level I.Q."

"You said that already. He's a genius. Geoffrey's a genius, Chris is a genius. That word's been redefined so many times, any kid is now a genius for learning how to tie his shoes in the dark."

"Are you going to let me talk?"

"Just don't repeat yourself."

"Bite me."

Nadine feigns umbrage, *tut tut*s under her breath.

"Please stop, Nadine. Don't get me started. Okay, what else did The Chess King do? Geoffrey says he worked at Los Alamos during World War II with special clearance to speak to Fermi and the rest of the physicists who built the bomb and never lost a game of chess to any of the big brains. He still carries a rolled up chess game—the board is a kind of sturdy but flexible rubber—wherever he travels. He keeps the plastic chess pieces in a felt bag. If he doesn't have anyone to play with he recreates great historic matches the masters of the game played.

"He's also a card shark and sleight-of-hand master who spent six hours a day in front of a mirror training himself to be able to deal from the bottom of the deck without being caught. No one wanted to play poker with him after he took the pot time and time again. The Chess King had a lot of free time on the base. When he got out of the military he fell into the lucrative business of importing optical glass and traveled to mines in South America and all over Europe. Geoffrey states he did a huge black market business in communist countries in the early '50s, optical glass, and gemstones."

"Somehow I can picture him as a spy, a short, bald

James Bond."

"According to Geoffrey he's a troll."

"I definitely would've liked to meet him."

"For a game of chess at least."

"Cross the troll's bridge."

"So, The Chess King traveled the world selling his glass and playing chess with other world champions. He hired a secretary in Paris to handle his growing business. The C.I.A. kept tabs on him after the war and even tried to recruit him because he had access to so much privileged information during wartime."

"Just like in that movie. Except the crazy part about the C.I.A. being imaginary characters."

"Yep. Basically he was a geek who loved getting away with scams. The C.I.A. showed up at his hotel room when he was in Rome once and almost arrested him for selling contraband to communist countries."

"What happened? The troll grows more interesting by the minute."

"Geoffrey's father isn't someone he likes to bring up in conversation, and I've always honored his wish."

"Until now."

"Geoffrey's done many more dishonorable things."

"Shhhh," Nadine says with a finger pressed against her lips for emphasis, "They may be listening."

"Who?"

"Geoffrey and his father . . . and the men in black suits, listening devices in their ears."

"Ha ha, well, by then, McCarthy was on his communist witch hunts and the C.I.A. questioned anyone who wasn't under their thumb. The Chess King was given a warning and a telephone number to call if he should ever fall into the hands of the enemy."

"Now I know you're making all this up. You do make a living by creating fiction."

"I assure you I'm not doing that."

"It all seems so farfetched; our little Geoffrey raised by a rebellious imp with a genius-level I.Q."

"174 to be exact. That's higher than Einstein in case you don't subscribe to Genius Quarterly. He did teach Geoffrey how to make the world's best Bolognese sauce. Taught to him by the Roman owner of a small dinner café. I think you've raved about it once or twice."

"It is the best," Nadine admits, "so maybe that part about Italy is true."

A nurse pops into Maddy's cubicle and says they're waiting to schedule a series of tests: x-ray, CT Scan, MRI and so on throughout the afternoon and early evening. The nurse is sympathetic to what's happening and that's why they've given Maddy the private trauma bay, even though it's very small. The press remain on the prowl outside the hospital and their numbers grow by the hour. Security stays doubly tight and the hospital administrator is in a snit trying to keep them at bay."

Maddy says, "I'd rather live in a world where Geoffrey's father has superpowers and his fortress of solitude is built in the shape of a rook, the grounds laid out like a chessboard. The secretary The Chess King hired in Paris was on vacation when they met. She was born in England. Mary. And he and Mary fell in love."

"It's all very romantic."

"She was a lovely woman. She was at our wedding, and died a few years after that." Maddy stays quiet for a few seconds before continuing, "But, The Chess King told Mary up front he'd be traveling up to six months a year. He told her he wouldn't be able to stay faithful to her and he never expected her to remain faithful to him either."

"A sexual rebel."

"Who knew? We covered this part."

"And this was the '50s?" Nadine asks.

"I guess he could be called a sex pioneer."

"And his wife agreed with his piggish conditions?"

"Completely. They were married in New York City. Tried London for a while before moving back to the East coast. Mary gave birth to Nell. She must've been a handful because eight years passed before Geoffrey was born. The thing Geoffrey says, and I believe him about this, is that his mother, even though she agreed to The Chess King's little sex loophole, never strayed."

"He grew up with someone who believed married people

didn't have to remain faithful from the get-go."

"And he followed in his father's footsteps."

Nadine quickly comes back with, "Remember the tarot cards called for major changes."

"Again with the cards. Let's drop the cards and never bring them up again."

"Life can be laid out so precisely sometimes."

"Yeah, and other times it can remain such a mess," and Maddy stays silent for a long time after she says these words to Nadine. She grows tired of Nadine trying to keep her mind off her ailment, me, alone, and she doesn't know what else to do.

* * *

Deepika has one true friend in the Middleton area. There're other friends she barely trades letters with once a year, all from her former life at Emerson College in Boston, her undergraduate and graduate school days spent toiling away. Then ten years living in the Boston area to stay close to her brother and his growing family. She loves Boston, the history there isn't fake; it's measured in centuries, not decades. Ever since she moved west, thousands of miles to Montana, with a two-year obligation and the promise of a continuing relationship if that went well (and that's not happening now), after a one-year stint living in Sun Valley, she tired of keeping up with most of her friends long distance; she's always the one who has to make the telephone calls. Just catching up. How are you? Her sentences became shorter and her listening skills deepened until she started uttering hello and goodbye with little or nothing in between.

It happens.

You decide to move. You're the one who left. Deepika heard this before from her own family. The ones back home in India now just getting over the monsoon season—drying out—and the brother who, after his undergraduate and medical school days, still lives in Boston with his perfect

Bengali wife and their three children, almost teenagers now—the trend today in America is to have three children and Deepika's brother has always followed the day's social trends. He chose a career of high esteem: a doctor. He followed Deepika to American colleges and spoke with an even harsher, yet still lyrical, accent; he's surrounded by more people telling him to please repeat what he just said than she ever was, but his writing is atrocious.

Deepika meets Liv, her one true friend, for tea at one of the college coffee houses in the late afternoon. The sky darkens with more rain clouds as if Middleton has been calling for a loud, seething party.

Liv is a longtime resident of Middleton who lives near the college campus. She has nothing to do with the school although she does make a comfortable living off the students and their parents who come into her Big Sky College Logo Shoppe. Didn't work for it; her life is totally separate. Doesn't have to drive through it to accomplish her daily errands. But she enjoys the fruits of the college campus nonetheless and wonders at the perpetually youthful crowd, as if she's the only one aging and everyone else has taken a sip from the fountain of youth.

Liv also owns the small bungalow Deepika lives in so technically she's her landlord even though they remain as instantly close as if they grew up next door playing board games together; they've only known each other a little over a year and made an instant connection. Deepika views Liv as a blessing. Liv accepts Deepika's rent check monthly, but has always wanted to tell Deepika she need not pay rent the last month of her stay. She didn't even take a security deposit; it isn't how she does business anyway. Liv believes this extra generosity will somehow taint their relationship so she takes Deepika's check when she hands it to her after they sit down. Liv quickly pushes the check down into the depths of her huge brown leather purse. She doesn't want to count how many times money comes between friends and acquaintances, and family too, turning the friendships into something bitter nine times out of ten. Deepika's already told Liv she's leaving early, moving away, and is overwhelmingly sorry to leave mid-term, gives her another month's rent on the check just to help even though Liv wouldn't hear of it. Liv will cash the check, though, and find a tenant within two weeks to take over the bungalow. I picture someone slovenly, clothes piled up on the floor, toothpaste hardening in the sink, a meditation chamber now in a horror.

How can I possibly know the future from this moment? This is new, and I don't like it because I can't see anything in that future direction that isn't murky. The present, the past, are clearer to me, but the future isn't laid out and feels like a book in the restricted section of the library, where you must ask permission before its contents can be revealed.

"That covers everything, Liv."

"You didn't have to. I told you."

"I realize that, but it's what I promised. I'll be leaving soon and with the house empty you can try to rent it to someone before the holiday season starts."

"How are you feeling?" Liv asks, trying to change the subject with an upturned smile. Her lips are drawn with a dark orange lipstick and heavily applied to compliment her dyed simmering-orange hair. It keeps the gray away and is so much more festive. Liv always says this to anyone who mentions her hairstyle.

"Honestly, not so—" Deepika searches for the right word: "content." She starts to stand and Liv asks what she needs. "Oh. The milk. As if contentment can be reached by imbibing dairy products."

"I'll get it. You just rest." Liv grabs the small container of whole milk and brings it to the table with the jar of honey."

Deepika has shared with Liv her love of taking her tea with milk and rich dark honey. Her mother and aunts would sit around most late afternoons drinking tea, and they put twice as much honey in and swapped stories. Most of the stories told were true but embellished into heroic proportions. Her mother's sister, Amman, who lived in the South, would tell the most colorful stories, these centered around her husband and his ongoing struggle to make ends meet. She always liked Amman's husband even though in the stories he came across as a loveable bumbler.

"What's going on with you? Did the power go out last

night like it did over in Crow Hill?"

"The electricity flickered on and off all night but I had my candles going." Liv takes another sip of her tea and mildly scalds her tongue.

Deepika doesn't tell Liv about Geoffrey. About the evening he showed up at her front door, out of the blue at the beginning of spring; she believes there isn't much to say. He sought comfort. Deepika opened her home to him with a perplexed smile. He said: I've been thinking a lot about what you said the other day—a faculty party where Maddy drank too much wine and slept on the couch in the spare bedroom and he was left alone with his thoughts—and I had to see you. Deepika never allowed Geoffrey to spend the night, never once. He stayed in a hotel room near his law office, spending money by the handful on dinners outside Middleton, presents, little trinkets to cheer Deepika up, even though she seldom needed to be cheered up; he behaved this way to make Deepika think she was special to him, to offer proof, but Deepika would always keep her skepticism bubbling beneath the surface. She was well aware of Geoffrey's reputation and he used her just as much as she used him. She gave most of Geoffrey's gifts away almost immediately after she told him to go back to my mother, to my father's wife. Deepika breathed a sigh of relief when she closed her door that final June afternoon. She vowed never to be the other woman, never again; it does surprise her how she gave in far too easily to a role she'd never imagined playing before. She wants to tell Liv everything; she knows Liv would understand; Liv has seen enough of the world to not be surprised by much, but Deepika doesn't want to ruin the friendship or strain it in any way; it's so hard to try to fit in, be assimilated, Deepika rarely tries anymore.

Liv smiles and realizes, for the first time, she feels impatience in Deepika's presence. She knows there are so many things Deepika hasn't told her and she always thinks: When she's ready. Maybe tonight she'll confide in her. Please.

"Did you go to your doctor last week?"

"Yes, for another ultrasound mystery tour."

Liv laughs and raises her mug to toast: cheers. "Is your

doctor still as funny as she usually is?"

"Yes. Definitely. There's something that makes me just squirm, happily, not with any regret, but with a sense I'm following in the footsteps of so many other women."

"You want this to be your singular experience and yours alone. Honey, when I had my kids the whole thing was so much more humane."

Deepika laughs.

"I remember being wheeled into my smart little hospital room as if I was a queen. I can't even remember my contractions. The drugs were that good!"

"You're not that old," scoffs Deepika.

"True, but when the nurse came in with the blessed magic knockout potion and I woke up with a baby girl I was very pleased nonetheless but still asked for more drugs. Two years later, the same vanishing memory occurred and I have a baby boy in my other arm. They wouldn't even let my husband into the room more than an hour a day. By the time I went home I thought I'd keep that habit up. George, you've gone past your hour limit today. I'd tell him this and we'd both crack up."

"It sounds like he shared your sense of humor."

"It's the most important thing in a relationship if you ask me. Both people have to be able to laugh together."

"And cry."

Deepika thinks of Geoffrey and how serious he always makes himself appear to be, and then tries and fails to remember a stray Oscar Wilde quote about equating seriousness with being shallow. She also doesn't remember Geoffrey ever laughing with her although she could get him to crack a smile through his ever-present ephemeral devotion. He was just scratching an itch. And she let him.

"Liv, I think we've just figured out why we can stand each other; we both laugh at life."

"So true."

Deepika exclaims that she likes her tea and then lets slip, "Did you know I was married once?"

"My, nostalgia must be in the air today. I didn't know you were married, not specifically, but I always assumed as much."

"Why?"

"You have that broken-in look. One of my neighbor's horses has that same wistful gleam in her eyes and it's not because I stopped feeding her carrots either."

"Ha ha—very funny."

"They moved the stud horse to a different pasture and the filly's never been the same. Besides, I read that short story you wrote about your divorce."

"Loosely based on fact," Deepika smiles.

"No, I always wondered why you had such a generic last name. Webber doesn't match your first name well."

"Deepika Webber. I guess not. My brother Ananda, the one who lives in Boston wants me to legally change my name back. He thinks my Americanized name distracts any possible legitimate, meaning Indian, suitors."

"Sexism at its best. I knew if I waited long enough, now that you've given me your last rent check, you'd let me know about your life in your own time. Life should be filled with mystery and revelation. I certainly haven't told you every little thing about my past."

"You were married once and had two children."

"Correct. I guess that sums me right up. See? You didn't even have to ask for any secrets or my personal philosophy of life."

"Okay. Was your husband your true love?"

"Now there's a question I'll shelve for later. He's been gone so long now. I still miss everything about him even when he'd trim his fingernails and forget to put them in the trash, just leave them about for me to find and shriek over."

"Ick."

"Yeah, but obviously, I even miss that much. Now, enough about me, what about this first husband of yours?"

"I married a fellow right out of college. We'd known each other three years, since we were sophomores. My family thinks I did it to receive my green card—my free pass into the United States. But I did love Andy. And the Green Card process is still a tiring ordeal for any couple. We were in love."

"You said that already," Liv interjects wryly.

"Yes, and I still love Andy. We weren't faking anything. We had a big wedding in Provincetown with all of his relatives who sat there in silence." God, Deepika thinks, all the alternative people running around in P-Town should not have been her first clue that Andy hid a rainbow flag on a back shelf of his closet. "Only a handful of my relatives could make the trip from India and they huddled together on one side of the church, nondenominational of course. I give them a lot of credit; they tried to mingle with my new in-laws at the reception. I later learned Andy's family was stunned and silent because they thought Andy would never get married to anyone."

"Why?"

"Oh, one major reason." Deepika raises her eyebrows to show shock and surprise.

"He was gay."

"Bingo. Liv, you're a good guesser."

"I have the gift. Did you know?"

"I don't think Andy knew. But, by getting married we silenced a lot of family talk on both sides of the ocean."

"How long did the marriage last?"

"Until I got my green card and Andy came out of the closet. We're still friends. I love him. He loves me. He lives in California with Terry, a great guy, life partner is how he labels his mate, and they're incredibly happy except about today's political climate, but who truly is happy about that? Either side can't be all that merry. We divorced and Andy applied to medical schools and went to Stanford."

"What's his specialty?"

"I told Andy I wasn't going to recruit more clients for him."

"He's a plastic surgeon."

"I promised Andy. And don't even begin to think you need any work done."

"I could use some freshening up."

"No, you couldn't."

"He must've really loved you."

"I know he did when he asked me to marry him. We could talk about the most intimate things just like any other couple. Even the sex was great."

"I've heard gay Indian sex can get pretty kinky."

"Don't make me laugh. We were married for over a year,

almost two. It took another year to get the divorce."

"You wrote a short story about it."

"As you remind me so well. Yes, if you want to call it that. My writing is about personal life but not necessarily always autobiographical."

"You and Andy Webber married because you were both considered outsiders."

"You know me so well."

"That's in your story. I'm almost quoting here verbatim. You can't pull something like that over on your number one fan."

"Don't put me up so high on a pedestal."

Deepika reaches over to a newspaper stand and takes the first section and hands it to Liv.

Liv says, "I read it this morning. Tragic."

"There's a boy in the hospital fighting for his life. Hooked up to machines because he met up with a group of raging juvenile delinquents."

"Not too far from where you live either."

"The boy had just left my house. In the pouring rain."

Liv's mouth opens to speak but no words come out. She stirs her tea and then stops. There isn't any liquid left in her mug.

"You're involved in this?" Liv finally asks. She places her hand on top of Deepika's hand, both lay flat and limp and then tighter when the contact continues.

Deepika wants to tell Liv everything—she notices Liv's eagerness beneath her humorously cranky surface; Liv is eager to know what happened to her and the choice she made last spring when she let Geoffrey Bullet into her house and then took him to her bed—and Deepika wants to let it all out as if she's in the world's largest panic room clearing her mind. Her thoughts race over the implications of my unannounced arrival at her door while the storm raged outside—just a time-loop recreation of Geoffrey slouching up her porch steps, raising a listless arm and knocking on Deepika Webber's door—and Deepika recreates her own face pinching tightly when she sees me, the son of the man she agreed to have sex with and create a child with, all of this blaring in her mind when she allowed me into her dry, cozy bungalow of lamp-lit warmth and true understanding. Why? Why? Why? Deepika asks herself this question again and again.

* * *

The lights in my hospital room glow dim fluorescent. The nurses check on my progress every fifteen minutes. I remain incapable of moving voluntarily. I don't feel anything. I shrink into the bed, stretching myself too thin.

If I could feel the pain in my head as the blood pulses through the swelling I'd scream for hours. One of my doctors, the neurologist, keeps an eye on me by *whooshing* into the room and making pronouncements to the nurses: Keep him stable and comfortable. The doctor must give a press conference in the front lobby of the hospital at seven p.m. and he's nervous, showing his tics, and the nurses want his demanding, pompous ass out of their way. They nod and keep their silence and tend to the business of letting me sleep and heal. The doctor still says to the nurses outside his door he doesn't know if the swelling will abate because there isn't any sign of that happening yet—things are still very much touch and go.

The police, with input from the city prosecutor's office, want to charge the three boys who initiated the attack as adults and the media will then get access to their names. Assault in the first degree, with the possibility of pleaing down to 2nd Degree assault—unless I die, which changes everything—I see the boys, the quartet, the bullies, tearing up at a future trial date, only a glimpse in the ether, and then nothing more.

My name, the victim's name, will remain largely unknown to the crime reporters who circle the hospital. Ellis Pallino, because he allegedly comes clean with the police first, and denies all wrongdoing, as if he only arrived late to a party, is seen as the least guilty—but the truth will out. With urging from his father, he sticks to his story: I'm a victim too, he somehow has the guts to say this when first questioned by the police the night before.

The police keep Ellis's name out of the newspapers since he's also a fifteen-going-on-lifer teenager, like me, and won't charge him as an adult, yet, they're reserving judgment, but they've heard deep bullshit before and know it when it so nervously spews out of Ellis's mouth. His story doesn't add up. They don't like it when Ellis's father barges into the police station. This helps the police imagine Ellis as one of the bullies who punched my lights out, the son like father thing. I won't remember Ellis doing anything if I could wake up; I blacked out and trauma victims have a hard time with memory. Try to think back to the street. Slick with rain. The way the three teenagers with the bat spoke barbs, anti-gay slurs, and punched me in the stomach first. The swing of the bat and my elbow shattering is a grainy digital photo engraved forever in my unconsciousness. The pain shoots sparks into my mind and I almost blacked out after that. My elbow in ruin and deep, deep pain. I know I tried to get up but I tripped and the bat rushing—

The three teenagers and Ellis will be separated and held indefinitely. Ellis's father raises a stink. He tries that old chestnut: Don't you know who I am?

The second detective on the case gets right up close in his face, seething, and says, "Do you know what your son did to that boy? Your good son hit him when he was down."

"Ellis didn't even touch that kid."

"You keep telling yourself that."

The father sputters and takes a deep breath before continuing his boorish behavior. He wants to protect his son from harm. It's understandable. "I believe my son."

"We have eyewitnesses who place your son there, along with the other three. And we have the baseball bat. Fingerprints. But it doesn't look so good for sonny boy, and we just want to know when the lying will end. Tell him we're very patient. Forensics will be back with the test results within the hour. We'll know more then. Won't we?"

Ellis's father's almost whining, "Ellis says he arrived only after the others were beating the . . . he says he tried to stop them."

"Is that the story he's sticking with?"

"It's no story. It's the truth."

"The three other boys and your son beat that kid with a vicious intensity. He's in the hospital across town struggling for his very life. You'd better hope he doesn't die, for your son's sake." The three other boys, who were almost old enough to vote in the coming election, were taken to three different rooms. Three different teams of police officers brought each of them into a solitary interview closet. One of the three, when the police arrived, was just leaving his house with a packed duffel bag. He threw it at the officers and hightailed it back into the house and was caught trying to climb over the chain link fence surrounding the backyard of the property.

Ellis's father fidgets in the uncomfortable, wooden, high-backed, scarred chair. He faces the detective with a permanent righteous air. He feels trapped by the abhorrent actions his son has taken. The media will have a field day and his name will be raked over the morning papers for weeks, if not months, years even, to come. The father wants to beat the stupidity out of his son. He and his mother are proper people, good parents.

The officer in charge of the interview begins, "Did you know the four of them called that boy Faggot? That they inferred that The Faggot had a crush on your son? That, because they thought that boy was weak, they went after him? Did you know that there's a witness to the whole event, someone who was walking behind them down the street? Another classmate who, when she heard what your son and the other three were shouting, hid behind a car across the street and watched the whole thing? She says, point blank, it was Ellis who delivered the final blow to that poor kid's head. She was too scared to try to stop it and you can't blame her because she's just a girl, effeminate, exactly what your son and the other three were accusing this boy of being—less than a man. Even if that boy was, is gay, that's no reason to beat him to a pulp. What your precious son did makes me sick."

This is news to Ellis's father. Ellis has lied to the police because he listened to his fatherly advice, a man who only wants to protect himself.

"I'll say it again in case you're having trouble processing things. Do you know what this girl witnessed at the end?" Ellis's father's shoulders slump in the chair and all the nervous energy drains from his body.

"The person who swung the bat at the boy's head—the very last hit—the boy who held the bat was your son."

"I don't believe that," Ellis's father mutters.

"Believe it."

"How could this happen?"

"Now, the three other teenagers, under separate questioning, all confirm this. They also say they never meant to hurt the boy at all. Blah. Blah. Blah. They're really angels without juvenile records longer than my arm. So, I have enough on your son to put him away for a long time, but since he's so young, any time he'll get from the system won't near be long enough. He lied to the detectives about what happened. I hope you can hire an amazing lawyer who won't try to distort the truth in any way. The city is calling this a hate crime, but you should thank your lucky stars that Montana doesn't recognize sexual orientation as a factor in their hate crime statutes. Your boy would be on a poster for this if it was law. You should go talk to your son. Get to know him, all of his secrets, the things you encouraged him to do."

"Now hold on there. You can't speak to me like this. I had nothing to do with this. You're walking on thin ice."

"Let me rephrase then so we can get back on solid ground here. I want you to go talk to your son and try to realize how much you don't know about him. If you don't think your saintly son is capable of such abhorrent violence against another person, think again."

"What do I say to him?" The detective believes Ellis' father may be the most pitiful man he's met in a very long time.

"Just listen to him. Ask him to tell the truth." There's a certain pedantic tone to the detective's words that makes Ellis's father cringe.

Ellis's father stands and leaves the police detective's office in a huff. He can't take the righteousness blazing there. He'll go see his son directly, sit across from him and wind up listening to the story he encouraged his son to remember after speaking to him last night. Then he'll look deeply into his son's eyes and he'll see someone he doesn't recognize at all. This handsome, young kid with so much to look forward to, and only then will he begin to cry softly. He won't wipe his tears away. They will fall. He's never cried in front of his son before.

Ellis will then also cry, but not for him—for his father and how badly he's let him down. For his mother—out of her mind with worry and incapable of composing herself—who left the police station that very morning and went right to bed after locking the doors and taking the telephone off the hook. The angry calls start almost immediately, trickling in after the first day and then escalating to madness in growing numbers. They condemn her and her husband and their parenting skills and she doesn't even begin to wonder how her son could be this monster people in the media are writing about; they don't even have his name yet some people are finding out; they don't know how kind and sweet he really is. She takes the phone off the hook. Ellis won't see the larger picture until his father tells him the jig is up and he needs to start telling the truth. "Don't lie anymore. I know I said I could get you out of this but everyone knows."

"What do they know?"

"They have a witness or witnesses who saw you take the bat and hit that boy." Ellis's father can barely speak in more than a whisper. He'll never be able to look Ellis in the eye again.

"Who?"

"They're not going to tell me that just yet but I'm sure it'll be in all of the papers soon enough."

Ellis fidgets across from his father in the small interrogation room.

"It was an accident," Ellis says. He hangs his head and his fingers fiddle with his prison jumpsuit pockets.

"How can four boys beating up a defenseless, smaller boy, be an accident? You tell me this because I really need to know how you can sit there and tell me it was all just an accident." His father's voice rises and a guard shoots his head into the room and tells him he better cool it or they'll take Ellis back to his cell.

"Okay," Ellis's father responds quickly. He knows their every word is being recorded, his actions in the room video recorded.

No one can believe what's happening there. Only the witness can remember Ellis hitting me at all. I was pushed to the ground holding my stomach, then my elbow, and I was trying to stand and then blackness after the bat swings closer once more. But now I don't see Ellis holding the bat, I reimagine all the boys with bats, waiting, hitting; it could've been any of them; it was all of them. How could Ellis do this to me? We just studied together? Algebra, remember that? And why couldn't I remember any of this? Well, because I was knocked out, and all the lights went out, the windows crunched and broken. Now, I want to wake up and confront the bastard.

Ellis still says, "I didn't mean to hit him with the bat at all. I thought the other guys were joking. Like a big practical joke."

"And that's why it's an accident? Just because you didn't mean to—next you'll tell me you had the best of intentions. Like your three friends? What were you doing hanging around those kind of kids?"

"I swung the bat but I didn't want to hit him. I only wanted to scare him. And those kids were my friends." Ellis's voice is weak, barely audible, and he's on the verge of tears, desperate for his father, anyone, to get him out of this. He doesn't tell his father about the drugs his friends supplied. "I think he fell into it; I think he tripped or something and I couldn't stop my swing in time, but I didn't mean to hit him at all. I can't believe it happened."

"The police think you hit him because he had feelings for you."

"What?" And this is the real shocker for him. Ellis wants to believe he has no idea I had a crush on him, and I know this is true: he easily ignored my presence at school unless he needed something. I can still picture him on the arm of the girl who pulled him from my cafeteria table.

Now this next reaction from Ellis is the interesting part because my crush on Ellis has been my biggest secret and it's finally out. I wrote about Ellis in my journal, in the cracked computer that's in my backpack protected by passwords. All he can muster is a weak: What? As if this is big, fat, startling news. "The three others were teasing him, teasing me, about it, calling him names maybe, bullying him, ribbing me, before they made the first shot. They hit him first. But I can't believe it. I never thought he was—I barely knew him."

"Are you gay?" His father asks this straight out without any emotion left.

"No." After all of his son's lies how can his father believe him? He's not even protesting too much.

"Then what's this all about? What the police say?"

"The other three. They were calling him names like I said."

"What?"

"You know."

"Ellis, tell me what they said."

"Fag. Faggot. The usual put downs—stuff you hear every day at school. I thought they were kidding but they acted like the kid had the biggest crush on me, like he was my girlfriend or something."

"And you took a swing at him? Do you know how that makes you look?"

Ellis sits there in silence puzzled by his father's questions; he hasn't pieced it all together yet.

"It makes you look guilty. You and those three other bullying halfwits beat up and almost kill, and by the way that kid may still die, a defenseless classmate of yours who, on top of everything else, may happen to be gay. Do you know what the prosecutor is going to do?"

Ellis will not raise his head to look at his father. He thinks he'll never get out now and says, "What can I do?"

"The other three are saying you took the last swing, that the boy was making sexual passes at you and the rest of them, that it made you angry—angry enough to take the bat and smash his brain in."

Ellis wishes he could vanish. Right then, he's thinking about disappearing as his father continues his tirade.

"There's another witness who heard what was said to the boy, what names were used, but I bet that same witness never heard that boy making passes at you. Am I right?"

Ellis stays silent and his father stands with his hands curled into fists pressing against the tabletop between them.

Ellis's father yells, "Am I right?"

The guard opens the door once more, quickly steps in and takes hold of Ellis's father's arm, guides him out of the room. The door closes on Ellis sitting alone at the table. He doesn't rise from his seat. He stares at his hands. Ellis then pictures me and the moment he joined his friends on the rainy street, shattered glass crunching under his Nike sneakers, and how he became the catalyst for their anger, how they turned on this kid who had just helped him prepare for an algebra test.

When the first boy hit me Ellis reached out his hand to make him stop. But ended up stopping himself because he'd thought about me being a fag who wanted him, and in that instant Ellis was with the group no matter how he reconfigured the event in his mind. Even after what his father said Ellis thought his father would get him out of trouble somehow. In his mind, he wasn't guilty of anything except being in the wrong place at the wrong time.

After composing himself Ellis's father searches out the detective he spoke to earlier to ask what his son's options are one more time. If his son could speak to him, speak the truth this time, and hash out a plea bargain of some kind.

The detective is busy for a half hour before he can see him and Ellis's father calls his wife but the line is busy or off the hook and he wonders why. She knows to wait for him to call her with any news. He wants to take his anger out on her, rage at her through the telephone about being so inconsiderate. When he finally arrives home he'll see the telephone left off its cradle and his wife shivering in sedated sleep. He'll place another blanket on top of her, touch his hand to her forehead as if checking for a fever and collapse into the easy chair next to his side of the bed.

* * *

The nurses who look after my every need page Doctor Gapestill when my breathing starts to labor and blood pressure weakens. He races into the room and tells the nurse that they need to check the ventilator. There's so much going on in my body, the broken bones, the concussion, fractures, the swelling, that my breathing is impeded somehow. Another machine is wheeled in and a different tube is pushed down my throat and the whole process takes less than thirty minutes. More needles pierce my skin. More drugs enter my stressed system. The nurses do what needs to be done in silence. They act like my condition isn't good, not that it was good before. They hope I don't feel anything. My mother only imagines these people working on her son's broken body. She doesn't know what they're feeling, what they're saying, what they're thinking. It's not hard to consider what may happen.

I'm dying.

That's a grave possibility, says one of the nurses when she takes her break with another nurse from the pediatric ward. But you didn't hear it from me. We're not supposed to be discussing this kid with anyone; I could get in trouble just saying that much to you, Tracy.

* * *

Geoffrey sits in his room, unshackled, messing with the tray of food the morning nurse, Bree, brought in half an hour ago. It was supposed to be an early lunch but it's breakfast again: soggy scrambled eggs and a dry English muffin, a carton of whole milk. No utensils. He's supposed to use the muffin as a cudgel, perfect. At least Maddy's insurance will pay for this.

After breakfast, a different doctor visits and another hour-long session of questions about his past and what happened to make him lose control so effectively. That's the opposite of what Geoffrey thinks of his suicide attempt: it was ineffective.

The doctors refuse to tell him I'm in the hospital. They

don't know his mind well enough yet to gauge whether the news of my beating will push him over the edge emotionally, crashing. They don't tell him about Maddy either and her news is almost as troubling.

* * *

Maddy rests in the E.R. the entire morning, afternoon, and into the evening, waiting there for test results, and distant family members to arrive. She wants the okay to go back to my bedside. She's in stasis, talking to Nadine, who's been a lifesaver. What's taking so blasted long? The blood tests all came back normal. Dr. Fusil says Maddy's cholesterol and blood pressure are way too high, but the stress she's in plays a factor here, and to follow up with her family physician about that later. Dr. Fusil schedules an x-ray of her lower extremities to rule out anything physical. Those films come back clear and free, as normal as any woman in her early forties.

Then her CT Scan hits the schedule but it's so busy in the hospital today she can't be fit in until early afternoon so Maddy waits and waits and asks for updates on my condition. She starts to have more feeling in her legs a couple hours later and Dr. Fusil makes another round of tests, moves her legs back and forth, up and down, testing reflexes. She smiles her brilliant smile and says she'll get to the bottom of this mystery. Maddy wants to scream.

MORBIDITY

THE NEUROSURGEON, Doctor Gapestill, stands under the hospital's large covered entryway in front of a jumble of microphones; he feels anger as if a solid form is close and stretches out arms to reach for him, in front of the squid-like jumble of cameras and lights shining in his face, hitting him in waves and he takes several deep breaths before he's composed enough to continue with the first official hospital press conference.

* * *

Before Doctor Gapestill stepped up to the front line he visited my mother in the emergency room. He read through her chart and spoke briefly to Doctor Fusil; now his own curiosity grew as Maddy awaited the patient transporter, why is there only one transporter per shift, for the journey to the MRI, a machine still not paid for by the hospital, but on loan, rented by a consortium of hospitals, who couldn't find the funding to purchase one of their very own. He and Maddy conversed—he told her how the media had overrun the hospital grounds and sought her permission to keep them informed in a timely manner. "I'll give them only the basic information."

"Please tell them Chris is doing the best he can. That he's still fighting. Alone. That the boys who did this to my son should be forced to sit next to his bed until he wakes up from his coma. That he's going to wake up; that his name is Christopher Bullet; I want them to know his name."

"Are you sure?"

"I'm positive." Nadine sat silently as Maddy spoke to the neurosurgeon. She kept her thoughts on Maddy's words, wishing she could call her husband and get him over here, too. He's Maddy's friend as much as Nadine's, but then he'd only want to find out how Geoffrey's doing—like I did, she thought—and he'd want to know all the intricate secrets of the past year, a good old boy to the end, but he could cheer Geoffrey up if he was permitted to see him—talk about the trout they caught on the Swan River, how I wiped out every time they took me tubing across the lake, how I enjoyed the feeling of skimming across the lake like a water bug, laughing even when Nadine's husband tried to make me fall off by cutting the boat in a tight curve at high speed, tumbling off the yellow and black inner tube, skipping across the top of Swan Lake, a stone tossed by some giant's hand. How Nadine remembered sitting up in bed next to her husband, Bernard—Bernie—before they turned off the bedside lamps and chatted about the day, the lake, their friends, Geoffrey, Maddy and me, knowing they could speak freely because their guests were tucked in far and away across the large house in their own separate guest quarters, sleeping, and talking about them just as fervently; Bernie sighed and said he thought I needed to toughen up.

"And I suppose you're just the one who's going to go about toughening up someone else's kid? Teach him how to be a man?"

"Sometimes he gives me the creeps."

"Because he's quiet. A bit too sensitive."

"No. His behavior is annoying, a know-it-all, thinks he's already smarter than most adults, and because he's a bit of a momma's boy. He doesn't enjoy anything and only comes in the boat because Geoffrey demands it of him."

"So what?"

"I'm only speaking my mind. Doesn't mean anything. I do like the kid."

"But you're not comfortable around Chris."

"He'd rather sit on the shore all day—reading."

"Again: So what?"

"I just want everyone to have a good time."

"Your good time. Maybe Chris takes after Maddy more.

Maybe he'll become a writer someday like his mother." Bernie sighed as Nadine continued, "Not all boys have to be Strong Men from the circus. Look at how our own children turned out."

"Don't remind me."

"Tony called today while you were out on the water."

"What did he want?"

"Nothing, you old grump," Nadine loved to tease Bernie. "He just called to say he and his new girlfriend are going to her parents' house for Thanksgiving this year."

"Figures."

"So I'm going to invite Maddy and everyone to our house for the holiday. We're closer to them than our own kids."

"Now that they've grown up and left the nest and can't find the time to come back home every year for even a short visit."

"Bernie."

"What?"

"Just try not to be so hard on Chris."

Nadine remembered this conversation and how her own husband spoke about me, and my sensitive nature, and she wrung her hands. Maddy, when Nadine invited them, said yes to Thanksgiving at Nadine's house; Geoffrey had to be cajoled into it; I shrugged when I was told, and Maddy happily said to Nadine she'd make the pumpkin pie from scratch and also the mashed potatoes and did her family prefer cranberries pre-molded out-of-the-can or the real berries; she could make her savory cranberries with caramelized onions? Trust me, it's incredible. Nadine wondered if all the planning for a friends Thanksgiving will even come to pass now. How could it if I don't wake up to eat stuffed bird?

Doctor Gapestill, almost imperceptible in such tight quarters, swayed back and forth on his heels, ready to leave just as the patient transporter popped her head into the room and, with perfectly rote robotic repetitive motion, informed Maddy she needed to take her to get the MRI. Maddy stood, wobbly, her legs completely usable now, and with a little embarrassment she planted herself in the wheelchair.

Maddy said to the doctor, "Let me know how the press

conference goes, would you?"

"Of course. I'll just make a simple statement. It'll probably only last five minutes. I'll come down in an hour. That should give me time to check on Chris and give the MRI experts time to find out what's going on with you." His voice remained light and sincere and Maddy appreciated all that he was doing. She believed I was in the best of hands as he left for the press conference.

* * *

Before turning Doctor Gapestill loose on the media one of the detectives finishes what he's saying, a bright light makes his face too pale and washed out. The reporters on the steps of the hospital remain fervidly eager for new information.

"A young boy was critically injured yesterday when four of his fellow classmates, allegedly, beat him with a baseball bat. This assault did not occur on school grounds and we're investigating every possible angle. After much consideration, the Montana attorney general's office filed second-degree assault charges against three of the boys who initiated the attack, and first-degree assault charges against a fourth boy. Now, this just in, all four teenagers will be charged as adults." With their stories changing, more charges may be withdrawn and refiled.

Across town, at the police station, the Pallino family attorney reads a statement in front of his own small press conference: "The Pallino family offers their heartfelt apology and deepest regret to everyone involved in this terrible tragedy."

Back at the hospital a reporter shouts out, "What if their victim dies?"

"I won't speak about hypothetical situations. Doctor Gapestill will update you about the victim's condition. Please save your questions until the end. Doctor?"

Doctor Gapestill tells the growing crowd that he's only one of the neurosurgeons consulted on the case, and that he's speaking on behalf of the family. Doctor Gapestill only sees bright shining flashbulb white light in front of him, blooms of light, and he tries to keep his eyes away from the pinpoints by staring down at the ground until one of the reporters heckles him into tilting his chin forward for the cameras, blinding himself. He's so glad he didn't go into journalism back in college, which he minored in so long ago. Pack of vultures.

"Chris Bullet is being treated in the intensive care unit. His bed is propped up to help keep the swelling in his skull down. He's hooked up to a ventilator and there's no telling when or if he'll be able to breathe on his own. Chris has involuntary movement in his arms and legs but he's in a deep coma. He has a severe brain injury that threatens his life and, honestly, this creates a deep concern for his future. He remains in critical condition. That's all I can say at this time."

I can't feel myself giving up—and I don't suppose I would. Am I a ghost? Don't I have to die first? I remain asleep in darkness. The machines make too much noise in the empty room and bring no comfort. There's a tube running into my mouth, breathing for me, taped in place across my face. With all of the bandages wrapping my head and the tape there's little of me showing. There's so little left.

The nurses come and go and no one has visited in a long time. Maddy's still in the emergency room, unsettled; at least she can move her legs and walk now. She's back from the MRI and awaits the results. She tells Nadine she should really return to my bedside, and Nadine tries to get Maddy to stay calm and rest as comfortably as possible against the pillows. Nadine asks one of the E.R. nurses when the MRI results will come back and the nurse checks the chart and informs Nadine it shouldn't be much longer now. The nurse also updates Maddy, almost every half hour, about my status, and it's so late in the evening by then there's nothing new to report.

"He's healing and that's all we can hope and wish for. I'll pray for him," the nurse says to Maddy before closing the door and leaving Nadine and Maddy alone once more.

"I wish I could pray," Maddy says.

There's nothing Nadine can add. Religion is something she's tried to get a handle on all her life. Maddy never talks about following any religion, and often says she doesn't have any need for it. Nadine was raised Episcopalian and still goes to church every Sunday. Her husband only attends church services Christmas Eve and Easter Sunday and complains about that and being perceived as a hypocrite, but Nadine puts her foot down and he gives in to his wife's insistence on this point. Nadine's asked Maddy if she'd like to join her some evening sessions when her church gathers for singing but Maddy has to teach her night classes during the week.

Maddy doesn't want to go to any church; her parents made her go to Bible School when she was of pre-school, kindergarten, age; they dropped her off alone, and then, later, Maddy would accompany her sister, Rhea. They drank Kool-Aid, grape or lime usually, and ate stale graham crackers in the early mornings. Maddy always wondered why her own parents didn't attend the adult services. She could hear murmured sermons through the pastel-green, painted ceiling of the basement room, voices from above.

You'll thank me one day, her mother always said. Millie and Frank didn't go to any church and they only made Maddy and Rhea go to Bible School to learn the Bible stories, socialize them, let them make up their own minds once they became thinking adults. Like her parents, Maddy, as an adult, doesn't follow any organized religion; too many righteous people sermonizing about how life should follow only one rigid path, one without sin. She tires of hearing about how religion is behind so many of the decisions from high government subterfuge, war on the world stage driven by religious zealotry, compassionate conservatives—ha—faith-based initiatives, family values, fundamentals murdering other people because they know exactly the word of God, and scarier if they believe God speaks to them, tells them to kill sinners in his name, all the way down to how to run a pizza parlor catering to the youth of today who believe abortion is a sin—another ha moment—that everyone burns in hellfire after casting the first stone. In the past, people used the Bible to justify owning slaves. Today, Maddy feels people still use the Bible to hide behind their bigoted opinions and I agree with her on that front. When I started going to the Baptist Youth Outreach Program every Sunday and Thursday afternoon I could tell my mother was worried, just a little bit, but I only went to be around other junior high teenagers who felt lonely and cast aside by their peers who had better cliques and groups to join. I didn't go to Bible School, knew nothing specific about anything in the Bible, but of course I hear all the names. I would play foosball, air hockey, board games when it rained, chess, talk about homework, go to PG movies or watch appropriate rental movies on an old 32-inch television donated to the Fellowship long ago. The other kids I got to know accepted me and I fit into the group with ease and an easy wit and a keen skill at game playing. They sometimes asked if I would like to join them for the regular church services Sunday mornings but I always had excuses. Occasionally the Youth leaders stopped their ping-pong battles and would convene in a circle. The group leader would ask the group if they really knew who Jesus was and if I was called on I'd bow my head and my face, redden in embarrassment; I don't have an answer to even the simplest religious question—and being smart doesn't help answer questions with multiple outcomes. Of course I know who Jesus was. People talk about him constantly, and if you don't think so, just stop and listen and watch, and you'll know I speak my own truth.

Nadine takes Maddy's hand in her own and squeezes gently.

The results of the CT reveal nothing, zip, nada. Dr. Fusil still works the room, all of the patients brought into the emergency room that day, all of the tests, double-checking every chart, initialing in the appropriate places. She's not worried too much about Madison Dakota and the lack of information because from the first moment she tested Maddy's legs and asked her questions about her puzzling immobility she's had this sneaking, intuitive feeling, 99% of the time willing to bet on her hunches, she knows what ails Madison but she wants to get everything just right before she reveals her assumptions. She's seen these symptoms before, close to textbook even with the variety the illness takes, not much, but every month there's someone new for her to try to learn how to soften an impossible-to-soften blow.

A lot of times a patient's dire symptoms are caused solely by the mind. Dr. Fusil doesn't want to bring this up. Stress can cause a healthy child or adult to develop breathing difficulties, asthma sometimes is suggestible and is definitely used to manipulate, she's seen children do it all the time—Mom, I'm having an asthma attack! Help! And the children only seek attention from busy adults—she's seen it all before. Is something stressful happening in your life right now? The patient says the family is dealing with the loss of a loved one, a cousin who has just died in a car crash, the heart attack of a grandmother, the father or mother has lost a job, the house is in foreclosure, and the doctor will try to say, delicately, maybe this breathing difficulty is really just a symptom of your grief, a panic attack, and not an asthma attack at all, and the patient does a double-take and thinks hard about what the doctor has just said and clings to this new information. The doctor says: The mind, when faced with disaster, sometimes tries to shut the body down.

Doctor Fusil hasn't said any of this to Maddy because she wants to get all her ducks, the tests, in a row first. So far everything lends credence to her theory: This poor woman is being put through the wringer; her family's falling apart and she's on her last leg—no pun intended. Then: Where are those test results? She demands this of the night shift nurse now in charge of Madison Bullet—no, Dakota, sorry, we've kept her down here long enough.

Then there's a loud disturbance, a woman's shouting voice coming from the waiting room where patients are first checked in for triage. The hurricane named Nell has arrived at the hospital.

Nadine and Maddy hear Nell's loud voice echoing all the way to their back room and they immediately start to cringe and giggle. They grab each other's hands and say: What will we do now?

"I'll protect you," laughs Nadine.

"Oh, my God. When you told me she was coming I

must've blocked it out until now."

"My brother is somewhere in this hospital." Everyone in the E.R. hears Nell's harsh, imperious tone.

"There's a lot going on today. Just bear with us please." A woman tries to soothe Nell with these words but she doesn't know Nell.

"My family is here somewhere."

One of the other admittance clerks comes out and says, "You're family to Madison Dakota?"

"Yes. She's the one who called telling me my brother is being kept here."

"Madison is here in the E.R. being evaluated but I have to wait for a nurse. Please take a seat and try to calm down in the waiting area or I'll have to call security." The clerk stands blocking the swinging ER doors separating triage from trauma areas. She has her hands on her hips.

Doctor Fusil shakes her head and twists her stethoscope around her neck as she exits the central hub of the emergency room and opens the door to the triage area. The clerk steps aside. Doctor Fusil studies an older woman awash in the colors of copper and bronze, butterscotch, leather shoes, pants, blouse, jacket, purse all a subtle shading of this color palette, the bronze so chic Doctor Fusil glances at her own cheap, sturdy shoes bought on sale. There's an aquamarine scarf wrapped around the woman's neck, with the diaphanous ends shifting when the woman places her hands on her own hips and turns to face the doctor.

"I'm Doctor Fusil. I'm taking care of your sister. Madison."

Nell doesn't even proffer her hand to shake, she's a major germaphobe, hates hospitals, the lingering infectious surfaces, and Doctor Fusil drops her arm.

"Follow me, please," says Doctor Fusil as she walks to the waiting room and sits on one of the easy chairs. She doesn't check to see if Nell follows her. If she didn't, Doctor Fusil would really get steamed. This woman doesn't know whom she's about to confront. Doctor Fusil's name will ring in the woman's mind for years if she steps out of line, but Nell sits in a chair across from Doctor Fusil. Nell lets out a huff and clasps her hands together. Before Nell can speak, Doctor Fusil smiles and tries to calm the situation.

"Your sister is doing well and I'll check on her after I speak to you."

"Actually, Madison is my sister-in-law and she isn't the one I'm worried about."

Doctor Fusil is taken aback—puzzling information.

"I want to know how my brother is. Maddy's husband? I didn't travel all day just to hear how my sister-in-law is fine and doing so great while my brother is locked away somewhere in this Godforsaken, rain-drenched, moldy hospital. I can smell the mold. My allergies are already closing down my sinuses."

"I'm not in charge of your brother's care." Doctor Fusil's at a loss now; she realizes she cannot predict human behavior whatsoever; she's a mere novice. Whatever she attempts to say to this woman in front of her, however Doctor Fusil predicts a response, it will all be nothing but fancy, a game she can study later when off shift, talking about patients and relatives with the other doctors who gather around a bar tabletop with a pint of Guinness in front of each of them.

"Your brother is being seen by the psychiatry department right now."

"Do you know when he was brought in?"

"A woman named Nadine—"

"Your sister-in-law's friend?" The stormy look on Nell's face makes Doctor Fusil almost turn red; she can tell in a split-second Nell does not take kindly to being interrupted, who does?

"Are you quite through?" Nell asks.

"Excuse me. Please. Go on."

"Nadine telephoned me this morning and told me what was happening up here. She said my brother was brought into your E.R. last night and admitted into the Psych Ward. I was lucky to get on the next available flight."

Doctor Fusil waits for Nell to keep speaking and then another second before she says, "I wasn't working last night but I can check the records and tell you anything that may help."

"I think it would help immeasurably."

"But if your brother was brought in here last night and he's where you say he is there may not be anything I or the hospital can do."

"What do you mean?"

"That floor, if he was admitted there, doesn't allow visitation for the first three days. It's a locked ward."

"You've got to be kidding me."

Doctor Fusil plows ahead. "I think you may want to speak to Madison first."

"Wait just one—"

"Listen,"—and Doctor Fusil almost has to shout—"Listen to me. I don't take kindly to being spoken to in the tone of voice you're using. I can understand why you're upset, angry even. Your family is going through something very difficult."

Nell stands without a word.

Doctor Fusil stands also and faces Nell. This woman is a stone pain in the ass, my Aunt Nell, but I think of her as a great deliverer. She gets things done. People fear her, but they don't know her like I do. "Let me get Nadine to come out and speak to you."

"Why?"

"Honestly, I don't want your energy around Madison."

"You can't bar me from seeing my family."

Now it's Doctor Fusil's turn to smile as if she cares so much. She says, "According to what you told me earlier it isn't your sister-in-law you're worried about."

"You can't speak to me like this."

"I suggest you take a seat."

"I will do no such thing."

"Gillian?" Doctor Fusil calls out to the Incoming E.R. Desk Clerk, "Please call security."

As if by instant magic trick, two guards appear, they must've been called down by the clerk just in case, and they walk over to where the two women face each other in a standoff.

"If this woman tries to get past the front desk or anywhere else in this hospital you have my permission to block her entrance."

"You can't treat me like this. I'll sue. You just wait."

Nonplussed, Doctor Fusil gives Nell her name and position. "Do what you want. Be my guest. I imagine you've become who you are by only doing what you want to do."

There's silence in the waiting room. That telltale silence of the embarrassed is palpable. There are three other people sitting huddled on the other side of the room, three young girls, one with a bloody bandage around her left hand. They look like they're watching reality television. Nell doesn't move an inch. She imagines calling a lawyer as soon as she gets back to her hotel room. She wishes she could speak to her brother and get him to sue this uppity witch of a doctor but then she remembers he's locked away in the loony bin and Nell's rudderless, a feeling she seldom allows, and she crumbles onto the cushions of the couch. She's not totally pulling a Zsa Zsa, feigning a collapse to gain sympathy; there's no one in the room who would bear witness for her in a favorable way.

"Now. Let me go get Nadine to inform you about where things stand. I'll leave it up to Madison. If she grants you permission to come back to her room, great, but I'm warning you right now about your behavior. You will not upset anyone else in this hospital. I can take it. Your sister-in-law can probably take it too, but I'm not going to give you the chance. She's under enough stress as it is. These security guards will be right here. Do you understand?"

Doctor Fusil doesn't wait for Nell to reply, and turns abruptly, her sensible shoes squeaking on the hospital-grade flooring, and gives an overview of her meeting to Madison.

Inside, Nell burns. I hope to soothe her at some future point, get her to laugh at a stupid animal joke. Knock knock. I've always made it a point to stay on her good side.

* * *

Deepika finds herself filled to capacity with nervous energy. She begins to contemplate and direct a magnifying lens at the mess she's in the middle of. The scarlet woman tears apart a family, but of course she feels she's not to blame for the whole thing, or any of it, and she won't take all of it on herself. She wants to make amends, to free her from any feeling of remorse in an easy, graceful manner. She comes to the conclusion that Geoffrey did something to make me snap and follow Deepika to her bungalow in an inconsolable, uncontainable rage. Did he squeeze his son's arm too, the pain becoming a burn?

She usually winds down at night after a block of writing. But tonight she can't stop pacing as she tries to focus. She concentrates on anger, an invisible controlling force, and the violent nature of some of her fictional characters. Anger and violence are now her main thematic issues. With everything happening around her, the anger becomes an entity in her story. American violence. Fear-based folly. She thinks of the violence done to me, how I could lay shattered on a street dripping with rain, unconscious, body in spasms. She thinks about me and then turns to her own fiction. She wants to use me for sport. She twists and reshapes my life, mirrors the violent nature of man, to create a history for her main protagonist, steeped in angry violence from birth to Sai's current station. Sai's (my!) journey will take her readers to a dangerous altitude where breathing is difficult, a lofty goal. Deepika will take her character back to a time before anyone coins the phrase hate crime. Her main character, Sai Amrashi, has found the stamina to tell his boss, the newspaper's editor, he needs to fly home and deal with his father's death. Deepika wants him to know why he makes this choice. She bows her head and soon is writing away, lost to this world.

* * *

Time flips backward in a rush, and I wish I could feel this; it's earlier in the day, before Maddy begins her battery of tests and sits and waits, when Geoffrey stares out his wire-reinforced window. The city of Middleton doesn't sparkle in the gloom of this fall day. At least the rain has stopped. He seeks a way out. He knows he's trapped for good now. He has no one to speak to; his wife probably abandoned him again; I ran away from him and probably wouldn't speak to him for a long time. If he only knew what I was going through: see how selfish my father's actions really are? Geoffrey wants to think about me finding him with Deepika, somehow go back in time and rearrange the tableau. There's no way he can be a father again.

The next doctor, the head of the department, will interview him in an hour. The staff does not allow Geoffrey to watch television in his room, or the communal gathering lounge. The news shows are filled with speculation about me, the attack, which they're all calling a hate crime, even if Montana wouldn't recognize it as such.

It's a mistake the doctors make without a thought towards Geoffrey, not telling him about his poor brain-damaged son because Geoffrey is a patient in the Psych Ward. They should know better; they haven't breathed a word yet about his family and he's going to ask about them the moment he's brought before the new mind-mucking physician. He can count on his wife to get him out; she'll still fight for him, unless she knows about Deepika and their baby, then all bets are off.

"How are we feeling today?" Harry, the morning nurse says. He's sick of hearing about how Geoffrey shouldn't even be here—"Just wait until my lawyer hears about this!" But Harry knows this man is the father of the victim of the beating.

"Is it okay if I say I'm not in the mood?" Geoffrey says with an edge to his voice. "I want to see the doctor and I want to clear up this misunderstanding and get the hell out of here."

Harry doesn't respond, as if he's dealing with a child, but at least he doesn't say: That's not going to happen anytime soon.

"I want to know what happened to my family. Are they waiting for me?"

This stops Harry. He's no fool. The ward doctor doesn't want Geoffrey to know anything. Yet. Harry thinks about how he wants to spin the information and realizes it's too big for him. Sheer stupidity allows this sullen and suicidal patient to remain so uninformed; usually they just decommission the TV power in each individual room. He'll go get the doctor in residence to handle the meeting.

"Let me take you to the doctor's office. It's Doctor Spitzer this early in the day."

"I can't speak to Dr. Minogue?"

"No. He was called away."

Geoffrey imagines a psychological emergency of the gravest proportions and the psych hotline pulsing red, Dr. Minogue racing to a nearby cliff side in Glacier National Park where a madman insists on taking his own life. Let me talk you down.

"But Doctor Spitzer said you can use the telephone now if you want to call your friend."

"My lawyer."

He asked first thing that morning to be connected to Lance. And this request went through the appropriate channels and Harry is the messenger boy. Harry leads Geoffrey out into the hall and down to a cubicle with a public telephone. Geoffrey punches in Lance's Michigan office cell number, remembering by heart even though he hasn't called Lance in over two months.

When are you going to call me, Buddy?

Now.

Lance connects on the first ring. He's busy in the office. Always working long hours every single day, morning to late in the evening.

"Hi, buddy. Long time no talk."

"Hello. Geoff?"

"It's me."

"Couldn't tell by your voice. It's all scratchy. What's wrong?"

"I need you to come out to Middleton."

"Whoa, buddy."

"Lance. I'm in a bit of a jam."

"What's going on?"

"I don't want to get into it over the phone but I'm being held in the psychiatric floor in the hospital."

This admission almost takes over and tumbles the

conversation into an unsteady silence.

"I need your help getting out of here."

"What's happening?"

"Can you take the earliest flight? I'll pay."

"That won't be necessary, and, of course I'll come. Sheila, too."

Geoffrey doesn't say anything about Sheila. Maddy won't approve, again, for sharing family secrets, but what the hell.

"I'm going to tell the hospital to let you in as my lawyer."

"I'm sorry Geoff. We'll be there as soon as I can make flight arrangements and close up my office."

"Lance."

"Yeah."

"Just get here."

"I'm on my way."

They both hang up. Geoffrey glances at Harry and stands up from the telephone nook in the public hallway. Lance calls his travel agent; he flies too much not to have one, and tells him to book two seats, first class, the fastest way possible to Middleton. Then he calls Sheila and tells her to pack two small suitcases. Hurry. We have to be at the Airport in less than two hours. They'll get into Middleton by dark, late, Central Mountain time.

Harry explains, "Doctor Spitzer is the head psychologist and you'd end up speaking to him sooner or later."

"It's a community of emotional touchy feely. I get it."

Harry tells Geoffrey to follow him down the hall to the offices and group therapy rooms. He knocks on a door and a man's prissy voice answers, "What is it?"

Harry opens the door and motions Geoffrey to sit on the chair outside the office. "I'll only be a moment."

"Yeah. I don't know what I'd do if I was left out here all alone for a long period of time."

Harry winces and shuts the door behind him. Geoffrey only hears muted conversation. Nothing of substance and he leans back in his chair with his head resting against the painted wall.

He waits ten minutes while rocking the chair up and down, front legs off the tile, slamming them back onto the

floor and then up again. A nurse with another patient—
wearing the hospital's industrial pajamas—walks by briskly
and they're gone in a flash.

Harry pokes his head out and asks Geoffrey to come
inside the office.

He stares at the Yoga Man, the gadfly from the park, who
righteously went off on the dog owner who allowed his dog
to wander leashless, chase small animals: Doctor Spitzer,
Protector of Squirrels. Of course only I call him Yoga Man,
and I'm the only one who knows this man is a snit. Watch
out, Dad. There's no other witness to this doctor and his
interactions with a stranger and his two dogs and his feral
bite, except for the handsome jogger, and he's forgotten the
public confrontation by now, as Geoffrey stands in front of
Doctor Spitzer, depressed, and angry at the world. There's
no one who can warn Geoffrey to prepare to get bitten.

* * *

Nell sits in the waiting room, steaming. Security keeps a
watchful eye on her and the petulant, but firm, doctor hasn't
come back yet. When Nell got exited the small airplane she
took out of Palm Springs she worked herself into a righteous
froth of anger. The first thing she did after renting her car
was race to the hospital to try to confront Madison, and now
she finds herself stuck. Madison should've called her
immediately when she found out Geoffrey was having
problems, the moment the ambulance took him away from
the house, but no, she waited until the next day, and she has
the nerve to have her friend call for her as if she can't face
speaking to her. Who does Maddy think she is? And now her
friend says Maddy is in the E.R. being seen for some
unfathomable reason? Nell wants to know who is taking care
of me, her nephew? Who is taking care of her brother?

These questions race through Nell's mind as she tightens
up. She grips the chair arm firmly and swears under her
breath. Her brother isn't crazy. Why would they put him on
the psych floor? Finally, Nell thinks, this is all Maddy's fault.

* * *

Lance and Sheila arrive in Middleton shortly after 10pm, a little more than four hours after Nell's airplane came in from Palm Springs. The three of them have one thing in common: they chose not to have children. It made it easy for them to just shut up their homes, lock the doors, get the neighbor to feed the cats, water the plants and turn on the alarm.

A long time ago Lance and Sheila started worrying about Geoffrey the very moment he told them he was finally asking Maddy to marry him after living together for three years, after having a child together out of wedlock. They thought he was crazy, not depressed back then, but too quick to only think about himself the whole time; he hasn't really thought things through. Lance knows Geoffrey craves his freedom above all else. Yes, they had a child together, and he and Maddy have worked out their problems but could Geoffrey really stick to Maddy, remain a hundred per cent faithful?

Lance and Sheila both also know about Geoffrey and his infidelities, the many girlfriends, the pattern of leaving one woman right when she fell in love with him by running to another woman. He lives an ongoing cycle of the cold-feet dash and the wishes for new and exciting sexual liaisons. When Maddy came into the picture she was different, aloof with her appraisals, more into herself and her needs at times, someone who Geoffrey could see had a plan and would follow through. They had a child but she wouldn't even consider marriage. And she knew about all of the women he listed in his past. One of these women even approached Maddy and warned her about Geoffrey. He's a dog, she said. No one would realize that Maddy did the same thing Deepika was doing in the present when she was first pregnant: neither of them wanted—wants—to marry Geoffrey. And the pattern continues.

Lance and Sheila drive to the Hyatt in the Middleton downtown city center and quickly check-in, drop their suitcases in the room and freshen up. They actually believe they'll have time (later on) to walk around and enjoy the

Montana scenery, maybe even take a romantic fall color-of-the-leaves trip up to Glacier after they sort out Geoffrey and what could possibly have sent him into a tailspin. They foolishly think this until they turn on the late evening news and hear the name Chris Bullet, victim of a hate crime come out of a reporter's mouth; they realize they have no time and this trip will not be about them or a vacation. They drive their rental car, a maroon Saturn sedan, out to the hospital, a mile into town, perhaps less.

Sheila says, "I knew we should've called Maddy first. Geoffrey told us to go to the hospital. Madison will be there. I can't believe Chris is in critical condition or what's happening to him."

"Just settle down."

Lance takes out his cell and rings Maddy's cell number. He hopes his phone is charged enough and will not cut out.

He hears an answering service and leaves a message: "Maddy, this is Lance and Sheila and we're in Middleton on our way to the hospital. Geoffrey called us. We'll help in any way we can. Call me back if you need anything but we'll be there soon." He wonders if Maddy will think he's brainless, considering her son is in a coma and her disturbed husband is in the Psychiatric Ward.

Lance and Sheila cannot believe what's happening in Middleton.

Lance cautions Sheila: they both should keep silent. Lance says, "It may be hard to get through the crowd and talk our way past security. This is big." They see the crowd of people gathering outside the hospital. How do these people have time to come here, make signs, yell and yell and yell.

When they drive into the parking lot it's full and there's a security guard blocking their entrance.

"Unless it's an emergency you'll have to turn around and park at the extension lot two blocks down 14th," the guard says with little enthusiasm.

"Look at that," Sheila says as she points out the enormous group of people massing in front of the hospital entrance. Most of the people hold candles, some flashlights. They look cold in the darkness.

Sheila believes this is all Geoffrey's fault even though she's only going by her intuition and what little information she learned from the newscaster about the beating I took. "Where was Geoffrey when Chris was going through"—She repeats, "He was always your friend."

"What did you say?" asks Lance.

"I can't believe this."

"I don't know why they moved all the way out here."

"I do."

"Why then?"

"Geoffrey wanted to escape and Maddy needed a change. They weren't going anywhere in Ann Arbor. He hated the gray winters and the University of Michigan wouldn't hire Maddy except as a T.A."

"He wasn't going to be happy anywhere. And if you haven't noticed, it's gray here too."

"That's not Maddy's fault."

"I didn't mean to imply that and you know it."

"Okay. Let's not fight."

Lance drives to the overflow lot and he and Sheila walk the wet, cold streets to the entrance, moving around people stalled on the sidewalks. Lance holds Sheila's elbow as they walk past the mass of people showing up for the vigil.

People are yelling and they witness another smaller group of ten to twelve people shoving for space and chanting and holding many bright signs which read: BURN IN HELL. FAGS SIN AND DIE. GOD IS WATCHING. A small child of about eight holds a GET AIDS AND DIE sign, and he's proudly smiling. The other people attending the vigil are yelling back at them to shut up or go away but the group fighting is unruly and there aren't enough police officers to really do any good.

It helps that Lance is an attorney when stopped at the front doors by hospital security, when Lance says he's the Bullet family attorney, and has a business card to back it up, the guard doesn't want to bar someone who's real and not faking, lying to gain entrance. What a mess, the security guard thinks.

Lance and Sheila approach the information desk and are told that all family members are still in the E.R. The old woman behind the desk, a volunteer, takes out a pamphlet with a map of the hospital on it and points out the route to take. The bug-eyed old woman treats them with obvious suspicion but hands them the special visitor's passes they're required to wear during emergency situations. Lance and Sheila clip them to their clothing.

"Thank you," Sheila says.

They walk to the E.R. and the Patient Care Coordinator tells them to take a seat in the waiting room. They sit down next to Nell.

"Do you remember us?" Lance addresses Nell. "It's been a long time."

Nell, shaken out of her stupor of grievance, replies, "I beg your pardon?"

"From Geoffrey and Maddy's wedding?" Lance remembers Nell as a forbidding woman who doesn't do well in crowds—heavy social anxiety issues, treats people horribly, but only to further a victimhood. They didn't speak much so long ago at the wedding of his best friend; he was the best man after all, but they made small talk and Geoffrey has already filled him in on how to survive unscathed when in his sister's presence. During the entire wedding weekend, Nell carried a large bulky Leica camera with a huge lens everywhere she went during the rehearsal dinner, the church service, and then the reception at the University Club on the second floor of the Union even though they'd already hired a professional wedding photographer. The camera was a shield, a prop to lean against, to keep distance from everyone. Sheila wanted to go up to Nell and tell her to relax. She worried that Nell wasn't having a good time that she was so shy, that there really wasn't any need to be aloof with Geoffrey's friends.

"Hello," Sheila says to Nell.

"Oh my," Nell replies. "I don't know how you got through that mess of people outside, but I'm staying put."

"Have you heard anything?" Lance asks.

"The doctor just left again. She's checking on Madison right now. I've been here all evening, waiting." Nell doesn't tell Lance the truth about her run-in with Doctor Fusil, and she's very glad they weren't there to witness the scene.

Maddy's test results must've got lost in the system.

"How's Geoffrey?"

"I can't seem to find that out. He's in a different part of the hospital. He can't have any visitors where he is." They realize Nell's on the verge of tears.

"And Chris?"

"He's under lock and key in the Children's wing. It's all so unbelievable. I still don't think Geoffrey's son is gay."

"Well,"—Lance says as he stands up again to stretch and take his jacket off—"None of us should go outside if we can help it."

"All of those people, most of them, probably don't even know Chris."

"The nutcases have arrived. There's a vigil. And a hate group."

"What a spectacle," Nell says. She picks at her scarf, rearranges it around her neck. There's no longer any warmth to Nell's voice and she's far from being on the verge of tears. She's reined in her emotions and locked them away.

"Do you know what happened? We heard a brief news report."

"Absolutely nothing. The doctor said she'd be right out, but that was hours ago." Nell doesn't add that she thinks the doctor is punishing her. She wants to tell them that the doctor is rude, full of herself, and it may be awhile before they're informed about anything.

Sheila takes her coat off and places it next to her on a rickety table.

"Maddy is being seen by a doctor, too?"

"They wouldn't tell me what's wrong with her. I think she may be too shocked or stressed by what's been happening. All of this may be too hard to take. Her friend, Nadine, said she couldn't move her legs. They're still waiting for test results."

* * *

It's strangely funny to skip backward in time. My mind

does it with ease now even if I can't control where I go, what I see, a flipping, somersaulting, following the thread of my father's cringing behavior in front of Doctor Spitzer. It's not funny. How can it be? I'm here and time ripples. I see everyone arriving in the hospital Emergency Room waiting room and we're all waiting for something. The psych meeting my father sits through ripples and keeps repeating in my mind as black as Swan Lake water at midnight.
"You're upset. Your family is going through a crisis of huge proportions. The quicker we get you settled down the quicker you'll be reunited. And I'd appreciate it if you would stop pacing and take your seat again."
"Can you blame me? You tell me my son has been hurt. That he's in a coma, beaten by other classmates, and that my wife hasn't even asked to see me—that my family is involved in something the hospital hasn't seen since it was built—and you want me to calm down? You want me to sit down now?" Geoffrey shouts the last of his words.
"No one is here to pass judgment on you. We're here to help you get through this."
"What about my family?"
"Take a seat. Please." Doctor Spitzer doesn't give Geoffrey a choice. Geoffrey stands in front of a desk, gray and metallic, the surface piled high with file folders and stacks of computer paper. There's a pen and pencil holder made of ivory, scrimshaw detailing the life of a whaler on all four sides of its surface. Geoffrey finally sits across from the doctor and slouches in his chair with his hands held behind his head. Relax. Relax. His mind calculates how his behavior, if it was good enough, could help him get out of there faster, help him get to his family. He wants to make the doctor think he's in control.
"Your family is being cared for."
"Can I get anything specific from you about my son's condition?"
Doctor Spitzer remains placid and he feels total control sweep through him in a rush. He gets off on conflict resolution, making the world step to his musical beat, his judgment—even if he professes to not being capable of judging anyone.

"We're not here to talk about anyone but you."

Geoffrey feels the doctor's conceited attitude wash over him. It hits him almost physically and he thinks about why he's even in this position and how stupidly he has allowed himself to hit bottom. He thinks of me, finally, comatose, brain-damaged?

He thinks of the music I listen to at full volume when I believe everyone is gone, something by Nine Inch Nails or The Eels or the mix from some teen angst show on TV, something distorted and electric, something angry and filled with a rage so raw. I didn't know, until now, about all the times Geoffrey snuck into my room and searched my small CD collection, small because most of my music is now in the iTunes format, but a lot of the older stuff's still on CD. He steals the music away and plays it on his office stereo repeatedly. By the time I got back from school the music was back in my room but I remember walking into my room and knowing something was amiss almost automatically. I knew my parents, maybe both of them in concert, had been snooping; I thought the worst, that maybe they believed I was on drugs. Geoffrey only wanted to listen to music to mimic his mood. He took The Fragile CDs every other day for a month and put them back in the same place before I got home. That was a month before my dad raced to the bathroom and I asked him where mom was and why was she so late and I pretended to be asleep when she finally arrived home, alleviating all of my worries.

"I'm going to be completely honest with you," Doctor Spitzer says, clasping his fingers together.

"I don't think anyone who claims to be my doctor should have to quantify his level of honesty."

I've got a piece of work in front of me, Doctor Spitzer thinks before his next thought carries him away instantly: no wonder this guy's family is so messed up. Doctor Spitzer scolds himself for thinking that, since it's too unprofessional and he prides himself on being right, if not fair, at all moments. All he says in reply is, "I mean you don't have to worry about your family."

"My family needs me."

"Then please tell me why you took pills and drank them

down with all the alcohol?"
"I didn't try to kill myself. I drank too much vodka. My head started splitting. I had the largest fucking headache and I must've taken too many aspirin."
"Acetaminophen. Did you know acetaminophen should never be used while drinking alcoholic beverages? An old study—causes problems—I'm very surprised you aren't aware of this."

Doctor Spitzer opens Geoffrey's hospital chart and scans the E.R. log sheets and closes the file with clean efficiency. He executes every action with equal ease. He's ex-military, long ago he made choices and ran drills and held someone's hand in a hospital so far away, such a long time ago, and this flash from Doctor Spitzer's past is present and then blocked, cast aside. He really wants to help my father, stay focused.

What Geoffrey says to the doctor: "I've been depressed lately." It's what Geoffrey thinks the doctor wants to hear.

What Geoffrey's done, what my father reveals to me with his thoughts, what he remembers but can't put into words for the good doctor, unspools: He was only eight when two sisters, the Amblyns, Diane and Rhonda, who lived two houses down from his in Greenwich, Connecticut, with its tree-lined streets, large lots for homes pushed towards the back, sloping down hills, leaves falling in autumn to make piles for the collectors to haul away, invited him up the driveway and into their garage.

Diane and Rhonda Amblyn were ten and eleven, a couple years older and much more sophisticated; a dreary worldliness cast a rich pall over their every gesture, giant girls who Geoffrey would obey to the end of days. They didn't necessarily ambush him at all; he stared at them whenever they passed his house or walked to the school five blocks away with older neighborhood boys, or splashed in the city pool if not invited out to Sag Harbor to be with their Aunt who sold beach art as a hobby in the summertime. They invited him into their garage and asked him if he would let them kiss him. First Diane, then Rhonda, one on either side of him. Waiting in the dusty garage, rusted-up gardening equipment littering the shelves and the smell of gasoline from the lawn mower pungent in the air.

Diane had dark brown hair and darker eyes the color of bitter chocolate. Rhonda had lighter brown hair she pulled back from her face with a slice of pink ribbon and blue eyes that stayed in shadow; Rhonda always kept her face tilted downwards as if the floor, the ground, the earth, keeping sight of it, was her only secure tether. But she and her sister now stared into Geoffrey's eyes.

"We're going to kiss you. Me first since I'm the oldest," Diane said, and Geoffrey's mind ached.

"Your face is so pale. Look at him, Di"—Rhonda remarked.

"Don't be scared." Diane laughed and Geoffrey remembered the high pitch of her little girl laughter as if she had inhaled helium before embarking on the journey to his first kiss.

"I'm not scared." Defiant and tiny and fists at his side pumping like a bird whose wings had been clipped, caught in a trap and unable to fly.

Geoffrey remembered Diane stepping closer and placing her small hand, a bit warm, gently on his right shoulder and quickly leaning in, her face a slant and she was pressing her lips against his mouth and he realized she wasn't stopping and he felt her lips move against him, insistent and probing and then he believed he couldn't breathe and that he was hot and his mind was on fire and she parted. He could feel her saliva still on the outside of his mouth and he licked with his tongue.

"Your turn," Diane said to her sister.

Geoffrey was struck speechless after that first kiss, and before he could close his lips Rhonda was pushing against him and her tiny tongue flicked inside of him and touched his teeth. He heard Diane tell him to open his mouth just a little bit as if she was now directing Geoffrey and her sister, Rhonda.

He followed her order and Rhonda kissed him open-mouthed and they touched tongues together and he was only eight and when Rhonda was done he wondered who had taught them how to kiss that way. But he never asked them.

He stumbled away and said, "I have to go."

Diane and Rhonda laughed but the sound didn't ring in Geoffrey's ears anymore and he would come back when they asked him and over the years they would teach him other things until they moved away the year after he turned thirteen. He would miss them terribly and Rhonda and Diane would lose his address after a month and Geoffrey never heard from them again. They would visit him numerous times in his dreams, and recently too, just last week, Geoffrey awoke with the fleeting image of Rhonda opening a door after he knocked many, many times, too many before he almost turned away, and there she was and Rhonda closed the door on him before he could ask where Diane was and he later tried to remember the two sisters and hopelessly forgot why Rhonda appeared to him.

"Have you sought any help for your depression?" Doctor Spitzer is unaware of the history of the patient in front of him. He's been prescribing for the mentally ill for so long he no longer sees the people who come into his office as anything but patients; he doesn't allow himself the weakness of getting too close to someone who may try to stab a pencil in his hand, which happened once long ago, and, he swore, wouldn't happen again. It's the quiet ones he needs to watch out for and the man, Geoffrey, in front of him, is in this category. Doctor Spitzer doesn't trust him one iota. Doctor Spitzer is one of the few people Geoffrey cannot charm easily.

"No. I haven't. I probably should have but I've been under so much stress this past year."

"Let's stay on that for now. Dig into your memories a bit more and try to picture what's been causing you so much stress. Tell me anything that pops into your head."

What Geoffrey says to Doctor Spitzer even though the good doctor somehow sees right through his bullshit: "I've been feeling very lonely, and I still feel lonely."

"When did this feeling of loneliness start?"

Geoffrey is being honest and as truthful as possible when he replies, "Since I graduated from high school, before that even, so long ago. I try to push this feeling away."

Doctor Spitzer stares at the file in front of him and waits for Geoffrey to continue. When he realizes Geoffrey isn't speaking anymore he says, "How long have you been successful at pushing your loneliness away?"

"Since last night."

"Somehow I don't believe that and I think you don't either. Try being honest with yourself."

Geoffrey wants to scream. He's trying to be honest. He's really, really, really trying his hardest to appease this doctor. He doesn't know what this doctor in front of him wants to hear. He hangs his head, stares at his hands, tries to think. Only I am a witness as my father pictures himself in high school once more trying to escape. His father, The Chess King, is gone once more, another six-month leave of absence, selling his optical glass to the laboratories of Germany, France, and England. His mother is lonely but rarely shows her huge sadness to her son. His job is to make her happy. Nell isn't even finishing at USC. She never tells them she dropped out. She lies to her parents and to Geoffrey. She escapes the house in Connecticut and flies across the country and seldom comes home, even for holidays, which The Chess King rarely feels he needs to attend either. Geoffrey remembers getting the infrequent call from Nell. He misses his sister; they were a team, and then she abandoned him, too.

"How are you? Staying out of trouble? The school girls giving you problems?"

"I'm OK," Geoffrey replies to Nell's teasing voice. She sounds so far away over the telephone line. "Are you coming home for spring break?"

"Not this time. I'm going to Mexico with Shirl and Mallie." Nell speaks as though she's kept her family informed about her friendships and classes and the intricacies of her life in clear detail, she speaks fast with no pauses; she doesn't listen, all lies. She calls to tell her family she's decided to lead her own life. Just remember to send her some money. "Can you put mom on?"

"Sure," and Geoffrey leaves the telephone to find his mother in the kitchen smoking, cupping her cigarette when Geoffrey appears as if she's able to capture the smell and the escaping smoke. "Mom. Nell wants to speak to you."

He thinks of Mexico, beaches his sister haunts, the ocean

far away, and then recalls the summer moments when his father would drive the family, or just Geoffrey, all the way to the Jersey Shore for a long afternoon. Sometimes they'd rent a cottage at Cape May. Happy days. Geoffrey would stare at the ocean. He was just a little boy, the back of his head seal slick. He watched the rolling waves crush the beach and laugh, run into the water and sparkle alone, figure things out in his head as his father watched, as his family watched on those occasions. If he could retrieve those happier moments more often, maybe the darkness within him wouldn't clutch at his heart.

Geoffrey escapes to his room and takes out his history book and tries to read and read and learn and learn. He wants to follow in Nell's footsteps. Get out of the house. Escape. He finds the World History reading too easy; his other classes just as simple. He can read something once and retain all of it as if his memory banks will never fill up. He takes tests without having to study and receives his "A"s without any joy—who's back at home waiting to compliment his performances? After an hour reading he calls Cecilia, his latest girlfriend, who has to study very hard just to get her frustrating "C"s and begs her to let him come over. He pushes, wheedles, and says, "I can help you study." She protests but relents when he tells her what he wants to do to her. Cecelia will be forced to break up with Geoffrey when her mother eavesdrops on one of his telephone calls. Cecelia cries even more when she finds out Geoffrey hasn't even put up a fight.

"Don't you love me?" Cecilia asks in the hallway two days later.

"Of course I do," Geoffrey replies, but he's with Linda the next week telling her all the things he used to tell Cecelia, recycling words, massaging her in all the tender places, caressing her softer curves and lying to her over and over again. Linda lasts almost three weeks before Geoffrey grows bored and meets a girl from a rival high school. Linda asks why he's being such a bastard.

"You're with someone else. I know it. How could you do this to me?"

Geoffrey takes it and takes it and then leaves Linda

crying on her front porch. He drives to the neighboring town to speak sweet nothings to his next girlfriend. Soon everyone will know everything about Geoffrey and his extracurricular pursuits, girls talk, Cecilia talked to Linda and they both talked to the next good girl, and his souring reputation. The girls are warned to stay away from him but Geoffrey is a ladies man and women always think they can change him; Geoffrey will go on and on and graduate with honors and leave for the Midwest. To college and a huge town like Ann Arbor where he meets many women who don't care who he's been with before. Where there are so many girls, where he can be anonymous, where he can study and play. Years later, after he passes the Michigan bar exam, he meets Dakota, my mother, and she's one of the few women who, without any pretense of naiveté, resists his innate charm and strapped-on charisma, and this girl is the one challenge he can't defend against in turn.

Doctor Spitzer takes notes while Geoffrey remains silent in front of him. Fifteen minutes of silence passes. "You seem very tense right now."

"Wouldn't you be?"

"I'm here because I want to be." Doctor Spitzer's tone of voice carries a sliver of condescension. Geoffrey almost feels it like a breeze wafting across the room. Geoffrey notices the psychiatrist in front of him never says, "I want to help you."

"How is my son doing?"

"I'll get information to you as soon as possible." Doctor Spitzer places his palm flat on the front cover of the DSM. He draws strength from it and is very eager to flip to the singular diagnosis for this weak man in the chair he has to deal with. His impatience is showing as he starts to rub the medical book's cover, gently rubbing in a circular motion.

"What about right now?"

"Right now we need to help you." Click. The doctor says we instead of I need to help you.

Geoffrey doesn't think of anything else to say. His mind is blank. He slinks down in his chair as if he's in a dark movie theater and there's so much tension in the room, on the screen in front of him, he cannot possibly escape it. What he wants to say to the doctor: Shut your smug face.

What he does say, "I'd really like some help."

"One step at a time."

Geoffrey wants to know which university was fooled into believing this doctor's bullshit. The clichés, the homilies, the frozen personality, if there was a course in bedside manner, this doctor has fooled everyone involved.

"Now," Doctor Spitzer continues, "there's something deeper you're not revealing."

Geoffrey shrinks even more. Inside he feels caught.

"Take me back to last night."

"What?"

"To when you felt like killing yourself."

"I didn't feel like killing myself last night."

"And yet here you are."

"I felt like I needed to numb myself."

"That's a start."

"And I couldn't numb myself with just alcohol. I had a crushing headache."

"Have you ever considered therapy before?"

"No. My wife—"

"What's her name?"

"Madison Dakota. She's a professor at the college. She's also a poet." Geoffrey says this as if he's never been prouder of her accomplishments. Somehow his words ring false even to him. He's unable to pretend.

"Continue."

"Dakota wanted us to go see someone this summer." He doesn't know why he's called his wife by her last name, maybe just to mess with the doctor. "I promised her we'd go see someone when I asked her if I could move back into the house."

"Okay. So. What happened before this summer? Why did you need to ask Dakota permission to come back?"

"Let me tell the story my way. Do you have to interrupt me so much?"

"Okay. Go ahead."

Geoffrey remembers meeting Madison for dinner at a small pizza place on Maynard St. in Ann Arbor a year after I was born, the happily unmarried couple. I wasn't happy, my small fists clenched and I was tightly wound up in the cracked leather booth, trapped by Dakota's body. She ached with loneliness. All she'd been doing day after day was taking care of the baby and not working on her writing as much as she wanted to and Geoffrey was at the law office until seven, eight, nine at night. They weren't married and Madison, more than a year after meeting Geoffrey didn't think she wanted to get married anytime soon. She knew the law firm Geoffrey worked for was putting a lot of pressure on him to have the chipper nuclear family and that the unmarried arrangement made Geoffrey suspect around the firm. He told her this much.

"I'm not going to marry you just because it will make you look better. How ridiculous. If you and I are compatible, I need more convincing."

"Honey," Geoffrey said, "I want you to be happy."

"I can't get Chris to stop crying sometimes. We sit at home all day and he cries."

"He seems fine now. Why don't you let me take him"— Geoffrey and Madison switched places in the booth and Maddy was amazed at how quickly I calmed.

"He loves you."

Geoffrey somehow doubted it. He could feel this doubt pouring from him in waves, this doubt that's stayed hidden.

"Where's your father?" asks Doctor Spitzer.

"I said I didn't want to discuss my father."

"I think it's important."

"Can't you just get off thinking you're psychology's greatest gift to the world and realize I'm just trying to make you understand that right now I need to be with my family?"

"You need to know your family is okay and I'll check on their status again after this session is over. How did your father treat you when you were a child?"

Geoffrey remembers leaving his law office, the downtown Middleton office one sunny lunch hour, with a huge grin on his face. He was free for the afternoon actually, not just for lunch, and he'd cleared the weekend, also. No work for the wicked. He was supposed to meet Maddy up at Flathead Lake after work, a weekend getaway lake rental. She was driving right that very minute with me seat-belted in the back. I was six-years-old. Geoffrey almost skipped across the parking lot. He got into his car and started whistling. He didn't think he'd ever remembered being this happy. I was humming in the backseat of my mother's Subaru and could barely see out the window at the farmland, cattle ranching fields, mountains approaching. Geoffrey received an urgent message from the hospital when he checked in at his law firm an hour later. He was inside a strange woman's apartment. He hadn't even taken his clothes off yet. He listened to the message from the hospital. Come right away. Your family has been involved in a car accident. Just get here as quickly as possible. And Geoffrey didn't feel any guilt. He just picked up all of his belongings and never sought out this woman again. She was disappointed and thought: Screw him. Just an excuse from a player. She didn't believe his family was really wrecked by a truck speeding through a stop sign. Screw her. Geoffrey arrived, flushed, at the emergency room and the doctor told him I was okay, a couple bruises, a few cuts, none too deep, and guided Geoffrey to a private nook outside the operating halls.

"Your wife's in a very fragile state. She's still unconscious. We ran a lot of blood tests. When we got the results something came up and we ran a different set of tests."

"Just spit it out," Geoffrey said.

"Your wife was pregnant, very, very early, in the first trimester. She was probably unaware of this."

Geoffrey almost collapsed against the doctor. He steadied his footing and crossed his arms against his chest, tried to puff himself up.

"What are you saying?"

"Please. Sit down." And Geoffrey sat in a chair at a nearby desk.

"Your wife lost the baby. There was too much bleeding and other physical damage. This crash your wife was involved in is one of the worst I've seen in the three years I've been here."

Geoffrey didn't know what to think. What would he do? What would Madison do when she learned she lost the baby? She never told him she was pregnant. Now he did wonder if she even knew. Did she keep it a secret from him?

He had his own secrets he kept from her. "How am I going to tell her?"

"There's more, and I already informed the police."

Geoffrey was too stunned to reply.

"When we tried to stop the bleeding there was nothing we could do. We had to perform an emergency hysterectomy."

The image of Madison lying on a stretcher somewhere, broken to pieces, unhinged Geoffrey so much he wanted to flee the hospital. It took all his courage just to stand. The doctor mistook his fear for grief. He could hear him breathe. I wasn't an only child. Then and now, but they didn't tell me about any of this. I know it now but I won't remember this if I wake up, and I doubt they'll ever breathe a word of it to anyone else for the rest of their lives. Geoffrey wanted to see his wife.

"Take me to her, please."

"She's still in surgery."

"I need to be with her."

"We're doing all we can. Your son needs you now. A few more stitches above his eyebrow and we can release him to you. Follow me."

Geoffrey didn't want to collect me. He wanted to jump out of his skin.

When Geoffrey was sitting next to his wife eight hours later she woke up, groggy, and in excruciating pain. Geoffrey could barely look at her. The bandages wrapped around her body everywhere. Just keep breathing.

"Stay quiet," he whispered. "Don't try to speak. You're going to be okay." And he kept hold of her uninjured hand, squeezed gently.

Geoffrey thought about my other unborn sibling, the only chance for a brother or sister vanishing like a fish jumping a dam. The doctor told the police, something he was legally bound to do—my father felt invisible blows, decking him, and viewed the years ahead as vacant. When Madison truly awakened and slowly got off the painkillers, Geoffrey finally told her and she closed down and told Geoffrey to never speak about the accident again. She cried alone, never comfortable letting anyone ever see her tears.

Weeks of rehabilitation flew by, she never remembered the specifics of the accident and wanting another child was something she kept locked within the deepest part of her. There were few people who even remembered her from the accident. The nurses on duty that day may still talk about it when telling stories about tragedy and how horrible it hits some families but no one else had to remember except Geoffrey. Why do bad things happen to such good people, one R.T. tech said to the nurses at the desk, and then pushed his cart down to the staff elevators and pressed the up button. Little did he know; it was all on the surface, rippling from this moment of betrayal, seduction, catastrophe, another quickie infidelity with a woman who forgot all about Geoffrey after he left. She now lives in Boca taking care of her sick mother and is no longer able to bring strange men back home without making her mother sicker than she already was. I see this blurry future and wonder if it's just a dream filtering into this black, hovering reality. I'm trapped. Back in a different hospital I bawled during and after my cuts were stitched up.

"Where were you daddy?" I screamed. Accusing. "Mommy's hurt."

"I know. I know. Mommy's going to be all right." He was thinking about this lost child of his but not me. This second baby Maddy and he created who died in the crash. Snuffed out. Then, the next second, he was thinking about the man who ran the stop sign and how he could seek a certain vengeance by suing him beyond what the state would do to him, which turned out to be nothing much, in the end. The man was a drunk, but not legally when he hit our car. Old. He blamed the crash on his diabetic sugar low. He found the Lord soon afterwards. He swore he really did. The Lord would help him out of the mess he got himself in. The court system had him. He was a poor cattle ranch helper, always worked the grazing cattle, taking them from one patch of land to another. Married and divorced long ago. Always a drink in his hand by 5:30, he'd eat very little and work in a somnambulant state for the rest of his days until he hit my mother's car and changed everything. He cut the booze the next day. Not two months later he died of a heart attack.

Sadness worked its way into his veins, the shock on his system spread, not knowing he shouldn't go on the wagon without being monitored. His estate didn't amount to much and there wasn't anyone for Geoffrey to sue in civil court, and, besides, he didn't want his wife's pain to be extended, for her to dwell on this lost promising child, and he got his wish. Life passed. Maddy woke up and her body mended over the next year. It didn't mend true; there's the limp, slight as it is, the tightness in her neck, and she gets these awful migraines that sometimes linger for days, but she was back and she's still healing within. Later, and only once, would my parents both cry as they held one another in their cold bedroom. Maddy cried because she didn't know if she ever wanted to have another child, but she wanted the option. Geoffrey cried because he had too many secrets banging around inside of him and they festered, and he didn't know they would simmer and simmer until they started a low boil.

"What?"

"I asked you if you feel okay. Physically. All of this information. Your family. It must be quite a shock."

"Yes."

"Have you ever been on medication for depression?"

"No."

"I think one of the goals of your stay here should be to find out what's causing your depression."

Geoffrey believes he shouldn't have to be told that as if he was a small child, spelling everything out. I believe the doctor is only going by procedure, following the rules, connecting the dots, and isn't doing anything wrong. My father has never been the most attentive listener, active in pressing his own egotistical need to be the one speaking down to allow someone else's opinion to form.

"The hour is almost up. I'm going to start you on some medicine to help take the edge off. Someone else will see you tomorrow morning, a specialist in cases like yours. Then I'll be with you again tomorrow late in the afternoon. I'm recommending you sit in on a group therapy session tonight just to observe. You won't have to say a word but the experience can be fairly motivational. Some use it as a time for personal meditation."

"What about my family?"

"I'll check on them and get back to you around the dinner hour. Six? We have a lot of work to do."

Geoffrey can't believe his ears. The doctor just seems so unprofessional to him but somehow he's worked his way into the number one position in this place and Geoffrey knows he'll have to stay on his good side. Listening to this man is torture for him.

"I can't make a judgment yet," the doctor drones on, "but if I had to, I'd say you still have a lot of childhood issues you haven't dealt with."

Way to go, Sherlock. Geoffrey mumbles, and the doctor doesn't understand what Geoffrey has said.

"For tomorrow, when we meet, I want you to think about your own childhood, your family growing up. What you remember the most. Happy or sad times. I'm going to prescribe an antidepressant. You'll take it tonight and tomorrow morning."

Geoffrey has no response. The doctor tells him to go back to his room and Geoffrey stands and says, "Please find out what's happening with my family. I'm begging you."

"I will tell you of any changes. Soon."

Geoffrey can't get through to the man and walks back to his room. Again, it's not that funny, Geoffrey's situation, yet Geoffrey starts to softly laugh and I laugh with him, at him. He laughs, mumbling, until he starts to choke. Tears roll down his cheeks as he rests on his bed. He laughs and laughs, but it's not that funny.

* * *

In the late evening, Nell, Lance, and Sheila sit silently in the waiting room. They've covered all the facts they know, what little facts each has gathered from Nadine, on one of her trips to tell Nell that Maddy's doing fine but she doesn't want any visitors just yet, and from the nurses and the newspapers. Sheila says, "Poor Chris. When will the doctor come out? Is Maddy hurt?"

"I don't know what's wrong with her," Nell states as she stares at the far wall. Nell would say she was never really that close to her brother. Really close. She was much older, almost eight years older, when Geoffrey had been born. She left home for a college in California, one of the few that accepted her application and her parents' money. Nell fooled around with art, architecture, and when those didn't work out someone suggested she try interior design. She was insulted, but she would've thrived there. She has a flair for the exotic. The counselor in the office blanched a bit but collected herself enough to quip: "Well, Ms. Bullet, it seems you've gone through the majors starting with the letter A, shall we try the letter B?"

Nell stood and left the persnickety woman's office immediately and the university soon after. She called her mother for money. Never her father, The Chess King, and didn't tell her mother she'd dropped out of college for almost a year. "How are your grades, dear?" They were everyone else's problem. Never Nell's fault. A victim of the times when women were still seen as feminine objects until the sexual explosion in the late '60s happened and Nell met up with a man who changed her world view. He was everything she wasn't: slick, skinny, wore clothes too tight, loud colors, longer hair (it was the time), a man who had easy access to drugs of all kinds and Nell rarely left his side.

She'd met Oliver at a campus party a week after she stopped going to classes. He made her laugh and she tried to forget that she was lying to her parents back home (never once thought about her brother and how much he missed her all the time, alone in the house back in Connecticut), her roommate in the dorm, who finally stopped speaking to Nell because they always got into huge arguments about all manner of subjects, usually the worst stemming from how dirty and unkempt Nell's side of the room was all the time and the late night interruptions, sneaking in and out of the dorm. "I'll never lie for you again," Nell's roommate sneered. "Consider this morning the last time."

"I never asked you to lie for me. I never lie for anyone. Go back to your books." And Nell would laugh in her roommate's face time and time again.

Nell paraded herself on the arm of her boyfriend all summer until she brought Oliver home to Greenwich to meet her parents. "You'll never believe it, Mom. Oliver asked me to marry him."

Nell's mother blanched. Visibly. Geoffrey didn't understand what was happening. Oliver treated Geoffrey like a little adult; someone he could speak down to. How could his sister be in love with such a charlatan? This was what Geoffrey believed and years later never could get a straight answer to. Nell's mother was so angry with Nell it was up to Geoffrey to intercede on her behalf: the little protector. And The Chess King hadn't arrived home yet from his trip to Bolivia, another buying opportunity down there but when he did get home he'd already made up his mind about Nell and her infatuation and couldn't care less. He arrived, met Oliver, shook his thin, tanned hand, gave Nell his blessing and inwardly said: And Good Riddance. Geoffrey's parents were eager to see Nell out of their lives and living with anyone else, someone else's responsibility.

They agreed to pay for a modest wedding—Oliver's parents never showed up—and they also agreed to never pay for anything for Nell again. She asked them for money once more, but by then they knew about her quitting school and wished they'd cut the purse strings long before. They flatly told Nell no. She didn't ask for any more money. Even when Oliver begged Nell to call them, to lie to them, to tell them you're sick, that's a good one, Honey. Oliver wanted to buy a fishing boat and start a business down in Puerto Vallarta where he could live like a king, have lots of servants, a cook even. Let's steal some of that money from the tourists. But there was no money coming and Oliver started to dream less and Nell no longer dreamed at all and woke up one day, five years after she married Oliver, and started to scream at him. Scream. Scream. Scream. She filed for divorce that very afternoon. She never heard another word from Oliver and she never spent time trying to dig into the past. Nell ended up crawling back to Connecticut when Geoffrey was one year away from graduating high school. The Chess King was, how strange, gone once again, but received a call from his wife explaining everything. Geoffrey's mother had missed Nell, but they circled each other and got on each other's nerves so readily. Geoffrey escaped the house on a date almost every night, with a different girl each week, and Nell noticed this and tried to tease Geoffrey but he turned his back and quick-as-a-whip he was out the door.

Nell took a job in a travel agency and studied to become a travel agent and did quite well for herself, started her own agency and sold it almost thirty years later, before the Internet made travel agencies inefficient. She lived in Palm Springs. She had lots of suitors but kept her vow to never marry anyone ever again. Of course she fell in love, but the feeling never lasted; Nell wouldn't allow it.

Nell remembered selling a honeymoon trip to an older man and a much younger woman. She told them they'd love Hawaii, a topnotch resort on the western shore of the Big Island, somewhere they could retreat to and not have to think about anything else. The blonde woman reminded Nell of one of Cinderella's stepsisters. There was something not quite right about her, the large cheekbones and the thinness of her skin spread over them, pointedly. There in the travel office Nell studied how the woman's mouth naturally formed a frown, and shadowed her tiny sliver-like teeth, how the woman never took her eyes off her husband-to-be, and how during the whole encounter the woman couldn't think of one happy thing to say. The man kept a tight grip on the woman's hand also.

"You'll have the vacation of a lifetime," Nell said, "A time to enjoy each other." Nell couldn't help but add that. And wondered about this couple now. She could read the signs. How happy they didn't act. How controlled. How studied this disrespecting older man and this calculating younger woman seemed to be. Nell wonders why this couple popped into her memories. They were probably in a large dual-housekeeper mansion sleeping in separate bedrooms, avoiding calls from their extended families. After all this time the in-laws couldn't quite picture them together but kept trying to bury the hatchet. This is the reason, Nell thinks.

Nell turns to Lance and says, "Are you going to speak to Geoffrey soon?"

"He called me here. I asked the front desk and he can't have any visitors, not even me. Don't worry. I'll be going up there within the hour as soon as we find out what's up with Maddy. Did the E.R. doc say when she'd be back out?"

"No." And Nell falls back into her silence. She doesn't tell Lance or Sheila she hasn't spoken to her brother in almost a year, since last Christmas; she doesn't need their judgment. Communication between family members always waxes and wanes, the closeness and growing apart, growing up.

* * *

Nadine sits next to Maddy and they whisper to each other.

"Geoffrey's sister is going to cause trouble," says Nadine with a dry tone.

"She always does."

"My brother is very much like Nell," says Nadine. "Always has an opinion. Freely given. Always interrupts. Too judgy, never listens well. Never compliments. He's single, too."

"Don't even wish that on them. Oh, to be single again. Sow some undone wild oats."

"What? We should set them up. Imagine. Our families linked by two of the world's most unhappy people."

"They're not the only ones who've been unhappy for a long time. Did the nurse say when we could leave? I need to get back up to Chris. It's almost midnight."

"It shouldn't be much longer. You can't wait in the Intensive Care Unit upstairs and you're protected here. The hospital recommended you stay here as long as you need."

"If I have to hear that one more time."

"How do your legs feel now?"

"Perfectly fine. A-OK." Maddy pushes up from the stretcher and stands, walks the length of the small room and back to the second chair next to Nadine. She sits down and grasps Nadine's hand.

"Do you want me to go get Nell? And what about the

other two?"

"Lance and Sheila? I can't believe they came all the way out here."

"Yeah. Lance said Geoffrey called them from the Psychiatric Unit sometime this morning. They got here on some fast connections. The news worried Lance to no end. So at least we know Geoffrey is doing better."

"I don't think I want to see them at all. I don't even know why they're here. I mean, I know why they're here, but I don't see the point."

"I can keep telling them you don't want to see them. They're not family."

"Then Geoffrey will find out and have a fit. Later. Lance is his best friend."

"He can't have any visitors yet? Not even his lawyer? That doesn't make a great deal of sense."

"What does here? I'm worried, Nadine. Not about me. I don't think Chris is going to make it."

Her doubt hits her almost physically. Nadine can't believe Maddy thinks I'm not going to make it. She's rarely maudlin and self-pitying and Nadine wants to tear her own hair out.

"Don't say that. He's going to pull out of it."

"I just don't know what I'll do."

"Don't think the worst."

At that moment a nurse and Doctor Fusil open the door and crowd into the room. The new night nurse asks Maddy if she's comfortable and if she needs anything—water—and then leaves. Doctor Fusil holds a stack of computer paper and her clipboard. Her expression is almost readable, studious, definitely serious, maybe preoccupied, and Maddy feels a chill along her spine where the thin hospital smock slightly opens against her back.

"Well," says Maddy.

"How are your legs feeling now? Any numbness? Discomfort?"

"The pins and needles feeling completely went away about twenty minutes ago even with Nell in the waiting room."

This makes Doctor Fusil smile and she presses her

clipboard against her chest. "The preliminary test results are back. I think you can go be with your son now. I apologize for the tests taking so long. I know everything must be hard for you and I'm very sorry for what's happening to your family. I'm going to recommend that you make a follow-up appointment with the hospital for more tests to confirm some findings. I'm not going to admit you into the system but I have some concerns."

"What do you mean?"

"You've been having these episodes off and on for quite some time, you said. Most of them mild or short-term in duration. The feeling in your legs. Some blurriness in your vision. But that went away and never reoccurred. Correct?"

"Yes," Maddy answers and squeezes Nadine's hand.

"When was that?"

"Over a year ago. I have migraines sometimes and I thought the blurry vision was associated with them. My vision cleared up after four weeks." Maddy never mentioned she was having trouble with her vision to me or to Geoffrey. The secrets Maddy keeps, her health, her resentments, cause as much damage as Geoffrey's secrets. Nadine wants to shake Maddy and tell her to take care of herself first.

Weary, Maddy and Nadine wait for Doctor Fusil to give them the news while I lay comatose, motionless except for the occasional involuntary tic, in an abandoned room in the children's wing of the hospital. No one's allowed to visit me but family and my family is busy elsewhere. I'm under tight security and my mother is about to find out what's been hobbling her body. What Maddy will never know: that her husband had affairs with three (not counting Deepika and the woman before Deepika who'd almost split Maddy and Geoffrey up three years in the past) different women since the move from Michigan to Montana, all of them long-term and ending at his insistence (but not Deepika; she called that one off) that he could never leave his family; that he had sexual liaisons, quickies, with many other women. Geoffrey had always lived with the fear that one of these women would break down and call Maddy, seeking a bitter revenge.

What she will find out: that I am truly gay; I wrote about it in my journals for years, the paper notebooks hidden away at the bottom of my closet, the computer journal secured by passwords easily broken later, and I know I'm gay (that word not in my vocabulary as a child; I just know what I'm attracted to, curious about) since grade school, maybe earlier, when I sat and played at the public swimming kiddy pool and stared at the fathers of the other children, fascinated by their masculinity and ignored all the other mothers in their one-piece and bikini bathing suits.

What she comes so close to figuring out: that I have a half-sibling about to be born into this world; that Deepika is pregnant with Geoffrey's child, since Maddy hasn't seen her and Deepika is packing to move away even at this moment; that Maddy, perhaps, she can only wish, will never again see Deepika, that the office gossip will never reach her ears, and not from a lack of tact on anyone's part, Deepika will become the nameless one; that I was with Deepika right before I met my fate straight in the eye: Pow! That I try my hardest to wake up but cannot even feel myself slipping away, adrift in the darkness.

HUBRIS

THE NEXT MORNING wakes everyone in Middleton with unquiet alarm and an infuriating feeling of unease. How can this be allowed to happen in our city? An upturned nose, an indignant wrist flick, *shoo* the shame away, people skim the headlines in the morning paper: **Beating Case Suspects Deny They Meant to Kill**. And isn't that putting the cart before the horse? Isn't there anyone out there who thinks I will pull through this?

Now that they've got their stories straight the four boys-quickly-turning-to-men admit they did assault me in what salivating prosecutors describe as a "savage, savage beating," leaving me in a coma, but they also say, plead, they had no intention of killing me.

The story begins: All four of them together, Terrence Jewell, 17, Paul Real, 17, Richard O'Connor, 16, and Ellis Pallino, 15, were formally charged yesterday with first and second-degree assault (attempted murder charges pending) for beating Christopher Bullet, 15, on S. Higgins St. three blocks from Tipu's Indian Cookery.

Maybe Deepika likes the food there. The names of the boys, so young, are given to the press because they're all going to be charged as adults.

Then there's speculation in the article about the victim's state of mind. How I probably didn't understand why I'd ended up in that area of Middleton, rain-drenched, still a short distance from my home on foot like I was. A witness will state I left school early and without permission. I missed a math test. And the same witness also brings forth the fact that she tried to take pictures of the beating with the camera on her cell phone but it was really dark and some of the photos didn't turn out very well, just enough to show shadowy shapes, a blurred darkness. The witness even asked when the police would return her cell phone to her, her lower lip puffed out with worry.

The witness doesn't recall me being disrespectful to the four suspects or doing anything to provoke them. She says: all four boys used slurs and foul name-calling to taunt the victim, right from the get-go. The witness only tells the police what she specifically overheard, cautioned by one of the detectives to try to not give anything to the media. All four suspects fled the scene leaving my body broken in the street hanging onto life.

In part two of the article, which appears the next day, the reporter delves into the lives of the four participants, the human-interest angle. Five young lives lay in ruins because of brutal, senseless, stupidity. What were they thinking? Who took the first swing? Why was this being labeled a hate crime? All of these questions will be answered, but not to the fullest, because I cannot speak. But even then, as in all things, the answers beget more questions. The reporter wants to dig into the lives of the four attackers to try to humanize them for some sad reason, and pointedly makes the pronouncement: We're all monsters. We're all culpable. Everyone. The catchall phase. Play on emotion, when so many people shy far away from anything touchy-feely.

The four attackers are all being charged as adults, a recap of yesterday's news. Terrence Jewell, the apparent ringleader, started smoking cigarettes when he was 11. By age 14 he was making weekly appearances in Juvenile Drug Treatment Center Court. He and a group of teenagers were caught with enough marijuana to send him to a drug-rehabilitation center. Terrence said, "I got frozen (disciplined) for it. Real bad." When his mother and his stepfather found out, Terrence told police he was kicked out of the house.

Someone from the court system intervened on Terrence's behalf and got him into a mentor program. His mother took him back after completion of this program and his juvenile court Judge said: "I appreciate your honest progress. You know you're far from perfect, but you're back on the straight-and-narrow. I'm happy you're beginning to blossom." Terrence fell out of line once more when he started high school and met up with his two cronies-in-crime, Paul Real and Richard O'Connor.

Terrence knew how to circumvent the system, being a child of this system. None of the three boys had strong parental figures, the product of broken homes, and fewer mentors willing to stick by them after the court obligations had been fulfilled. Three tough teenagers finish their time on the streets of Middleton. You (and the reporter wants to point fingers at everyone sitting in offices and coffeehouses reading his morning words) passed these children every day (inferring that we, as, a, society, we're all responsible for the beating).

One of the bizarre twists the city of Middleton plays witness to is that Ellis Pallino didn't come from a broken home and had a friendly school relationship with the victim. The youngest of the accused, Ellis Pallino, had every opportunity in the world. A good kid. A kid who was part of the jock crowd and played wide receiver for the football team. One of his coaches said he showed promise on the field, even as a freshman; maybe even college ball is in his future (nope, not no more). A celebrated junior high athlete, Ellis worked hard. His family remained prominent in Middleton sporting events and sponsored several charity benefits. Ellis Pallino was the son of a city council member. A spokesperson for the Pallino family reiterated the family has no comment at this time (and never will). Ellis Pallino's father resigns from the city council the day his son is formally charged. This gives him time to spend on his son's defense, to distance his son from the other three, obviously more troubled, boys.

The article doesn't say what happens if I die, only that the boys didn't mean to kill me, but there are so many who think differently; I was there, beaten to a pulp. I can't tell anyone my truth.

* * *

The Chess King sits in his first class seat humming softly, annoyingly, and notices the woman in front of him adjusting her noise-canceling headphones. His airplane will touch down in Middleton in thirty minutes, the fasten-your-seatbelt signs blink, and The Chess King may take a taxi to the same hotel Nell lodges in. He hasn't decided to go there yet. She booked him into the adjacent room, took care of all the details, and didn't say a word to anyone about his arrival. All for the best.

My grandfather stops humming and thinks about what little information Nell told him when she called him from her house in Palm Springs. Stop whatever you're doing and fly to Middleton now. Do you hear me? The Chess King hears Nell—he usually does the opposite. He hasn't always acted on her persuasive orders in the past. His behavior annoys Nell as much as it has annoyed Geoffrey. He's not flying all the way to Montana to save Geoffrey even if Nell believes it to be the perfect opportunity for The Chess King to apologize to, reconcile with, and reunite the family. All for one and all that, but Nell is a dreamer, and past history show her dreams rarely have come true. Their family, as a family unit, has never been a central concern for The Chess King. The center of their family died when The Chess King's wife died.

But that's not true. I've seen the ocean, the beaches, the trips to Cape May. These happened. I see The Chess King staring at his son, my father, as he plays chicken with the Jersey Shore waves, laughter. I see a shadow next to The Chess King—my grandmother? She's gone. My father just a boy in a red bathing suit left alone while his father watched, watched others, watched the ladies in their skin-baring get-ups under striped umbrellas—and, I knew The Chess King liked to travel to this beach alone more than with his family. There's Nell flying away like a gull.

Of course, Nell's bullishness flowed over The Chess King, and now he has to laugh. She did get him to fly all the way to Montana, and that's something, so maybe there's more of a tethered connection. He may or may not check into the hotel. He may or may not even see Nell. But he will go to the hospital to see what happened to me. His grandson is on his mind. I am. This grandchild he remains distant from, unknown. It's Geoffrey's choice keeping me away from The Chess King. In the end, and it all comes down to this, The Chess King wants to meet me; wants to see what I'm made of.

* * *

Flying in from San Diego, and arriving early in the morning, Rhea doesn't know I'm showing signs I will never wake up. She starts to drive to the hospital and rehearses what she'll say to her sister.

Maybe I'll wait until mom and dad get here. They should be here from Ohio in the late afternoon. She practices this silently as she drives.

Rhea turns the rental car around and drives to Maddy's house. She knows where Maddy hides the spare key, off the back deck under a fake rock, but no one tells her Maddy didn't have the sense to lock the house up, just a little forgotten detail in all this craziness. Rhea doesn't even try the front door; it must be locked. She goes in search of the key, finds it and enters through the back door. The stench of rotting Chinese food hits her senses like a sledgehammer and she backs outside quickly.

She's torn about how she's seldom able to communicate with her sister without judging her. She vows to try to keep things even, keep everything down deep, doesn't want to bring up old wounds, certainly not rise to the occasion; this isn't the time.

There were three cars and a news van parked along the roadside almost blocking Maddy and Geoffrey's driveway. They've been waiting like poachers. Rhea doesn't get miffed. She noticed the drivers of the cars stepping out of their vehicles into the cold gray morning but she kept driving on up the long driveway. One of the men motioned for her to roll down her window and Rhea gunned the car and spewed rocks behind her. Who are these people? What did Maddy do?

Rhea steadies herself, covers her mouth with her sleeve

and braces herself for the smell. She gives the Chinese food, in cartons on the kitchen island, a wide space and eventually finds a Hefty bag under the sink. Quick as a *whoosh* Rhea places the offending odor into the garbage can in the garage.

Rhea and Maddy have been so distant the past couple of years Rhea barely remembers when she stopped trying to interfere in her sister's life, made decisions based on a familial love for her sibling rather than insisting Maddy open her eyes and finally get out, distance herself from a man she couldn't trust.

Three years ago Maddy told Rhea she was going to come visit her for Thanksgiving—just her. She sent me to be with my grandparents who were down in Florida. "We can take Chris to Sea World," Millie exclaimed. And Rhea sensed she had no choice. She said, "What about Geoffrey?"

"He has a lot of work to do. So much he can't possibly get away," Maddy said.

And that was that.

Rhea opened the front door. Her two kids were playing Nintendo Smash Brothers Party Bomb or something like that in the family room but the noise they made was loud and cheerful and competitive, and Rhea pulled Maddy to her, a quick hug and a smile. Maddy was tight in her arms, a stiffness that was the result of the car accident long ago, but Rhea felt like her sister couldn't warm up to her and never could. Rhea took things too personally.

"I'm so happy you're here. I've got the meal all planned." Rhea didn't say it would feel like a real family holiday.

"Did you get the stuffing recipe from dad?" Maddy asked.

"He didn't want to reveal his secret but you know dad. I could tell he really wanted to be here with the grandkids."

The first arrow flew into the air. Maddy let her sister's words flow over her, and replied, "Well, it'll be good for Chris to have some alone time with them."

"Oh, of course . . . I didn't mean."

"Well. Let's go see my nephews." This comment worked to get Rhea back on track and the living room opened up to reveal two pushing, loud, squealing, adorable kids.

"Your Aunt Maddy is here!" The oldest nephew turned

back and said hello but they couldn't leave the game. Loss of points. Loss of battle. Maddy understood and took her sister's arm in her own and said, "Let's go to the kitchen."

"Is everything all right?" Rhea asked. She felt like Maddy was too quick to get away from her children.

"I don't know."

"Is it Geoffrey?"

"Let me ask you to do one thing. Okay?"

Rhea nodded and said, "Sure."

"I'd appreciate it if you do not tell me 'I told you so'."

"Can I get you some tea? Coffee?"

"Tea, yes that would be terrific."

"Peppermint with honey?"

"Sure."

While Rhea was moving around taking out cups and saucers and filling the teakettle, Maddy said, "Geoffrey has been having an affair. He doesn't know what he wants anymore."

Rhea turned the gas up on the burner.

"He says he doesn't love this other woman." Maddy hadn't really confided in her sister in a long time. Her sister liked to tally misfortune and place her perfect life in comparison to any of her missteps, and continually bring up the sad times. "He says he still loves me and Chris and he doesn't want to disrupt the family and it's all so much bullshit."

"Have you told mom and dad?"

"No. You're the only one I've told."

Rhea was preening inside but tried hard to not show her sister this.

"Please. Don't let mom and dad know. Geoffrey and I need some time apart. Chris doesn't know anything, but he's old enough to suspect something isn't right between his father and me." This was the woman Geoffrey took up with before Deepika. He ended it, and Maddy so wanted to believe her husband would never do it again. She wanted her life to be simple; Geoffrey complicated things.

Besides Maddy's first confession to her sister the Thanksgiving weekend went off without the predicted traumatic moments. The bird was a little tough, but not much, and the sausage stuffing earned raves and the gravy hid the toughness. Rhea kept her own counsel. Maddy believed she could count on her sister. Thanksgiving night Geoffrey called and Maddy spoke to him using the telephone in her sister's master bedroom.

They talked for an hour and Geoffrey begged Maddy to come home early. Please. Please. Please. Maddy still loved him. That's what it came down to.

Geoffrey said it was truly over between him and this other woman. It was just sex. He could never love anyone else. He made Maddy feel culpable. When was the last time we had sex, Maddy? He actually asked her this question. She told him she didn't agree with that, his ego was coloring everything he was searching to blame. Maddy didn't want to feel any guilt but somehow she took it on. It came down to Maddy, who still felt comfortable with Geoffrey. She'd always felt this way. She'd known he always played the field, too. It was part of his nature, and she knew he believed himself to be sorry and sincere about wanting her home. He missed her. He missed Chris. He missed his family.

But Rhea knew one of her sister's deeply hidden secrets now and a year went by and Rhea couldn't help but let this secret out to Millie and Frank. And Maddy realized how stupid she was to confide in her sister.

"I was only trying to help. Mom and Dad want to help too."

"Rhea," and Maddy was almost shouting, "you had no right to speak about my marriage with mom and dad. You told me I could trust you. Once again. I'm such a fool." And they don't speak much anymore. Each waited for the other sister to call, hurting.

Rhea remembered her own folly. She hadn't been to visit Maddy in Montana in over three years. And this made her mad because her kids needed to be around their Aunt Maddy. Rhea put every bad thing off on Maddy and didn't understand why Maddy was being so selfish. This new problem is certainly linked to the past somehow. And Rhea believes this, and would be happy to be proved right time and time again. Poor me. Rhea blamed Maddy for this. She was always so unaware of her shortcomings.

Rhea waits in the stinky house. She turns on lights and airs out the bottom floor by opening a window in each room for thirty minutes before closing them, cold fresh air. The doorbell rings and she refuses to answer. She knows it's one of the reporters and wonders if she could call the police to get rid of them. Is it illegal to ring someone's doorbell? Is that trespassing? She goes upstairs and does the same thing she did to the first floor, airs it out. She stops in Geoffrey's office and all the piles of paperwork make her curious. All the bills, with dunning notices, build mountains. All the magazines and newspapers, spam mail, junk up the corners of the office, and the smell of sweat is cloying. Has she been too hard on her sister? Is this all Geoffrey's fault? Had she so misjudged her own sister? She sits down and starts to organize the letters. Most of them are unopened. These she piles in one stack. The bills that are open and not paid she places next to the first. What was Geoffrey thinking?

Beyond this thought Rhea cannot wait for her parents, Millie and Frank, to arrive. Boy, it gets worse—Look at this mess. Geoffrey hasn't paid anything, credit cards, electric—the power's due to be shut off in a week; I guess, I can pay that one now and Maddy can pay me back—cable, athletic club . . .

Rhea can't wait, settles in to straighten out the least of our mess.

* * *

Deepika sits in her home office and reviews the past six months. She has a lot of planning to do. Her skin itches around her elbows and she rubs moisturizer into the dryness. She can't get me, my last visit (possibly my very last) out of her mind. She remembers how I appeared fragile and frantic, as if about to melt and drown, how I acted stunned by the news. She now understands how Geoffrey must've, Maddy too, kept everything a secret from me; they try their best to keep everything hidden. The baby kicks Deepika hard and she winces. She remembers being sick a lot. It was early in the summer, June, and she planned another trip to Boston to get away from Middleton and the people she didn't want to see anymore—least of all the great white way and lack of diversity, minus a few students from out of state.

    A test run. She planned to leave Montana for good. She'd bow out of her future commitment to the Big Sky in the fall when she was showing more. Her philosophy of every act playing out exactly where it was supposed to be, and every consequence being exactly true was one of her guideposts. She rarely felt what some people call guilt. There was remorse when her actions, intentional or not, brought out Shiva's worst side, but there was also contemplation and reaction and a great deal of human kindness. We all have our demons.

    In late June she wasn't even showing yet. Her doctor said maybe four, five weeks. The doctor never once entered into a conversation about who the father of Deepika's child was. A reason Deepika kept seeing her. Her brother, Ananda, welcomed her into his home in Boston and she would help with his family, get up early, if the morning sickness took hold even more—the doctor said this would pass once she reached the second trimester, a promise—head to a coffee house and work on her book. She had a lot of research to do and the library was close to her brother's medical office complex. She researched psychology mostly, motivational impulses, birth order, and familial relationships. She told Liv she'd be away for most of the summer and early fall and paid her another check for the rest of the summer months. Deepika didn't even try to find someone to sublet her place.

    Liv sensed something changeable in their relationship and decided to be true to her own nature: whatever floats your boat, Toots.

    Deepika, by telephone, told Liv she was pregnant in early July. She was the first person in Middleton Deepika revealed this to, and Liv couldn't be happier for her. Because Liv didn't ask whom the father was either, Deepika, relieved, decided to never talk about Geoffrey Bullet. The last time Deepika saw Geoffrey was right before she flew to Boston in late June. He was in his car driving to work, sipping a coffee from Starbucks and driving with one hand. He almost caught Deepika watching him as he sat waiting for the light to change, but his thoughts were bumping and jumping in his mind; Madison was about to take him back in, his job was going downhill, a slow grinding of gears, and his face was pale as if he never ventured outside even in this sunnier Montana weather. Deepika shivered and turned her back on him. He would never know.

Deepika moves into her meditation room and starts the process. She concentrates her energy on Shiva, destroyer and creator, a god of asceticism and of procreation. Deepika relishes Shiva's dichotomous nature, and has ever since her mother bowed, praying before a *linga* on her bedside alcove, meditating on a neighbor's perverse shortcomings; he was always pawing at her, whispering crudities to her under his breath. Shiva, called by many people the Lord of Yoga, smeared with the ashes of renunciation and the cremation ground, was also the source of the Ganges. You wash your sins away in a river that gives life and death. In spite of the multiplicity of forms in which he appears, Shiva is mostly worshipped through the *linga*, a symbolic, semi-abstract representation of the phallus. A sexual deity. And this sexual component of one of the strongest gods, instead of being hidden and shunted away in a closet of denial, is embraced. Deepika takes on Shiva's energy.

Deepika's mother told stories about Shiva all of her childhood: the myth that came to pass in ancient times during dark times and floods, when there was no understandable written language, when people lived on the plains at the foothills of the mountains and cultivated the land.

Vishnu and Brahma argued:

"I'm ever the strongest." Vishnu breathed heat at Brahma. "Your godhood is suspect."

"I'm the greatest to walk this land, this world." Brahma breathed flame. "Your beauty cannot distract me." Deepika made up dialogue to suit the gods, the myths; the stories she could believe and discard.

Each god declared himself to be the greatest of the gods. Infantile and bewildering, the battle between them raged for days, weeks, the passing of years in the blink of an eye.

Deepika pictures civilizations wiped out in the battle. Raging. Her mother continued her stories without embellishment: When suddenly a great pillar of fire appeared from the waters—it was so tall that it seemed to be unending, the sky was roaring flame and the sound of the burning sky was filled with a thunderous snap, a fearful crack. The two gods, both undaunted, both trying to outlast one another, spoiling, set out to discover the height and depth of the pillar. Vishnu assumed the form of a boar and dove into the water, while Brahma turned himself into a swan and flew as high as he could. Both returned amazed that they had failed to find the pillar's extremities. Shiva appeared—and Brahma immediately concocted a lie so pale Shiva denounced his hubris; Brahma wanted to save himself embarrassment and competed against Vishnu for the betterment of all; Brahma told Shiva he had measured completely the upper flame.

Liar.

Shiva denounced Brahma's lying nature: "No temples will be built in your honor to the end of days"—maybe this really was why there were very few temples for Brahma in India—and Deepika always hated the way her mother pronounced Shiva's entrance as preordained, like a magician on stage smugly sawing a woman in half and opening the box later to find the woman whole again: "Whaalaaaa!" And the magician's arms held high, all-powerful, knowing how the trick was accomplished—and Shiva explained—the god really had only one purpose in the story: to tell—that the flaming pillar was the cosmic form of the *linga*, a phallic symbol, the earthly emblem of his incarnate power.

Give the gods some human attributes, make them argue and fight like dogs, let her hear their words. Yet Deepika takes this ancient myth to heart; in remembering the stories she was told as a child she seeks knowledge and understanding. What has happened to her is part of a cosmic form. She's part of the flame. Is Brahma strong within her?

At the beginning of last summer, Deepika fled back to Boston, and spent two weeks with her brother, Ananda, before she gathered a small suitcase and flew, alone, to India to visit with her family, her mother, her siblings, and all of her aunts and uncles and cousins—some brazen in revealing their secretive thoughts that she'd become too Westernized now. There was a party to celebrate her arrival and Deepika fell into familiar days and nights, afternoons reserved for visiting, early mornings to her writing. Her mother placed palms against her stomach and made blessings on the child.

"You will come home more," her mother said, "I can watch her while you write"—while you find a husband who wants a woman with a child—this last thought unsaid to Deepika but it was there in the room nonetheless. And then she was back in Boston for the end of summer and early fall and returned to Middleton late September to finish up her book and tidy up loose ends. Deepika made plans to finish her work in progress and leave.

A week before Deepika drove to Geoffrey's home, the week before I caught my father holding Deepika's forearm so tightly it would leave a bruise, she was in her bedroom stretching to pull a suitcase from under the bed when she found one of Geoffrey's undershirts balled up and wrinkled, hidden from sight. Deepika held this shirt and remembered how tender Geoffrey appeared to be. How he made love to her—a handsome devil of an enigma. How they created a child. Deepika's thoughts turned to Geoffrey, but it was another week before she came to the conclusion she must reveal her secret to Geoffrey. She called the law office and Glynnis smoothly told Deepika that Geoffrey no longer worked for the firm. It was the second week of October and Deepika wasn't sure what had made Geoffrey quit—she felt Glynnis would be all too happy to give her every detail but Deepika hung up the telephone and contemplated her next step. She would come clean and absolve him of all responsibility, and say goodbye.

She finds her resolve through meditation, the lighting of her oil lamp. Maya is everywhere and everything; her karma runs throughout her system. And one early afternoon Deepika finds herself in her green Saab driving to Geoffrey's house. She knew Maddy was teaching a class after calling the office pretending to be an insurance agent, oh, when will she be back? She didn't know anything. She really thought she was doing what was right, what was good, what Shiva didn't need to rely on in search of a truth; Shiva was the truth. Deepika was there, Geoffrey was there twisting her skin, holding her arm tightly when I arrived, startling them both, catching them together, and Deepika could only think about the puzzle pieces she interlocked, a series of events she blamed herself for and no one else.

She needs to settle things, another human weakness.

Deepika takes all of her clothes out of her closet and discards the shirts and pants that don't fit anymore, stuffs them into a large black garbage bag. She won't take much with her to Boston. The trunk space in the Saab isn't large. She'll soon need a whole new wardrobe anyway, as her belly grows larger.

She sits in her chair and telephones Marjolaine at the administrative office. After Deepika explains she must leave immediately Marjolaine's tone of enmity is deafening.

"There's no one else," says Marjolaine.

Deepika plows ahead. "I'm very sorry."

Marjolaine's voice turns screechy. "Do you know the position you're putting me in?"

"I do realize you're in a bind."

"There isn't anyone else to sub for Madison while she's out. She has the emergency. You do not. She needs your help."

Deepika pictures the group of sullen, needy students in Madison's Creative Writing class and breathes deeply. "There's nothing I can do about that. I feel for Madison, but I have to think of my own situation."

"I can't believe I trusted you," Marjolaine says.

It's the only weapon Marjolaine wields, a barbed comment.

"I do wish you the best," Deepika says before hanging up the telephone without listening to Marjolaine's intake of air and sputter when she hears only the dial tone. She doesn't blame Marjolaine for being so condemning; there isn't anyone else who could readily sub for Maddy without doubling his or her own teaching load. With budgets so tight and the cuts already stripping the Creative Writing Department of detritus, the English Department asserting more control over an ugly-stepchild of a program like Fiction and Poetry Writing, Marjolaine will probably have to cancel the courses if Maddy doesn't come back after a week or more. A problem Deepika doesn't have to worry about. She doesn't answer to Marjolaine anyway; she answers to the Director of Creative Writing, the overlord of the M.F.A. program, a good, sensible man who wrote happy, sensible stories about farmers, Montana historical figures and the taking of the land from its original owners, but she's compelled to get all her Big Sky College business in order. She already has a teaching position at Emerson lined up for the following fall in the Visiting Writer series. She omits this fact to Marjolaine, but she's probably aware of it anyway; she has her ears to the wall—why would she want to hear it anyway? Everyone's life is in flux, even those who think of their lives as the most regulated, and change makes or breaks the world. Destroys or creates.

Deepika calls the department director and because he's teaching a class on The Art Of The Screenplay he's unavailable and she receives his voicemail. "As you've probably heard by now, Sheldon, I won't be returning. I'm in deep regret about my decision to leave such a beautiful and warmly welcoming place, but I know there are several quality writers waiting in the wings for just such an opportunity. You can reach me on my cell. I will miss you and my students. Thank you."

Deepika feels lighter now. Saying goodbye has never been a tearful task for her. She, like anyone else, will miss certain aspects of the Montana landscape, but she really only misses one person, Liv, her crankier-than-thou on the outside, heart-of-a-lion on the inside, friend and landlord who opened up her arms to her wholeheartedly the second they met.

Her mind wavers. Is she just running away? Will all of her decisions create a fetid badness within? She presses her belly and thoughts of her child grow larger, stronger, and she wonders if this child will someday, with curiosity, inquire about the circumstances surrounding the birth, still several months away—this thought pings in her writing mind and she jots down "birth moment" on a piece of paper, wants to get back to that with her characters.

Will Deepika have the nerve to ever speak the truth about what she did? When the child asks about her real father, how will she respond? (How do I know it's a girl? A new half sister? I just know.) Deepika, like Brahma, believes: No temples will be built in my honor.

One task finishes, another begins, and Deepika takes out her PowerBook and peruses her final story. Sai seethes with familial bitterness and sorrow. Deepika imagines his anger boiling. She's turning him away. Does he wonder about his own birth, his creation? Who were his parents? Why did they hate him so?

Deepika wonders if what's happening to her, her own child, her child's father, her child's half-brother, me, and the woman who sits next to my bedside, my mother, are forcing her fictional characters into a rage so specifically tied to birth and tragic family lineage Deepika might possibly be confusing my family with her own empty, airless people— our lives printed on cheap copy paper. She wants to get into Sai's mind. Discover what breaks his view of the world? How he will cope with a father who turns his back on him and a mother who is no longer able to respond to his love? I cannot move, speak, yell: stop using my life as your blueprint!

Deepika writes the last section of her final story and senses she's lost track. For the first time in a long time she's abandoning her words, finishing a project she started well before she opened herself up to Geoffrey's world of hurt. Her editor wants the end; another email says as much when Deepika logs onto the Internet. Get me the pages soon— Quick!

Most of the packing in the small house is finished. Deepika leaves everything and throws away what doesn't fit anymore. She stretches her arms above her head after an hour and feels her hunger. She makes a final trip to her favorite lunch place. A walnut salad and an apple. Deepika calls her doctor at the hospital and, when they finally connect after a nurse searches the office, says she's feeling a dull pain; could she possibly fit her in, see her right away? Of course. Please come in. The doctor senses Deepika needlessly worrying, chalks it up to the first time mother-to-be acting anxious and waits for Deepika to show up. Deepika takes a right turn and drives to the hospital before she can stop herself.

* * *

It's a chilly gray outside the window in my room. This is when the doctor decides to move me to a more secure and private room. The machines still blink. A nurse in the room says, "I hope it snows—early in the season for it—a good blanket of covering snow."

Another nurse, later, tells an RT tech she thinks the sun will come out again before it snows. Put it off until Thanksgiving. We need more sun. The RT tech pushes his machine onto the elevator and wishes her a nice day.

Maddy's back next to my bed. Her skin pale, arms and legs lagging. She bows her head and holds my unbroken hand. Nadine speaks to Lance and Sheila and Nell in the crowded waiting room. Nadine tries hard to keep things on an even keel but Nell pushes her buttons; her condescension picks at her patience, how it's present in her tone of voice, or a flick of her wrist. Nadine vows to handle anything. They speak in whispers.

Reporters for CNN, FOX, ABC, CBS and NBC are waiting outside the hospital for the next report on my condition, salivating. With all the news of gay rights, a moral decline, please bring family values back to the home, gay marriage, gay fashionistas decorating straight people's lives, don't let them into your homes, your schools, they recruit, don't you see them signing the unaware up to be gay, protect your children, your animals, everywhere, it's happening, fear that, if we allow them to distort what marriage really means where will this Christian nation go, there seems little time for gay beatings and what the press call hate crimes. It seems hate crimes are shuffled and swept under policy rugs. The national press covers hate crimes in increasing numbers but with a built-in, wary, distance—statistics shout there's an upswing of violence against gay people—probably as a result of all the constant news coverage and hatred from the President on down, hate the sin not the sinner a catchall booby trap since it's disingenuous to think any of them would welcome a gay person into their midst and truly love them in a Christian way. It's in the back of the President's mind, whisperings from his religious constituents: our country needs a constitutional amendment to protect the sanctity of marriage, and the country remains divided, but the most strident of these followers bully and threaten and act as the President's bodyguards of negativity, make him seem compassionate while whittling away at the peace idol, I'm the kind of President you can have a beer with nonsense, even in the heartland and way out on the Montana cattle ranges. Spread the word: gay people shall be put in their place and made to keep their abnormal lives silent. Don't ask, don't tell. Keep the checks coming folks. We need money to protect the family and all the children, and the money rolls into campaign headquarters at a heady clip. Every vote counts in this election year.

Last night, while Geoffrey sat in a social worker's group therapy conference room aching for Lance to swoop in and save him, Doctor Fusil told Maddy she had MS, Multiple Sclerosis, onset: a disorder of the nervous system. Maddy didn't really react. It was the way she always responded to any news, good or bad. A day or a week later, alone, she would break down. Maddy didn't know if her son would be around to see her when she did crack.

Dr. Fusil explained, "No one knows what causes MS." MS could stand for Mystery Syndrome, Maddy thought.

"I can walk now. My legs feel fine."

Doctor Fusil suggested a neurologist for follow up. "We'll get you lined up here with some of the best neurologists in the Pacific Northwest."

"What else can I expect?" Nadine held onto Maddy's hand tightly. Maddy thought her body was on a seesaw. Up and down. Up and down.

"You're in what is called a relapsing-remitting phase. This isn't a death sentence. I need you to believe this."

Maddy gave back only silence. She liked Doctor Fusil, and then wondered why she even cared to like her. I have

MS. Multiple Sclerosis. It's really not that big of a surprise to her. She knows one other person who has MS in Middleton, someone who wheels himself to the theater, always takes the handicap parking spaces at the supermarket, but also someone who couldn't drive himself, and she thinks about Geoffrey and wonders if he'd give up everything else to drive for her. She doesn't know why he's in so much pain. No one, not even his sister, does, not after all he's done. He thought about killing himself well before Deepika ever showed up.

"From what you told me about these attacks and you've only had three or four—with the vision coming and going— the relapsing-remitting phase can last many years, decades even. Your MS may not progress to the second stage. Some people never do."

"What's the second stage," Nadine asked for Maddy? Maddy felt fine. What could she expect? There were tears in her eyes and she absently wiped them away. She didn't want Maddy to start bawling. She couldn't remember ever seeing Maddy cry. She wouldn't cry either.

"Disabilities increase in the secondary progressive phase. But recovery comes too. It's a seesaw." And the doctor's phrasing made Maddy smile knowingly—I just thought of that. "Of course a neurologist has to work up your condition. There are a number of medicines to help give ease during episodes. If you're having attacks now, you will find they'll come in waves and usually more often once you have a diagnosis. People go, sometimes for years, without being diagnosed; they think their body is playing tricks on them but never seek help until the body gives out." Unsaid: Like yours did. "But, in this first phase, the number of episodes tend to settle down. We just have to find out where you are."

Maddy and Nadine stayed silent, passive, while the doctor continued. Doctor Fusil talked because she'd seen the look of disbelief before. But I feel so healthy otherwise; most patients said this adamantly. Doctor Fusil understood this, too. The next stage was denial. She continued, "It's a disease many doctors feel is in its infancy. There's no cure. Many people with MS do very well and you'd never even know they have MS unless they tell you. We don't know why MS hits people differently, but the people it doesn't affect greatly have what we call Benign MS." Nadine hoped this was the case with Maddy. "Benign," she repeated. Just as Maddy was thinking the same thing: Benign. There was something to hope for. Doctor Fusil continued, "Of course MS can, and I'm not one to sugarcoat anything, seriously and significantly disable, even if a person can get around moderately well. Your neurologist can give you better statistics about this disorder. And a much better outlook. We're making great strides in research, but I can tell you, honestly, we're not doing quite enough." Maddy and Nadine couldn't make themselves respond. I won't cry, Maddy thought. I can't think of myself right now. Let me get back to my son; he's the one who needs my help now.

Doctor Fusil tried to downplay the news as much as possible and said, "We notice the people who are most disabled by MS, but there are so many other people with MS who you'll never notice."

Yeah, Maddy thought, because they're shut away in their homes. Maddy could imagine herself in the future surfing the Internet and wheeling herself around the first floor of her house, teaching her classes by remote television monitors. Turning the downstairs family room into her bedroom, and never leaving her riverside home again. Staring out the windows at the magpies, hating their insistent calls even more.

Nadine couldn't help tearing up.

Maddy remained stoic and her mind couldn't get around the enormity of what the doctor in front of her was saying.

"I've contacted the neurologist who sees the most cases here in Middleton and his office will be in touch with you to schedule an appointment when things settle down." Doctor Fusil didn't have to say what settling down meant. "If you need to speak to anyone about this you can call me anytime." Doctor Fusil touched Madison's arm. Maddy glanced at the doctor's business card and noticed the handwritten home telephone number.

"You're free to leave. Your family and friends are still in the waiting room."

"Give me a moment. Please."

Nadine clasped Maddy's hand the way Maddy would like to clasp my hand one more time. There were many things she would still like to do. Things she could only imagine and could only now dream of doing. If I could imagine the things I would never do it would be a short list: I would never experience that first kiss, from another boy, or kiss anyone myself anymore. I would never fall in love. I would never tell my mom or dad I loved them. Despite everything that'd happened, in all of this craziness, I couldn't even feel regret if I wanted to.

* * *

My mother has an illness that sleeps inside of her and will wake up in her system periodically over the next ten, twenty, thirty years. No one can read what a shock this is to Maddy. She doesn't speak yet. There's no one waiting for her to speak.

* * *

Finally, Maddy softly said to Nadine, "Don't tell anyone."

Nadine remained silent.

"I don't want anyone to know what I have. Not when so much else is happening. Not when Chris is—"

"Oh, Honey."

"I mean it, Nadine. I feel normal. You're not to tell anyone. Not even Bernie."

"My husband will be the last to know."

"I want to go back to Chris now."

"Sure. Let me get your clothes." Nadine felt a roiling bitterness and frustration. She could tell Maddy she's been too self-centered for so long her family was falling apart way before all of this insanity started. But she won't. She'll do her duty and protect Maddy from her family and Geoffrey's family and then slip away back home to her own silent, funny, stodgy husband, Bernie, who didn't really want to understand the intricacies of a family he's known just as long. As if he'd given up on them long before Nadine opened her eyes and all along had consciously hidden this fact from his wife.

"I've been away from Chris for so long. He's all alone."

"Rhea's on her way. Your parents, too."

"Not a word."

"What do we tell Nell? She can't believe you're even down here when your husband is locked away somewhere."

"Just tell her my body gave out. Exhaustion."

"Okay."

"You're a true friend."

Nadine had no reply. A true friend would've been able to do more. And instantly, Nadine felt guilty about having such negative thoughts sneak in about Maddy.

* * *

Maddy and Nadine wash their hands and faces in the small sink attached to the wall in their hospital room and adjust their clothing. My mother signs some papers the nurse left for her. Maddy reassures Doctor Fusil she'll be in touch. Really. Maddy somehow isn't worried about her diagnosis.

Nadine and my mother greet Lance, Sheila, and Nell in the waiting area. Nell is on her feet quicker than the rest and comes so close to opening her mouth to scold Maddy about how much time she's wasting down here in the emergency room when her family is falling apart, but Nell is able to contain herself and even gives Maddy a short hug.

"Let's go up to Chris," Maddy says to the group. Maddy holds onto Nadine's hand to steady herself—what if her legs give out again—and the small group of people walk down the long hospital corridor toward the tunnel to the children's wing.

Maddy asks Lance if he's spoken to Geoffrey.

"Not yet. I called when you were still being seen. The

head of the department up there hasn't given his okay yet. He wants to meet with Geoffrey one more time. I probably won't be able to see him until tomorrow. We'll just have to wait."

Sheila says, "Maddy. I'm so sorry."

"Thanks for that. I'm glad you're all here." The hallway fills with an uncomfortable silence.

"Nell?" Maddy asks.

"Yes."

"Can you call my parents? I think they're flying in, and they must be delayed. I'll give you their cell number. It's early morning there and they shouldn't be driving all night. I don't want to worry about them too."

"I have to make some other calls anyway."

Maddy only wants to get people moving, thinking of anything else—the mundane tasks. Nell leaves the group to make her calls of reassurance. Afterwards she'll head back to her hotel room to rest and prepare to talk to her brother's doctors later in the day.

When Maddy enters my new private room she remembers the way she left, stiff and scared on a stretcher. My condition hasn't changed much; at least I can't feel the changes.

Doctors, nurses, family members, sitting beside people in unresponsive conditions, always act as if the person— maybe there's a possibility, maybe it's not just reaching— feels, hears, acknowledges the outside world (it's true, folks, talk talk talk; I'll hear every word), maybe with just one blink of the eyes, maybe there could be meaning in one physical involuntary response. A nurse on the ward, whenever she comes into the room to check on me starts singing softly, old standards from the '50s and early '60s. A bit of Frank Sinatra, Peggy Lee, appropriate, she sings, like a DJ's running commentary to me. I have no idea who Peggy Lee was but I like her Fever song the nurse sings to me. She thinks it'll help me even if I never listen to Frank Sinatra, but I promise I will if I wake up; she thinks my eyes will open and react to her voice, the tone of warmth and the longing to get better. My system is too crushed and some of the doctors and nurses grow very worried. I can't feel myself slipping away, not that I could before.

There aren't enough chairs in my room and Lance and Sheila stay a couple minutes, standing, before they tell Maddy they'll be in the waiting room and make a trip to get food if anyone is hungry.

It's late in the evening, early, early morning, and Maddy spends the entire night by my side. The feeling in her limbs doesn't desert her again. There's so much she tries to work out. The police want to speak to her again. The doctor keeps putting them off. She's not up to it.

In the morning Nadine brings Maddy a change of clothes from her own home, comfortable clothes. Nell stays in her hotel room awaiting news. Rhea is in Maddy's house, sneaking through rooms, opening letters in Geoffrey's office, searching for clues to the disintegration of her sister's family. Millie and Frank are in the sky flying over South Dakota, they couldn't arrange an earlier flight, and they worry for their daughter and me, and both grip the armrests of their seats as tension fills their minds.

That same morning a different consulting neurologist comes into my room to assess my condition. He peers into my eyes, shines a penlight into my vacuous stare, lifts my limbs, checks the machines, my blood pressure, and leaves without speaking to Maddy. She hates him for this. She reads sorrow in his expressionlessness. She feels there's something he's withholding and she's reminded of the first neurologist who spoke to her like a robot as if the humans around him didn't have emotions. Maddy worries for me even more.

* * *

The Chess King arrives in Middleton and takes a taxi to the hotel Nell mentioned to him earlier in her message. He checks in and enters his room and reads a message Nell slipped under the door:

Please call my room when you get in.

Lots to tell.
l.
N.

He crumples the note up and throws it away in the wastebasket. He's silent as can be, knowing his daughter rests in the adjacent room. He tiptoes out and makes sure the hotel door whispers shut. Nell can always wait. The Chess King hasn't thought much about his family since his wife died, since Geoffrey stopped answering his infrequent calls over ten years ago. Nell stays in touch. He calls her back and they speak, both never bring up the past. He heard about the car accident long ago from Nell, but didn't rush to his son's side to comfort him. What good would it do? He understands his son's estrangement and deep inside he applauds it. His son always takes a distant course filled with blame.

Nell speaks to The Chess King, her father, as if he's a fallen angel. A brilliant angel so smart, her brother, Geoffrey following in the intelligence department, and a small resentment there as she's always wondered why she didn't inherit a high IQ. She wonders if my IQ is also causing me so much trouble, a trait to be admired turned into a family curse passed down from generation to generation. If I could speak to Nell I'd say: I'm no genius—look where I am, Aunt Nell. She's learned long ago never to bring their father up when speaking to her brother, and Geoffrey almost cut her off for mentioning where The Chess King was, somewhere in Patagonia, eight years previously. In the back of her mind she's gathered enough determination to believe she will, at some future date, orchestrate a tough reconciliation between Geoffrey and The Chess King.

The Chess King never takes off his puffy, dull orange winter coat. He places a snug black knit hat on his almost hairless head and asks the hotel desk clerk to call him a taxi. He returns the hotel room key, startling the desk clerk into asking, "Was there something wrong with the room?"

"No. I've changed my mind. I've decided I can't stay overnight in Middleton. I have business to attend to and then I'll fly home on a late flight." He tells the desk clerk to give his daughter a message when she asks after him. My absent grandfather is coming to see me. It's there in his mind. He wants to lay eyes on his grandson, to tell me he's sorry.

For what?

No one will ever really know. He shoulders his soft, but durable, carry-on bag with him, leaving nothing in the hotel but the message for Nell.

* * *

Doctor Spitzer welcomes Geoffrey back into his office with an awkward swing of his arm that's meant to be reassuring and convivial. Geoffrey is slightly insulted by his show of hospitality. He cannot believe this man ever has truthful human reactions. I cannot believe how petty my father truly is, how pained, how hurt. I can relate to his angst but still want to shake the sniveling snot out of him.

"Please, take a seat."

Geoffrey is stone-faced. He's numb, as if his body is weighted down by concrete. The new antidepressants have kicked in and Geoffrey feels hollow.

"Now," Doctor Spitzer says, "I started you on Lexapro last night. It should be too soon to notice any changes, but I think this is a good starting point." When Geoffrey asks about the side effects of the drug, he's slapped with: nausea, dizziness, and a decreased sex drive. Geoffrey takes the pills with a grimace.

"How did you feel during group therapy last night?"

"Annoyed." Geoffrey's not slurring his words, but he's slowing down. He's on an increased dosage of Lexapro and still depressed. It's not the instant cure he hoped it would be.

Doctor Spitzer writes in his notebook.

"Group therapy can open up a whole new way of looking inward."

"The social worker who ran my little group therapy session was a real idiot."

"Why do you say that?"

"She couldn't find a shoe in a shoe store." Geoffrey hears her tinny voice in the back of his head: "Picture a toolbox. Inside this toolbox are all of your coping skills. Geoffrey, what's the most important tool in your toolbox?" Complete idiocy. And the demeaning way she speaks so slowly to everyone as if the group hadn't graduated from kindergarten yet. He wants to have a talk with her, ask her how much it costs to buy a vowel.

Doctor Spitzer doesn't find Geoffrey or his comments amusing. "We're all trying to help you here."

"Then don't assign more group therapy sessions."

"There aren't any this evening."

"When can I see my lawyer? His name is Lance Copler. He should've called?"

"Yes. He's downstairs with your wife. We spoke earlier."

Geoffrey feels some small relief.

"He'll be up after this session. You can meet with him for fifteen minutes."

"We have a lot to discuss. I don't think fifteen minutes will be enough time."

"I don't want to stress you too much. Your mind and body need time to heal. You've shocked your whole operating system."

Geoffrey screams inside. The man in front of him is a robot.

* * *

Millie and Frank arrive and drive to Maddy's house to collect Rhea. They're tired from their flight and look it. They've always been so easygoing, not in the best of health, but chugging along on the right prescriptions, Lipitor, Synthroid, high blood pressure medication, and after prolonged exposure to the Atkins Diet doesn't seem to work—they both love pasta too much—they balloon around their waists even more: just chugging along. Rhea seldom worries about them but she'll tell Maddy to bug them about their health whenever she speaks to them. They're not getting any younger. Maddy always wants to tell Rhea to fight her own battles, but resists; the outcome will always be hurtful, and bring up unnecessary arguments and sharp judgments about love, loyalty to family, and trust.

"Hi, Mom and Dad." Rhea greets them at the front door and ushers them in, quickly looking behind them and up the driveway for any news vans, people scurrying behind bushes. This is such a farce, Rhea thinks. She hasn't been to the hospital yet and only knows about my condition through what's been playing on the small kitchen television. Rhea doesn't want to face her sister alone. She's waited for backup.

"Hello, Kiddo," Rhea's dad says.

"I waited to call Maddy until you got here. I thought it would be easier to only go over everything once." Rhea believes her words sound false and doesn't say anything else. Let's it lie.

"I think we should go to the hospital now," Rhea's mom says. "Just let me wash my face."

"There's more." Rhea barely conceals her conflicted emotions. Just wait, she wants to say, it gets much worse. She purses her lips with a stern tightness and hands her father a stack of bills the width of a layered club sandwich.

"What are these?" he asks.

"There's more to this than Chris and Geoffrey in the hospital. No one has paid any bills in months. I've gone through Geoffrey's office and found all of these. I wasn't snooping. The house smelled of rotten food and I was airing it out. I was cleaning up. Some of them are threatening to turn services off." Frank sifts through the stack and his expression darkens.

"I doubt Maddy knew anything about this. She always told me Geoffrey handled the accounting chores, taxes."

"I sorted them in the order they need to be paid. We're talking a lot of money here."

"And I'm sure they're good for it."

"Geoffrey hasn't worked in a couple of weeks, maybe months, either."

Millie and Frank both look at each other with a growing sadness. For their eldest daughter, for me—I'm there in the back of their thoughts—not yet at the center of their attention, and for Geoffrey too, out-of-balance, and lastly, for Rhea, the daughter they always try to calmly restrain, rein in her natural instinct towards spite, jealousy, and neglect. The daughter who always brings them news with a negative criticism attached. A role Rhea takes to with the spirit of a woman hedging her concern so much no one will ever believe she even cares that much about what happens to her sister or her sister's family. Only her husband, Carl, will be able to console Rhea and tell her how sorry he is that her family never sees how good a person she is. Years ago, Millie once told Maddy parents are only as happy as their unhappiest child. Maddy replied: Rhea means well. She's happy in her own way. Millie doesn't respond but she knows Maddy defends her only sibling, as she should.

Frank takes the bills and places them in his overnight bag. Rhea wants to say something—Dad, those bills aren't your responsibility—but resists the urge. She'll remember how Dad and Mom bail Madison out as if a big tally sheet has just been marked in the wrong column.

"How are the grandkids?" Millie asks to mask the empty feeling creeping inside of her.

"They're doing very well," Rhea responds. "They send their love." Rhea can talk about her kids for hours and Millie listens as they freshen up to go to the hospital, wash the airplane atmosphere from their faces and hands, change into less wrinkled clothes. "Carl was just promoted to systems manager for the national gas company. A move is on the horizon." There's a gleam of so much pride in Rhea's eyes it's hard for Millie and Frank to respond.

"That's great. But we need to get to the hospital now." They honestly understand why the kids and Carl aren't with Rhea. For whatever reason, there's a distance between their two daughters, and Millie and Frank are tired of it.

"Let's get going," Frank says.

* * *

In his office space, the neurologist confers with two of his colleagues, neurosurgeons, about my condition. They're sweating too much and pontificating about theories and abstract medical practices. The doctors need a consensus for what they're about to say to Madison Dakota. What it comes down to is this: How do we tell the parents of this child? The worst part of being a doctor—it never gets any easier.

Doctor Gapestill then walks down the hallway in the children's wing too slowly, and pokes his head into the waiting area. Nell never told Maddy that Geoffrey's father is flying in; the last she heard his airplane was on time. Nell couldn't take the waiting and left hours ago to rest in her hotel room, to be there when her father does show up; she needed to change clothes again as well. She'll be back with coffee for everyone. Lance and Sheila sit there with Nadine. Maddy rests in the chair at my bedside. She says she wants some time alone with me.

Nadine wants to be in the room with me more than any of them but she doesn't want to overstep. Maddy's entitled to her alone time. 'Only family' is the security guard's motto. He walks up and down the hall and Nadine thinks anyone can just walk right by him, even Bernie. Family only. Strict rules to follow now and the nurses imply they won't cut them any slack this time. Too many people are watching them to make mistakes. The security guard continues to patrol the hallways.

"Should I get Maddy?" Nadine asks.

"No," Doctor Gapestill says. "She's with Chris? I need to speak to her. Please wait here." He closes the waiting room door and walks ten yards down the bustling hallway and into my room where I sleep, my mother next to me leaning on my arm.

Maddy straightens herself up in her chair.

"What's happening?" Maddy asks this question without strength. After her diagnosis she hasn't been able to focus on anything but me getting better, waking up, lifting my side of the seesaw up high in the air.

"I'm afraid I have some very serious news."

Maddy sits as if she expects a physical blow, about to flinch. Her shoulders curl forward and her lip quivers.

"I don't want to hear what you're about to say."
Doctor Gapestill sits next to Maddy and takes her hand. She tries to pull out of his grasp and shudders. She vows she's not going to cry. She will not cry. She has to keep her focus, give me her strength. She will not cry in front of me; that won't help me.

"There must be something you can do. Something you haven't thought of?"

"The damage is so severe. We've tried to relieve the swelling but if it continues . . . his brain cannot take the stress."

"Oh, my God." And then Maddy falls apart, an uncontainable cry filled with sharp, wailing pain. Long and screaming nothing, nothing, and Nadine rushes into the room regardless of the rules and the security guard's startled expression and Maddy collapses into her arms. And only then does Maddy start to cry and I'm too far-gone to wonder if she'll ever stop.

* * *

Lance, Sheila, and Nadine guide Maddy to a conference room where they will confer with the doctor. She doesn't want anyone speaking about me, what will happen to me, within earshot, if I can somehow understand what is said. Shutting me down, off, end. The doctor says this is only one possibility. I could wake up. I still could. The swelling could reverse itself. Somehow. And Maddy wills this to happen. She wants Geoffrey.

"I want him here," Maddy insists through her tears. No one has ever seen Maddy break like this, ever, and it unnerves the entire room, brings Sheila and Lance to tears also.

"Lance, I need you to get Geoffrey down here right now. I can't make this decision on my own. Surely the hospital will let him out. They can put him back in forever afterwards for all I care but he needs to be here now. Let them know they have my permission if it matters."

"I'm meeting with the head psychiatrist in ten minutes. Doctor Gapestill, can you come with me?"

"You don't need to ask. I'll do my best. It won't be easy." He's familiar with Doctor Spitzer and doesn't hold out much hope. He follows the rules and knows that only those in power try to break rules and Gapestill and Spitzer have had their battles in the past.

"The nurses will be right outside if you need anything. As I explained, I would like to call for a hospice nurse. With your permission of course."

Nadine can't believe my condition has deteriorated so quickly—none of them can. There's a one-sided fight, and I'm smacked with a baseball bat, over and over again. They arrest all four classmates who tried to kill me. Soon it won't be *tried*; they'll have succeeded.

Maddy returns to my bedside. I won't be able to recognize my own mother's face if I awake right at this moment. If I awake, I imagine I'll forget everything important or trivial, and my smarts will be a thing of the past. Will I drool? Speak in monosyllables? Brain injury crushes only gift—curse.

Lance and Doctor Gapestill leave. They take the elevator up to meet with Doctor Spitzer. They enter the Psych Ward, ushered into the main office by a meek woman who collects all the patient charts at the end of each shift.

"Welcome," Doctor Spitzer says. "What can I do for you? Is there any change in the son's condition?"

Lance stays silent as cautioned by Doctor Gapestill.

Doctor Gapestill clasps his fingers together and says: "Time is of the essence here. Mr. Bullet's son, Chris, has withstood too much trauma. If his brain hemorrhages, more than a slight possibility at this point, he won't hold on much longer. I know it's not part of procedure to allow patients in Mr. Bullet's condition out of the ward for any reason—"

"That's correct. We have a protocol in place especially for those patients who are deemed to be a danger to themselves."

Lance cannot believe how righteously prissy the psychiatrist sounds, a formulaic button-pusher. Lance would dislike anyone sitting where Doctor Spitzer sits. It's nothing personal. "Are you aware of the situation with Mr. Bullet's son? Do I need to spell it out for you? He's dying."

"I can't let any outside information interfere with the patients I take care of on my ward."

Again Doctor Gapestill says, softer this time, "His son is dying. Good God, man."

This emotional display slaps Doctor Spitzer. He's only following procedure. Life, he's witnessed so many patients filing through his office, watching them, only able to help a small percentage of them, shuffling the others off with drug therapy (they won't get healthier) is tough, veiled, filled with loopholes.

"What do you need from me?" As if it's all about Doctor Spitzer.

"We need Mr. Bullet and his wife to speak. They need to sign the appropriate forms if the worst happens, if their son, Christopher, will not survive the beating he took. His condition is deteriorating and it's of the utmost urgency we get the bureaucratic side of this finished. Will you let Mr. Bullet out?"

"I'm not sure if Mr. Bullet can take the news you just told me."

"Well. He's in the best of hands. I don't think many people could take the news we're about to share."

"I have to think of my patient."

"And I have to think of mine."

"You can bring Mrs. Bullet—"

"Madison Dakota is her name."

"Up, here. You can conduct your meeting in the conference room. I'll be with you in the room. Mr. Bullet is in a fragile state of mind and this could push him over the edge." Doctor Spitzer still doesn't view his actions as unreasonable. He has a suicidal patient on his hands. I think he's being perfectly rational. My family situation may be the cause of my father's depression, and more and more thoughts of family dysfunction only make a grimace cross Dr. Spitzer's face. I wish I could grimace as easily. What family does function? He's buckling, bending the rules, even though he'll monitor the proceedings and call everything off quickly if Geoffrey's state goes funny farm. If he only knew, like I do, that my parents are once again facing the death of a child ten years after they lost another child. How could my father not be depressed? How could my mother not care to see how depressed her whole family situation really is, sweep the negative away and never come to terms with the outcome of that accident so long ago. The phantom face of this unborn child, distorted, yearning, haunting her dreams, and she never speaks a word about this upon waking.

Lance steams. He needs to punch the self-serving face in front of him. His hands turn into fists but he keeps them below the psychiatrist's sightline. He doesn't believe it's possible for his best friend to be in such a mess. He's glad he went into the practice of law if medicine turned out people like Doctor Spitzer by the hundreds.

"We'll go get Madison immediately. Please get Mr. Bullet ready."

"We'll be waiting."

* * *

This is the part no one could've predicted, what most stories Deepika writes, what her characters have been waiting for. The serendipity of life and chance meeting and coincidence plays a part in everyone's life. She knows every member of my family, one intimately. She sees my mother walking the Big Sky campus halls, views her as this aloof woman with a deep ability to concentrate, someone who is rigid and who rigidly sticks to a protocol. She views my father as a lost cause, someone who begins an adventure and fails to connect because he's unable to welcome emotion, a weak and weakening man, and Deepika wants to run far away the last time she saw my father. She sees me as a product of these two unhappy people but she doesn't regret the affair; she is with child. God, how she writes now. She has all the details, all the differing characters to draw from.

If I hadn't cut school I never would've caught my father with Deepika. She's thought about this for a long time. No one knows she's leaving town as soon as possible like a deserter during wartime. Who's there to really know? They assume she's already left. Geoffrey's trapped and meets with Maddy in a few minutes to contemplate signing a form condemning me to my death, a painless, sorrowful, slow death. Geoffrey will be shocked anew because he's only seen his wife cry once, and he wishes he could hold her tighter, change their fates, and mine, and he'll remember her tears and speak of them to every therapist he ever sees in the future. His actions are to blame, and he wants to change all three of us, rewind far enough back and view a fourth member of the family, smiling, a sunny sibling for me, gluing the family back together, make him skip his meeting with a pouty, sexy, flirtatious stranger, drive home from work, pack up the car with us, leave that differing timeline and enjoy a weekend at the Lake.

There's Deepika entering, passing through security; is she just another ghost no one can see—there's no guard at his station, and this shouldn't be possible during such a crisis, she strides past an empty receptionist's desk, up the elevator, and into the OB/GYN wing.

"I have an appointment," she says to the receptionist. Deepika's resplendent in a loose-fitted skirt of amber, too tight, and yellow blouse with small birds embroidered around the cuffs in blue, one size too small. Her jacket is black and she's noticeable in the ensemble, worn to accentuate her pregnancy so that if she's stopped she'll have an excuse to be there, walking the hallways in search of my room.

Deepika heads to the nurses' station and listens to them talking until someone notices her. She asks Deepika if she can be of help.

"I'm looking for Chris Bullet. I'm his Aunt Deepika." Don't reveal too much but make sure they hear your name clearly. They may have made a record of her earlier approach. If anyone checks, it has to be perfect.

"He's on the secure floor. Right, Tara?"

"The rest of the family is there." Less said the better. Deepika's making a guess here but it's one of the thrilling things about her nature. Deception and deceit walking hand-in-hand with good intentions.

"That's the sixth floor. Let me make a call."

"No need. I have an appointment right now." She pats her belly. "I know the way. I'm not feeling right. Maybe it's all the shocking things happening to my family."

"You said you're married to—"

"The father's brother." And these words slip out so naturally Deepika can hardly believe it. Geoffrey doesn't have a brother. "What's the room number?" Deepika relaxes.

Another nurse asks for Deepika's doctor's name.

"Dr. Marina. I think I have to be there in five minutes. I'm sorry this city has to witness such brutality." Deepika means what she says.

There's nothing the nurses can say. It's all too big. They reveal too much information.

They watch Deepika move down the hall. Limping, it's almost too theatrical, with her pregnancy. She lays it on a bit thick but gets the job done until one of the women actually calls her back to the desk. Deepika turns and waddles back, says, "Yes?"

"Here. You need one of these passes to be in the hospital now."

"Oh. Yes." Deepika doesn't know what the woman is talking about, plays it cool as the nurse hands her an extra visitor's pass. She clips it onto her black jacket collar.

"I don't know why they didn't give you one downstairs."

"There was no one at the reception desk," Deepika says. "No harm done. Thank you."

When Deepika's out of sight the second nurse calls Doctor Marina's office: "Do you have a—sorry I can't pronounce—Deepika? Is that right?"

"Yes. She's scheduled for an appointment in a few minutes, just a drop-by—I didn't put it on the calendar. She's just worried. Is there anything else?"

"No. Just checking on something." The nurse hangs up and wonders about all the security surrounding the building, trying to keep the wrong people out, slowing down people who need to get in, the crowd she has to drive through when she leaves for the night, the chanting candle-holding vigil, and she thinks of me up in my room and shakes her head: how do we handle such brutality? Dr. Marina tells Deepika she has nothing to worry about. She touches her, takes her blood pressure, slightly elevated heart rate, asks if Deepika is under any stress, and sends her out the door ten minutes later.

After the appointment, Deepika takes the elevator to the sixth floor and the hallway in front of her empties, the security guard's back is turned and he's moving away down the long corridor; her luck must be phenomenal; she walks confidently, I belong here, past the waiting room where Sheila sits alone, her head bent as she works her Blackberry. Nadine is absent because she's rushed home to shower, change clothes, and return with Bernie. Maddy and the doctor are upstairs with Lance. Sheila sends messages to her friends back in Michigan. She's engrossed in her task. She doesn't see Deepika enter my room. The security guard is now facing the vending machine alcove when Deepika steps by. The nurses gather for shift change, patient updates, which is usually quick, and doesn't take much time. Karma.

Deepika slips into my room and closes the door behind her. She sees my body on the bed and all the bandages and comes closer. She expects a confrontation with Madison, imagines her calling her names, yelling how selfish Deepika is, and worse, scratching her eyes out like a cat, but she and I have the room alone for the moment. Deepika takes a deep breath. She recalls me as I surprised her at her house a couple days ago, bright, angry, and seeking so much promise: a final explanation. Hurt and bewildered by Deepika's presence in my father's life.

She sees me as studious, very cerebral—definitely my father's son, a bright, slight boy. The few times Deepika observed me at faculty parties she'd liked my quiet reserve. As if I knew how important familial duties became when the center of the family unit is out of balance, if only to keep up the charade. Most teenagers she meets want attention to be focused on them at all times. The strong ego is to be celebrated, coddled, smothered, the brashness of youth adulated. Just look where it places them when they reach adulthood and don't get as many pats on the heads just for breathing.

She takes my hand and rubs my palm. She's unable to think of anything to say after coming all this way. She needs to say goodbye but her voice has left her.

The door opens, startling her. She drops my hand and turns.

"It's okay," The Chess King says, holding up his old arms. "I didn't mean to give you a fright." He lowers his arms, clasps his fingers together in front of his orange coat. He still has his black winter hat on indoors as if he isn't staying long either.

"Excuse me. I shouldn't be here. I'm sorry," says Deepika, "I mean, I thought you were someone else." Deepika touches her belly, waits a silent moment and then says, "Obviously, I'm not family,"

"You thought I was a security guard?"

"Yes. I mean no harm. I just needed to see Chris. Extend my apology and sorrow."

The Chess King walks slowly to the bedside and sighs. "I never knew my grandson. He's my only grandchild."

"I didn't really know him that well either."

"Yet here we both are," The Chess King says evenly. "I hope my son can forgive me for not knowing his child."

"You're Geoffrey's father." It isn't a question and Deepika's only talking now to calm her nerves. This third male in the Bullet family, shaking her composure by showing up suddenly, unsettles her. What would Shiva do to conceive such a family dynamic?

"Yes. I still exist."

"Geoffrey told me little about you." Which is a lie Deepika tells just to keep the conversation going, a lie to keep ill will at bay. Geoffrey only spoke of his father once after she asked about his parents, sheepishly, as if the very act of telling Deepika about The Chess King could absolve him of guilt, anger, and abandonment. He acted like his father was his nemesis. Deepika remembers Geoffrey in one of his rants, long monologues of cynicism, speaking about his father as if he was dead to him. Geoffrey then tried to act as if he didn't have a father, but Deepika knew he repressed his past, bottled it up inside so tightly she was frightened for him and of him. The rage he thinks he must keep frozen. It will destroy him. And Deepika thought this about Geoffrey back in the spring.

"What did you do, I mean, what brought you here?" The Chess King asks softly.

"I couldn't love Geoffrey. Completely. And that isn't enough. It sounds like you never loved your son enough either. I'm truly sorry."

"You had nothing to do with that; we've kept it all in the past. Decades have passed both of us by. But, just from looking at you, this condition you find yourself in, you've still got a couple months before your due date. You had something to do with Geoffrey's situation, and this." The Chess King doesn't say what this he is referring to: my condition or the child in her belly. Deepika's rarely so scattershot, confused.

So she changes the subject, "Geoffrey did say your I.Q. was too high to be rated." Deepika immediately reconsiders her shallow opinion of The Chess King; why base her opinions on Geoffrey's broken dreams of a perfect childhood? Such a misunderstood troll, Geoffrey's word, of a man painted unflatteringly by a sullen prince. She watches as The Chess King rubs his wide lower lip. Geoffrey never said his father was misunderstood but Deepika now looks at what Geoffrey said with a skeptical eye.

Deepika turns to me, leans down, hovering over my bandaged face for a second, and chastely gives me a kiss.

"I'm sorry," Deepika says softly to me.

"You said that. No need to say it again. I believe you."

"For you and your family."

The Chess King asks Deepika, "Did you love him?"

"Geoffrey?"

"Yes."

"No. From the little time I spent with him—"

"Enough time." The Chess King means the child she will have, the child growing within her.

"Yes. I've released Geoffrey from all responsibility." She doesn't add her dark thought: and this is why this boy is here, crushed. I set the first wheel turning on the mousetrap.

"When all of this is settled. One way or another. I want

you to call me." The Chess King hands Deepika a card with a telephone number on it.

"I'm leaving tomorrow."

"I don't expect you to call me but I would like to know what happens to my next grandchild. And I would like to help. I've been away for too long." Deepika wants to ask why he's allowed his son to dictate his actions. Why he's such a coward. You have to fight. You have to stay.

She ends up saying, "I won't make any promise." Deepika remembers her former lover's cloying feeling of unjust abandonment, a deep and longing infection within Geoffrey. He says he never wanted to discuss his father, but did all the same, as if she was his worry stone, therapist, and absolver of guilt. He gave her vague intimations of unfulfilled wishes and a desire for retribution. Geoffrey's last word on his father: I won't give him the satisfaction.

"Just a consideration. I won't reveal anything about you to Geoffrey. Ever."

"Thank you for saying that. I have to go. Maddy must be around here somewhere. I know she definitely wouldn't appreciate me being here and she doesn't know about—"

"Yet you were willing to brave this confrontation. Please call me."

There's nothing left for her to say. She can feel tears on her cheek but can't remember when they started; they aren't tears of sadness.

Deepika leaves The Chess King alone by my bedside, walks briskly to the elevator and steps out of the hospital feeling lighter. All her secrets are held safely within. She feels joy overwhelm her even in this dreary hospital, even after leaving my broken body.

Who can blame her for feeling happy? She is with child. She's leaving a town where she's felt like the usual outsider, but then again, she never allows herself to feel a part of anything. She grows and grows. She didn't love Andy completely, and vice versa, but she got married and got what she wanted: she could stay in the country that beguiled her. Andy got what he eventually wanted, too. They both made choices. She didn't love Geoffrey either, and wonders if love is something she will ever feel, and then scoffs at herself because she loves; she knows she loves as she places a hand on her belly and drives away from the hospital.

The Chess King bends down and kisses me on the exact spot Deepika had minutes before. From his shoulder bag he takes out a rolled-up rubberized chessboard and places it on the table next to the bed. As the board is laid out he sighs. He then takes out the felt bag of tiny plastic pieces and sets up the game. He makes the first move—a center white pawn moved forward two spaces.

The Chess King then leaves the room. In the crowded lobby of the hospital he passes Rhea, Millie, and Frank as they're checked in by security. He marvels at the fact that Deepika, in all her glorious mother-to-be appearance could bypass the system and appear at his grandson's side so effortlessly. He wonders how she did it as his mind always wonders at the work of true magicians and the secrets they would never reveal to any living soul. He removes his laminated security badge and places it on the receptionist's desk. Good karma.

* * *

Millie and Frank and Rhea take the elevator to the sixth floor of the children's wing and a nurse greets them from the nurse's desk halfway down the hallway. "May I help you?"

"Our grandchild is here," Frank says. The nurse has met so many family members she shrugs and tells them to take a seat in the waiting room for a minute so she can check if I'm presentable. And to see if the other older grandfather has left yet; she didn't see him depart. The head nurse of the day shift says they've lifted the ban on number of family members because the mother wants everyone to have access.

"They're okay." That's how The Chess King got in to see me. His charm alone wouldn't be enough. In the waiting room Sheila sits now with Bernie and Nadine, who are visibly relieved when the door opens and Millie, Frank, and Rhea reintroduce themselves. They met Sheila and Lance at the wedding, of course, and they met Nadine and Bernie several times on numerous RV trips, and memorably when the families spread out down near the river at Maddy's house during a 4th of July gathering. How long ago was that? Sheila remembers being there after Lance finished a case so hazardous to his health, stressing, that the early Montana summer was a salve and a blessing, but it's another event that will never take place again. Rhea just feels left out once more, presses her lips tightly together.

Millie asks Nadine: "How is he doing?"

Nadine can't bring herself to say anything but Sheila answers, "Maddy is meeting with Geoffrey right now." The door opens and everyone who isn't facing that way whirls around. The hospice nurse, Kiki Miles, stands in the doorway, calm, serene, all the courses and workshops she took preparing her for moments like this—building a bridge between the living and the dying—and no one envies her a bit.

* * *

The Chess King departs the hospital without a second glance. He doesn't go back to the hotel where Nell awaits his arrival in a slow-simmering fury; she's never used to him letting her down; who could be? He tells the taxi driver to take him to the airport and buys a one-way ticket to New York City. The airplane departs in a little over two hours. He's back in the country, jet-lagged, downing dozens of multi-vitamins, and he's done viewing his son's actions from afar, washing his hands of loss. In two days he'll be playing chess in a shop near Columbia University against professors who still try their best to beat him, and have for decades, always unsuccessful in their endeavors. Maybe Geoffrey will contact him, maybe he won't. He's made the first move.

* * *

When Madison finally sees Geoffrey she wants to take him into her arms and hug him until his sadness breaks them both apart, but she can hardly bear the sight of him. Her tears remain slow, a steady stream now, but she looks strong across her face. She doesn't even wipe them away anymore. Geoffrey sits in his chair drugged to the rafters next to Doctor Spitzer.

"Geoffrey," Doctor Spitzer says, "we're all here to support you. There isn't anyone here who can harm you."

Lance is able to say, "Hey, good buddy," but he can't look his longtime friend in the eye.

"Chris is dying," Madison says. "Geoff. Where were you? What did you do?"

Doctor Spitzer intervenes, "Mrs. Dakota. Please. No judgement. This isn't the time for accusations." Doctor Spitzer shoots Doctor Gapestill a warning glance: See? This is why my department follows the rules.

"Okay. Okay," Doctor Gapestill says, "Mr. Bullet, we need your permission, if the time comes, to turn off life support. Chris's condition . . . there's nothing more that can be done. We still need to wait and see. Hope he heals." The doctor's voice falters towards the end.

Geoffrey can't think straight. He witnesses his wife in tears for the first time he can recall, through the antidepressant haze, and he again wishes he were dead. But he doesn't say that out loud in front of Doctor Spitzer. He thinks of how he's tried to avoid his father, push him out of his thoughts for over ten years, ever since his mother passed away, and I'll never get this now, even though The Chess King has never revealed it. The image in Geoffrey's mind at that moment, the doctor's badgering him to open up about his childhood, his father—Geoffrey, a handsome, tall, striking teenager, older, wiser, beyond his age—coming home early one evening after telling his father and mother he had a date coming up, an important one, and please could he borrow the car, home by midnight? It's a Saturday, c'mon. Everyone set up like bowling pins: mother away for the weekend, anyway, caring for an ailing sister who lived in New York City. She took the train from Connecticut that very morning. And the girl Geoffrey had a date with resisted his charms, a girl from the right side of the tracks, a girl from a neighboring high school, a girl who, nevertheless, heard all the rumors about Geoffrey, but was more than willing to give him a chance. Her mistake. Something in the car, something Geoffrey had implied was going to happen didn't sit well and the girl insisted he turn the car around and take her back to her house. She wasn't that kind of girl. Whatever gave you that impression? Geoffrey obliged with a sickening smile, happy to be rid of the ungrateful prude the second after he dropped her off. He'd never taken rejection well and it didn't happen often, rejection just made the challenge sweeter and he pulled back into his driveway and most of the lights in the house were out. His mother was gone. He knew his father was home, not traveling, on the road again in a week or two and when he opened the door he heard the scrambling of doors and footsteps on the upstairs landing, his father fastening an old rust-colored bathrobe, hair mussed.

"Geoff? What are you doing back so soon?"

And Geoffrey knew. It was so damn intuitive of him. That's all it took.

"You bring them to the house? Dad? You couldn't wait?"

"Don't run away," shouted Geoffrey's father, but much too late, because Geoffrey was back in the car driving away. He drove until his mind ached, until he didn't feel anymore, and when he couldn't feel anymore he tricked himself into thinking he felt much better.

When he returned the next day his father was alone in the house and gave Geoffrey his space. They didn't speak and Geoffrey wouldn't speak to him that day or the following week. He went straight to his room and then to school day after day and accompanied girl after girl out on the town. He thought of that night and how close he came to ramming his car into a brick wall, how very close he'd come. He'd pressed the accelerator down flat, speed rising, his father's image so large there on the steps, and he could've done it. He could've done it too, many times.

Doctor Spitzer worries about his patient, and only his patient. The rest of Geoffrey's family isn't at the forefront of his decision-making process. It would be unprofessional for him to break protocol, word would spread, the rest of his colleagues could use this as a wedge, and he would have to grant favors. He's prepared to deny the next request as soon as Geoffrey collects himself enough to speak again.

"I want to be there." Geoffrey says this softly and without any inflection, a toneless quality that speaks volumes if anyone but Doctor Spitzer were listening for signs of deterioration.

"I don't know if I can allow this. I think such a huge shock will be a setback you may not be able to easily recover from."

Maddy sighs. "My husband needs to be with me . . . when we say goodbye to our son."

Doctor Gapestill sets his elbows on the table and joins in, "I will take responsibility for Mr. Bullet's whereabouts. I'll escort him downstairs and then back to your ward. This is an extreme sacrifice you'll be making Doctor Spitzer."

"Don't belittle my intelligence by speaking to me of sacrifices that need to be made. That's clear. Presently, this man's mental health is what is at stake."

"That is also clear. No one is denying that."

"Please. Everyone calm down." Voices start to rise and Lance breaks in. "As Mr. Bullet's attorney I believe he has every right, and I, although not well versed in Montana law, believe both parents need to be present to make this decision." Lance knows nothing of the sort but his voice is strong and pressing. He cannot fathom how Geoffrey is under Doctor Spitzer's care. What a joke.

"I don't take kindly to threats. Legal or otherwise," says Doctor Spitzer.

"After we see Chris, you can keep my husband here for as long as it takes," Maddy interjects. "Just let us say goodbye. Please. You're supposed to want to heal someone in a hospital. Your words just come across as so much bureaucratic heartlessness."

"I beg your pardon." It's all Doctor Spitzer can retaliate with as if he's the one offended. "Okay. Doctor Gapestill can take you. I'll release Mr. Bullet into his care. He's to return"—and Doctor Spitzer cannot bring himself to say: when it's all done. Even that sounds heartless in his mind.

"Enough talking then, please, these people have been through enough," Doctor Gapestill says as he pushes himself away from the table with both arms. "If all of you will please follow me."

* * *

Doctor Gapestill's urgency is lost on me; I can't get my broken head around the idea that they're coming back to my room to say goodbye to me. I don't feel anything. Even resignation is lost in the darkness.

PART FOUR

*He whose face gives no light,
shall never become a star.*

~William Blake

THE GREEK CHORUS II

WHEN DOES DEATH BEGIN?
The doctors confer, all the neurologists. Some remain dour and insist on defining my condition as a persistent vegetative state. Two other internists actually are hopeful of a slim recovery. These two opposing sides argue back and forth, strict, heated whispering—God forbid anyone overhear this debate. My lapse from comatose to vegetative is kept as a confidence until more tests are done; it's as if some of the doctors want to be proven right, but have no inclination to deliver the bad news themselves. I'm still in a sleep-like state; I cannot be aroused by anything: a loud noise, the blaring of an alarm clock, the clapping of palms above my ear, any drug known to man slipping into my veins. I don't feel the needles, the multitude of pinpricks dotting my unresponsive skin, a roadmap of pain I can't feel.

I want to feel this. Nothing supernatural works either, even though I can't really claim my mother's kiss as proof of this. Maybe a kiss from a virgin, boy or girl, would do it. Realistically, though, not a chance.

Another doctor on staff speaks to one of the many journalists outside on the steps. The media flocks to him like a group of western meadowlarks, searching for the story, crying. The doctor says: People are rarely in a coma for more than a month. They recover, enter a vegetative state or become minimally conscious. He's studious, irritatingly ponderous, as he gives the hoard his simplistic definitions. He's never known me as anything but unresponsive.

He continues talking and the media takes notes, pupils in a classroom, jostling one another, half deciding not to print the doctor's words because another story about the growing mass of supporters and protesters outside the hospital is brewing. An official spokesperson for the Hospital will give his press conference. She'll make the mistake of starting with the words: We are all in mourning. Doesn't someone have to die first?

The doctor continues—patients may appear to be more responsive, but they show no awareness of self or their environment. Duh. My brain is about to explode according to Doctor Gapestill. He wants my mother and father to confer. When they enter my darkening room—how do you turn up the lights in here—my parents wonder about the chess set and the game in progress. They keep their thoughts to themselves. Mother thinks of the board as just another practical joke and will find out who brought it if it's the last thing she does—she's too saddened to grasp a thought about The Chess King, someone she's only rarely spoken about, memories dredged up from the depths, but my father knows instantly who set it up, who was there, and there's a light in his eye; he avoids looking at the one lone white pawn three spaces ahead of the white king in line—his father's words: always have a plan, Geoffrey, even with the first move—he will turn his back to the old portable chess board and try to forget. He'll have a talk with Nell if she ever shows up. Now that they know everything, now that Geoffrey is sitting next to my broken body, Doctor Gapestill's words are meant be soothing. Not to me. He thinks if he can make them understand the severity of my injuries they'll consider doing the right thing. He's on the side of the doctors who don't think I have a prayer of a chance. He hopes he can get the parents to sign off on pulling the plug, if that becomes necessary, of course, to save me from suffering more. Giving up. No one in the media will know this until much later.

* * *

Kiki Miles steps next to my bedside and checks the chart marking my progress. From what the doctors have told her specifically Kiki thinks calling for her services is a bit premature. The boy is still fighting. She doesn't want to approach my mother and father and tell them what a hospice nurse is supposed to do, what her purpose is, how she can help. She's finding it hard to open her mouth. Usually the patients she's brought in to facilitate and comfort are still able to speak. This is a rare case. Children are always the toughest and Kiki thinks of her own child, a son, she only had one, who is with his father watching a TiVo'd Ultimate Fighting Championship while she took the call. The hardest part of her hospice orientation is to learn what keeps people holding on. The one thing. I want to tell her I'm not holding onto anything, but of course she can't hear me. People under hospice care worry so much that they haven't made their mark yet, left a mark on the world, and hold onto this worry, lets it dig into them. You have been loved she wants to tell all of them.

Let go. I haven't left a mark in my shortened lifespan, but if I die my death will leave the largest stain for some time to come. Even if I somehow open my eyes, my living, my struggle will stain Middleton—become myth. I can feel this. My death will leave a mark. My life will ring bells. Kiki holds my mother's hand and stays silent. Part of her job is also to ask for permission from the living for organ donation. I don't know why she can't bring herself to ask. I wish I could tell them to take everything. I won't need anything anymore. Kiki asks my mother if she could talk to her while my father spends some time alone with me. She leads my mother out into the hall and tries to be reassuring even if she's following procedure every bit as much as Doctor Spitzer tries to. He's upstairs wondering about his next article about psychiatric practices and new breakthroughs in varying pharmaceutical wonder drugs, and how the Bullet case can be a PR advantage for the hospital. By the end of Kiki's prepared, mournful speech, my mother gives her consent and the two women return to speak to my father. Geoffrey can't get his head around the death of his son and refuses to give his consent. I want to say to my father that my organs will help many people lead healthy lives. The decision is taken away from me, too. Just another thing. I wish. My mother and father start to argue once more. Everyone else leaves the room. I don't want to die.

"Geoffrey."

"Yes."

"I just needed you here. There was no other way to get you out. Doctor Gapestill will take full responsibility with your doctor."

"You mean Chris is going to be okay?"

"No one knows. The swelling in his head isn't going down."

* * *

Mrs. Plesher sits in Deepika's fictional kitchen surrounded by thirteen fictional cats and a brother too old to care about anyone but himself, his sister be damned. Deepika has inferred Mrs. Plesher's murderous intentions. Don't turn your back on her. The neighbors who cross her should watch out, and I think of Deepika creating such a woman and how much she enjoys conflict and the hateful side of human nature. Nearing the end I know I've been upsetting Deepika as much as she's disturbed me. I know nothing will happen to Mrs. Plesher. She's not real. She's still sitting in her kitchen yelling at Shorty who's stuck in a dark, unseen living room forever eating heirloom tomato sandwiches.

* * *

Ellis Pallino can't know I'm about to make a choice, so close to death. If he did he'd shake even more. He lies on a bunk in a police station, locked away. I'll be in his thoughts forever. Somewhere I once imagined being. He can't hide, but it's not worth it anyway.

* * *

Andy Webber and Terry Elias will read about me in the *San Francisco Chronicle* and think about barbarians in the country, rednecks, backwards people killing homosexuals rampantly and they'll never know the truth until much more time passes. Andy will say: doesn't Deepika live in Middleton? I should probably give her a call. And when Andy does get around to finally calling Deepika her telephone will be disconnected without a forwarding number. Terry will say: Let her get in touch with you. She always does.

* * *

Ms. Phyllis Deafers reads the paper and can't reconcile her feelings. A boy who sat in her study hall is dying. The whole thing disrupts her school, her city, and the national news is cycling a 30-second story every hour on the town and how far civilization has come. Man versus man. They compare his fight to live with the political battle and this sickens her. But her study hall isn't giving her trouble, and never really did, even the worst of the kids seem meek. And gay, she thinks. Maybe he deserves what he got. Let God sort it out. She thinks of the rumors flying around the school, the blackest being I had sex with the toughs who sit in jail; there must be a reason more complex to explain their actions. As if gay people should be beaten to a pulp on a regular basis. Cleanse the sin away. Ms. Deafers is too old to really care what happens. She's looking forward to going home.

* * *

Amos Morataki sits at the dinner table. He's been silent, withdrawn. His parents don't know what to do. If Amos doesn't come out of his funk they'll take him to a grief counselor. They can't imagine why he feels responsible for my situation. Amos knows I left school because he told me one of my father's secrets and this eats away at him.

* * *

Mary Follick thinks of herself as something of a local celebrity now that she's the star witness for the prosecution. She came late to the party. She asked me to dance and I refused. She acts like she's better than anyone else and keeps talking and talking and talking to everyone about how well she knew me. A prosecutor will have to sit her down and tell her to stop—shut up, shut up already. Just stick to the facts. The pics she took with the camera in her cellular telephone are all washed out and not really going to make or break the case. Even the one blurry photo isn't all that good; technology isn't sharp enough yet; there wasn't even a flash to combat the darkness.

* * *

Edy Augustyn daydreams about the years ahead. She imagines writing Ellis Pallino a letter. She'll want to because she believes he's innocent. One of the few. It's there in her head. She'll eventually write him a letter and tell him he's a good person and not to give up hope. She'll remember him only from Biology class, a required pre-college course, and his good looks, his swagger, and how she did everything in the labs, and not particularly well, because Ellis couldn't be bothered. He's much too important, popular, even as a new kid, and she did the lion's share of the labwork happily, reverentially; his handsome aura there to make her feel like she's the only girl in the room.

* * *

After another long shift, Dr. Fusil finally makes her way home. Her legs feel like rubber doorstops. She breezes by security and winds through the growing crowd of people at tonight's vigil. Someone pushes a candle into her hands.

Someone else dips and her candle is lit. The crowd isn't moving, just standing still, and Dr. Fusil closes her eyes and stays in place for a long time.

* * *

Maddy's wayward student, Travis, sees the Class Canceled sign taped to the room and doesn't even know why he thought there would be a class anyway. He never mailed the card he bought for my mother. He never even wrote his feelings within it.

* * *

Ananda tells his wife to make up the extra bedroom. Deepika is coming soon and he wants her to be comfortable. His wife will have someone to talk to when his patients take up his time. They will welcome Deepika into their home. Ananda will be superior and proud and take Deepika's situation for what it's worth, as if he can be a savior. They'll laugh about old times and plan trips to see their parents and how the world hates America, and how there's nothing they can do about it. Pakistan and India vow to bolster their peace efforts. Politics after dinner.

* * *

Harry, the psychiatric nurse, sets his alarm clock. On his last shift he had to stay two hours extra and he's not feeling well. The psychiatric drain of his job wears on him and he's thinking of moving to another department. He'll seek an application next week. He's good at his job. He doesn't take shit from anyone, but he's compassionate with a dry sense of humor. This is what he tells himself.

* * *

Lance sits next to Sheila in the waiting room. Their backs are stiff. Sheila's been in that room all day, sitting, staring at the television, standing, getting coffee, food from the cafeteria, rushing back when she thinks too much. Lance clasps his hands together and rests his head on them. He whispers to Sheila: There's nothing left. Sheila rubs her husband's back and massages his shoulders. Sheila says: You're a true friend. That's what's important.

* * *

Mrs. Gallows notices the hole in her classroom immediately, my empty seat in the front row; she seats people alphabetically. She doesn't fill it the next day either. She doesn't want to be seen as dispassionate, but there's a class to run and my empty seat is a distraction. After more whispering, the shuffling of feet, the slack eyes, Mrs. Gallows asks the people behind my seat to move up. The students in my row don't move. They can't comprehend why this teacher is so insensitive—but of course they don't say it out loud. The boy now in my seat isn't too comfortable but the third time Mrs. Gallows yells for the row to move up and take their new places the boy shrugs and slouches into my seat. The whole class seems picked up and shaken.

* * *

Mr. Roffiger and his family, his smiling wife, who has a great singing voice and sings in the church choir, with their eight children, are outside the hospital. All of them, except for the two younger kids, are grasping candles and swaying. They pray for me. Mr. Roffiger misses a math team practice for me. I want to give him a demerit.

* * *

Millie and Frank stay in the conference room away from the other members of the party. There's a couch Millie can stretch out on. She has a migraine, like mother like daughter. A cold front is moving in and the cloud pressure hits her hard. All the sorrow. Frank takes out the stack of bills Rhea gave him and sorts through them once again. Tomorrow he'll pay each and every one of them as if doing penance. He won't ask Geoffrey to pay him back either. He'll never bring them up. They sit and wait and wait.

* * *

Glynnis wants to drive to the hospital but she can't bring herself that far. She takes out stationary and writes a note addressed to my father. She wants to say how sorry she is. She leaves out the law firm. This is her apology. She thinks the firm is culpable in my father's depression.

* * *

Rhea will call her husband Carl from a telephone tucked away behind the nurse's station. She'll be in tears. She hasn't even had time to speak to her sister one on one, and this drives her to speak to her husband. She's trying not to take anything personally. Her sister is in trouble here and she wants to help. She misses her kids and can only think about what she'd do if one of her kids was lying on a hospital bed, dying, clinging to life, what she'd do if one of her kids turned out gay.

* * *

Nancy Followatta takes her sister, Valeria Brandow, a

large bowl of chicken noodle soup with lemon grass and ginger. Nancy feeds Valeria her pills, strong anti-psychotics and anti-depressants, and calls her a good girl. Valeria's naked streak through the streets made the news and embarrassed Nancy into a stupor. Valeria also caught an infection, maybe from the hospital, maybe from all the police officers putting handcuffs on her and pulling her into their police cruisers. But Nancy has to take care of Valeria and spoons chicken broth into her slackening mouth. See what happens, Nancy says to her sister. You've got to stop.

* * *

Officer Ken St. Amour will distance himself from the investigation. Washes his hands of my case; he's only on patrol, at a lower level, too few years on the force and under his belt. He has the image of my mother's face etched in his mind, the sadness and confusion, and he wonders when he'll have to give bad news to the next mother.

* * *

Mr. Abrassini pisses and moans. Marjolaine called him with the news he has to take on my mother's classes for the short term, starting early next week. Deepika is leaving and there's no one else. As if he doesn't have enough to do. He has his own writing to think about, which he never does, slouching by on his past achievements, not producing anything of merit in a long, long time.

Marjolaine hangs up the telephone and sighs with relief. She's made her arrangements work. All of my mother's classes are covered and no one will thank her. She thinks once again of retirement and the cutting, cold winter approaching. Her joints ache.

* * *

Nell returns to the hospital after calling the front desk to see if her father has checked in and learns he's also checked out. The nerve of him. It's just like him to only think about himself. She can finally see why my father refuses to communicate with The Chess King. She enters the waiting room and sits next to Sheila who brings Nell up to speed on the decision Geoffrey and Maddy have to make. Geoffrey is in there right now, Sheila says, I guess it was a real battle to get him out—Nell doesn't want to be here, she doesn't want all the sadness to rub off on her, she doesn't feel needed but she can only be so helpful, she can only think of herself, even at this late hour, and she wonders where her own father is flying. Back into his shell.

* * *

The Chess King amuses the flight attendants on the trip back to New York City by making dirty limericks using their first names: There was a young lady named Amy . . .

* * *

The printer hums in the background as Deepika takes out one more overstuffed trash bag full of old writing magazines and the last dregs from the refrigerator. She hears Liv making a joke, saying, "You'll be back before I quit smoking. I know you."

Which means Liv believes she'll never see Deepika again. A bittersweet relationship. Two women who take care of themselves first and foremost. Liv leaving with a tear in the corner of her eye, not letting Deepika see this tear, after helping Deepika pack up the belongings accumulated over her almost two-year stay. Liv gives Deepika back her damage deposit in full. Business is business.

"I'll ship those last two boxes next week when you call."

"I will call. And I will stay in touch."

Liv grumps. But doesn't respond.

Deepika clucks Ha! And says, "Don't be so hard on me."
"It's in my nature."
"I'm going to hear that in my sleep."
Liv gives Deepika a final hug and she departs. No guilt. No regrets. Keep them at bay. The printer bustling right along. The end of the story. I'm holding onto the hope of finally figuring things out by reading over her shoulder, so to speak. Deepika hears the teakettle whistle and moves to cut the sound short. She's larger around the middle in just one week's time, almost a magical transformation.

She takes her teacup and steeps the strong Darjeeling for a couple minutes before adding her milk and honey. She thinks of this land as her Bhoga Bhoomi, something she's still capable of deriving pleasure from, but she knows her mother would disagree with her tell Deepika she's had too much American influence. I never will understand why you live in a land that's lost the dream of materialism—Maya, she calls it—a land that will now suffer as India has suffered in the past. Deepika's mother believes India has now matured after suffering through a lesson of defeat—only speaking in economic terms. You and the country you live in have lost the American dream, and Deepika's mother can tell the exact moment this dream came to an end: When the assassinated president's son died in an airplane crash, there was a solar eclipse right at that spot over the water—a beginning solar orb—and the eclipse ended over the Bay of Bengal. Do you know what this means? We reclaim this dream. India will prosper now. This is a strong sign.

Deepika doesn't say anything in response to her mother's prognostications and pronouncements because she knows her mother only wants her to come back home. Why would you not come home? America is going to suffer, suffer, and suffer until it loses its breath. Bauble, please come back to a country that wants you to succeed. Deepika tells her mother she'll be home at the end of November but she has to stop in Boston first to get her life set up. She's going to let Ananda and his wife and children look after her while her story collection begins the next stage of revision.

She'll have her child and go on a short book tour in New

York City, Boston, Chicago. She'll try to forget the people in her past, even Liv, without remorse. But she can't get me out of her head. Likewise. She thinks about murderers back home in India and remorse taking over guilt and how the murderers when caught shed all clothing for 24 years, grab begging bowls, and earnestly beg for food, wandering the land, doing penance to try to erase their violent natures, but it never works. If I die what will Deepika's penance be? How will she erase this stain on her conscience? She doesn't have an answer. The past is the past and cannot direct her future. She believes this. Her fate is her own.

Deepika takes the last sheets of printer paper and sits to read her story. The papers tremble, an almost unnoticeable tremor, from time to time, in her hand—reading, editing, and trying to divert the way her mind keeps remembering what pain really feels like. She writes. (The End. The last section Deepika prints out to follow the other parts—I don't need to read this now, perhaps later—why bother, you're almost at the end, my end, already. Read this final chapter after the lights go out—when the book is published: *A Great Distance* by Deepika Webber. In her final section I know Sai is angrier than he's ever been and I can relate. Deepika thinks she is Sai, but I know different. I am Sai. My mother and father are Sai's parents, each of us falling down long dark stairwells. All the blood, the birth imagery, violence, Deepika's own worry splashes across her pages for all to see.)

* * *

The machines keep beeping. There is no peace.
I'm not breathing on my own. Not for a long time now.
Sai is—here. Where Deepika waits.
The doctor, the hospice nurse, and my mother and father are in the room with me, all together again, changed, changing, and I know I will wake up. I can still feel them wanting me to open my eyes.
I will.

I open my eyes, just a sliver. It feels like they've been gummed up for a thousand years.

When I finally focus I don't recognize anyone in the room. I don't know anyone. I can't speak with a tube stuck down my throat.

This woman is so happy. I can't place her. The room grows dark.

"Chris." A man rests his hands on my legs and looks up. He's crying. He is strange to me.

I don't know who he is now but the man who I will come to know as Doctor Gapestill calls for more nurses and they start measuring my impulses. I'm so tired after waking up. The Doctor is afraid I will immediately relapse right back into my comatose state. My brain is on fire. My body hurts. My mouth is dry and doesn't seem to function; the ventilator tube rises.

"Don't close your eyes," Doctor Gapestill says. "Chris. Look at me. Look at this light." He holds a penlight in front of my face and I try to follow his every word.

TRIAL

THE OFFICER of the court retrieves Deepika from the witness room.
"Ms. Deepika Webber?"
"Yes," says Deepika. She's finally ready for this moment. No one could realistically be ready for it, but Deepika is calm. Inwardly, she pumps herself up: You're ready to speak your truth. There are so many stories circling around Middleton about Deepika, her truth, she perceives, will not be believable, and the defense table salivates, spins her stories into deeper circles of deception.

It's so many months later, the same President has won back his office. Deepika's mother must be crowing. My court case is wearying Montana. They just want it closed, finished and put to bed. The same protesters who stood in the rain outside the hospital now line up behind courthouse barricades. Their signs are new but say the same old things: one sign states the holder, a young woman with long black hair, caught on news film, wishes the four boys had succeeded in killing the fag, that I deserve to die just for being me, and my parents try to shield me from this mob. They are together again. They help each other more, listen more, help me all the time try to put my past together, but only my past, they never talk about their past. I have to come in through the side exits, surrounded by my parents, my grandparents on my mother's side, and Nadine. Everyone wants a good photo of me, and I don't give interviews to anyone.

"They're waiting for you." Deepika follows the guard to the courtroom door. He holds it open for her. "Just walk straight down the middle of the court to the witness stand

and face forward."

Deepika quickly surveys the full courtroom, and tries not to make eye contact with anyone. Media cameras click, still photography, and video monitors whir in the back corner. Court TV, every newspaper, local, national, even some international press from India where the last year of stories has ripped into the atmosphere circling the globe, coldly recording the proceeding. They bunch across the far back wall. All eyes are on Deepika. She doesn't feel like a star witness—far from it. Liv sits on the hard bench to her right, three rows in, as Deepika passes. Liv holds Deepika's baby, now almost six months old, a tiny quiet child, a baby girl Deepika has named Sabrina, after Sai's mother in her story. She's always loved the name, the playful quality. Sabrina's features are dark and full, the black hair from Deepika's side of the family. She has Geoffrey's eyes, a startling dark green flecked with gray near the center. She's a beautiful child. Sitting next to Liv is The Chess King. He also has green eyes, and he tries to balance his wayward life. My father says he'll meet with my grandfather at the end of the trial, but not before. My father sits four rows ahead of his own father and feels the weight of his stare. He tries not to fidget beside my mother.

Liv ducks her chin towards Deepika, which is her way of saying: You're doing great.

As Deepika approaches the front of the courtroom she can't help but notice Madison, Geoffrey, and me sitting behind the prosecution table to her right. Madison holds a cane in both hands and grasps it tightly. Nadine rests her hand on Maddy's thigh to steady her, as if she pictures my mother climbing out of her seat to start a catfight with Deepika. Madison stares right at Deepika as she passes and vows not hate her so much she will blame her for everything, but somehow, just thinking that, doesn't take her bitterness away. She's partly to blame, for everything. Geoffrey won't make eye contact with her. He rarely makes eye contact with anyone anymore, and he has such handsome eyes. He'll be on antidepressants for the rest of his life and he feels enervated 24/7. He seems too loose in his suit, his tie limp, but at least his shirt has been pressed and his brown hair combed over into his usual conservative style. His law firm took him back on a trial basis, called his absence just that: a leave of absence. He's in weekly therapy, and group therapy once a month, and he can be caught smiling from time to time without feeling self-conscious. Looking upset isn't hard for either of my parents to do.

None of the four boys—teens—responsible for my assault have pleaded guilty after all the handwringing and detective posturing, even after the prosecution pressed for the worst possible outcome, no plea-bargaining, all the usual prosecutorial bells and whistles just a little more than empty threats, and ineffective. The trial has slowly approached this moment. Ellis Pallino sits with the three other boys at the defense table on the left. They have separate lawyers, but their cases are being tried concurrently. Their parents and family members crowd that side of the room and they look mean, unsympathetic, and if someone lights a match . . . the two warring sides remind Deepika of weddings, where the two families and friends will always choose sides to back, even at the beginning, for better or worse.

"State your name for the court," says the bailiff.

"Deepika Webber." She stands there much thinner, having lost most of the pregnancy weight, in an amber blouse, light, for the end of summer. She has an intricately abstract patterned, yellow and orange skirt to compliment her blouse, little makeup, barely a dash of soft red on the lips. Geoffrey stares at her now for a second and cannot catch her eyes. He thinks she's always looked this confident.

"Please speak a bit louder. You may proceed," the judge, a woman with silver hair and a friendly but firm tone speaks out. Friendly or not, she holds court with a no-nonsense air.

The prosecutor stands and moves with smooth efficiency out of his seat, up to the witness stand. He stops four feet in front of Deepika and turns to the jury. "May I call you Deepika?"

"Please."

"Are you here of your own free will?"

"I don't understand the question."

"I'll rephrase," and the lawyer-speak takes over. Of

course Deepika is here of her own free will, but the defense will spin Deepika's words into something that could possibly let the four boys off the hook, bring in that varying sliver of reasonable doubt. It goes to the victim's, my, state of mind after I left her home. "You came forward rather late in the proceedings. Just six months ago you made yourself known to the court."

"I am here because I want to do the right thing. My own free will."

"Good."

"How did you know Christopher Bullet?"

Maddy stares at Deepika, and she will not give her any comfort.

"I wouldn't say I know Christopher Bullet well. I'd only seen him twice before that night."

"When did you first meet Christopher Bullet?"

"His parents had a college faculty party at their home a year before. 2003. I was introduced to Christopher by his father, Geoffrey."

"Did you speak to him about anything particular?"

"No. Just small talk. Nothing more."

"And the second time you met?"

"Another party later on in the school term. Again, we barely said more than hello to each other."

"But you spoke to Christopher's father, Geoffrey Bullet, quite a bit."

"Yes. He was very interested in the work I was doing."

"And what was that work?"

"I was writing a collection of short stories that year. I must've been at the very beginning of that work."

"This book is out now?"

"Yes."

"These proceedings have helped with sales?"

"I can't imagine why that's pertinent, but yes." She says this and I may be the only one who knows there's a bitter irony in her tone.

"You came forward of your own free will. I'm just trying to refute what the media has been saying about your motivations on the stand. You could've stayed in Boston. Lived your life. No one here would've been the wiser. People are buying your book in larger numbers because of your connection to this case." Deepika doesn't respond to the statement. She's trying to help the prosecution. "Are you being paid to be here?"

"Absolutely not. Notoriety is a double-edge sword."

"Your conscience getting to you?"

"Not at all, but it's very difficult to disprove a negative."

"Yes. It is. When did your affair with Christopher Bullet's father begin?"

"Last year, early springtime, 2004."

"And who initiated this affair?"

"Geoffrey showed up at my door one afternoon."

"And you let him in?"

"Yes."

Deepika knows her words cannot be easy for Madison to hear. She, however, feels relief flowing through her. Even though the prosecutor treats her as a hostile witness—something she fully understands—she begins to feel at ease.

"He came to my door and we started a short affair."

"Purely sexual. You didn't come to love each other?"

"No."

"Yet you conceived a child?"

"Yes." All the cameras now focus on the baby Liv holds in her arms. The Chess King's kind expression startles my father when he watches the evening news later in the day. My mother refuses to watch.

"Let's go forward. The day of the attack on Christopher Bullet you paid a visit to Geoffrey Bullet's home?"

"Yes."

"What was your reason for going there?"

"The answer to that question begins in the spring. Let's go back, please. In June I broke off the affair with Geoffrey. He loved his wife. And he always will. I was just a diversion for him, and he was just a diversion for me as well. We both knew there would be nothing more to our affair. I left Middleton at the end of June and found out I was pregnant about the same time. The day of the attack, but an hour or so before the attack took place, in October 2004, I went to Geoffrey's home to tell him he was going to be a father."

"Why?"

"It was the right thing to do?"

"But look at the consequences. Do you still feel it was the right thing to do?"

"No one can undo what has already passed. I went there to absolve Geoffrey of all responsibility as the father of the child."

"How did he take the news?"

"He was upset. Manic even. I don't think he fully understood that I wasn't asking for anything from him."

"But you were. Wouldn't he have to legally sign away his rights as the father of the child?"

"Yes."

"And has he signed anything formal relinquishing his rights as the father of—Sabrina Bullet?"

"No."

"Have tests been made proving that Geoffrey is even the father of Sabrina?"

"No."

Maddy rests her chin on the top of her cane, a long hard dark wooden cane with a metal top, inching up in her chair. She has tried to prepare herself for Deepika's words but it still feels like being hit by another truck.

"Why not?"

"Geoffrey and I both know Sabrina is ours. We've decided to handle it without court interference. The way most things should be handled." Deepika doesn't want to go on, make a speech about how complex Americans are, fighting their battles, spending so much time and money on courts and lawyer fees and how it's amazing when something good comes out of the process.

"What happened next at the Bullet house that day in October?"

"Chris surprised us both. He'd skipped school. He came in and saw us there in the kitchen. Geoffrey was holding my arm too tightly. It left a bruise. Geoffrey was angry. Chris ran away up the stairs. I left the house as soon as Geoffrey let go of my arm. He didn't mean to hurt me."

Geoffrey shrinks in his chair. He never means to hurt anyone. He's clinically depressed. He is truly ashamed of his actions but he can't show it in court. He keeps it hidden. This shame can overwhelm him as it has many times over the past year.

"You left and then what?"

"Chris showed up on my doorstep maybe a little over an hour later. He'd walked all the way from his house to mine in a pouring rainstorm. He was soaked to the skin."

"He was angry at you."

"And his father. Who wouldn't be?"

"I'll ask the questions."

Deepika stays silent. She's always hated being reprimanded, even for small things.

"You came forward, and we're grateful that you did; otherwise no one would really know why Christopher Bullet was, allegedly, so angry when he confronted his attackers on that stormy night. Because of Chris's traumatic head injury he has no memory of even going to your home. Too bad he cannot corroborate your story."

The defense interjects, "Is the prosecution going to start making speeches now?"

The judge says, "Please move along."

"Chris was angry, but he wasn't raging. He came in and sat down. I gave him some hot tea to warm him up. There was a fire going in my home. He really wanted to understand. He was out of the loop. No one told Chris about us, Geoffrey and I, nothing specific anyway. He knew his father had an affair the spring before. He knew something was wrong at home between his parents during that time. Geoffrey wasn't even living in the house. He was in a hotel room."

"So you told Chris what happened?"

"No. We spoke about the child. He was asking about his half-sister-to-be. He was angry at being in the dark for so long. About everything. He left angry at the world like any teenager, but he didn't seem out of control, whatsoever."

"In your humble clinical opinion, but you're not a doctor."

"No." The image of her brother, Ananda, *tsk-tsking* her behavior once more, flashes for an instant in her mind and is gone.

"Was this the last time you saw Christopher Bullet until

this day?"

"No."

Madison and Geoffrey both look at each other.

"When did you see him again?"

"In his hospital room. I snuck into his room before he woke up."

"Why would you go visit him when you knew his mother and father wouldn't want you there?"

"I wanted to say I was sorry."

"And that would make everything better? The world revolves around you and the absolving of your guilt?"

"That's an unanswerable question."

The courtroom paints Deepika as a fallen, marked, calculating woman, an outsider. The defense loves Deepika's words, tries to play up the anger in me as I left her house, but she plays back and reiterates that we merely had a conversation. I left with more knowledge, but rage didn't control me and I wasn't looking for a fight no matter what the defense intimates. She says I wasn't capable of starting a fight, then or now. Deepika replies no one deserves to be beaten to within an inch of life, scarred, left broken, with years of rehabilitation ahead. I'm still relearning how to speak clearly, I have seizures, which scare the hell out of me and my parents, and, like my mother, I have blazing repetitive headaches. My father has already formed the basis of a huge civil suit, and those papers will be filed after the outcome of the trial. My huge hospital bills will be paid and more.

Deepika answers the last question and leaves the courtroom with Liv, Sabrina, and The Chess King. My slump-shouldered grandfather finally looks his age, and more and more like a shrinking fairytale troll, diminished by a lifted spell. Nell chose not to share the spotlight and remains in the desert; she wishes she could be there for her brother's reconciliation tomorrow, but not enough to fly back. The journalists do their best to not let Deepika's posse pass through their massing body of pointing media equipment. The din hurts their ears. Maddy, with me at her side, follows them out of the building. She awkwardly limps with the cane. The MS has progressed incrementally, little by little, hobbling her gate. Geoffrey left us alone once again to bring the car around. Every one of us is boxed in by the crush of the camera crowd, and the confrontation between me, Maddy, and Deepika is caught on tape for the evening news, the three of us circling each other.

Deepika holds Sabrina tightly with both arms wrapped around her. Liv gets behind the wheel of her new spring green Volkswagen Beetle and inches to the curb. The Chess King sits in the back and his presence with Deepika must hurt my father and mother anew. It's a wonder they've agreed to meet after so much time, but chalk it up to Dr. Spitzer's weekly therapy sessions. He's finally getting through, clearing the cobwebs of the past out of my father's cluttered head. My mother, Deepika, Sabrina, and I are left on the curb, waiting, silent.

The cameras catch the moment Deepika hands Sabrina over to Maddy; the child, a sweet baby girl with dark, almost black, hair, looks warily at Deepika but she's not even close to crying. The scene plays over and over again every half hour on CNN that day. Maddy hugs this child, my half-sister, cooing, innocent and happy until Maddy gently places the tiny child in my spindly arms. I don't want to drop her and fear this happening. And, at least for the present, I let her tiny hands grasp at my face, laugh as I hand Sabrina back to Deepika without any of us ever saying one word to each other.

* * *

What happened to my attackers—my bullies? After much bluffing and bluster by the police detectives, only two were charged and tried as adults—something courts love to do these days, lock them away, rough justice. Terrence Jewell and Paul Real, both 17 years old and almost adults anyway, were convicted of first-degree assault, resisting arrest, drug possession with intent to sell, from various substances found on them when arrested (though not attempted murder, because the prosecutor couldn't prove intent) and sentenced to 15 years in prison (with 8 years suspended because the judge felt the sentencing guidelines were a bit excessive), with the possibility of parole in 4 years. Richard O'Connor, age 16 at the time, didn't have as extensive a criminal history as the two older boys, and would go to juvie. He received 10 years for first-degree assault (8 years suspended at the whim of the judge), with the possibility of parole in 2 years, ten years of probation and more than a thousand hours of community service. And Ellis Pallino, at 15, the youngest "half-hearted" attacker, and most believably remorseful, received only 7 years, with the possibility of parole once he reaches the age of 18 as the last sent to a juvenile detention center—the same amount of probation concerns and hours of community service attached. Will I see him at some future point dressed in reflective orange picking up trash on some dirty Montana highway? All four could've received longer sentences—up to 10 years longer, but Montana doesn't have a hate crimes enhancement. It's ironic that if I'd died, there would've been murder charges and maybe they'd never get out—unless the judge continued playing favorites. In studying previous cases before her court, she favored the new State Constitution against gay marriage and thinks all crimes are hate crimes. I survived; they will pay for the rest of their lives for what they did to me—even if they *do* get paroled, and, upon waking, this Western justice is barely tolerable.

ACKNOWLEDGEMENTS

To **my mother and father**, whose creativity will always inspire me. Thank you to my sister, **Jesse Ellison**, for allowing me to use the "Ocean Boy" painting in the creation of the book jacket. I love that this painting of our father's hangs in your home.

ABOUT THE AUTHOR

Born in Allentown, Pennsylvania, and raised in Pullman, Washington, and Granville, Ohio, Justin Bog, or, with his given birth name of Gregory Justin Bogdanovitch, is an English graduate of the University of Michigan and an MFA in Fiction graduate from Bowling Green State University. In its original form, *Sandcastle and Other Stories* was named one of the BEST BOOKS OF 2013 in the SUSPENSE ANTHOLOGY category by *Suspense Magazine*. It was also chosen out of over 400 titles to be a FINALIST FOR THE 2014 OHIOANA BOOK AWARD. Several of Justin Bog's short stories have won regional awards.

Long ago Justin joined the workforce as a babysitter, a Licking Memorial Hospital cafeteria worker, only lasted two weeks at McDonald's, enjoyed a 4-year stint as a U of M Campus Games Center clerk and 9-ball novice, and apprenticed as a University of Michigan Bookstore clerk, both while living in Ann Arbor, a Nippersink Resort Expediter and Waiter, a University of Michigan Hospital Patient Care Coordinator, an English Comp and Creative Writing Teaching Assistant in Bowling Green, a Between The Covers Bookstore clerk in Harbor Springs, Michigan, an Ex Libris bookstore clerk in Sun Valley, a Chapter One Bookstore manager in Ketchum, was a Pop Culture Correspondent and Editor at the online travel and culture magazine *In Classic Style*, and is an Editor at The Author's Advocate.

Justin is a member of the ITW: International Thriller Writers organization.

Justin currently lives in the San Juan Islands with his mate of almost thirty years, his two long coat German Shepherds, Zippy and Kipling, and his two barn cats, Eartha

Kitt'n and Ajax the Gray.

Author's Note

I highly recommend *I Don't Want to Talk About It: Overcoming the Secret Legacy of Male Depression* by Terrence Real. It's informative and dedicated to the author's sons, Justin and Alexander, a coincidence I like because my twin brother's name is Alexander. Also, *Multiple Sclerosis: The Facts You Need* by Dr. Paul O'Connor. MS is a disease that still needs a cure. It strikes about one in a thousand North Americans. Because the disease involves the central nervous system, its effects are wide-ranging and difficult to predict.

Wake Me Up takes place in 2004. There were 7,489 incidents of hate crime reported in the USA in 2003, and 1,239 were linked to sexual orientation. In October of 2005, an abhorrent coincidence occurred: two University of Montana students were severely beaten in downtown Missoula by young attackers who thought the students were gay. Four of the assailants were charged with assault and robbery, but many others fear filing charges in rural, conservative Montana. The police force in Missoula now has an officer who works in close liaison with the gay community.

All the places and people were used in fictional ways. This is still a work of fiction, and mistakes do happen. I try hard to get each detail right, and any mistakes in medical, legal, or Montana fields within these book covers, are solely my own—artistic license is up to date.

A READER'S GUIDE

For Book Clubs

1. How did the situation, a boy is beaten by bullying classmates and ends up in a coma, resonate with you?

2. Did the narrator change throughout the course of the book, or was it the situation that forced a change?

3. Did you like the strengths and weaknesses Deepika spoke about all people having? Could you relate to her situation?

4. Did you feel sorry for any of the characters? Why?

5. Was the narrator consigned to his fate?

6. What did you think about The Greek Chorus?

7. How important were the short stories included in the body of the novel? Was Deepika using the characters around her, the narrator's situation, to create her own fiction?

8. Was Sai supposed to be Chris? If not, who was Sai?

9. What other stories or novels have you read where there is also fiction written within the storyline? One of the author's influences was the novel Aunt Julia and the Scriptwriter by Mario Vargas Llosa. It was turned into a film under the title, Tune in Tomorrow, starring Keanu Reeves, Barbara Hershey and Peter Falk.

10. Why did the narrator's mother feel like she needed to shut down her emotions?

11. What did Geoffrey Bullet do to make himself despair and choose death as a way out?

12. Did The Chess King's antics resonate?

13. Wake Me Up is set in 2004, yet its themes are important during many future election years. Do you see progress or setbacks for a civilized society?

14. The point of view of the narration is First-Person Omniscient. This allowed the narrator to observe actions beyond his comatose state. Did the ending surprise you?

15. If turned into a film, who could you see playing the different parts?

16. Deepika is a catalyst in the action of the narrative, touching each of the main players. Is she "guilty" of anything? If so, is her belief in fate and karma stronger or weaker than the guiding systems in the other characters? Or is her belief system running along beside actions taken?

17. What happens to the narrator next? What about the other characters? Where do you see them in a year's time? Ten years from the ending?

18. What do you make of Ellis and his interactions with the narrator? Do you think he's hiding his own secrets?

19. Would you like the power to see and observe people from a distance? Hear what they are saying? See what they are doing?

20. Did the characters change over the course of the book?

Thank you for reading Wake Me Up and sharing the book with others. Please recommend it to your Book Club!